iii

Rough Justice

There was no smile now, no acknowledging the support of his silent crewmembers. Yukio's head seemed to shrink into his shoulders, and he pushed himself slowly away from the rail.

Then everything happened at once. The moment the sailor attacked, Teora knew that her Herdsman hadn't a chance. As the huge arms grasped Daegal around the waist and hurled him to the deck, she vaulted from the cabin top to land beside the two men.

Yukio had grasped his opponent's throat in his left hand but as he raised his right to strike, Teora laid her fingertips gently in front of his fist.

"You've proved your point, I think."

The man froze, staring at her blankly.

"Are you going to hit me?" She kept her voice calm.

Then the focus came back to his eyes, and he rose, backing away to lean on the rail, breathing heavily.

Teora glanced at Daegal, who stumbled to his feet, shaking his head. He started to speak, but she stopped him.

"I saw it all. You didn't need to let it go this far. You'd better go to your quarters. Mayna, you stay here. We have something to straighten out."

"We certainly have." Teora spun to face the new voice. Palani was standing behind her, slapping a coil of rope against his leg. The circle of sailors faded like smoke in the wind. "Yukio?"

To her surprise, the stocky sailor sighed. "I'm sorry, sir. I was just havin' a bit of fun with the girl, there, and..."

"Yukio, we do not have a 'bit of fun' with the passengers. Male or female."

"I know, sir, I know."

The officer looked grimly at the heavy coil of tarred rope in his hand. "Down. Hands on the rail."

The sailor shook his head slowly, sighed again and knelt, his hands grasping the rail, the tendons standing out with the intensity of his grip. With no ceremony, Palani stepped forward and slashed the coil five times across his naked shoulders.

Teora, shocked by the sudden brutality of the punishment, heard Mayna gasp behind her. The girl rushed from the deck, her hands to her face.

"Sorry you had to watch that, Lady. It was best to get through it quickly."

"It was good that she got to see the results of her foolishness, I suppose." Teora spoke more sharply than she intended. "My man was equally at fault. Do you expect me to mete out equal punishment?"

He worked the rope in his hands, and she winced to see a fleck of blood on one coil. "No, of course not. If Yukio was messing with the girl..."

She shook her head. "It wasn't that serious. She could have handled it. I expect better of my people than to go brawling with sailors." She grinned evilly. "I suspect he got a bit of a shock when his back hit the planks. Up until that point, he probably thought he had a chance."

"Speaking of taking chances, I don't think you should have jumped in like that."

"What would he have done? Hit me? I take worse than that at least once a month in training."

"I suppose. But if he hit you, it would have gone hard with him."

"And I'm supposed to be sympathetic?"

It was Palani's turn to grin. "You're not exactly the sweet young lady you seem, are you?"

"People keep finding that out."

The Power to Serve

Gordon A. Long

AIRBORN PRESS

Delta, B. C.

The Power to Serve

Gordon A. Long

Published by

AIRBORN PRESS

4958 10A Ave, Delta, B. C.

V4M 1X8

Canada

ISBN: Softcover – 978-1-988898-38-4

eBook – 978-1-988898-38-4

Printed by Amazon

Cover Design by Gordon A. Long

This is a work of fiction. All the characters and events portrayed in this book are fictional, and any resemblance to real people or incidents is purely coincidental.

Contents

Thanks to Cas Peace for her eagle-eyed editing

Prologue: A Difficult Decision

The girl stood relaxed, her gaze drifting off across the rolling prairie to the haziness of the distant horizon. She seemed unaware of the huge beast that paraded ponderously off to her left, pawing the dirt, fixing her now and again with a large, intelligent eye. Slowly, her concentration narrowed. Her body straightening, she pivoted to face the hulking animal.

At that moment his demeanor changed, the uncertainty gone. Without warning, he lowered the vicious hooks of his horns and charged. As his immense weight accelerated, the ground quivered under the power of his driving legs. Dust from the arid soil boiled around him, sweeping up behind like smoke from a prairie fire.

Teora stood completely still: head up, her short, light robe fluttering against her thighs in the hot breeze. As the thundering bull approached his full speed, she raised her arms and held that pose, willing her compact stillness into stark contrast with the destructive power closing on her.

Barozon had now achieved his stride, massive weight transformed into headlong movement. At the last moment, when his head lowered for the impact, she took two measured steps forward. The broad poll swept upward, and she dove into a forward roll between the horns, her arms spread wide in counterpoint to their sweeping curve. A fingertip's touch on each side set her balance to perfection.

The force of his rush and the thrust of the muscular neck beneath her body lifted her and, for a heartbeat, she stood upright atop his shoulders. Then, as his momentum carried him through beneath her, she ran lightly along the tapering back and leapt down to land precisely in her original position. The bull, with dexterity out of keeping with his huge bulk, spun to face her again.

Flushed with the exertion and the pleasure of accomplishment, she waited. The bull did not move. She waited longer, then made an imperious motion with her hand. The beast shifted, his blunt nose rising and falling.

"Come on, Barozon, once more. That was almost perfect!"

Her huge companion gracefully (to the degree it was possible for him) declined.

"Barozon!" The stomping of her small foot was dwarfed by the restless shuffle of the massive hooves confronting her.

She moved closer, surveying him critically. *It is not like him to refuse.* Then her experienced eye noted the lathered darkness marring his tawny shoulders, the dust smudging the short, tight curls of his mane, the laboured quality of his breathing. In contrition, she ran up beside him and reached her arms around his neck as far as she could.

"I'm sorry. It's too hot to be working so hard for so long. But we were just getting it smooth. You've been a real trouper to put up with me. How about a swim to cool off?"

The nearest eye rolled doubtfully up at her.

"Yes, that's it. A swim!"

An ear twitched in hope.

She batted him on the cheek to start his head turning and vaulted onto his back. "To the river, Barozon, but take your time. We've done our work for today."

She sat crosswise on the curly mat of his hump, her heel kicking his sleek brown shoulder in time with his stride. In response, he turned and ambled through the stunted prairie shrubbery towards the green line of willows that marked the nearby water. As they rambled along, she chatted to him about their training session, discussing the finer points of her moves and letting him know what she needed from him.

The other Dancers considered this habit of hers eccentric, but she was convinced that the bulls understood much more of what was said to them than most people thought. She knew that Barozon enjoyed it when she spoke to him. His mobile right ear always flicked backwards, and he sometimes bobbed his head or snorted in response.

Besides which, Father says you must always finish a training session by going over what you have learned and deciding what you need to work on next. This is my rather personal method of obeying instructions.

When they reached the river, several Dancers were already relaxing in the shallows with their Partners. Others lay in the shade of the huge old willows that lined the banks while their bulls rested with them or grazed on lush, deep-green grass nurtured by the flowing water. Barozon splashed towards his favourite spot deep under the hanging branches and settled in the water with a satisfied groan. She rubbed him down vigorously, cleaning and combing his hair with her fingers until he glistened.

Finished, she took to the water with a sigh, floating with her head and upper back resting on his half-submerged side. She was picturing, one by one, the motions of the vault she was perfecting when her attention was drawn by low conversation and a stifled snicker. Opening her eyes, she recognized the couple relaxing against the trunk of the tree above her on the bank. Her pleasant mood vanished, replaced by one of cautious defence.

The girl tossed her wavy brown hair and spoke, pleasantly enough, although her smile was overly sweet. "Oh, Teora, I was just saying to Fenaris how well you and your animal suit each other."

An inward burning began. It wasn't Teora's fault that she was stockier than the others. Even some of the boys were slenderer than she, some of the youngest trainees taller. And who could have known, when they were Partnered so many years ago, that Barozon would grow to such proportions? She knew that the other girl's snide comment was rooted in envy, but still it hurt. Fenaris had the grace to look uncomfortable. Teora wondered what to say.

She was saved from answering by a languid voice drifting up from behind a rangy black bull that lay, an indistinct blob, in the deep shadows nearby.

"Harida, you mustn't plague my sister. You have to show some sympathy, you know." A sleek head separated itself from the midnight of the black bull's mane. The pale, clear skin of the girl's face accentuated her dark eyes. Her smile matching Harida's for sweetness, Linea rested her chin on the backs of her hands. "It's difficult, you know, being Partnered to the prime bull of his generation," the smile softened theatrically, "and having to deal with all that envy."

The black bull, sensing his Partner's tension, heaved himself to his feet. As his head rose, the dark-haired girl laid a hand near the tip of one horn and drifted up to a standing position. Teora was struck again by the grace of her younger sister's every move. Insight flashed to her. *There is no way that trick could have been improvised. Linea worked on it in private to make it that smooth. It's not something I would have even thought of, let alone spent time on.*

3

Linea turned to her sister and smiled. "If you're finished, let's go home. I was waiting for you and got sidetracked by a little nap. See you, Fenaris." She nodded in a friendly fashion to Harida and swung lithely up onto her bull's back.

Teora nudged her Partner, taking firm control over her emotions as he was beginning to respond to her distress; his head rising, eyes searching for the cause. He heaved his dripping bulk out of the shallows, and she slipped up on his back in her own economical way. As they mounted the bank, she nodded politely to the two under the tree, neither of whom had figured out Linea's response quite enough to understand whether or not they had been insulted.

"Thanks, Little One." Teora slowed Barozon as she came alongside. "You know, I'm the big sister. I'm supposed to do the protecting."

"Don't let her get to you. She's just jealous."

"Of me? I'm no competition for Harida. She's the Senior Dancer! I'm a full year younger. Unless some unheralded wonder comes in from the provinces, she is sure to win in this year's contest."

Linea slammed her palm on her Partner's thick shoulder, hard enough to cause him to start. "It just isn't fair."

Teora regarded her sister with concern. Theatrical as Linea was, it was unlike her to get seriously upset, and even more unusual for her to show it, especially over such a trivial incident. "What do you mean?"

Linea glared across, anger marring her smooth face. "The whole system. It isn't fair. Why can't there be a contest every year? Look at Harida. Sure, she's going to win this year. But you're so close, and getting better every day, you work so hard. Then, next year, when you will be Senior, there isn't a contest!"

"I know."

"And when the contest comes around in two years, you'll be nineteen and past age. It isn't fair."

Teora shook her head, her lip twisting. "My dear sister, you are once again off in the land of the poets, where power is only used for the purposes of the Deity, and faith conquers all."

"I know. I must be realistic." Linea tossed back her hair. "But I don't have to like it."

Teora shrugged. "That's the way the Deity has planned it. She doesn't need a new Consort for her herds every year, I suppose. You shouldn't be complaining. That's sacrilege, you know."

4

The younger girl looked guilty, then smiled. "There, I've given you a chance to act Older Sister. Now we're even."

"Not really. Your interruption was very handy. I was starting to get steamed, and you know how Barozon reacts to that."

A predatory smile flitted across the pale face. "Yes. And given the chance, he would tromp her mangy 'Teddy' into the ground."

"Linea! A fight between bulls is intolerable, and a true sacrilege. The Consort of the Deity would never forgive me if I allowed one of His avatars to injure another!"

Her sister's expression did not waver. "I have a feeling that the Deity Herself might intercede for you in this case." She shook her mane of hair, so like that of her Partner in its glossy black, so unlike in its long, straight flow. "Besides, the idea of that witch lording it over us for two whole years is not a pleasant one. That's not fair either."

Glancing once again at her sister's slender form, Teora reflected that there were other types of unfairness, but dismissed the thought as unworthy. "At least they'll have someone nicer for the following two years."

Linea regarded her, straight and deadly serious again. "You think I could make it, don't you?"

"Of course. And so do you."

"Will you help me?"

"I've always helped you."

"No, I mean, will you work with me, coach me? I'll listen. I promise I will!"

"What about Father?"

"I'll still go to all my regular classes and practices with him, but you know he hasn't enough strength left for any more than that. I mean extra work. The kind you do all the time anyway. Please, Teora?"

The older girl considered. She knew what her sister meant. If Teora herself were to concentrate, there was an outside chance that she could win this year. *A very outside chance. A large tree falling on Harida and about three other top Seniors would do the trick. And the number of large trees in the Haven is vanishingly small.* If she were to spend her extra time helping the younger girl, her own chance would disappear. Her sister, in two years' time, was a different matter. She had beauty and athletic ability, and her Partner, Leathad, was an exceptionally graceful and intelligent animal.

5

It was hard to give up the dream. Now Barozon would never be the Consort; would never stride in his unyielding pace at the head of the Consecration Parade; never be the Sire to the Herds of the Goddess. She would never see her father's wan face brighten again with pride. If she were to give up now, then soon Barozon would be sent, with all due ceremony, to the ranch of some lucky lord as a reward for services to the Land. His Partner would follow him to the honourable, dull life of herd husbandry for which she was trained.

She snorted in disgust with herself. *Who am I fooling? Even if I did, by some whim of the Deity, win this year's contest, what would change? Two years of glory that I don't deserve, then the same fate anyway.*

"I'll work as hard as you do. Well, as much as I can!"

She looked over at her sister, beautiful even in anxiety, those dark eyes alight with enthusiasm. Now there was the one who should be Priestess, and what a Priestess she would make! What honour to their family. She would not retire to obscurity at the end of her reign. If she were ever allowed to leave the Haven, it would be as the bride of the lord who deserved her Partner.

Teora suppressed a sigh. *I have always known this time would come. Deep down, I always had the hope that, somehow, if I worked hard, the Deity might, just might...*

That was the dream. It was what kept her awake through the long, hot nights, when the dry wind sucked the sleep from her. Teora knew the reality all too well.

If you lived in the Haven, you earned your place. If you no longer earned a place, then there was no place for you. It came as a wrench to her, but if her father died, then the only reason her family would remain was because she and Linea were Dancers. If neither of them became Priestess, the family would have to go. That was it. No reprieve, no second chance.

The dream had to end. A physical pang shot to the centre of her being. *Today is the day.*

Teora smiled ruefully across at her sister and reached out to lay a hand on her arm. "I guess we couldn't do better than to bet on a sure thing, could we?"

Linea's responsive smile made it almost worth it, right then.

"All right, then, Little One. The work starts tomorrow!"

My purpose is clear. I have made the choice. Will the Deity ever tell me if it was the right one

1.   Celebration

Teora stood in the cheering crowd, eyes full of pride and tears, as she watched the joyful scene at the altar. *If only Father had lived to see this moment: the fulfillment of all his years of encouragement and support.*

The black bull's head swung from side to side, taking in the mob of people below him, the sounds and the smells of the ceremony, the decorations brushing his hide. Then Linea, tall and slim, strode across the wide stone platform, her silken dress and hair flowing, and offered the wreath from the Blessing. He calmed under her touch as she deftly wove the flowers about his spreading horns, ending perfectly with the huge orchid in the middle of his forehead.

Then, in the traditional symbol of entreaty, she stepped backward, and he followed her down the long, sloping ramp to the pavement of the Way of Horns. There she turned with sedate steps and began her walk to the Temple of the Consort, the tall black animal a few paces behind. Her head was high, but her glance searched from side to side, and Teora wondered what she was looking for. Then the dark eyes met hers and held. A quick wink, a slip of an impish grin, and then the new Priestess resumed her stately demeanour. Soon, the procession had passed, and Teora was left, the only stillness in the shuffling crowd as people followed, trying to stretch out the contact with joy and hope for a bit longer.

There had been precious little joy, she thought, glancing down at the sunbaked stones. The past two years had not been kind to the Haven. The drought had been longer than any in recorded history, and all the effort the people had put into new pumps and aqueducts to bring water from the mountains had barely sufficed to keep the Herds alive. There had been a poor calf drop this past spring, and more than the usual number of deaths among the weaker animals. This was just as well – small herds were best in drought time – but the political situation was also serious.

Even in the Haven, cushioned as they were from the outside world, they heard rumours of the weakening of the Binding Treaties. What effect a breakup of the Joined Kingdoms would have on the Land, who could know? Would a new, better order arise, as some said, or would all disintegrate into chaos and war? How could the Deity allow such a disaster?

Teora roused herself from the lethargy that held her. *Who am I to be having such morbid thoughts? This is the day of my sister's triumph.* The shadow of uncertainty that had descended on the family at the death of their father was gone, at least for the next two years. That was plenty of time to carve a new place for themselves in the Haven if they wished.

With that thought in mind, she looked around. She caught a glimpse of her mother leaving the shaded viewing area. A pang of...something...dashed through Teora. Manora was a young widow with new status, now that her daughter was Priestess to the Consort. The gentlemen of the solicitous group that had formed might have more on their minds than good manners. She watched as her mother impatiently pushed aside the proffered hands and stepped down to street level, brushing at her eyes.

In that moment, Teora forgot the crowds, the staring people, the regal display. She rushed forward to be clasped in those strong, soft arms, to be enfolded in the familiar warm scent that had always meant security to her.

After a moment, she pulled back to look into her mother's tear-stained face. "He would have been so proud!"

"Of course he would. Of course he is. He always knew one of you would make it, and I'm sure he knows now." Her mother smiled softly. "He will soon, anyway, with Linea in a much better position to transform our prayers. He will be so pleased." She paused to look at her elder daughter. "He wanted it to be you, you know."

"Oh, Mother, you didn't have to say that."

Manora pulled her daughter in beside her as they walked along. "I didn't just say that. I believe it. He loved Linea, because he was her father, and, well, because everyone loves her. But..."

"But everyone doesn't love me."

Her mother grinned and cuffed her shoulder. "Well, you could try a bit harder." Then she took Teora's arm and leaned towards her. "But he had a special place in his heart for you, perhaps because of that, and I know he really wanted you to be happy, to do well."

The older woman chuckled fondly. "I remember the first time he figured out that you were going to be the wrong age to be Priestess. He was so angry! You were only about three years old at the time. I laughed at him and told him how silly it was to have such plans for one so young. He laughed with me and lifted you and bounced you up and down and then apologized to you very politely, you giggling in his face the while. Still, I remember how it bothered him at first." She gave Teora's shoulders a squeeze. "I suppose it was one small dream he had to let go of. We were very young, then."

Teora stopped and looked across at her mother for a long moment. "Mother, in a little while, when you want to, you find a nice man and you marry him. I won't mind. I will do my best to make him feel welcomed."

"Why, Teora, what a strange thing to say on a day like this. What put that into your head?"

Teora leaned forward, her hands on her mother's shoulders. "This is important, Mother. You are young. You can marry again. Now is a good time. Look!" She tossed her head back towards the crowd of her mother's friends who had been following behind, respecting the privacy of this conference. Sure enough, there was a considerable number of unescorted gentlemen. She took Manora's arm and led her on through the crowd along the dusty street.

"Now is your chance. You have status, allure even, as mother of the Priestess. Don't hold back because of us. Father wouldn't mind...won't mind either. We all want you to be happy."

Manora looked at her daughter strangely. "So, you have given me two years to find myself a mate, because I'm more...marketable?"

Teora shook her head miserably. "I know I sound like a breeder at the stock fair, but that's not what I meant. I didn't think, it just came to me, and I spoke. I didn't want to start a fight; I wanted you to be happy!"

A shake of her arm turned her to look at her mother, who was laughing. "Teora, you have always been the strangest girl. You are so used to being everyone's big sister that you even do it to me sometimes. Now, don't worry. In a while, if I find someone I want to marry, I promise you I won't hold back for any silly reasons. But don't you dare start parading dignified elderly gentlemen past me." She shook her daughter again. "Promise?"

Teora slipped her arm comfortably around her mother's waist. "I promise. Now, let's catch up to the procession, find a cool drink, and see Little Sister installed properly in her new home."

Manora paused, looking around. "Have you seen your brother?"

"Don't worry about the Stretched One. He's around somewhere, basking in reflected glory."

9

"Teora! Do not tease your brother about his height. He is at a very sensitive age right now."

Teora laughed. "Nonsense. He puts that on to get attention. He's so proud that he is finally growing that he can barely contain it." A wicked grin crossed her lips. "And if he's going to be that much taller than me for the whole rest of our lives, he's going to pay now!"

"Teora, you aren't the type to be jealous."

The girl looked straight across into her mother's eyes and smiled smugly. "Oh yes, I am. We short people are very vindictive."

Her mother's response was instinctive. "Oh, you really aren't that..."

"Yes I am, and so are you. We short people are also realistic. So, stop pretending that you don't know I'm teasing you and let's go have some fun. I'm sure Brother and his obnoxious friends with their strange haircuts are off having a great time, and there's nothing to worry about." She paused, smiling an invitation back to her mother's friends. "We have a celebration to attend."

* * *

After two days and nights, the party was beginning to wind down, thank the Deity. Teora could barely keep her eyes open. She wandered the empty street, focusing on the dust swirls lifted around her feet by the ceaseless wind. She had stolen a few hours of sleep when she could, but it was never enough. Now all she thought of was getting home for a quick nap before the Vigil of Fertility started at sundown. Despite the happy nature of the occasion, she was at the moment feeling downright grouchy. Hoping it was only lack of sleep and could not be attributed in any way to jealousy, she did her best to hide her feelings from the others. She also kept away from her Partner so as not to disturb him with her negative emotions. *Leaving me alone, which is good, because I'm used to myself when I'm like this. I'm the best company I can find.*

"Say, Teora, where are you headed?"

She sighed and squared her shoulders before she turned. There in a nearby tavern doorway stood a group of Dancers: from her year and Linea's, a few lucky younger hangers-on. A friendly face, edged by unruly black curls, answered the smile she dredged up.

"Hello, Renelal. I'm going home, I think. I'm so tired I'm not sure anymore, and I must get some sleep, or I'll never make it through the Vigil."

He straightened from his leaning position and stepped closer, his smile widening. "I could get you through the Vigil all right. Definitely keep your mind off sleeping!"

A tiny point of excitement wiggled upward through the smothering layers of fatigue. Renelal was one of the better Dancers of her year, flamboyant and undisciplined. They got on well together, although he always had too many of the other girls hanging around him to find time for her. She moved in to speak privately.

"Now, Ren, you know I can't join you. The family of the new Priestess has a more decorous ceremony to attend." She grinned at his disappointment. "Don't worry, you'll get over it. Once the novelty of Linea's position wears off, you can see me as a fellow performer again."

A hurt expression crossed his fine features. "That's not it at all, Teora. It's not because of your sister. I've always liked you! It just came to me, you know, and I thought..." He wound down, then looked seriously at her. "I <u>have</u> always liked you. You always treated me so well, not like..." He tossed his head in the direction of the group. "You know."

She shook her head. "I understand what you mean, and I wish I could say I know how it feels. But I have never had your problem. Sometimes I wish I did!"

"No, you don't!"

She stopped him with a raised finger. "Renelal, are you actually complaining about how the girls come running if you even tilt your head?"

His old, cocky grin returned. "Well, not really, I guess. But sometimes it gets to be a bit of a bore, and you wish some girl would talk to you normally, without that look in her eye...oh. I'm sorry. I guess I just did that same thing to you, didn't I? I mean, I treated you like..."

Smiling, she rescued him. "No, Ren, you didn't. You made me a perfectly honest and very flattering offer, which I unfortunately must refuse. It won't change anything between us. Don't apologize. I'm not completely business, you know. The attention of a popular man is a great compliment."

11

His head rose to its usual slant. "Some other time, then."

She thought a moment, gazing up at his handsome face. "Probably not, Ren." She shrugged. "It isn't my style. You know." Reaching up, she pulled his head down and kissed him on the lips, taking care that his followers could see clearly. A whoop and several whistles erupted from the inn doorway. Then she was away down the street with a lighter step, leaving him to saunter back inside. After a parting like that, he would need to make no excuses to his rowdy friends.

She continued homeward, her head and body buzzing with warring excitement and fatigue. This was an aspect of her new situation she had not considered.

The Consecration ceremony and celebration took exactly three days, starting the first morning with the serious religious rites at the Temple and ending with the Vigil of Fertility through the final night. Different people had their own interpretations as to how an all-night vigil might honour the concept of fertility. In some sections of the city there would be a great upswing in business for the midwives nine months later, and no one commented on the family resemblances of children born at that time.

But on that last night, the family of the new Priestess attended a private ceremony, allowing them one final night together before her duties took her from them for two years and sometimes for the rest of her life. The part that Teora had also tried to tell Renelal was that she would never spend the Vigil in the way he had envisioned. Only when she was married, when the gift of fertility from the Deity would bring her something important and wonderful. Without that purpose, the act would be meaningless.

Still, it was impossible to ignore the surge of excitement his offer had brought. She wondered if there were others who saw her differently, now. Ren was right in one thing; he really had helped her. It wasn't going to be hard to stay awake tonight.

With these thoughts winging her along, it was a considerably more cheerful Teora who skipped into the tiled hallway of her mother's house. "Anyone home?"

"Someone sounds happy." Manora was in the public room, resting on the embroidered horsehide couch that her husband had bought for their house-entering day. Teora could not help but wonder what her mother was thinking. She often got a faraway look when she sat there. Probably remembering.

Teora sat down and laid her head back against her mother's outstretched arm. "I suppose I am happy. It sometimes seems as if nothing has happened, and then I remember, and I get excited all over again."

"Me, too. What reminded you this time?"

Teora glanced over at her mother, then straight ahead. "I got an invitation for tonight."

Manora laughed happily, with a touch of pride. "You did? And what poor young man has thrown himself at your feet?"

Teora shifted her gaze again to her mother. "Renelal."

Manora's smile faded. "Oh. That kind of invitation. You didn't..."

Teora waited, then gave in. "Of course not, Mother. I don't even know how serious he was. He must have known I had to Vigil with Linea. He knew he was safe. Still, I was flattered. He's very popular, you know." She thought a moment. "And very nice."

"They often are."

Teora stared at her mother. "They? What do you mean by that?"

"Men with too many women around them. Some are very pleasant people, but with a certain wildness which is somehow attractive. Others are quite different. They have a streak of mean selfishness once you get through the surface charm. Every mother worries about that sort of thing, you know."

Teora stared at her mother, trying to keep the anger from boiling up. "I think you're making a lot of assumptions, Mother. You know, that was one thing Ren was just saying to me. Every woman regards him as if he were some...thing. The younger ones want him for it; you fear him because of it. But none of you treat him like a person. But he is!" She couldn't stop now, even though she knew her voice was rising. "And he isn't one of the 'mean ones' you're worried about, because I know him and I've worked with him and I've Danced with him for years, and he's as considerate and friendly and selfless as anyone I know!"

Without warning, her mother collapsed in tears, her face in her hands. Teora sat, stunned. *What did I say? My mother is made of tougher stuff than that.* Helpless, she put her arm around the older woman's shoulders.

"Mother, what's wrong? What did I do? I'm sorry, it's just that everyone is mean to him, and it bothers him. I didn't mean you, specifically."

13

Slowly, Manora lifted her face from her hands, fighting for control. Finally, the sobs subsided, and she regarded her daughter. "Oh, Teora, it's so hard. I worry about you girls so much, and your brother, and there are times when I don't know what to do. Here you are, talking about this wild young fellow, and I'm so worried, but I know if I argue, you'll go running straight to him! Sometimes I wish so hard that your father was here!" She buried her face again, and slumped there, unmoving.

Teora reached out and took her mother's wrists, gently forcing them apart until the two women faced each other. "I do too, Mother. I'm sorry I made you upset. It's all the excitement and the lack of sleep. But don't worry about me. I'm not about to run off with Renelal to his wild life. I have very little interest in it, even to experiment. Don't worry. I'm smarter than that. Come on, let's get cleaned up. It's almost sundown, and we're due at the Temple of the Consort." She smiled. "Linea's temple."

Manora wiped her eyes. "I suppose so. I'll need to wash again after this." She ruefully gestured towards her tear-stained face and got up from the couch. Then she turned back towards her daughter. "But don't think that intelligence is going to keep you safe. When love comes into it, even the smartest people do the dumbest things." A reminiscent smile curved her lip. "At least that's what my mother told me when I said I was marrying your father." She turned and left the room.

Wondering what that story was all about, Teora followed.

As the sun fell past the edge of the plateau, the Family of the Priestess presented themselves at the Consort's gate. Three young priests, stiff and serious, met them with the ritual challenges.

"Who seeks entrance to the New Consort's Home in the time of his Ascension?"

"The kin of his Priestess seek entrance to his Home."

"What would you with the Consort's Priestess? She is His alone and can no longer spend her time with the earth-bound."

"We know this is to be, and seek one last time with her."

"Where is the Mother of the Priestess?"

Manora stepped forward proudly. "I am here."

"Where is the Father of the Priestess?"

Everyone knew the answer, but the ritual must be completed. Manora lifted her chin higher. "The Father of the Priestess has gone early to the Last Haven, to prepare the way for his family."

"Who else comes to Vigil with the Priestess?"

"I, her elder sister."

"I, her younger brother."

Teora glanced sideways at Sovestin, standing there stiffly in his best suit of clothes. He really had grown. *Good for him. Now, if only he would grow up enough to get a decent haircut...*

The priests continued, speaking in unison now, their trained voices rolling deeply across the wide stone ramp that led to the huge doorway. "The Consort will consider your plea, but for this night only. With the rising sun you must leave His Priestess to her duties. While she serves Him, never will she eat at your table, nor sleep in your home, nor walk with you in your pastures. The Deity demands all from Her Consort, and the Consort demands all from His Priestess. Still, for this one night, He may have pity on you, who have loved him. You may enter His presence."

At those words, the massive doors opened. Teora had never been past the threshold, and she gazed around with interest as they entered. The main hall was a huge room with rows of pillars holding up the stone roof. In the centre, where light spilled down from square openings in the ceiling, was the largest stall she had ever seen. The sides were low, but carved with stone heavy enough to resist the hooves and horns of any bull, living or mythical. At one end, the walls rose and were roofed over, open to face the main doors of the hall, with an arched lintel carved to represent the constellations of the heavens and symbols of the Land, the Sea, and the Mountains.

And there, looking forlorn and small, stood Leathad, black and shiny, munching in a bored way on some bovine epicurean tidbit. When he saw the family approach, his head came up, his ears twitching. He was so pathetically eager to see familiar faces that Teora wanted to laugh, but the presence of the three serious young men stifled her.

They were led in a stately procession towards the stall and stood in a row facing the entrance. Technically, this was a test. If the Consort would not accept them, they were not supposed to be admitted. There was certainly no problem today. Leathad trotted over to see them and stuck his nose over the stone wall. With a glance at the priests for permission, Teora stepped forward and rubbed him under the chin.

15

He loved it, turning his head to expose scratchable spots to her fingers.

With a hint of a grin tugging at the corners of his mouth, the priest intoned the ritual phrase. "You have been accepted by the Consort." With a relaxing of tension, they all moved around behind the stall.

There, on a throne attached to the back of the stall, illuminated by crisscrossed shafts of light from the roof, sat Linea.

Teora stopped in some confusion. This was not the quiet, languorous sister she remembered. This was a powerful priestess, with upright posture, her austere beauty an appropriate counterpoint to the massive stone of her Temple.

They lined up humbly before her, and the three priests continued the ritual. "O Priestess of the Consort. Your family desires to spend one last night with you before they lose you entirely to your duties. What say you, Lady of the Deity?"

As the ceremony droned on, Teora regarded her sister. Was it some trick of the light, or did Linea seem sterner, more imposing? This was not the girl who had winked at her in the street. This was not the sister who, the night before the ceremony, had been so frightened about not knowing what to do. This was a mature woman, confident in her power, upheld by the belief of her society.

When the ritual was over, the priests withdrew, and the illusion was broken as Linea ran stumbling down the steps to throw herself into her mother's arms.

"Mother, you don't know how glad I am to see you!" She took Manora and Teora's hands, including Sovestin with a toss of her head, and led them towards a door: a normal, human-sized door, obscured by a pillar.

On the other side was a pleasant public room, cool and well furnished, with food and drink set out on trays, and soft couches spread around. Leading her family to comfortable seats and tossing the tiara from her head, Linea was bursting with talk.

"It's good to see you here. I am so tired of all these people who won't talk to me. Me, you understand. Oh, they talk to the Priestess, of course, and give her no end of instructions. They act as if I'm not really here. I'm only a body to hold up the Circlet of the Priestess."

Teora laughed in relief at this Linea-like outburst. "Don't let it get to you, Little Sister. These people live here and do this job all their lives. The Priestess comes and goes; a new one every two years. The beginning is a tense time for them. What are you going to be like? You will have a lot of control over them. They are probably trying to assert their power first, while you are still new. Ground they gain now will be easier to hold. Mother, why are you looking at me so strangely?"

Manora was staring at her older daughter in awe. "How did you know that?"

"I didn't really know it, but it stands to reason, doesn't it?" Teora was puzzled. *It seems so obvious.*

Her mother sighed and smiled sadly. "Of course it does. To me. It's just that I was surprised, that's all. You are both growing up so much." She turned to Linea.

"You know, I had planned to come here and have a heart-to-heart talk tonight, explain things to you, prepare you for the next few months. Now, it seems, you should talk to your sister."

"Mother, I've been talking to her for years and I still don't understand how she figures out things like that. I'll have to muddle my way through as I always do."

Sovestin stared at the laden table in front of them. "Hah! If I read the signs right, you have at least three followers already, and you'll have the rest falling in line before the month is out. Do you think we could stop worrying about nonessentials and get to the appropriate hostess duties?"

Manora gave him a mildly reproving frown. "Don't always think about your stomach, Sov. What do you mean, followers?"

"He means," Teora draped an arm across her mother's shoulders, "that those three young men out there were positively, pathetically anxious for the ritual to go smoothly, stumbling over themselves to ease our way. Can you imagine what a relief it's going to be for the people around here to have Linea as the Priestess, after suffering two years with Harida?"

"What do you mean, suffering?"

"Oh Mother, don't try to be correct." Linea poured a drink and handed it to her brother. "Even when she was Priestess, everyone said what a twit she was. Now you take this plate, Taller Brother, and enjoy yourself. Mother? Teora?" She passed plates and cups, then set herself to play the hostess, serving them all before she partook herself.

She gazed up at the sunlight, fading from the mirrors that created the lighting effect. "I'm sure we all have plenty to say to each other."

2.   Envoys

Teora was perfecting a dance move in the inner courtyard when Sovestin charged through the street door like a bull headed for his feed, his hair flying in all directions. She paused and regarded him, then broke from her pattern. She felt good today. The moves had been going well, and the breeze cooled the sweat on her skin. She grinned at his restless pose.

"Obviously the city is falling around our heads, there has been a new song in the market, or something of equal importance has happened. What are you jumping around about?"

He was too excited to be affected by the usual sisterly squashing. "Where's Mother? There's news! Din sent me over to get you both!"

"Who is this Din that he can send for us with such authority?"

Sovestin jumped and spun to face his mother, where she stood in the dark shadow of the archway. "Din...Dinnan, he's... a Junior Priest at the Temple. One of Linea's... her... well, you know."

Teora laughed. "We know. Linea hasn't wasted time in finding allies. I told her it wouldn't be hard. How are you so familiar with this priest?"

The boy's eyes dropped. "Well, I've been around there a bit, you know, and the Temple's pretty slicey, you know."

"I doubt if the Consort of the Deity would like his Temple referred to as 'slicey', but I suppose your approval is the main thing. You haven't been trying to see Linea, have you?" Manora's voice was sharp, but her glance at Teora behind Sovestin's head was much softer. A boy could find worse things to do in his free time than hang around the Temple. In fact, he probably had been finding worse things to do since his father's death.

"Oh, no! Well, not really. She does a lot of public appearances, you know, and sometimes there's not too many people there, and she smiles at me, you know, and..." he went on more quickly, "...and sometimes at the Temple the Priests are sitting around. They have free time, too, and I talk to them. Dinnan's the youngest. He's only been here two years, and he was a Dancer before, like you!" The boy's voice lowered. "I don't think he liked Harida very much, and she was the only Priestess he ever knew. Then when Linea turned out nice, he was pretty surprised and pretty happy. Now he's nice to me, and we talk about her." He grinned, but then his face became serious. "And he wants us to all come to the Temple right now. He told me privately, so we could be prepared, he said."

"Prepared for what?"

"I don't know for sure, but it must be something to do with those horse riders that came in yesterday. They sure looked different today, let me tell you. All fancied up in their robes!"

Manora was confused. "What about the riders? What kind of robes?"

Teora smiled. "I can answer the first part, Mother. An embassy of some sort rode in yesterday. I can't figure out what a bunch of horsemen could have to do with the Temple, though. I thought they were traders or something. Dressed in riders' leathers."

Sovestin was practically jumping now. "What they had to do with the Temple is that they're Priests!"

"Priests?" Manora frowned. "But they were riding horses!"

He nodded emphatically. "Priests. One of them, at least. They came from a long way away, and they must have carried a real important message. They were received at the Temple this morning, and Din says you have to come right away so you'll be prepared."

Teora glanced at her mother, abruptly silent and still. "What do you think, Mother? What's wrong?"

Manora put a hand on a shoulder of each. "The only thing we have to be prepared for is Linea going away. She must be needed somewhere." She straightened her back. "Come, children. It was thoughtful of Priest Dinnan to give us some advance warning. We must go to the Temple."

Sovestin frowned. "So, what's wrong with that? We knew she'd be going on lots of journeys. That's why it's so slicey to be the Priestess!"

Teora understood. "It's the politics, isn't it, Mother? Emissaries coming in a hurry like this, and the problems with the Treaties. It doesn't sound like a normal Tour."

"No, it doesn't. Where would Priests of the Deity be coming from that they would need horses? And why did they go to the Temple of the Consort, not the main Temple? This is serious, and the roads are unsafe right now and I hope Linea doesn't have to go!"

"It can't be that bad." Teora put an arm around her mother's shoulders. "Here we are getting all upset, and we don't even know what's happening."

Sovestin was right behind her. "Sure. What are we standing here getting all lathered up for? Let's go over to the Temple and find out. Maybe it's something good!"

Manora smiled and shook her head. "I wish I shared your enthusiasm, but maybe I worry too much. What the Deity has planned will happen; what's the use in fighting it?"

As they left the house, Teora kept her comforting arm across Manora's shoulders. *She feels so...small.* Teora had put on a late growth spurt, but not until now had she realized how much taller she was. It gave her an uncomfortable feeling. She had always thought of herself as short, and her mother as much bigger and stronger. It somehow wasn't right to be larger.

When they reached the Temple, Sovestin led them confidently down a narrow alley to a door that pierced the thick outer wall, letting them into a garden. Following a winding path through clumps of trees interspersed with plots of vegetables, herbs and flowers, the boy brought them to an open courtyard, where several Priests and servants were busy. *Housekeeping and gardening. Normal chores.* It certainly was a different perspective on religious life, and Teora regarded her brother more closely.

"You seem to know your way around."

"Sure. I've been here quite a bit. I help out sometimes, too. They're all real nice. Oh. Here's Dinnan."

He introduced them correctly to a tall young man, on whom the normal priest's robe looked somehow fashionable. Teora took in the stylish blond hair and sharp, pale blue eyes. *This is not a man who means to stay at the lower levels of the Priesthood.* She cautioned herself about making snap judgments, but the impression remained, strengthened by the firm tenor of his voice and the smooth manners he displayed.

He took them into a small office just inside the main Temple building and offered them chairs and a cool drink. Unhurriedly, he dispensed the amenities until Teora was starting to squirm. As she was getting up her nerve to ask, he leaned back in his chair and smiled at them.

"Now, this is all unofficial, you understand. I'm not supposed to be bringing you in and telling you all this. Officially, they'll let you know in their own good time. It's just that they don't take your feelings into account when they make these decisions. I've been talking to Sov, here, and I know a bit about your family, and I thought it would be more obliging to let you know what was happening. Then you'll be ready for whatever they decide."

Manora was still sitting in a formal pose, ignoring the young Priest's relaxed approach. *As if she is steeling herself to receive a blow.*

"I'm sure we appreciate your thoughtfulness, sir. May I assume that what you are preparing us for has something to do with my daughter's position as Priestess? Is she being called upon for some unusual duties?"

"A shrewd guess, Madam Manora. But please call me Dinnan. As I said, this is hardly an official occasion. I will not keep you in suspense any longer. I am sure Sov has told you about the emissaries?"

"We knew about them. They must come on an urgent mission, to be riding."

"Well, the riding is not that unusual. They come from the Enclave at Aeru. The people there are friendly with the nomadic tribesmen of the area, who are the finest horsemen in the world. However, this group is on an urgent mission, one that will affect us. You know of the political troubles down on the Flat?"

Manora and Teora's eyes met.

"I see you do. That will help you understand the problems facing the Aerans. So far from the Haven, they must either depend on peace in the Kingdoms to keep contact with us, or else break away and try to become independent. At the moment, neither option seems open. The peace is seriously threatened, while at the same time their stock is dwindling. Poor calving, many stillbirths, weakness in the breeding lines."

This was Teora's area of expertise. "It's the drought, the cold spring. We have had the same problems."

"Not as much as they have. Certainly, the weather has been difficult, but theirs is a deeper fault. They think it lies in the blood of their stock. Far as they are from the Herds of the Haven and with dwindling resources, they have not been able to afford good new blood in their herds. And it is not only the cattle. The leaders feel that the people have a weakness as well. Their faith is fading along with their stock. They need both practical and spiritual strengthening from us. After all, that is our function. But the political situation makes it difficult to comply."

Manora's poise was beginning to waver. "And they want Linea and Leathad to go all that way to rebuild their Herd bloodlines and give their people renewed faith? But it's so far! So dangerous! Who will provide the soldiers? Will the other Kingdoms, the ones who don't worship the Deity, let such a strong party pass through their lands during troubled times?"

The priest laughed: a low, friendly sound. "You are a practical lady, and you have pinpointed the main problems. The discussion has been taken over by the full Council, as it should be. The answers are out of our hands. I merely thought to prepare you."

"But they want Linea to go."

"That is one of the solutions."

"One of the solutions?"

Dinnan spread his hands in graceful denial. "I'm only a Junior here. They don't tell me much. Probably right. Look what I'm doing with the little information I have – spreading it to the general public. That's all I was told. The Priestess is only one of the solutions. I was as surprised to hear that as you are. But that's why those people have their positions, because they can come up with several solutions where you and I have only one or two."

"What is your alternate solution?"

The priest's quick eyes pinned Teora and, for a split second, she could see the calculations going on. Then he grinned. "Sov told me about you, too. He said you were always one jump ahead of everyone."

Her brother responded with his usual, 'Would I tell a lie?' expression, and she had to smile as well. "If I'm that quick, you're not going to put me off by changing the subject. What is your other solution?"

"I'm a bit ashamed of it, as a matter of fact, and I doubt if the Council will even consider it. But you have to at least look at any idea." His enthusiasm rising, the young Priest leaned forward. "I thought maybe an even bigger project."

"You don't mean a full Herding? Like the Aerans had when they first left the Haven?"

He nodded, his eyes bright.

She considered a moment. "No. Sorry, but no."

"Why not?" His face fell. "It has been done."

"Weather and politics. The Aerans left in a time of peace and plenty in a year of rains. We've already discussed the problem of moving a small guard through a stranger's land. How about enough soldiers to protect a Herd? Besides, I doubt if we have the stock or the soldiers here." She shrugged. "They aren't the only ones with political and spiritual troubles."

He shook his head as if not too disappointed. "I said it was out of line."

"And your third solution?"

"I only admitted two."

"Right."

"Teora!"

She looked at her mother.

"You mustn't question him like that, dear. He is a Priest."

The blond head lifted, and a deep laugh rolled out. "Don't worry, madam. I deserve it. It is unworthy of me to play such games." He leaned forward again, and once more Teora could sense the power of the intellect and spirit that drove him. "Please, ladies, and you, too, Sovestin. Any ideas I have are only conjectures, even wilder than the one I gave you. It would be irresponsible of me to share them with anyone. Be reassured that I would like to help you. I have my own reasons, you may be assured, but mainly I would not like Linea to take on this task. Oh, part of it is selfish, of course. She is such a pleasant change, after the past two years. But also, I don't think she should be the one to go."

Manora sat straighter. "Perhaps you think she could not handle the task?"

The priest raised his hands. "No, no, not at all. I have no doubt about the fitness of the Priestess for her duties." He grinned at Sovestin. "In fact, I suppose Sov has told you what I think of her."

This admission of human failing had the desired effect, and Dinnan said no more. The interview seemed to be over. Manora allowed herself to be escorted courteously to the door. As her mother turned, Teora caught the man's eye, determined to let him know that she wasn't fooled. He smiled and glanced heavenward, with a quick mopping of his brow to signal relief. She was forced to smile back, aware that he had worked his magic on her, too, but not really caring. With a friendly word to Sov, the priest let them out through the alley door, promising to call them the moment he got word.

The three trudged along, each caught up in deep thoughts.

"So that's your friend the Junior Priest, is it?"

Sov looked up at his mother with a grin. "Whaddaya think?"

"Some Junior Priest."

"He is! He wouldn't lie to me! He's only been there two years, and that makes him the lowest one in the Temple. He comes from the Capital, though. From a big family, he said, and he can't inherit. His only options were war, merchant travelling, or the Priesthood. That's what he told me."

"Mother, you know the Capital. What kind of a family has all those choices available to them?"

Manora smiled up at her daughter, striding purposefully along, now, as her mind worked. "You know the answer to that, too."

"A very powerful family. That one has a long way to go in the Priesthood."

"So, the question remains..."

"...what did he want with us?"

"And why did he pick Sovestin to be friendly to?"

"What are you two talking about? He likes me, is all. The other people in there are all caught up in the religion, and I'm not."

Teora thought. "And you know what's happening in the city, and he asks, and you tell him about it."

"Of course. He's interested. He listens." He glared accusingly at his mother and sister. Then his face fell. "You don't mean he only wants me as a source of information! But he likes me!"

Manora put her arm around her son's waist and matched his stride. "Of course he likes you, but there's no reason he shouldn't like the person he gets information from."

"Put it another way. Is there any reason why he shouldn't get the news from his friend?"

"Thank you, Teora, you put it much better. After all, Sov, at first you thought he was talking to you because he liked your sister. What's the difference? It means you're doubly important to him."

The boy's step was regaining its usual lilt. "You think he'll still be my friend?"

"Of course he will. What has changed? He needs to talk, and he probably still finds the conversation in the Temple pretty restricting. The question, though," Manora included Teora in the conversation, "is what plan he has that needed our visit."

"Well, Mother, as you said before we came, if the Deity wills it, then it's probably going to happen, so there's no use worrying about it."

"I have a feeling that if the Deity wills it and a certain young, blond Priest is involved, then all doubt is erased."

"Dinnan said that, actually." Sov nodded. "He said if you want the Deity's help, you go out and help yourself."

Teora ruffled his hair. "I also think that if Dinnan has anything to do with it, it can't help but come out to Linea's advantage. That's the impression I got."

"Well, Older Sister, as usual, we will depend on our impressions." Laughing, they turned in at their doorway.

3.   Chosen!

The next few days were a frustrating whirl of rumour, a conflicting mix of certainty and doubt. The news Dinnan had given them privately was common property long before they could have spread it. The major question, of course, was whether the Council would refuse the Aeran request. Some said yes, some no. 'Certain truth' circulated hours ahead of sure denial. Despite their reluctance, Teora and her family were drawn into the storm, although they refused to make any public comment.

Finally, official news was announced. The petition was denied. The Council had decreed that the Consort could not leave in such a time of turmoil. Desperate though the need might be, He might be in more demand closer to the Haven, should the political storms blow stronger. The Consort and His Priestess would stay in the Haven.

Manora rushed into the courtyard where Teora was helping Sovestin with some simple dance moves. This was unusual, as he had always firmly refused to get involved with the activities that took up so much of his family's lives.

"I heard the announcement in the courtyard outside the Temple. She's not going!"

"That's great. You're sure she's not going?"

"That's what the Speaker said, on the steps of the Main Temple. They made the announcement to keep people from being upset by the rumours."

Sovestin turned a clumsy cartwheel. "Slicey!"

Manora turned to her daughter. "You don't look completely happy."

"Yes, I am happy." Teora considered the strange feeling welling up in her. "For us. But what about the Aerans? Are we to turn our backs on them? I have always been taught that we at the Haven have one purpose: to act as the centre and bastion of the power and the belief of the Deity. What can we say for ourselves if someone comes with a real need, and we turn them down? What is our purpose, then?"

She could feel something building. "We have been selfish, Mother. Linea must go. Our feelings don't matter here. These people are an enclave of Followers of the Deity. If we allow them to fall away through our own selfishness, what will She think of us? What can we think of ourselves?"

Manora stared at her daughter. "You really mean it, don't you?"

"Of course I do. Why else would I say it?"

"You would prefer that Linea go into all that danger."

Teora seized her mother's shoulders and faced her. "Mother, she must. It is her duty. The task of the Priestess has a lot of luxury and glory, but it also has a purpose. She represents the faith of the people. It is selfish of us to want only the easy part for her."

"So, what do we do?"

The simple question took Teora aback. "You mean you agree?"

Manora's lips twisted with a sort of humour. "Do not take it for granted that your generation owns the market of wisdom or pride. Hard though it is to send my daughter into danger, I know that we must. I simply don't understand how the Council could fail to see the same."

"Then we must talk to them!"

Sovestin stared at them, aghast. "You mean that, after all this, you're going to the Council to ask that they send Linea away? What if she gets hurt, or killed, or never comes back?"

Manora reached out her hand, touching the boy's cheek. "You must understand how hard it is, so soon after losing your father, to send another one of the family away. But it must be. Come with us. Listen. Perhaps you will understand."

"Where are we going?"

Teora stared at her mother. "We can't just go to the Council and say, 'Hello, can we talk to you, we think you've made a big mistake.' They'll laugh at us."

"I haven't lived here all these years without making some friends, you know. I wasn't twiddling my thumbs all the time you girls and your father were messing around at your dancing. Come now, before my resolve weakens. Let's go get some answers." She strode out the main door and down the street towards the Main Temple, her son and daughter following, awed. It wasn't often that their mother acted this way, but they knew from experience that when she did it was best to stay well out of the way.

As it happened, they weren't the only ones who needed that advice. They had barely entered the main street when they bumped

27

into Dinnan, hurrying in their direction with un-Dinnan-like haste. He seemed somehow relieved to see them, although he was also a bit taken aback when Manora swept past him, forcing him to turn and scramble to catch up with her.

"How convenient, madam. Just the people I was coming to visit."

Manora smiled politely but did not slacken her pace. "I'm sure it is pleasant to see you again, Dinnan, but we have no time for chat at the moment. Would you like to come around later this afternoon? I'm sure we could arrange a convenient time."

By this time, the long legs had made up the distance, and their owner was regaining some of his aplomb. "I wasn't exactly coming on a social call, madam. I was sent for you ..."

"How unfortunate. Whoever wishes to see us will have to wait. We are on an important errand." She favoured him with what her family called her 'polite face.' "Do come along, Dinnan, if you please. When we are done, there will be time for whatever you wish."

Teora allowed herself a tiny inner chuckle. *So, Mister on-his-way-up priest with the piercing eyes and the thoughtful mien. It's good for you to get set back a bit. Not every woman falls over herself to accommodate your good looks and commanding presence.*

Dinnan opened his mouth but decided against it. He then started a bit of small talk, but that gambit was stifled as well. He glanced back to Teora, who returned her own version of polite interest. Sovestin shrugged expressively. Finally, the priest simply strode along with them, as if that was what he wanted all along.

He hesitated as they approached the entrance to the Main Temple. Then, as they turned in, he followed again. He seemed happier at this. *Very strange. I wonder what his original errand was.* If he had been sent to get them, this would be the wrong Temple.

Manora was oblivious to this by-play. She marched straight through the Worship Area and, as if she knew where she was going, turned to the left, through a large doorway that Teora thought perhaps led to the administrative offices. Correct. Soon, they were stopped in a small room with a large desk, and an imposing lay apostle guarding it.

"What may I do for you, madam?"

Manora smiled pleasantly at him. "You're new here, aren't you? I am Manora, and I will see Rhondona, please."

The man settled uneasily in his chair. "I'm sorry, Madam Manora, but I'm not sure that the Head of Council can manage another appointment. This is a very busy time, as you may know," he was getting back into his stride now, "and she has many weighty matters to decide." He pulled a huge book towards him as he spoke. It seemed to give him strength. "Perhaps we could fit you in early next week…"

Manora froze the patronizing smile as it formed. "You misunderstand, young man. I did not say I wanted an appointment. I merely indicated, for your information and peace of mind, that I would be seeing the Head Councillor. You will facilitate matters greatly if you would inform her that I am here. I assume that is why you have been placed in this convenient location."

The man's hands slid slowly off his appointment book as the superior look departed his face. "Well, madam… I don't quite know…"

How Manora would have dealt with this, Teora and her amused brother would never know, because Dinnan stepped forward. "Don't worry, Jarel. I have been sent to bring Madam Manora and her family to the Councillor."

The layman looked relieved, but Manora seemed to have already dismissed him from her mind. "How convenient, Dinnan. You can lead the way, then, without us bothering anyone." But she hadn't forgotten. She turned pleasantly as she left the room. "Don't worry, Jarel, you'll catch on soon. Thank you for your help."

Teora followed, nudging Sovestin sharply to cut off an anticipated giggle.

One thing that somehow did not surprise Teora on this exceptional day was how well Dinnan knew his way around the Main Temple. Several long hallways and confusing junctions later they halted before a nondescript door. Knocking and waiting briefly, the priest pushed it open, motioning them to precede him. Teora followed her mother into the room, her curiosity piqued. She had little time to notice more than the huge, busy-looking desk before the tall, gaunt woman who sat there attracted her whole attention.

She had never seen the Head of Council this closely before. A reclusive woman who was known to prefer behind-the-scenes manipulation and hard work over the more obvious politics of the rest of the Council, she rarely appeared in public. During her tenure, which had been as long as Teora could remember, she had led the Council in a retreat from public exposure as well. Yet it seemed that even in these difficult times the administration ran as efficiently as ever. It was interesting to see her in her sanctum, surrounded by papers, books and cabinets, the symbols of her power. She was dressed plainly in a square-necked dress with little trim.

It was more than interesting to see her greet Manora in such a cheerful and familiar fashion.

"Well, Manora. Sorry to pull you in with no warning like this. Didn't disturb anything important, I hope? Do sit down, all of you. I have sent for tea."

They settled into serviceable but comfortable chairs in a semicircle in front of the desk, Manora at the centre. Teora chose the end chair, from which she could easily watch her mother, the Head, and Dinnan. She observed how her mother settled herself: relaxed, yet firm.

"Actually, I was on my way to see you. We happened upon Dinnan in the street. Rhondona, I'm not up on your deliberations, and you know I hate to interfere, but I have some reason to be involved."

"I couldn't agree more. You are involved. You and your family." The woman steepled her fingers and sat back. "So, what is it?"

"Something isn't right, here. I know it is a difficult decision, but it seems to me that the Priestess must go. There is precedent: the Rashida crisis; the herd deaths at Kalika; several minor pestilences. Always, the Priestess has gone. Always, we have sent what we could and more. We can afford it. We have plenty, and I don't mean riches. I mean support and belief. How can we turn the Aerans down when they need us, perhaps more than any of those we helped before?"

Rhondona propped up her long, bony arms, hands folded under her chin. Her gaze swept the group slowly. "Very interesting. And how does your daughter feel about this?"

"Of course, I haven't talked to her. But I know how she must feel…"

"No, this daughter. Does Teora agree with you?"

Teora started. *How does this woman even know my name, let alone care about my opinion?*

Manora paused. "Well, it was her idea. I confess that my first reaction to the news was relief. We are all aware of the dangers the travellers will face. It was only after Teora brought up the plight of the Aerans that I realized we must help them."

"Tell me about it, Teora." Rhondona leaned back, inviting an informal response.

Teora marshaled her thoughts. She didn't know why she was being asked, but she wasn't going to let down her mother or her sister at this point.

"Madam, we must send help. Otherwise, our whole reason for existence is meaningless. Our detractors say we are parasites, with no real use; we say we are important. This decision will prove them right."

The Head Councillor nodded. "But we are sending our Consort and Priestess into danger. What if we lose them? What if this is the first step in the weakening of our faith and our power, and in the end we fall?"

"Well, what if it is? If we refuse to fulfill our basic function, if we react selfishly, that will surely be the beginning of our downfall. And Linea will feel the same. I know she will. She will want to go."

"As it happens, you are right." Rhondona regarded Teora. "She said similar things to me this morning. She is also upset at our decision to keep her. Her arguments echoed yours."

"So she must go."

"If we were considering the faith alone, you would be right. But the ugly head of politics raises itself at every opportunity. There is reason to keep ourselves strong, to keep our Priestess in her glory. No, we must look to other solutions."

"But what? We have no armies, no money. At least, none that I know of."

"We have others to send. Other good stock."

"They are not Leathad. He is the Deity's Chosen one, the Consort of Her Herds, and Linea is his Priestess. They have more than material worth."

The seamed face wrinkled in a smile. "Our Consort and his Priestess were most deservedly chosen this year. But there is perhaps one other - good stock: the best, some say. Yet never Chosen. Some have wondered why. Why was the best bull in decades matched to a Partner who would never stand a reasonable chance of being Chosen? The will of the Deity, many would say. But why? Might She have some other task in mind? What do you think, Teora?" Those ancient eyes stared intently at her, then flicked aside, just for a moment.

Following the glance, she was confronted by Dinnan's level gaze, his pale blue eyes looking into hers, interested in a detached way. Then it all came clear.

"You! This is your 'other plan' that you wouldn't tell us. You want me to go instead, so Linea will stay here with you." She turned to the Head. "Can't you see what he's doing? It's only selfishness. I can't go in Linea's place! How could I? She would never forgive me! She has worked for this all her life. I worked with her. I know how hard she tried. She's not as strong as I am, but she kept up with me. You can't take this from her. I won't let you. I won't do it!"

A slow smile spread across the stern face in front of her, but the eyes bored into hers. "You are telling the Council of the Haven that their decision is wrong, and that you will not help them in it?"

Teora edged back in her chair, a thrill of horror coursing through her. *What got into me, laying down the law to this powerful woman?* Then she thought again. *What got into me? The truth. That's what it was.* Her back straightened. "I suppose, if you order me to, I will have to go. But don't you see that it will be wrong? It's not Barozon. Everyone knows that he's wonderful stock. It's me. I'm not the Priestess. I don't have that kind of aura. Those people need spiritual help more than anything else. They need faith. They need the Priestess."

"And if I told you that the emissary has been apprised of your qualities and he agrees, in theory at least, that you might be what they need?"

"He doesn't know me. With due respect, madam, you don't know me. You're going on the opinion of someone," she shot a look of fury at Dinnan, "who has only met me once and thinks he can use me for his own selfish ends."

The ancient eyes in front of her hardened. "Young lady, do not suppose that the Council of the Haven takes its decisions lightly or without proper information. We have talked to many who know you well, and while there are uncertainties, it is generally agreed that you should be the one to go. But you will not be ordered. If you decline, then someone else will go, be sure of that."

"But that's not the point! Linea must go. There is no one better. You can't send anyone who has not been Chosen by the Deity."

Rhondona was unperturbed. "We are all agreed. There is no one better. But the Priestess will not go. That is decided. That leaves you. You have the power of refusal. That is all. Do not think that even in your holy righteousness you can sway the Priests of the Deity. At least, not yet. Perhaps some day." The shrewd eyes bored into Teora for a long moment.

32

Teora squared her shoulders and stared back.

"I think you should talk to your sister."

This sudden change of attack threw her. "But I can't. I mean…"

"Normally, the family of the Priestess must leave her to her duties. But this is one of her duties. She must persuade you, if no one else can." She nodded to Dinnan. "Escort her to the Temple of the Consort, young man. Manora, you will stay here. We have things to talk of. Your son may stay, also. He has interesting insights into the minds of both his sisters." She turned her smile away, and Teora was dismissed.

Meekly, yet still unbending, she followed Dinnan through the winding corridors and out into the sunlight and heat.

As they left the Temple, he slowed, allowing her to walk beside him. Intent on her thoughts and not making any effort to be polite, it took her a while to realize that he was glancing over at her every so often. When she caught him at it, he spoke.

"She's some old bird, isn't she?"

Teora eyed him coldly. "She is the Head of Council."

His dignified countenance broke in a friendly grin. "Right. And she's some old bird."

Thinking about it, she had to agree. "How do you know her so well?"

"I don't. Before I went to her with my plan, she had no idea I existed."

"Yes. Your plan." Teora's anger swept through her again. She stopped and faced him squarely. "What right have you to meddle in our lives?"

He did her the honour of pausing thoughtfully. "I'm not going to answer that. I'm going to take the advice of one who is much older and wiser than both of us. I'm going to let you talk to Linea."

"To the Priestess." *How can he consider my sister as anything else?*

He motioned that they should walk on, then continued in his calm, conversational tone. "Yes, but to Linea as well. This is a complex issue. The Dancer must speak to her Priestess, but you must also speak to your sister. Both will be satisfied."

Calmer now, Teora restated her question. "What makes you want to meddle in this?"

He considered again before he answered. "I'm not completely sure myself, except that it comes naturally to me. I'm always thinking, you know, always puzzling over things. When I was younger, I had trouble keeping my nose out of places it shouldn't have been. Almost got it snapped off a few times. You see, I was sure I knew how to solve everyone's problems. It took a few mistakes before I realized that sometimes problems are more complex than they seem, or that often people don't even want them solved. I soon learned to think much more carefully and make my suggestions much more subtly.

"In this case, the problem was public property, so I felt no hesitation in putting my mind to it. It's a simple situation..."

"Simple?" She stared up at him. "Have you learned anything since you were young?"

He accepted the jibe in silence, then bent to her as they walked. "No, it really is simple, if you consider only the factors that can't be changed. Aeru must have someone. The Consort can't go. There is only one other solution; someone else must go."

"Very simple."

"Yes. That answer was simple. The problem was finding someone who could do the job. The list of candidates was short."

"Harida?"

He looked down to see if she was serious, decided she wasn't, and only smiled. "When I heard Sovestin talking about this elder sister of his, I didn't make the connection at first. I thought it was perhaps just brotherly pride. Then I thought, 'Wait a minute. The younger sister is special. The brother's no slouch, no matter how he tries to hide it. What about this other sister, with the Partner who is so perfect?' I checked the names on the list again, and there you were. After I met you, I was sure, and I bulled my way in to see Rhondona."

"Past the Guardian of the Gates?"

He grinned again. "Jarel's a pushover. You saw how your mother had a halter on him before he even got started. No, the main problem to get over was my own fear. She's a formidable woman, the 'old bird.' But she heard me out politely. She had come to the same conclusion I had, that someone else must go, but hadn't thought of you yet. She would have, I'm sure." He looked at her, his head tilted. "I don't understand. If you are as good as you are supposed to be, why hasn't anyone heard of you?"

Teora's pride was piqued. "I'm as good as they say. At least, I was. But when I realized that I couldn't win the contest and started working with Linea, I stopped performing in public. Word went

34

around that I had peaked too young. It happens. My father was not displeased. He understood, and he appreciated my help, especially when his illness became worse. It made the transition easier for the Trainees he was teaching. It wasn't hard to arrange."

"But not easy for you. You didn't have to stop, did you?"

"It wouldn't have been good for Linea. We are very different, and in areas like strength and stamina, she can never match me. I could still be her worst competition, just by Dancing. If I wasn't around to compare, they would forget about my style and all talk about hers." She shrugged. "Besides which, I couldn't really train her and keep up to my own best. I guess it worked. She won."

The young Priest was silent as they approached the Temple of the Consort. "Did you ever consider for a moment that the Deity chooses Her Consort Herself, and all this scheming of yours had very little to do with the final outcome?"

She glanced up at him. *Well, he has been frank about his personality. I can be equally open about my beliefs.* "Once, when I was about ten years old, I realized that if we all followed that philosophy, everyone would sit around waiting to be Chosen, and no one would work for it at all. No, you earn the right to be Priestess. Both Partners earn their honours, and Linea and Leathad earned theirs. They were Chosen, and that's why they must go!"

Her anger was rising again, and she strode away from him, across the stone floor to the huge pen, shining in its rays of sunlight. Leathad was glad to see her, pushing his head against her arm for a chin scratch. She caught herself looking him over critically to see if he was being treated right, then laughed at the idea.

She stood, drinking in the familiar aromas, the cool shade of the Temple, the sharp shadows against the light that limned the carvings over the stall. Her anger eased, and she smiled at Dinnan as he caught up to her. He led her, all business and deference now, to the room where they had sat vigil with Linea. He made her comfortable, then went to tell the Priestess that she had a visitor.

Teora had barely settled herself on a comfortable couch when the door flung open and the Priestess strode in. Teora stumbled to her feet, unsure of how to react, but was swept up in a very Linea-like hug, to which she gratefully responded.

"I wasn't sure how to... I mean, how do I address you? You know, I'm not really supposed to even be here..."

"What do you mean, you're not supposed to be here?" Teora saw a flash of something new in her sister's eye. "You are here on my request. I will see you if I wish."

"I know I'm here on business, so that's all right, but about the rules...?"

Linea laughed comfortably and pulled the older girl down beside her on the couch. "Don't worry about the rules. I'm the Priestess, remember? I do as I please!" This was accompanied by a careless toss of her long, dark hair, caught loosely in a single twist of braided gold that flashed in the light spilling through the open window.

This did not sound like the Linea she knew. "But aren't the rules there for a reason?"

"Now I've got you all worried. Of course they are. When I was first here, I followed them to the letter. But now I know what the rules are for. I do what I please, now, but they are good rules, so, in general, I choose to obey them. Does that make you feel better?"

"Well, I suppose..."

"You really have no respect, do you? Here I am, Priestess to the Consort, you haven't been with me for two minutes and you're Big Sistering me as if I'd never left home." Linea was grinning, enjoying herself immensely.

"You have settled in."

"It was easy. Well, at first it was all stiff and formal, and I was quite homesick. It's a good rule, you know, not seeing your family. If I'd had Mother's shoulder to cry on, or yours, I'd have cried too often. You can't be the Priestess and still be tied to your family. I can concentrate on my duties now that I'm used to it all. However, if I get a chance like this, I don't mind taking advantage of it."

"If you feel that way, then I don't mind either. Was it easy, once you got used to it?"

"Much easier than I expected. After all, the system is set up for people like me. The rules are to protect us all, especially at the beginning while we get used to one another. After the early stages were over, we sort of worked ourselves into place, and it all runs smoothly. It wasn't like Harida said at all."

"Harida?"

"She told me all about it. In the part of the ceremony where the Outgoing sits the new girl down and fills her in on the details of the job. She was nice, by her standards. Told me about how I would have to really put my foot down and not let anyone push me around, about how everyone would use the rules to keep me from getting anything I wanted. How everyone had their little powers and would try to get more while I was new."

Guilt brought a rush of heat to Teora's cheek. "That sounds familiar."

"And you were right! But it wasn't like she said it. When they found out I wasn't going to be any trouble, they stopped pushing. I'm sure Harida brought most of it on herself. The people here just reacted."

"So, are you happy?"

"Of course I'm happy! This is what I worked for all my life! And I remember who helped me. Who set her own career aside to work with me. I'll never forget that, Teora."

Teora sat glumly, her hands folded on her knees, staring straight ahead. "And now they want me to take it from you."

"Take it from me?"

"Yes. They want me to go to Aeru in your place. How could they even consider it?"

"Teora, do you want to go?"

She stared at her sister. "Linea, I can't go. It wouldn't be right!"

"That's not what I asked. Could you do it? Could you leave the Haven, perhaps with only a few Herdsmen to protect you, and travel all that way through an unsettled Land? Are you able to even think of doing that?"

"Of course I could. That's not the point. It's whether I should or not."

"No, it isn't. If you could go, would you want to?"

"If I could, without taking it from you? If I thought I could be of help to the Followers in Aeru? I never thought of it." *To have a purpose. To help the Land.* "Yes, I suppose I would. I would love to be of service to the Deity."

Linea's eyes sparkled with suppressed laughter. "Think of it, Teora. A whole Enclave full of people to Big Sister."

"Linea, this isn't a joke!"

Linea sobered. "No, it isn't. It's a serious matter, and there's one thing you haven't taken into account."

"What is that?"

The Priestess turned to face her sister and spoke softly but seriously. "I don't really want to go."

Teora took this in. "But the Head Councillor said…"

"She probably said I was angry when they wouldn't let me go. That's not the same as wanting to go. Help must be sent. If it had to be me, I would go because it was necessary and because those people need me. Not because I would enjoy it. I'm too lazy."

"Lazy! What are you talking about? Nobody who is lazy gets to be Chosen. I trained with you, remember? Lazy!"

"Not that kind of lazy. If I want something badly enough, I'll pay the price to get it. Being Priestess is what I wanted. I paid the price, and I love it. I love the luxury, the beautiful things to wear and the respect. If I was called upon to go to Aeru I would go, because that is part of the price and because it is right that someone go. But I wouldn't enjoy it. Come now, Big Sister. Picture me, camping in a forest somewhere, washing in a creek, performing nature's functions," she shuddered delicately, "behind a bush? No, I would not enjoy it."

"And you think I would."

"Yes, I do. It would be another challenge for you. Tell me. Have you been happy the past few months, since I saw you last? Haven't you been the slightest bit bored?"

"It's been good to relax after all that work and worry."

"But what about the letdown? Any crying spells? Sleepless nights?"

Teora looked at her sister, again noticing the new expression, the subtle changes of bearing. "How do you know about that?"

"I'm the Priestess, remember? I have time and reason to think. It's part of my duty. I consider my people, what they need and how I can give it to them." She smiled, a more serene expression than Teora had ever seen on her face. "I'm sure the Deity doesn't mind if I practise by thinking about my family." She took Teora's hand. "You would enjoy going, simply because of the challenge. I know you. You fight for the joy of fighting. You don't care who wins. You love the fight."

"But what about the people of Aeru? I'm not the Priestess. Oh, Barozon will be fine. He's what they need. But they also need what you have. I can see it in you. You're not just my sister anymore. You're the Priestess, and I can't be that."

"You can't be the Priestess, but does that mean you can't have what they need? If the Deity sees fit to send you, do you think She will send you unprepared? Have faith, Sister. When you get to Aeru, you will be what you need to be."

Teora stood slowly, her head whirling, and her sister rose beside her. "And you don't mind if I go?"

"Teora, you are the only one in the Haven who can do this task, and you are the one least sure about it. I must make you sure." She faced Teora. "You will go, Teora. The Priestess is speaking now. The Deity commands you, and you will go."

Teora looked up at the woman facing her. The presence of the Deity shone around them. The familiar lines of her sister's face blurred and sharpened into a different form. The Priestess. She felt shy. "Will you send me with a Blessing?"

Linea's voice was changed, yet still her own; somehow fuller, more resonant, but at the familiar pitch. "My sister, whom the Deity has chosen for this task, do you not realize that you have been blessed from the day of your birth? You have been blessed in your family and your Partner." Teora felt hands on her shoulders, but all she could see were the dark eyes, pouring into her, lifting her up.

"You have been blessed in your training, your knowledge and in your compassion. Daughter of the Deity, take your appointed post. Bring help to those in need, as your conscience tells you. Be Her emissary from this moment. Her power will uphold you in your time of need. Your faith will be your strength. Go, my sister, to the purpose for which you were destined."

The silence stretched out. Warm sunlight poured through the window from the courtyard outside, a burning shaft in the dimness. Then, as the feeling faded and the room came back to her, a soft hand touched her cheek, a small voice spoke. "And please come back safe and tell me all about it."

After a moment, she shook her head and looked around. She was alone. Bemused, she wandered out the door.

Leathad was standing where she had left him, ears perked up, his dark horns sweeping gracefully away from his soft eyes. She rested a moment beside him, scratching the base of his right ear. Then, with confidence returning to her step, she strode out into the sunlight.

4.   The Company Meets

"So, where is this woman you are foisting on us as a substitute Priestess?"

The grating voice stopped Teora, and she stood in the hallway, wondering. *Go ahead now, confront the accuser? Go ahead and pretend the words haven't been said? Wait a while, then go in as if we haven't heard anything, but with the risk of hearing worse as we wait?* She had a fleeting impulse to turn and go home, leaving the Temple and this angry voice behind. She turned to Dinnan but the Priest, too, seemed unsure of what to do. She tossed a nervous grin at him and stepped into the room.

No one noticed her. Everyone watched, with varied degrees of concern, to see how Rhondona would react to this challenge. The moment of respite gave Teora a chance to take in the scene. The Councillor sat at her desk, her eyes boring into those of the priest from Aeru. Heavyset and dark-browed, he stared back, his posture uncompromising.

Lounging against the wall to her left was the Rider who had guided the party: tall, lean, his flowing hair knotted to fall freely down his back like the mane of his horse. His clothing was plainer than at the formal presentation; a light cotton shirt and a tooled leather vest partly concealed the decorative tattooing which covered his chest and shoulders. Still, he had no place inside these stone walls: a figure wild and somehow strange and free. Seen up close, he was younger than she had suspected, about her own age, though it was hard to tell. He had an air of toughness that none of her contemporaries could claim. His pose reminded her of Sovestin when he was pretending not to care.

Opposite the horseman, sitting upright but relaxed, was the third member of the Aeran party. This man was older, closer to forty, and a hard forty years at that. His face was weather-beaten with small scars here and there. His hands, clasped casually over the hilt of his sword, were big-knuckled and rough. The sabre hung on a plain but sturdy belt, and a shiny spot on the opposite hip signalled the absence of some other piece of equipment. He was not in uniform, but his military-style jacket had brass buttons. He seemed to be watching with mild interest, but his very lack of reaction spoke volumes. *This isn't an important problem. Let's get it over with, so we can get on with the job.*

Rhondona sighed, and the tension oozed from the room. "I know, Goianor. You would like to return with the best solution, but it simply cannot be. We cannot send the Consort at this time. His Priestess must stay here to maintain the morale of our own people." She fixed the priest with a hard stare. "So let us not indulge in games. You have been given the Heritage of the bull we are sending. That, at least, you cannot slight." Her head tilted forward in challenge.

"Madam, the suitability of the beast was never in question. We are honoured beyond doubt. The lack of the Priestess is the problem. Our herds are weakening, true, but there are other solutions to that problem, and closer to home than bothering you here at the Haven. Our main problem goes deeper into the hearts of our people. We have been too long alone, surrounded by other faiths, worn down by misfortune. The appearance of the Priestess of the Consort is what we need. This substitute, no matter how good a Dancer, is merely a woman. We need more."

Rhondona maintained her steady gaze. "You know about this young woman because she has been described to you. You agreed then that such a person would be equal to the task. What has changed?"

"At that time, we were speaking in generalities. At that time, you had not informed me that you were keeping the Consort and his Priestess to yourselves! At that time..." The sweep of his arm brought him around to catch sight of Teora and Dinnan. "Ah. And this would be the young lady herself."

Teora forced a pleasant smile. She could understand his disappointment; in fact, she agreed with him. "I am Teora, sir. It is an honour to meet one who has travelled so far in pursuit of his duty to the Deity and her people." She bowed formally.

Before the priest had time to react, Rhondona took over. "Nicely put, Teora. This is Goianor, Priest of the Deity from Aeru. The Rider is Corquée of Curicuiriari, in charge of travel: mounts, trails, provisions. This gentleman is Tourantij Niverdhal, responsible for your safety. He will lead six of our best Herdsmen for your protection. Gentle sirs, this is Teora, the most accomplished Dancer in the Land in decades."

The soldier rose and presented her with a much more correct salutation than she had expected. *This one is more than he seems.* She surveyed his face but could read nothing beyond polite interest. She turned to the Rider, who flashed her a momentary smile that lit up the dark face and erased the hard lines, then disappeared as quickly as it began.

She had time for a partial grin before the priest rose to confront her. He was not much taller than she was, perhaps explaining his pugnacious attitude. "I have heard good things about you, my dear, and I congratulate you on your accomplishments. However, I feel it would be unwise to start such an important undertaking with any misconceptions. This does nothing to detract from your personal abilities, but I am deeply concerned that the Priestess does not return with us." .

"So am I, sir. Please believe me; I would never undertake such a task unless I had received assurances from all concerned, including the Council and the Priestess herself, that this is the best compromise." As she spoke, she could feel within her a small, warm echo of the presence of the Deity that had swept through her in the Temple. She basked in it, willed it to grow. The Priest looked deeper into her eyes, puzzlement growing. Then a wall dropped across his face, and he frowned.

The pause drew out, became long enough to make it too late for Goianor to make an honest and unfeigned acceptance. *So that is how it's going to be. Well, what more could I say? Am I supposed to go on?*

Apparently not. Rhondona rose abruptly to her feet. "There, sir. You couldn't ask to hear it straighter than that. Teora has been Chosen in her own right for this task. When you speak to the Priestess, she will reassure you on that score."

Teora could hear the 'take it or leave it' tone in the old woman's voice and looked to the priest for his reaction.

He smiled sadly. "I only mean to do the best for my people, within the will of the Deity. Perhaps it would be best if I speak to the Priestess." He turned towards the door.

"Good. Then we will proceed. I have set aside a room for your group's planning. It is on this hall, but nearer the Priests' Door. You will find it convenient, I am sure. Dinnan, will you escort Goianor to your Temple? I imagine your Priestess will find the time to speak to him."

Dinnan bowed and motioned the elder Priest to precede him, shooting a glance at Teora as he left the room. Teora allowed him to glimpse the smile she was suppressing. Imagine, this secular leader confidently scheduling someone an audience with the Priestess! And there was no doubt the Priestess would comply. A smooth and subtle demonstration of power for the benefit of the visitor.

Taking her cue from Rhondona, she led them along the hall to where an acolyte in a long white working apron was holding a door open. Teora glanced to the Councillor for confirmation, then entered and took her place at the big table there. The other two Flatlanders sat. Rhondona motioned the acolyte forward.

"This is Mocuara. She will assist you in any way she can. She knows our systems and can ease your way in the ordering of supplies and equipment. I will leave you now." She smiled. "I have a few other small duties to attend to." Left unspoken was the fact that her other duties included the running of a large city. The tall old woman turned unhurriedly and strode away.

Teora considered her new companions, remembering the Dance classes she often led. This was a crucial moment. Habits could be formed now that would continue throughout the journey. *Well, Rhondona gave me the lead. Take charge.* The fact that these two knew much more about what they were planning meant little to the personal dynamics of the group. This was her home, her territory. Ground gained now would be easier to keep. *I need all the help I can get. Well, here goes.*

"So, gentlemen. It seems we have a journey to plan. Mocuara, we will need paper and pens. Also maps." She turned to the horseman. "Do you have maps, or have you kept it all here, as I have heard your people do?" She tapped her forehead.

The wide smile appeared again, as the Rider imitated her move. "All up there, madam." It was the first time she had heard him speak, a clear tenor voice with the faint rolled 'r' typical of his people. "We have no need of written things."

She returned his smile. "Please, call me Teora. It would be awkward to continue with formalities in such a small group. Mocuara, would you scout out some maps for those of us who are not as fortunate in our mental skills? I don't even know our basic route at the moment."

She had addressed the Rider, but the other man spoke up. "From here to Coalantha, then by ship up west coast north from there to Port Hawkeston, thus avoiding the two local Kingdoms in between, and once more on land from there to Aeru."

"Perfect. Mocuara, can you find those maps?"

The girl nodded and made a note.

43

Teora turned to the soldier. "Tourantij, I will want to know what arrangements you plan for our safety. Which method do you use for organizing an expedition?"

The man's hands opened. "Standard military procedure, Teora," he pronounced her name slowly and with formal emphasis, indicating that he was doing so because of her instruction, "although this is a unique party, and we will find ourselves out of the established patterns at times."

"So we will improvise." *Fine with me, since my knowledge of military planning is severely limited.* She turned to the horseman. "Corquée, what about you? Will that suit?"

His shrug was expressive, utilizing most of his upper body and face. "We will cope. The planning will not be difficult."

"I know you both have much more experience in these matters than I do. However, the main area of difficulty will be in the needs and abilities of my Partner, and in that I have the most experience. We should make a good team. Have you ever met one of our bulls?"

"I have been to the Pastures many times. But met one? Face to face? I keep a good distance from such animals unless I am on my horse. Huge and cumbersome they may look, but I know danger when I see it."

The soldier also shook his head. "Any animal with horns as long as my sabre, and I maintain discretion. Good soldiering is often a matter of staying out of situations that require demonstrations of bravery."

She laughed. "Oh, Barozon isn't dangerous. You'll love him once you get to know him. He's actually very sweet."

She could see the two exchange glances, and the first sign of a smile appeared on the soldier's hard face. It occurred to her that these two had put in many days on the trail together and could quite possibly have a strong bond of friendship. It also occurred to her that they might be politely laughing at her attempts to gain control. *My first task must be to form a relationship with them. The Priest could be difficult. If I get off on the wrong foot with the rest of the party as well...*

"Why don't we go now? We can't make any decisions without Priest Goianor, anyway."

Again, a glance passed between them. Then, as if agreement had been reached, the Rider spoke. "Oh, we most certainly can't. That's one thing we don't do: make decisions without the Priest. It makes him quite upset. Let's go see this sweet and lovable Partner of yours."

They all rose. "Do you agree he's going to be sweet and lovable, Tourantij?"

The soldier looked serious. "And not dangerous. Remember that those long, sharp horns are not dangerous."

So, they wanted to know if she had a sense of humour. *My sense of humour has a bite, and they'd better get used to it.* She smiled sweetly. "He isn't dangerous most of the time. But have you heard about the emotional bond between Partners? He only gets upset when I get upset." Leaving them to chew on that, she turned to the acolyte. "Mocuara, would you like to come with us?"

The girl shook her head. "I believe I should stay here, Teora." She also managed to make the use of the first name sound formal. "I would love to meet Barozon, but I must find those maps. Is there anything else you will want?"

Teora included the two men with her raised eyebrows. Corquée was smiling, but the soldier was all business.

"A list of the usual travelling supplies your people use, and the availability of food and equipment. I would also like to meet these Herdsmen I will be leading. I have little idea of their capabilities."

This admission cued Teora's concern. "You mean you haven't even met them?"

"I don't even know precisely what a Herdsman is. I understand the qualifications here are different from those in Aeru. I hope he isn't an old man who has worked his way up the Temple ladder, or some young lad with a long stick who follows cattle around all day. We are going through dangerous territory with a valuable charge. There could be fighting."

Teora grinned at the soldier. "Well, you're quite right but quite wrong about our Herdsmen. They do qualify as 'young men with sticks.' But Herdsman has a capital H. It is a title of honour. Guns and other weapons are forbidden in the Haven. These men are the closest thing we have to soldiers or police. They go through a lifetime of rough training, and only the best succeed. I don't know much about fighting, but you will find that a Herdsman with staff and dogs is a pretty formidable unit."

"Mocuara, please find our Herdsmen and send them to us as soon as you can. If you want to bring them out to the Pasture, then you can visit with us and still do your job. We'll worry about the maps and other things later." The girl nodded and hurried off. *Hmm. I'm giving orders to seven different people now. Not bad.* "Shall we adjourn our meeting to the Pastures?"

Turning as she left the room, she heard Tourantij mutter something about "Dogs?" answered only by Corquée's elaborate shrug. *Well, I'm not going to tell them everything. They'll find out.*

5.   Strangers

Even before they reached his Pasture, Teora knew that Barozon was upset with her. The strangers she brought gave him an excuse to be difficult. He had seen her, but as she approached the fence he ignored her, pawing and snorting at the other end of the field. She waited a moment, then called his name softly. His head came up, and he stared at her as she mounted the stile and descended into the Pasture, motioning the others to follow. Positioning herself so she could watch the two men's reactions, she called again, reinforcing with the hand signal.

He tossed his horns. *How dare She leave me alone all morning? It was truly boring, and I needed some fun. She said come, so I must. But She didn't say how fast.* He started forward at a trot. *There were others with Her. Who were they?* He pushed into a canter. *Maybe they were what had kept Her away.* He lowered his head and put on more speed. *That felt better. Running felt good.* He sighted his quarry between the tips of his horns. *This is the way it should be.*

The beast thundered forward at full charge.

Teora did not look at her companions, but felt them watching her. *They know this is a test.* But things could go wrong, and they had no special reason for confidence in her. Still, they had no choice. If she stood firm, they would as well.

Barozon rolled into his best pace.

He felt good. This was his greatest pleasure, his hooves digging deep into the dry earth, the dust in his nostrils, a target in front of him. He got closer now, and he could see Her more clearly. *She doesn't look ready to Dance. Why isn't She moving into position?* He moderated his pace. *This isn't going to be a practice. Why won't She come and play? Maybe it's those two with Her. Maybe they're why She won't play with me. Maybe She needs me to protect Her. No, She doesn't feel afraid. Anxious, maybe.*

Maybe they'll run. They often do. That would be fun. Then I could chase them. Will She let me chase them? Yes, She is feeling like fun, I can tell.

But they weren't running. They were standing very still. *Too bad; not interesting at all.* He looked at Her again. *Maybe at the last minute She'll play. No, it doesn't look like it. She wants me to stop. Well, I better stop then. Oops! Going a bit fast!* He braced his feet, felt his hooves dig into the soil, slice through it, dig deeper, slide, stop. Right in front of Her like he was supposed to. *Hi! Can we play? Will you scratch my ear? What's that smell? Horses? Got a snack for me?*

As the wind carried the dust away, Teora pushed Barozon's head from where he was nosing at her pocket.

"No treat today. Sorry I didn't make it out this morning, but we've got a lot of planning to do. Don't worry about exercise. You're going to get as much as you need and more in the next month. And you better not get tired, because guess what's at the end of it? A great big herd of winsome heifers, and all waiting for a big sexy bull like you. Are you going to love that?"

She glanced up at her companions, smiling. "See, he's a big sweetheart, isn't he?"

She saw Tourantij's smile for the second time, this one bigger, with a touch of relief in it. Corquée, for some reason, had turned his head away, almost as if he were embarrassed. She couldn't think why; he had stood as rock steady as his friend when the bull had charged. *I must have said something I shouldn't have. Well, there are bound to be some problems, with his people being so different.*

"Well, isn't he? Come over and be introduced."

The soldier, as relaxed as she had seen him, strolled over to be snuffled. He chuckled, pushing the huge nose away as it checked for pockets.

Corquée stood back, regarding the animal. He had forgotten whatever it was that bothered him, for his concentration was completely on Barozon. He walked a full circle around the bull, then approached him head on. When he was sure he was accepted, he made a closer examination, looking to Teora for permission before lifting a massive hoof. The other two watched in interest until he finished.

"Well, I don't know about how sweet he is, but he's a beautiful animal!" He slapped Barozon on the shoulder casually.

The bull tossed his head around in interest. *I like this one. He sure knows what he's doing. Smells of horses. And grain. Does he want to play with me?* He pivoted into his 'ready' position and waited for the signal.

Corquée watched intently as the bull faced him, head lowered. Then he spoke to Teora, his body still. "He's not angry. What does he want?"

Teora let loose a peal of laughter. "Make a 'come here' movement with your right hand, and I'm afraid you'll find out! NO! I was joking." She quickly slipped between bull and man, signaling "Finished."

"What did he want?"

"I've never seen that before. He must really like you. He wants to Dance!"

"You mean he was about to charge?"

"That's right. He would have come straight at you, expecting you to do one of the standard vaults. We work out with the other Dancers a lot, especially to train the younger ones. I've never seen him want to work with a stranger before."

"I'm not quite ready to work with him yet." The Rider made a sweeping gesture to the bull. "Perhaps another day, when I have more experience." He turned again to Teora. "After all, I have never seen a Dancer work with her Partner. Is there any chance you could show us something?" He looked her up and down. "I suppose you aren't dressed for it..."

She laughed again. "No Dancer would ever be caught wearing clothing she couldn't dance in!"

Again, she signaled to Barozon, and he responded joyfully: trotting away, his head high, tail swinging. He started in a wide circle, and Teora moved to the centre of the paddock. As his path spiraled in towards her, she began swaying, her arms sweeping in time with his hoof-beats, and soon his head was swinging in rhythm as well. The result was that when he passed close to her, their movements were completely matched, so that the tip of his horn missed her by a finger length. He began to weave in a figure of eight with her at the centre, passing her closely on either side, still sweeping his horns back and forth.

Once more he passed her, very close, and this time she pivoted and placed her hand on the tip of the horn as it slid past. Running a few steps beside him, she then used both hands to swing herself under his horn, and he tossed her up and over in front of his face in a complete arc, to end up sitting astride his neck.

Barozon's pace settled to a lope around the edge of the pasture. As he glided along, she sat on his head, did a handstand on his horns and struck several poses standing on his hump. For a finale, she galloped him to a skidding stop straight in front of the spectators, sliding headfirst down his neck and swinging around under his left horn for a dismount the reverse of her mount at the beginning.

She leaned casually on his poll to receive her applause. "So, Corquée, would you like to learn a bit of that?"

He smiled, but his response caught her off guard. "He's not breathing very hard."

"No, of course not." She was only a bit warmed herself, a pleasant tingle of sweat starting on her arms and upper body. "That wasn't much of a run. Sometimes when we are polishing a routine, we will work for two hours straight, and he will be running that speed for half of the time. Oh. You're interested in his travelling speed, aren't you?"

The expressive shrug, a touch apologetic. "Yes, I need all the information I can get, to plan our travel. I really did like your riding, though."

"We don't call that riding. It's Dancing."

"Oh. We call it riding."

"You can do that?"

"Not quite, but the same idea. I'll show you some time, if you would like."

"Of course. I would love it." Teora returned his smile. This was not going to be hard, especially if Barozon liked him. She included the soldier in her glance. "What about you?"

"I won't be Dancing with him. Can he fight?"

"Fight? The bulls are never allowed to fight. Think what would happen if they did."

"He has never fought?"

"Not for real."

Tourantij mused on that. "He fights for fun?"

Teora was starting to catch on to how the soldier's mind worked. "You are trying to figure out how he might help against dangers on the road."

"That's right."

"What kind of dangers are you speaking of?"

The soldier considered. "How about men?"

"That would be difficult to predict. Some of our Dances are mock battles, so he is used to being attacked with spears and swords. However, at least at first, he would not be expecting to be hurt by them. If one of them poked him or hurt me, he would fight for real. I hope he doesn't have to fight. It would probably spoil him for Dancing. Others could never trust him again."

"Fair enough. How about other animals: wolves, lions, bears?"

"I have no idea. He has never seen a bear or lion. He's very strong and agile, so he should be able to fight well. However, he has led a very sheltered life. I don't know. Wolves are different. He has worked with the dogs quite a bit, and he knows how they attack. He could handle wolves, if there weren't too many, or he had help."

"Dogs again. What kind of dogs?"

"We have two kinds, though most Herdsmen work with just one. A small, shaggy type who does the herding, and a larger one who protects the herd. The bulls have to work with them so that they can get along together. Several of our group Dances include Herding sections. Are there any other dangers you want to know about?"

"A wild bull might challenge him."

Horror coursed through her. "No! He must never fight another bull! It is forbidden!"

Tourantij's face softened. "Teora, on this trip, we can't always choose what we will or will not do. What if he is attacked?"

"I don't know, but he must not be allowed to fight another bull. That is one of the Deity's main strictures, and to break it would be to place the whole expedition in jeopardy."

"You don't understand. This is a simple military problem. The bull must be protected, as he is a main reason for the trip. If he is attacked by another bull, he is the only force we have strong enough to repel the attack. Thus he must fight. Of course, we would do what we could to help. If we stop him from defending himself and he is killed, our mission is a failure."

He has it all wrong. He must understand that now, before we go any farther. She stepped forward. "No, no. You are the one who does not understand. If it were simply a military problem, I would agree, but it is not. This is a religious mission. The bringing of a new stud animal to the Herds of the Enclave is a very small part of it. The bringing of the Consort of the Deity is all-important. If Barozon were to fight another bull, he would no longer represent the Consort and we might as well turn around and go home at that point. Barozon does not fight!"

The soldier bowed deeply. "I understand, madam. The bull does not fight."

51

Teora paused. Was he making fun of her? Had she gone too far? No, he was deadly serious. She felt a presence at her back, and turned to find Barozon close behind her, his head swinging slowly from side to side, his right front hoof lifted until only the tip rested on the ground. Immediately, she went to him and calmed him, stroking his ears and nose until he settled. When he stood comfortably again, she turned once more to Tourantij.

"I'm sorry, I must have got carried away a bit. It is very important that you both understand the nature of this journey. I hope I didn't sound too pushy." She laughed shakily. "I guess I must have sounded a bit pushy."

Glancing at the bull, the soldier stepped forward, took her hand. "Please do not apologize, Teora. I have learned something important. When you are serious, you are very serious. I begin to realize why you were chosen for this duty. I will not take your suggestions lightly again." He nodded, as if to himself. "And I had been wondering how a girl your age could possibly be so important as to make all this fuss."

"I'm sorry I snapped at you. I know I shouldn't do that sort of thing anyway, and especially when Barozon is around."

"Does he always react like that?" Corquée's voice came from off to the side, considerably farther away than he had been. Teora turned to see him strolling towards her.

"I'm afraid he does. I have to be very careful before a performance, because if I get nervous, he will too, and we'll be dreadful. It also works the other way. If I'm in my best form, he is too. It has a great deal to do with how well we Dance."

"Well, let's keep you happy, then. Believe me, when he started with the pawing, I got out of his line of march. I'm not as brave as the soldier, here."

Tourantij gave a sheepish grin. "I didn't notice the beast at all. I was too busy being afraid of his mistress."

Teora looked around for a way to change the subject. "Here comes Mocuara with the Herders."

Dogs, in a mass too large to count, flowed through the fence and came tumbling towards them, a jostling, sniffing, barking mob that milled at the feet of the humans and exchanged sniffs with Barozon. By the time the dogs had lost interest, Mocuara had arrived, followed by six rangy young people who carried steel-tipped staves. "Herdsman" was misleading, as two of them were women. They arranged themselves in a rough line, shifting uncertainly, the dogs weaving about their feet. One of the men whistled a quick, sharp note and every dog dropped to the ground. For a moment of silence, the two groups surveyed each other. Then Tourantij stepped forward and walked down the line as if reviewing soldiers on parade. Teora introduced each by name as he passed. He regarded them, then turned to Teora.

"Very impressive. They are in excellent condition." He turned. "And you can fight with those staves? Wolves, lions, men? Men with swords?"

He was answered with wolfish grins.

"Good. We'll work together, evenings, while we travel. About the dogs. We can't take them all. What about three of the big ones?" He turned to Teora.

"And one herder. They are more intelligent and can be very useful."

"Fine." He pointed to two of the guarders. "That one, that one, and the one with the black ears, wherever he is. You choose the herder."

A murmur, then a discreet cough came from the Herdsmen. One stepped forward, a tall man with a craggy face. "Sir, if I may ask..."

"Certainly, lad. It's Daegal, right? What's the problem?"

"Well, it's about the dogs. I don't know how you chose, so quick an' all, but, well, especially the one. I don't know, sir."

"The black-eared devil?"

"Right, sir. Spar. He's mine, sir, and I...well, I haven't had him long and I don't quite trust him yet. He's not quite comfortable, if you take my meaning."

"I'm a soldier, not a herder. I'm not choosing these dogs for herding, but for guarding. Where is he now, the black-eared one? Hiding behind Barozon is where he is, keeping a good eye on the strangers. Watch this." He half-drew his sabre and took one short step towards the bull. Barozon didn't even stop the rhythm of his jaws as he stood chewing his cud. But right from between his front legs the dark dog appeared, his head low, his forepaws spread, a curve to his upper lip. The dark ears were flattened into the mane that was rising slowly on his shoulders and neck. He did not move to attack, nor did he back down. He simply crouched, waiting, the fangs gleaming briefly under the wrinkled lip. Tourantij sheathed his sword. "That dog, I want with us."

That seemed to agree with the Herdsmen, and the party, with a great to-do about saying goodbye to Barozon, headed back to the city.

On the way, both Tourantij and Corquée pumped the Herdsmen for information about their abilities and their needs on the road. When they reached the Main Temple, before they sent the men and women and their dogs away, Teora called them all to silence.

"Having all met and discussed our various concerns, is there anyone who feels that we cannot leave the Haven soon? Within the next few days, perhaps?"

There was a general silence, everyone waiting for a negative answer that did not come. Finally, Corquée spoke.

"I would prefer to leave soon. My horses are rested. We cannot carry that much in the way of supplies. Unless there is some reason to hold them from us?" Mocuara shook her head. "Then it would be better if we left as soon as we can. The rains have been poor in this area lately. Some of the water holes below the Rim were shrinking badly when we came this way. Unless there is rain, I would be much happier on the road."

Teora looked around for dissension and saw none. "Then, unless the priest has some reason for staying, I suggest we plan to leave in two or three days. Herdsmen, Mocuara will be in contact with you tomorrow with more information. Unless she informs you otherwise, that will be our schedule."

They nodded and strode off, a buzz of enthusiastic conversation drifting back on the warm wind. She regarded her companions. They did not seem as thrilled. "What is it? Have I made a mistake?

"Oh, no. You haven't made a mistake. It's just that if you believe we should leave in two or three days, then we will leave in one or four. Guaranteed!" With that observation, Corquée spun on his heel and strode in his rolling gait towards the Temple. Teora looked to Tourantij for help. He merely nodded soberly, then followed. She stood a moment helplessly, then followed.

What could they mean? They don't seem angry with me; in fact, both agreed with my decision. The only other factor to consider was the Priest. *What is the problem with Goianor? Corquée mentioned something about not making decisions without him. I'll have to be very diplomatic, it seems. Well, I have dealt with difficult people before. Too bad I have to be going on such a long and important journey with one.*

When they returned to their meeting room, the two Priests were sitting there in silence. Goianor looked tense, a vein throbbing in his forehead. Dinnan was much more relaxed, Teora thought, but when she glanced at him, he rolled his eyes briefly. *What was that supposed*

54

to mean? Presumably, Linea had worked her talents on the man, but he still didn't seem happy. She put on her most genial smile.

"So, Priest Goianor, I have been introducing our companions to Barozon, and also to the Herdsmen who will be accompanying us."

"That is a bit unusual, wouldn't you say?"

She considered. "In what way?"

"Unusual in that I had not given you any instructions to do so. Until I spoke with the Priestess today, it was not certain that the expedition was even going forward."

"Oh, I understood that. I felt that if we were going, it was best to start our planning immediately, with the dry weather and all. If we weren't going, then no harm was done."

"I suppose not. Still, it would be best for you to remember that I am the one who must make the decision. Oh, I know that we all have our areas of expertise, and in those areas, the expert's opinion is more important than mine. But I am the one who must answer to the people of Aeru, thus I must be the one to make the final choice." He smiled at her, but she couldn't help but notice that the vein still pulsed.

Teora nodded. *That sounds reasonable.* "I gather from what you said that we are going?"

"Yes, I have made my decision. The Priestess was most persuasive. Unfortunate for us that she is not coming. A great loss indeed. And Leathad: such a fine animal." He paused, as if recalling himself back to the present company. He dusted his hands and moved his chair to the table. "In any case, I suppose we shall make do. First thing is to set our departure."

"Yes, we were discussing that as we came in. I suggested, perhaps, in two or three days? I could be ready by then, and the Herdsmen too."

The Priest moved close enough to smile down at her. "Well, perhaps you think you could be ready in that time, but this is not the afternoon stroll you may be used to. We had best let those with more experience do that aspect of the planning. You make sure that you and your animal are ready to depart, say in four days' time."

Teora glanced around. Tourantij was diligently cleaning his fingernails with a short dagger he had pulled from somewhere on his person; Corquée was staring at the ceiling with great interest. Dinnan was the only one looking directly at her, and she saw sympathy, but no support there. She nodded. "That is your choice, of course. I hope you will, as you say, consult everyone else before you decide."

"Of course, of course. Don't you worry yourself about it." He turned to the others, giving Teora a chance to get a grip on her temper. "Now, gentlemen. What are our sources of supply here?"

Teora waited long enough for the priest to realize they were waiting for her response. Then she motioned to Mocuara, who laid a sheaf of paper on the table, precisely halfway between Goianor and Tourantij. The Priest immediately stretched out his hand; the soldier made no move. When he had checked the papers over briefly, Goianor tossed them on the table in front of Tourantij.

"Good. I'm sure you and the guide can decide what we need there. Now, about these Herdsmen. I gather you have met them. Are you satisfied that they will be enough?"

"Quite sufficient. Any more and we would start to attract attention. Also, we should take some of their dogs."

"You want to take their dogs?"

"Yes, a few of the Guards, for security. We'll sleep better with them there. Of course, it's your decision."

The Priest beamed pleasantly. "No, no, that is up to you. If you say they are required, they come. No question. As long as they are considered in the provisioning." He leaned back in his chair, surveyed the room with a satisfied air. "That is all for today. If you would start preparing yourselves for departure four days from now, we can get all the rough edges smoothed out by that time. Gather equipment tomorrow, assemble it for inspection and packing the next day, mostly ceremonies the following, and then we can go." He stood and looked down on Teora.

"You see, young lady, it must all be done in a methodical manner. No running off and doing what seems a good idea at the time. Methodical and thorough, that's the ticket." He smiled again and marched out of the room.

Tense silence reigned as his measured footsteps faded along the hall. Then Teora swept the group with her gaze. Again, only Dinnan would meet her eye. She made a weak grin. "Thanks a lot, fellows. For all the help, I mean." She paused, then dropped her hands and gave a mock shiver. "I thought for a moment he was going to pat me on the head!"

Tourantij sat up, his knife disappearing, his face tense. "We have a month on the road with him. Get used to it as soon as you can."

"But why do you put up with it? Corquée, why didn't you say something about the water holes?"

The elaborate shrug. "Wouldn't have done any good. He doesn't like me much. I stay out of his way; he ignores me. I can handle it for another few weeks."

Dinnan stood up. "Come, Teora, there are some things we need to talk about. Mocuara will have what these gentlemen need."

"By all means, Teora. Mocuara and Corquée and I will have this planned out in no time. You go about your duties."

"Are you sure?"

The soldier nodded. "If there are any problems, I'm sure Madam Rhondona will smooth our way."

"Well, don't make any decisions without me." Leaving them with that ironic reminder, she followed the young Priest into the hallway.

They left the Temple and Teora expected they would turn either towards her home or the Temple of the Consort. But Dinnan steered her into the town centre. "You need some relaxing after that," was his excuse.

They sat down in the cool, white depths of a cafe, looking through a trellis of vine leaves to the outside heat. A frosted drink arrived before Dinnan commented.

"Having second thoughts, yet?"

"From the moment I saw that man. If you'll pardon the sacrilege."

"No excuses needed. He's going to be a problem, I suspect."

"Oh, I suppose he won't be that bad. After all, I'm not much of a challenge to his authority, am I?"

"Who knows? Be thankful you're not taller than he is."

"Like you are."

He grinned. "He put me in my place before we had gone two steps. All very nice and polite, mind you, but somehow he had managed to allude to my youth and inexperience and his great contributions to the cause of his people, coming all this way. It's because I'm so much taller. Maybe I'm just being sensitive, though."

She returned his smile. "I suspect your sensitivity is well placed in this situation. Don't worry, we'll be out of your hair in a few days."

Dinnan leaned forward, his brow wrinkling. "But how are you going to handle a month on the trail with him?"

"I don't see why you're concerned. We'll work things out. I can get along with just about anyone. Actually, he hasn't said anything I don't agree with, so far. Once he figures out I'm on his side, we'll be fine."

"I'm not so sure. I have heard some rumours."

"Rumours? He only came here with two other people, and they don't seem the type to blather."

"We keep in touch with the Enclave, you know, and we have an idea of what's going on. I heard about Goianor before he showed up here. In fact, I'm not surprised they sent him. Probably wanted him out of their hair for a few months."

"Does that mean they don't consider this journey is important?"

"Not at all. There is a conservative faction in their Temple that holds Goianor in high regard. He's a 'word of the law' man, as you have probably figured out. I can't understand how someone who gets along with people that poorly can become an important Priest, a job which is largely concerned with people."

"He should be a money-books."

"Ah, that's where he started out, with the Temple accounts. The rumour says that he made the right friends but the wrong arithmetic, so they found him something else to do. He told me that the 'diplomatic experience' he gained on this trip was going to stand him in good stead for a position as a High Priest."

"Him? A High Priest?"

"Frightening idea, isn't it? Well, perhaps the Deity has something else in mind for him. That shouldn't concern you, if you can survive the trip. What do the other two look like?"

She considered. "The soldier, Tourantij, seems very nice, but he is holding something back. He's much better raised than he seems, but that's not all. Every once in a while he stares off into space, and you're not sure he's with you. The rest of the time he's fine. I like him."

"And what about the long-haired one with the crooked legs?"

"He's pleasant enough. Beautiful smile. A free spirit. He and Goianor don't communicate at all, I gather. Barozon likes him."

"So, you might have allies in the party. Good. That can make all the difference. How are the rest of the arrangements going?"

"Fine. They did give us the best Herdsmen. I know I can count on them, though not much for company. They're a shy lot."

"Of course they gave you the best. You're a valuable item, you know."

"'Why thank you, sir,' the lady said, blushing,'" Teora quoted.

Dinnan laughed out loud. "I can't see you as the blushing type, Teora."

She pointedly ignored him and continued. "More than likely, they want to protect Barozon. He's valuable."

"So are you, Teora. Don't forget that. You are Chosen by the Deity for this. By the way, there's one other thing. Word has it that you have another little job to do on the way."

"What kind of job?"

"Some sort of standard Temple business, I suppose. I gather you're going out to the ocean and north by ship, because it's safer and faster. There's a town you'll pass through down on the coast: Coalantha. They have sent a request for something, and the High Priest was saying that you could handle it. He also said something about 'getting her prepared', whatever that means."

"Getting prepared. I'm not sure I like the sound of that."

"Don't worry, Teora. They wouldn't give you something you couldn't cope with."

"Having met Goianor, I'm not that confident in the decisions of the upper clergy anymore."

"Well, I'll scout around, and if I find out, I'll let you know."

She looked up at him, her eyes narrowed. "Yes, you do that. Just remember whose idea this whole thing was in the beginning. You owe me something."

He laughed as they got to their feet. "I suppose I do, even if it is simply to make sure my plan goes well."

Teora pounced. "Hah! You have officially admitted that this is your plan. If anything goes wrong, I will officially come back and haunt you for the rest of your life."

He sobered. "Deity willing, I hope it never comes to that."

It was her turn to laugh. "So do I, Dinnan. So do I."

6.   Departure

The next three days contrived to fill themselves, despite Teora's anxiety to be away. Her travelling kit was carefully selected, packed, and repacked. It was decided, on Corquée's insistence, that Barozon would be steel shod for the trip. It was a new experience for him, and he was funny afterwards, lifting his feet with care and shaking them.

Friends, more than she had known existed, visited to say goodbye. Renelal dropped by several times: only briefly, but enough to let her know that he would miss her. He was the same old carefree joker, but Teora noticed a new gravity in him, especially when he talked to Manora.

The third day, they attended an official sendoff by the Council and another by the Priestess of the Consort. This time, Linea was in her full ceremonial persona: powerful, charismatic and distant, at least until the final moment. When she laid her hands on the shoulders of the travellers, Teora got an extra squeeze and a longer benediction. Then Linea was gone again, and the Priestess of the Consort bade her representatives farewell.

Teora spent that evening with her family in a smaller version of Linea's vigil. Not much was said, but she knew that both her mother and brother were feeling this parting. She lay in her bed for a long time before sleep came.

She rose with the first daylight, ignoring her drowsy body's desire to stay in bed. Manora was before her with a fire going and a kettle on.

"You may be cooking over a campfire tonight. Best enjoy this while you can." She made Teora sit until she had drunk her tea and eaten a bowl of porridge and milk. "You know, it doesn't look to me as if they are carrying much in the way of comfort for you. After all, you are Chosen by the Deity. And you have to sleep in a little, wee tent all by yourself and eat sitting on the ground? Do they really value you that low?"

Teora laughed sleepily. "Don't worry, Mother. Your little daughter is being treated just fine. This isn't a ceremonial tour, with Consort, Priestess and seventy-three Priests. This is a long, hard journey, and we don't carry a feather of extra weight. No fancy, gold-trimmed pavilion for me. A simple tent is fine. Suits me better anyway."

They let Sovestin sleep until the last minute, then rousted him out.

"Come on, Little Brother. I need your long and lanky help to carry my kit out to the Pasture. Where's that brotherly duty and respect?"

"Somewhere left behind in my blankets," he grumbled, but he looked proud as he swung both her packs over one shoulder and strode out the door.

If Barozon was surprised to see them at such an hour, he made no sign, but greeted his Partner with the usual enthusiasm. She strapped on his travel harness and hitched her kit to the tie-downs. Then, swinging up onto the pad, she was ready.

Glancing down at her mother, in that sturdy stance with one arm around Sovestin's shoulders, Teora realized how small her family was, now. Overcome by a feeling of loss, she jumped down and flung her arms around them both.

"Come, now, girl. No tears. Up on your beastie, and away you go."

Sov also made an effort. "Sure, Elder Sister. This is going to be the trip of your life. I envy you a whole lot. By the time you get back, I may have some news for you, too."

She looked up at him, noticed that his face was thinner, older somehow, and that he had grown even more. She hugged him one more time. "I bet you will, Brother." Another silent squeeze for her mother and she was mounted again, turning through the gate for the main plaza.

There, the rest of the expedition was assembling. The Herdsmen were ready, travel cloaks slung in a roll across their shoulders, staves leaning comfortably along one arm. The four dogs, pleased at the idea of an outing, frolicked more than usual. The small Herding dog pestered Spar to play with her, nipping and shoving at him until he finally planted a heavy paw on her shoulder and flattened her. He stared down at her in mild amusement for a moment, then let her up. She frisked away as if nothing had happened. *I hope the humans in our group can solve their problems that easily.*

Corquée was fussing over the horses, adjusting packs and twitching straps. Just as he finished the last saddle, Tourantij strolled up, a worn travel cloak and pack over one shoulder, his sabre in one hand. It was a measure of the importance of this mission that he was allowed to carry it at all; ordinary people sported no weapons in the Haven.

Reaching his mount, he checked all its fittings before strapping his pack behind the saddle. It was only a quick once-over, but Teora could tell that he had tested the tension and firmness of every strap or buckle that Corquée had adjusted. She wondered whether the Rider would take offense at this, but he seemed not to notice. *Must be standard procedure.* With a tilt of his head to the Rider, Tourantij mounted: a quick, efficient motion.

Teora turned her attention to Corquée. He was about to mount his own horse, a tall chestnut mare with an incredible length of mane and tail, lighter than the rest of her hide. She was much more spirited than the rest of the animals, and before his offside foot hit the stirrup she was away in a series of short jumps and turns. He whooped joyfully and urged her on, not bothering about the stirrup. As she bucked, he was sometimes in the saddle, sometimes behind it, once leaning forward to tap her on the nose with his forefinger. Then she reared up to full height, and he stood away from the saddle on his near stirrup, right hand raised in salute, left hand negligently curled around the twin saddle horns. As she landed, he slipped back into the saddle and rode her, completely calm now, back to the watching group.

"We must have that every morning, I'm afraid. She likes to remind me how she used to be free." He and the horse were breathing quickly, both thoroughly happy.

"If we have finished our little show, could we begin our journey? There are water holes drying up as we stand around watching the nonsense."

Teora couldn't help but notice that the priest had been the last one to arrive and that his kit looked as if it had been tossed together in haste. Realizing his disadvantage down there on the ground, he flung himself and his equipment on a horse. Then he arranged himself in a dignified manner and turned to the group that stood nearby.

A surprising number had turned out to watch them leave, Rhondona and the High Priest among them. Goianor made a short speech of thanks, then grandly signaled Corquée to lead out, leaving the local dignitaries no opportunity to respond.

So it was in relative silence that the party wound away from the plaza, the Rider leading, the other mounted members behind him, and the Herdsmen and their dogs trailing in single file.

Teora had just noted that there was no representative from the Temple of the Consort when Dinnan appeared, swinging in to stroll beside Corquée. When they reached the next intersection, the Rider allowed himself to be led, not towards the Plains, but on a route that led past the Consort's Temple. She tried to read Goianor's reaction to this, but could get nothing from his stiff back ahead of her.

At the Temple, Linea and Leathad were posed on the presentation platform in front. As the column rode past, the two stood without moving: statues, except for the breeze ruffling Linea's robe and hair.

As he passed them, for no apparent reason, Barozon stopped. He turned his head to stare at the two poised figures. The other bull raised his head. Then the Priestess bowed. Not a short, polite bow, but a full sweep of her hand and head: the formal kind used by equals greeting equals on state occasions. Teora was paralyzed. She felt a brief reminder of how it had been when Linea had blessed her. The feeling of power, of rightness. Then, before she had time to decide what to do, the moment was broken, and Barozon was moving along, catching up to the leaders where they had stopped to wait in some confusion.

Dinnan spoke again to Corquée. Then, with a quick wave to Teora, he disappeared down an alley. The Rider moved on, and Goianor's horse followed. The Priest himself seemed preoccupied, several times twisting in the saddle, first to look at Teora, then at the Temple steps.

Teora did not look back. She knew the Consort and his Priestess would remain there, immobile, as long as the party was in sight. It was Linea's symbolic sacrifice, bearing a small part of the discomfort her sister would endure in her stead.

Soon, they had left the city and were moving along the road that led dead straight across the plain towards its edge. Teora noticed that Corquée spent a lot of time turning back to check on his charges. Finally, he pulled his mount aside and allowed the priest to pass him. Moving in beside Teora, he frowned at her.

"How long can Barozon keep this speed? We have a good distance to cover today."

She considered. "How many breaks will we take? How long will we be moving?"

"We will travel about eight hours. We break just after noon for food and about every hour all day to get off and stretch our legs."

"Could we make our midday stop longer, and later in the afternoon? The animals could graze during the hottest hours of the day that way?"

"Yes, that would be fine. Given that schedule, what pace should we set?"

"Is there anything wrong with this one?"

"Not at all. But those Herdsmen are walking."

Teora glanced back at the Herdsmen, sauntering in a group now, the dogs running back and forth exploring everything. "Look at them. Do they seem like they are pushing it?"

He grinned. "Not really. What about your Partner? This is a faster pace than any cattle herding I've ever done."

"He moves along all right. Not as fast as your horses, but he moves along. He can maintain this pace indefinitely. My weight on his back means basically nothing. I hope he doesn't get bored. I hope I don't get bored."

"It always seems that way at the start of a trip. Then, after a few hours, your mind settles into the rhythm and the day seems to flow by."

Tourantij pulled his mount up on Teora's opposite side. "How are we doing?"

Corquée answered. "Teora says this is a good pace, if you can believe it."

The soldier nodded. "If she is right, we will do well."

"I assume I'm right, although we have never travelled more than one day at a time before. Are there any safety procedures you would like to discuss?"

"Not here. On the Plateau, we need only keep our eyes open. I have spoken to the Herdsmen, and down on the Flat the order of march will be different. For the moment, enjoy yourself. This will be the pleasant part of the journey." He reined his horse in behind her, and Corquée returned to the front of the column.

Teora gazed around. The road certainly was pleasant at this time of the morning. The cool of the night lingered, and a light dew kept the dust down. Birds called from the shrubs beside the road, and myriad small creatures were still going about their business. She looked ahead to where the pale blue of the sky was cut off by the sere brown edge of the Plateau. It was going to be another hot, dry day. She uttered a short prayer to the Deity to end the drought, something she had done so often recently that it came habitually to her. Today, it did not seem as meaningless.

She reached back and touched the slim leather pouch strapped to her pack. She had no idea what was in it, but she was curious and a bit worried. The Head Priest had been very serious and ceremonial when he handed it to her the day before. She was to deliver this, with full ceremony, to the Head Priest at Coalantha and to wait for his instructions. That was all. She did not feel it her place to question the Head Priest of the Haven; she merely assured him that she would do as he said. Now, she wished she had been braver. Dinnan had been able to discover nothing. Compared to the publicity surrounding Goianor's request, this task was a dark secret. It did not sound like her kind of dealing, and she hoped that her part in it would be minor.

The party rolled on, pacing the distance slowly as the sun rose higher and the air began to quiver. Reaching a small stream as the day got to its hottest, they thankfully dismounted and unharnessed. Corquée was about to hobble the horses.

"Is that necessary?"

He glanced up, about to retort, when he noticed the four dogs milling around. He included Tourantij and the Herdsmen in his glance. "I'm not sure."

The Herdsmen all grinned. Mayna, the shorter of the two women, waved her hand. "Where would you like them to graze? The west bank? The east? Where would you like them watered? Upstream, downstream? Now or later?"

Corquée looked to Teora for confirmation. She simply imitated his shrug.

Tourantij had been listening with interest. "It would be a good opportunity to check our capabilities."

The Rider grinned. "Fine. You know, this could get quite easy. How much more of my job are they going to do?"

"Do you feel it appropriate to be trying to shirk your duties this early in the journey?"

Teora could see Corquée's shoulders stiffen at the sound of the Priest's voice, but the Rider smiled as he turned. "Why no, Master Goianor. Simply making sure that work is spread evenly, so that everyone carries his or her own share of the burden."

"If there are to be any changes of general duties, I should know about them."

"Oh, you will, don't worry. You will know."

Teora watched Corquée's back as he sauntered over to his horse, reading the tension in his shoulders, noting the instant agitation of the animal, even though his touch seemed gentle. *If I ever have a run-in with the Priest, Barozon had better be far away.*

65

They settled down in the shade of some willows to eat a simple lunch of sliced meat and fresh bread. Radman, the Herdsman handing the food around, smiled at Teora. "Better enjoy it while you can, Lady. The fresh food will only last another day in this heat."

"Please, call me Teora. Formality is too complicated in such a small group."

"Teora." His smile was uncertain, then warmed. "Enjoy your lunch, Teora."

She smiled in return and took a bite. It really was good, and she was hungry. Looking around at the group, she considered the social interplay that was bound to happen. The Herdsmen formed a straightforward bloc. While self-confident and proud, they had no pretensions. Goianor, at the other end, had a natural assumption of authority that she could never master. In fact, she hoped she never assumed authority so blatantly.

In between these two extremes, Corquée, Tourantij and herself floated. Each had reason to exert power in certain circumstances, even over the Priest's head, but none had definite superiority in general, or seemed to want it, which was probably just as well. In fact, the Herdsmen would refuse any line of action that they considered unwise. *A period of settling in is necessary. I hope we can accomplish it before the dangers of the journey start.*

They rode on in the afternoon, the sun's heat seeming no less, although Teora knew the worst was past. Nearing sundown, the horizon edged closer; they were approaching the Rim. This observation aroused her from the semi-doze into which she had retreated due to the heat and boredom of the road, and she surveyed the area with more interest. There was a line of willows ahead, and she was relieved when Corquée turned aside from the road to dismount and lead his horse to the trickle of water at their feet.

Barozon drank, then snorted and pawed at the water. When he began to dip his shoulder as he pawed, she signaled him to turn out of the stream. "I know you're hot and dirty, but there isn't enough there for you to have a bath and leave any for anyone else. You drink a bit more, and then you can have a roll around in the dust to scratch your back."

She stripped his harness off and slapped him on the shoulder. He took this as a signal to follow her suggestions.

"Does he always do exactly what you say like that?"

She turned to see Corquée rubbing down his mare. "Not really. He has quite a mind of his own."

"But you talk to him a lot. How much does he understand?"

She grinned. "Who knows? He doesn't understand many actual words. He doesn't think that way. I use mostly hand and body signals when we Dance, but when I talk to him, he's more in tune with the tone of my voice."

"How do you steer him? I noticed you don't use a bridle."

"I don't know. Oh, sometimes I slap his shoulder or neck if I want him to turn, but, in general, he seems to go where I want to go."

"You don't know how you steer him?"

"No. I've been riding him since he was young. Think about it. When you are sitting down and you want to get up and go somewhere else, do you think, 'Lean forward, left foot goes there, right foot behind, push with the legs?' No. You stand up and your feet do the right things. That's how I ride. If I want to go somewhere, he goes there. I suppose I could figure it out if I tried."

"I wish I could teach my horse to do that."

"You don't teach that sort of thing. You learn it together."

7.   The Flat

Their descent occurred early the next morning. When they got close enough that the edge of the plateau was in sight, they were closer than Teora realized. She approached the Rim with a stirring of excitement and a twinge of fear. She had never looked out over anything from such a height. Mindful of her mission, she dismounted a good distance back, told Barozon to stay there, and moved ahead cautiously, alone.

At this point, the top of the plateau was a flat slab of granite like a piece of broken cheese: sharp but uneven. Afraid to stand, she got down and crawled forward on her stomach. She edged out and stretched her neck until her eyes neared the edge. The closer she got, the more the rock seemed to slant downward, the more she felt she might slide over, although it had seemed perfectly flat before she lay down.

Taking her nerves firmly in hand, she squirmed forward and looked over. Her eye travelled down the face: down and farther down. The rock was a uniform brownish grey, with long faults slashing across, stained darker where the dampness had seeped out in wetter times. Far, far down, she could see rounded bushes that must be the tops of trees. She had no idea how tall, or how far down.

"About a hundred strides, I've been told."

She jerked and would have started to back up except she was afraid to move too quickly. Instead, she turned her head slowly. Corquée lay beside her, relaxed, although she noticed that his head was no farther forward.

"How long is a stride?"

"The distance between the hoof prints of a running horse. A bit more than my height."

She turned slowly and let her eye try to get a sense of the real distance. It was impossible. All she got was a gut-tightening sense of fear, and a feeling that her head was twice as heavy as the rest of her body, ready to overbalance her and send her plunging downward. She held still long enough to prove to herself that she wasn't running away, then squirmed back.

A short way back from the edge she started to get to her feet. Suddenly, she was seized by the arms and hoisted into the air. It happened so quickly that she had no time to be afraid before she had been swung around and carried rapidly away from the edge. Her anger was starting to rise when she was set down, and she spun quickly to face her assailant.

It was Tourantij. In the heartbeat before she spoke, she took in his stern, controlled expression, the tension of his muscles, and she reconsidered. She calmed herself.

She glanced left and right. No danger. *What made him like this?* A strange mixture of fear and anger filled his face, rigidly held in check. His voice, too, was a mass of tension.

"What do you think you are doing?"

She hesitated, wondering how to answer him. *It's the first time he has ever touched me. What's going on?* As her pause lengthened, she realized it was the best thing to do. The cords of his neck relaxed, and his shoulders lost their iron. Then she spoke as softly as she could manage.

"I might ask you the same question."

His jaw came up. "Madam, I am in charge of the security of this expedition. It would be a shame if I were to allow the most important member of the party to throw herself over a cliff on the second day!"

This was no time to argue, but she could not let it go completely. "I thank you for your concern, Officer Niverdahl, but next time, perhaps a simple spoken warning will do. I like to keep my feet on the ground when I am at the edge of a cliff."

She could tell the shot struck home, as a touch of red crept up the whiteness of his face. She turned and walked over to Barozon, her knees quivering. Leaning on his shoulder, she stroked behind his ear and wondered what it all meant.

A soft footstep beside her made her turn abruptly and speak more sharply than she had intended. "I believe I have been surprised enough for one day."

Corquée stepped back apologetically. "I am sorry, Madam Teora. I did not intend to startle you." A brief grin. "At least, not this time." He was serious immediately. "But I do not know what happened with my friend, Tourantij. I have never seen him like that."

"You haven't?"

"Never. And there was little danger. The rock is solid, no one was nearby, and the animals were calm; I was watching. I cannot see how you might have fallen. I don't know why he was so angry."

69

"Angry and frightened. Is he afraid of heights?"

"Not that I know of. He seemed quite comfortable, even at ease, during the climb up."

"Well, something certainly bothered him. I will ask him about it another time. Did Goianor notice anything?"

Corquée grimaced. "The priest was too busy bullying the guards to see anything important going on."

The talk had relaxed her, and Teora was able to focus on the rest of the party. Four of the Herdsmen had placed themselves and the three guard dogs in a casual line that kept the horses well back from the edge. The smaller dog, Nipha, patrolled self-importantly up and down inside. The other two Herdsmen were standing deferentially nearby, waiting for her to notice them. When she turned their way, they hurried over.

"Is everything all right, Teora?" The taller one had a worried frown.

"Of course, Daegal. The soldier is concerned for my safety near the edge." *No sense hiding anything. These are my own people, and the more they know, the more help they can be.* "Overly concerned, I would say."

"Yes, he did seem upset."

"No harm done. I'm glad to see everyone worried about me. Shall we see about the arrangements for the descent?" She smiled and slapped Daegal on the arm, turning him toward the guard tower at the top of the road.

By the time the rest of the party reached the tower, Goianor had verified their credentials with the mercenaries on guard, and the armoured gate was swinging open. Teora hesitated, wondering who would lead. Tourantij evidently considered this a security decision; he started his horse forward.

"Teora is to follow directly behind me. Corquée after her. Stay within sight of each other, but not too close. The Priest follows, with the pack animals behind him. Your dogs have done very well, but I would like them last, with Herdsmen between them and the horses. No sense spooking an animal by mistake."

Teora noticed that the priest was not objecting to Tourantij's planning. In fact, the older man was obviously nervous. *Perhaps this type of adventure is not his favourite part of the trip.*

Tourantij started his horse down the trail, glancing back at Teora every few strides, and the tension returned to his face. Barozon was happy to follow. The way led along the north side of a fault, cracked far back into the surface of the Plateau, allowing space for a narrow trail to be hacked from the living rock of the face. The other side of the fault was near, although too far away to provide any safety; still, it felt comforting to have it there.

Then she turned the last corner, out into the wide-open air along the face. They were a good distance down, now, and the freedom and openness around her frightened and exhilarated her at the same time. Tourantij turned sharply at her indrawn breath and stared at her. She could see his shoulders stiffening again and she smiled and waved cheerfully. He turned his attention back to his horse's path, leaving her to wonder again what was going on.

Despite his concern, the trip down was uneventful, with Barozon and the horses coping easily with the firm, if rugged, surface of the path. As they wound northward along the cliff face, Teora was soon regretting the loss of the vista she had seen. She called Tourantij to stop.

"Could you show me where we are going?"

"It would be best if we saw the party down safely."

"Officer Tourantij!" She put enough steel in her voice to bring him to a halt. He turned in his saddle, and she moved Barozon close in behind the horse. "Tourantij, if there is some danger here of which we are unaware, it would be better if you told us. If there is no other danger, I wish you would explain this strange behaviour!"

He regarded her a moment, his face stony. "Do you not consider this enough danger?" His hand swung out over the abyss.

"Yes. Enough to make me very cautious. The most dangerous thing I have done today is to bring Barozon's horns this close to your horse's rump. I will be as safe as one can be on this trail, unless, as I say, there is some other danger I don't understand. Otherwise, it would help for me to know, at least for the next day or so, what our route is."

She could see a quiver start in his hand, gripping the cantle of the saddle. Then, with a visible effort, he calmed himself. "There is a lookout ahead. Perhaps your Herdsmen would like to see as well." He started his horse down the path again. Shaking her head, Teora followed.

A few minutes later they reached the lookout, a place where a part of the Rim had caved away, perhaps during the cataclysm when the Haven was born, leaving a huge pile of rubble half the height of the Plateau. Above it, the wall rose sheer to the Rim, but below them, the trail wound down between huge boulders on an easier route to the bottom. It had been the proximity of the slide to the upper fault that had induced early path makers to chop this route to the top. From where they dismounted, it was possible to stand quite safely and see far out over the plains below. They left the stock on the trail, guarded by the dogs, and scrambled up on a nearby boulder for a better view.

Off to the south, a glint of water showed where the river meandered away westwards from the foot of the cliff. Following its path, Teora's eye was drawn by an interminable plain, covered with sparse forest nearby, thinning out to bare grassland beyond.

"I've never seen anything that flat!"

"It just seems that way from up here. Actually, it is gently rolling like the Plateau above. If your eyes are good," Tourantij pointed out to the west, "you will see our next barrier."

Teora had always considered her eyes to be good, but it took a moment of straining before she recognized those vague shapes, half-hidden in the haze, as another range of mountains.

Corquée grinned down at her from her other side. "Two days travel for a Rider of the Curicuiriari on his horse. How long for us, would you say?"

Tourantij snorted. "Whenever he starts talking about the talents of his people, cut any claim in half and then don't believe it." Teora noticed a thawing in the soldier's face, although he still stood protectively between her and the short drop-off before them. "I suggest four days. We will take the first two gently, because when we leave the river there might be no water until the mountains. That water hole east of the Rock was drying fast."

Corquée came immediately back to business. "We might have better luck near the Dead Forest, but we will have to dig. The last day, going up the long slope to the top with no water, will be a killer."

The soldier considered. "We should head for the Rock. If there is water, we can go straight on. If it is dry there, we will detour to the Forest. If there is no water there…"

"Then we will have a long, dry walk ahead of us, and we will have wasted a day on the detour."

"Can't be helped."

"Could have been." The Rider glanced meaningfully back to the trail. Teora realized that Goianor had not joined them.

Tourantij followed the look. "Best if we get down there before he starts to pull out the maps." To Teora's puzzled expression, he explained. "He would have a route planned by himself, if he could."

"Based on what knowledge?"

The soldier shrugged off the question, but he moved with alacrity when he saw the priest heading for the packhorse.

Thankful that at least this time she did not have to interfere and that Tourantij's attention seemed distracted from her safety, she enjoyed another gaze around, then followed slowly. By the time she reached the path, the argument had already wound down. The vein in the Priest's forehead was evident, but he seemed to be giving in.

"But why don't we follow the river? According to the map, it goes within a day's march of the pass."

Tourantij was all patience. "But what does the map say about the ground along the river?"

"Why..." the priest looked again, "it doesn't say anything."

"Very suspicious."

"What do you mean?"

"Read the map. Some areas have good details, others are blank. The gaps are where no one has travelled. There will be a very good reason why the path does not follow the river. Even if we feel otherwise, we are not the expedition to try to find new paths. The route we have discussed has been travelled may times before."

"But not after all the drought."

"Perhaps, perhaps not. The main point is that while we have our own opinions, it is our scout's job to choose the best trail. Whether his knowledge is based on personal experience, the lore of his people, or merely a hunch, he is still our best chance."

Whether this reminder of the Priest's own words had any effect or not, he finally shrugged. "Well, if he kills us all, it will be no pleasure to say, 'I told you so', but I suppose..."

Corquée, who had been standing to one side like an uninvited guest at table, evidently decided he had heard enough, and turned away to remount his horse. The soldier, too, departed, and Teora thought she heard a soft snort of derision as he left.

As the priest swung heavily up onto his own mount, Teora hesitated beside him, then made up her mind. It went against her nature to confront anyone, but she felt she must establish her right to question the affairs of the group. "Is it wise to continually insult Corquée like that?"

Goianor smiled down on her. "My dear, when you have been dealing with these people as long as I have, you will understand the necessity of keeping them in their place. They have an amazing ability to get above themselves, with no morals or schooling like you and I have to keep their pride in check." He winked. "Just you watch. He will be falling all over himself to do a good job now, to prove me wrong." He clucked to his horse and moved off down the path.

Teora swung up on Barozon, wondering how this bunch had made it all the way to the Haven in one piece. It occurred to her, half as a joke, to wonder how many there had been in the party when they started out. *I would rather not ask.*

They had not gone far down through the tumble of rock when a Herdsman called her name softly. As she turned back, puzzled, he hurried up beside her.

"The dogs are restless. There may be trouble."

She had been too concerned with the mountain to consider this. "What should we do? The others are quite a way ahead."

"I'll send Spar ahead. The captain will know he is there for a reason."

"Good idea. Thanks, Daegal."

The man grinned and whistled. Instantly, the black-maned dog stood beside him, and Teora could see the vigilance, bordering on menace, in the animal's stance. Barozon, too, could sense something, and he moved restlessly underneath her. At Daegal's signal, the dog crouched nearer the earth and slid off down the side of the path. They followed, eyes and ears alert; four of the Herdsmen had her surrounded, with one man and his dog ranging, with difficulty she was sure, through the jumble on either side.

They only rounded the next corner when they came upon the other members of their party, their horses huddled together in the narrow trail. The Priest's voice rose in peevish anger, cut off suddenly by a harsh movement from Tourantij. The silence was broken only by the click of her Partner's shod hooves on the stone. As she came up to the men and stopped, that too was stilled. The soldier's head swivelled slowly, taking in the deployment of her guards, and he nodded.

"This is a good place for ambush. It is still too rough for a mounted scout to range the sides of the trail, so we must go blindly ahead. I am beginning to see the advantage of your people, especially if they can keep up, out there. If not, we will move more slowly."

Daegal smiled and pointed, left, then right. Teora could see nothing, but Tourantij seemed pleased.

"Good. Our scout should perform his usual function?"

Corquée inclined his head.

"Would you like a man and dog with you?"

The Rider pointed at the dark dog. "I have great respect for that one's nose."

Tourantij nodded. "I'll follow. Next Teora with two guards, then Goianor with your quickest man behind. Any questions?"

Teora tried to swallow the dry lump that threatened to cut off her speech.

"What kind of attack do you expect, and why?"

The soldier gave a tight smile. "I don't expect any attack, because there is no reason. However, this is an ideal spot, and the dogs are uneasy. That is enough for me. If an attack comes, it will be with single-shot guns and arrows. A small group of men, not overly brave. Well hidden, at least at first. If it is a much larger group, or if their weapons are more modern, our minor precautions will be of no use. In that case there will be no fight. They will simply stop us, and I hope our credentials will be enough to get us through. A small group of bandits is likely. Those, we can scare off or fight off, especially if we are forewarned. Shall we go on?"

Oh. He really is asking my permission. She swallowed again, but words would not come. She nodded and settled herself firmly into the harness. She could feel her Partner's muscles tensing as he shifted his weight. It was comforting to remember how he reacted when she was in trouble. It should have been reassuring to notice that both Corquée and Tourantij now carried rifles, and that the bare spot on the latter's belt was now filled with a holstered pistol. They would have been left with the guards at the Rim upon entry to the Haven.

"Then say a prayer for us as we go. You too, Priest. We can use all the help we can get." The soldier gave what she assumed was another reassuring smile and turned his horse away.

As she started forward, she caught a glimpse of Goianor's face, grey and sweating, and she knew why the priest had not interfered in their planning. He was quite as frightened as she was. And riding in a more vulnerable position, she had to allow. Even in the middle of the line, her shoulder blades twitched at the thought of a bullet or arrow. She was beginning to get a new understanding of the idea of prayer. She dug down inside for that new courage. *Surely the Deity has not Chosen me to be injured or killed here, this early in the trip. Of course not.* With a bit more confidence, she edged Barozon forward.

They moved slowly down through the massed rock, all eyes peering intently into every crevice that revealed itself. The trail began to flatten out, and the boulders became even bigger. Several they passed were the size of houses: huge chunks of granite with sheer sides, some topped with trees and bushes, leaves shrivelled with the drought. Teora could hear brief whistles and wished she knew the codes the Herdsmen used. The shadows between the rocks were a two-edged weapon; they provided shade from the sun's midday blaze, but also deep shelter for any number of imagined foe. Slowly, sweat beading her brow and staining her shirt, Teora moved forward.

A sharper whistle brought her guards to a halt. Teora stared around, but nothing moved. Another signal, and they moved on again. Rounding the corner of yet another huge boulder, they came upon a tableau. The dark-haired dog stood in his attack position, with three small, scruffy men facing him, their backs to the rock and their old-fashioned pistols wavering between the dog and Corquée, who sat his horse casually, his rifle pointing across the saddle in their direction. Tourantij seemed to have no interest in this scene as he scanned the rocks around. Finally, he seemed satisfied.

"And what have you to say for yourselves, gentlemen?" He spoke in a calm voice, but there was an underlying ice that made Teora shiver.

The men's pistols lowered a fraction. The middle one started to step forward, glanced at Spar, and thought better of it. "We was just walkin' up the road, sir, mindin' our own business, like, and this huge animal jumped us. We didn't know it was yours, sir, and you had such good control of it, like. Mikx, here, was all for shootin' it, but I says, 'no, my friend, that's no wild beast. That's a dog belongs to someone, and that someone will be along any minute.' And sure enough, here you come."

Again the cold, deceptively calm voice. "And you were just walking up the trail by yourselves?"

"To be sure, yer honour. Just lookin' for some sheep what strayed off."

"And what about your two friends up there in the rocks?"

The man's eyes leaped far enough for Teora to notice the ledge with the dark shadow along it. Something gleamed and then was still.

"Yes, those two. And a few others down the trail. Call them in." The soldier's voice rose a fraction. "All of them, or they'll come in feet first."

"What others, yer honour...?"

The man's protest was cut off by a yelp from the other side of the trail, and a youth of about fifteen, in tattered clothes and a large slouch hat, slid down a narrow avalanche path to dump in a heap at their feet. Neither Spar nor Tourantij even glanced around. *They make a fine pair, those two.*

"That other, for example. Call them in NOW!" The last word was like a whip crack, and the three men actually jumped. The leader recovered, shrugged, and gave a high, wordless yodel. It was answered by a crashing in the rocks above, and several men slid or climbed down to the trail level. One was holding his right forearm tightly with his left hand. To his leader's question, he snarled, "There's another dog up there," and slumped sullenly against the rock.

Tourantij glanced at Teora. "Would you...?"

She jumped down fast enough but hesitated before moving ahead. Daegal snapped his fingers and Spar glided forward, neatly cutting the injured bandit away from his friends. Facing the dog, the man backed towards Teora. A herdsman closed in from either side.

As the man approached, she was overwhelmed by the smell of him, a mixture of sweat, tobacco, and general decay. He grudgingly held out his arm, and she turned her head down, away from his foul breath.

Blood seeped from between his fingers, but not a lot, and when she persuaded him to open his hand, it revealed a tanned, dirty arm with two neat, shallow fang punctures a few fingers' width apart. Turning the arm over, she found two similar holes on the bottom, these barely breaking the skin. She grinned up at the man.

"Why, I don't know what you're so upset about. He only wanted to hold your hand." She noticed the flintlock pistol, thrust left-handed into the waistband of his homespun pants. A bit of anger stirred in her. "And what were you planning to do to him?"

The man pulled his arm away. "Just protectin' myself."

She took the arm back firmly and regarded it again. "I don't think you'll be crippled for life. When you get home, you wash these with clean water, keep a clean bandage on and you'll heal up fine. Let it get dirty, and you may lose your arm." She released him without much hope for his interpretation of "clean," but she had done her best. She had no plans to stay around long enough to do the job for him.

Meanwhile, Tourantij had been conversing with the bandit leader. He walked over to Teora, and Corquée edged his horse nearer to hear what he had to say. "These are quite harmless to a party our size. They live nearby, working at being shepherds. I suspect that they augment their living with what they can steal from unprotected travellers. I doubt if they would have attacked us once they realized our strength. Now they have become very friendly.

"They have invited us to visit their home to share the midday meal. That means we will provide most of it."

"Do we go?"

"There is little reason not to. First, I do not wish to offend anyone in this difficult country. They have their own twisted sense of honour, and to them the invitation is quite important. Also, I would like to see their camp. Any bandit group existing this close to a patrolled road must have a very strong or very well-hidden spot."

Corquée shrugged and smiled. Teora looked over her shoulder meaningfully. Goianor still sat on his horse, staring around as if waking up from a nightmare.

"I will clear it with the expedition leader. He isn't in any state to refuse." The soldier strode over to the priest and conversed a moment, then returned to the bandits. Soon, they were off down the path, their new hosts interspersed among Teora's party. Her herdsmen, freed from checking the trail, were now concerned with keeping an eye on the light fingers of their hosts.

They reached the bottom of the rockfall quite abruptly. The flat prairie seemed to flow right up to the bottom of the cliff like the ocean that Haven scientists said had once lain there. A welcome forest of taller trees shaded the path, which ran north along the base, detouring now and then to miss one of the huge boulders that had fallen at one time or another. The main trail turned aside before it reached a larger pile of these, angling off to the west and the distant mountains. The bandits turned in among the stones.

The boulders were huge, with so little broken rock around them that they sat upon one another like a child's blocks, with caverns and passageways beneath and between. Through a narrow crack between two the size of houses, and the party was in a tight, high-walled corral, the floor thick with years of sheep droppings. There they left their stock in charge of the dogs and two Herdsmen. Ducking under another stone, this one rounded and perched high on two neighbors, their guides led them to another enclosure, roofed over by a partly shattered plate. A comfortable amount of light got in around the sides, and the smoke wafted easily out. A boy sat lookout above them on the edge of the slab.

There was little evidence of the spoils of the robbers' trade. The people for the most part dressed in homespun, with leather moccasins or, in the case of the working-age men, boots. A few near-naked children scurried over the uneven rock floor, staring up with curiosity at the visitors. Teora wandered over to the largest fire, hoping that the cooking would be at least clean enough that she wouldn't be sick. One glance and she determined to eat only what had been brought in her party's own packs and handled by their hands.

Fortunately, the 'shepherds' stood on little formality. Since the acceptance of their invitation, they had become effusive. Teora needed the help of her Herdsmen to serve her and maintain a social distance from their hosts. Tourantij and Corquée had no such qualms, she noticed, chatting freely and eating copiously of whatever was put before them. Corquée even spent some time trying to get the children to talk to him, but all were too wary. Goianor had regained his hauteur, but since the Herdsmen made no effort to feed him, he was forced to join with the others. He ate very little, but managed to get down a portion specifically offered him, with a slightly green smile for the woman who brought it.

Teora started to relax. No danger threatened. These people lived on the fringes of the law, but no doubt considered themselves quite upstanding. They held to the forms of hospitality, especially with the honour of such an important group visiting them. They were aware of the importance of the Haven and were impressed at Tourantij's tale of her own mission. She began to feel guilty about staying aloof from the common conversation, but Tourantij seemed happy with the situation, so she stayed where she was. He was busy getting all the information he could about trail and political conditions in the vicinity, and she didn't want to spoil the intimacy he had achieved with his informers.

After they had all eaten, he strolled over for another informal meeting.

"The news isn't good. They confirm my fears that the water holes are drying up faster than usual this summer. They say they would never take a flock over our route at this time, although they have done it at a better time of a better year.

"The political situation is not great, either. This area nominally belongs to Lord Kilyan, from the north across the mountains, but the Duke of Chajna, who owns the land below the river, is pushing his influence north. The soldiers of the Joined Kingdoms who are supposed to be keeping the peace have been pulled back, leaving the small guard of mercenaries you saw at the Rim. Not that they have any worries. Five men could hold that trail indefinitely. But it means we could run into trouble earlier than I had hoped."

He was about to go on when a low whistle sounded from overhead. The boy on watch was beckoning to the shepherds below. Tourantij and Teora followed them up a cleft between two boulders to attain the roof. Tourantij was ahead of Teora, and as his head came level with the top of the rock he crouched down and motioned her to imitate him. They crawled over to where their hosts were peering over the edge of their vantage.

Taking care not to put her head higher than any other, Teora joined them. The main path to the west was close, but far below them. At first, she saw nothing, but then, guided by Tourantij's gaze, she saw a dust cloud approaching. Not a large cloud, just a blurring of the trees along the trail. It did not take long before the moving figures under the cloud became defined as marching men. They came closer, and details came clear. They were soldiers: light infantry, it seemed, carrying long rifles with bayonets attached. A few men rode horses. Nearer, and she saw that some did not have rifles, and that they were by no means marching in close formation.

"Is something wrong?"

Tourantij stared another long moment. "They aren't retreating, at least not at the moment, but they've been in a tussle, that's for sure. They're in a hurry. Light packs, no artillery, officers mounted. Chajnan uniforms. I suspect they were pushing up towards the pass and ran into a spot of trouble. They will be setting up camp at the base of the cliff near the river. There's a spot to fort up, easily held and surrounded by rock, near the trail. Custom-built for anyone who wanted to keep track of who was moving."

"Or to hold on until reinforcements arrive." Corquée had stretched his lean form beside them. "They might have come from the pass. Should I go down and ask them about the routes?"

"Perhaps not. We have no idea what our reception might be in general, and a group as worn down as that could be touchy. We'll wait for them to pass, then scoot off westwards. You'll have to scout ahead a bit farther than usual, to give us time to get off the road if anyone else was coming."

"If I backtrack them and figure which route they took from the pass, that might give us an idea of what it's like out on the flat."

When they broke the news of this decision to Goianor, he was not as enthused.

"Let me get this straight. You sit here in this den of thieves, proposing that we hide from the forces of the official owners of this land? What kind of people are we? To whom are we allying ourselves? This party is on an official mission for the Temple of the Consort. Believe me, I have no plan to slink through the country like a bunch of criminals. I carry with me letters from some of the highest powers in this land, requiring anyone whom I meet to give me all assistance." The priest paused for breath.

"Now, I have a counterproposal. We will immediately quit this foul hole and approach the soldiers of Chajna. I will show my letters and demand an escort through the pass. That was the intention when the journey was planned. That is how we will conduct ourselves. The armies of Chajna are disciplined men, with officers of the appropriate class. They will treat us properly and provide us with a more experienced guide, I am sure."

Teora managed to shift her weight casually to hook her leg in front of Corquée's shin. This sudden movement distracted him at the moment he was about to move. She pressed her elbow, not gently, into the pit of his stomach and pinned him in place against the rock wall. He felt solid, partly because he was rigid with anger. Tourantij was speaking calmly.

"That may be, Goianor. It may happen as you say. On the other hand, that is a band of soldiers who have just been in a fight. There were officers mounted and officers walking. There looked to be little in the way of supplies. If we go down there, we may get the help we need. We may also end up with no horses or supplies and, if they were to decide we were spies, it could be much worse."

Corquée had relaxed slightly. He slid from Teora's hold and gave her a hurt stare. Then his gaze swept past the priest disdainfully, and he focused on Tourantij and spoke one word. "Magali."

The soldier looked at him, as if calculating the truth of his statement. "The men's hair was very pale."

"Chajnan officers, Magali men."

"I know that formation. If it is so, this changes things."

"It is so."

Tourantij turned to the Priest. "No other tribe I know has that white-blond hair and dark skin. If that's a bunch of half-trained Magali who have lost a skirmish, I don't want Teora, Barozon, or any of the rest of this party anywhere near them. Chajnan officers or not."

The white had returned to Goianor's face. First, he began to speak, then he stopped, threw up his hands, then tried again, failed. Finally, his eye fixed on Corquée. "How...how do we know this boy speaks the truth?"

This time it was Tourantij who stepped between the two men. The cold note had slipped into his voice and his eyes bored down at the Priest. "It is not appropriate to question the veracity of your guide, especially if that guide is a Rider of Curicuiriari. In the first place, it weakens his usefulness to us if he is not trusted. As expedition leader, I should think that would be your concern. In the second place, if he should decide to turn against you, you would do better to take your chances out there with the Magali."

The soldier gave a harsh laugh and turned the priest away. "Come now, Master Goianor. I know it would be nice to find us an escort to protect us and speed us safely on our way. But this lot is not what we are looking for. Besides which, they are headed the wrong way, and we have no way of knowing that they aren't going all the way to the Rim. But I agree with you. It is time we bid our noble hosts farewell and return to the road. With the extra precautions we will have to use in the next two days, it will take us longer."

Teora and the Herdsmen took this as a cue and began moving towards the opening that led to the outside. After a moment, Teora checked back to see if Corquée was following. He wasn't. She returned and stood in front of him.

"Come on, Corquée. You heard Tourantij. We need you out on the trail first."

The Rider looked mollified but unmoved.

"I'm sorry I elbowed you. I thought it was necessary. Did I hurt you?"

That got through. "Hurt me? With your elbow? When did you elbow me?"

So, he's going to play tough. Well, at least it was a response. "What were you going to do? Hit him? He'd fall to pieces and cry. Kill him? That would be fine. You'd lose your job, the money or glory or whatever it is you expect to get from it, and you wouldn't even be able to go home, because the Priests at Aeru would put up such a fuss."

"Sometimes a man's honour is worth more than these petty details."

"Right. Sometimes it is. But is this one of those times? Is he worth it?" She made a guess. "Would it be honourable to hit or kill such a one, who would never fight back?"

He considered that. While he was distracted, she pulled his arm and sent him along towards the exit. "Now, let's get on with the journey. You have always known that he was this kind of person. You have put up with him this far. Keep on."

She left her arm through his and continued in a conversational tone as they walked. "I'm beginning to learn that doing one of these tasks is not as simple as it seems. You know, you start out being worried about the bandits, the desert and wild animals, but you discover that most of the time they are nowhere to be seen. The real problems are things like boredom, getting along with stupid people, and going without a bath until you're itchy. I suppose you must have found that out a long ago with the journeys you have been on, but for me it is a new thought." She glanced up at him.

He looked down thoughtfully. "Yes, I know what you mean. To have made this discovery is an important aspect of your personal growing. I, too, made this growing a few years ago. It leaves one not quite as anxious to go on long journeys," he smiled proudly down at her, "but it also makes one realize that those who have journeyed understand these things, and that it is a great honour to be accepted among a group of people who have paid such a price."

Then his face became more formal. "I see where you are leading me, Madam Teora. I have done some personal growing today. Thank you for this insight."

Teora managed to keep a serious demeanour. "We have all grown today, I suspect. Even Goianor, perhaps?"

"I seriously doubt that, although it is possible, I suppose."

She felt that now might be time to laugh. "Possible. But not around the waist. Did you see how much he ate for lunch?"

The Rider threw back his head and laughed, clapping his hand against her back. The others looked up, surprised, as the two entered the corral and strolled over to mount their animals, still chuckling.

8.   The Rock

Barozon snorted the sand out of his nose and peered ahead. He was tired of following that stupid horse. *Oh, he's a nice enough horse, skinny and weak though he might be. But if he keeps going in the wrong direction much longer, the Herd is going to get very thirsty.*

He raised his head. *She is not paying attention, either. Soon I will have to do something.* He snorted again. *She must have a plan. It is not for me to lead.* He lowered his head and trudged on through the swirling dust, his every sense on his Partner and the ever-present pull of Rightness that came from the left side of their path.

Teora spat, or tried to. Nothing came out, not even the grains of sand lodged under her tongue. She wrapped the scarf tighter around her face and peered ahead through the swirling dust. Nothing. At least, nothing that she could see except the tail of Corquée's horse, always receding towards invisibility. She willed her Partner to speed up. His head rose slightly, and an ear flicked her way. He did not seem as bothered by the storm as she was, and he plodded onward, keeping a decent distance from the horse ahead.

She wondered how the Rider knew where he was going, with the visibility this poor. She had to remind herself that, according to the others, this wasn't really a sandstorm. There wasn't enough wind, apparently. *Well, it's enough for me. Any wind enough to lift the dust into the air is too much.*

She wondered if it had been long enough since her last drink. The bottle sloshed an invitation from its place at her hip. *It hasn't been long enough.* She shifted the scarf until the sweat-dampened part cooled her forehead. For a brief moment. Then it was warm and sticky again.

She pulled herself out of a daze to realize that Barozon had stopped, and that Corquée, a dim ghost ahead, was swinging off. She stayed put where she was safe.

Corquée turned his horse and brought her the reins. "I'll check on the others. Don't move Barozon. Keep him pointing exactly the same way." He disappeared towards the rear. Goianor was a miserable lump in the saddle close behind her. She had a moment's pity, then a touch of admiration for the older man. He hated so much of this. It was amazing that he had come, that he continued. She resolved to forgive him for some of his minor pettiness.

Corquée returned, his feet scuffing up clouds of dust that danced away downwind behind him. "All's as well as can be expected. Not much farther now."

"How much is 'not much farther,' and how do you know you're going to hit wherever it is we're going?"

His grin looked strange, with the dark lines of dirt filling the creases and lining his lips. She was glad her face was covered. "I'm not too sure how long, but don't worry. The Rock is a bit hard to miss. Unless the wind picks up, we'll find it in the next hour or so."

He swung back into the saddle and moved on into the swirl. Barozon did not need to be urged. She felt a surge of love for her Partner. *He is so brave, so uncomplaining. So comforting.* She slapped his hump affectionately, then was sorry, as an extra puff of dust whirled up in her face.

As she bowed once more into the wind, she thought again about the mysterious bond of Partnership. The road gave plenty of time for thought, and she took advantage of it.

She was beginning to get a different perspective on her relationship with Barozon. Up at the Haven, the Partnership bond was a useful tool in the forming of a performance routine, and little more. She was beginning to see how it might have been different, a thousand years or more back in the mists before recorded history. The protection of the herd against predators, human enemies and raiding wild bulls must have taken a great deal of intelligence and strength. Her brief experience with the dangers of the trail so far had made her much more aware of Barozon's strength and how much her peace of mind depended upon him.

She thought of her far-off ancestors, ploughing through similar storms with the many dangers of their age surrounding them, and she realized the wisdom of the Temple in sending traditional support with her. The Herdsmen and their dogs, with their mobility and senses, were a perfect complement to the strength of the bull. Having the Rider ranging farther afield was a distinct advantage. She wondered what the old-timers used in that respect. Probably their fastest runners. The soldier was a necessary addition to cope with modern military problems.

Yes, for a minimal-sized party it was the best that could be found. Not one wasted body. Then she thought of Goianor. He probably represented the power of their Faith. Up to this point, he had not proved his worth. *I wonder if that's the main problem in Aeru. If the*

Priesthood has become a useless appendage, no longer providing the spark that made life meaningful, then there is an unfilled hollow in their people, which the strongest outer defences can never cure.

She hugged herself around the warmth of her own Choosing as she slumped into a half-drowse, her thirst receding. Even without the Priest, this was one party that carried true fullness: strength without, strength within. *It's my duty to keep the two connected.* She rode on into the storm, resolved to do her part.

She was aroused some undefined time later by an uneasy feeling beneath her; Barozon was swinging his head to the left. Lifting her scarf a slit, she could tell that the wind had increased. Larger grains of sand were carried in the air now and they stung when they hit bare skin.

It also seemed to her that they were moving slower than before, but that might have been the effect of the wind. Barozon was following Corquée closer as well, but she could barely make out the Rider's form, dimly outlined against the lighter area that might be sky in front of her. Her Partner swung his head again, off to the left, and broke his stride, then continued to follow the horse.

"What is it, fellow? What's over there?"

The bull's ear flipped at the sound of her voice, and his head turned left again. He couldn't be looking, because his eyes were slitted against the dust. She concentrated on her Partner, opening all her feelings towards him. She could sense eagerness, not danger, and he was beginning to drift slowly to the left, now. She nudged him back onto the invisible trail behind Corquée's horse, but he immediately began to drift again.

She let this go on for a few minutes until she was sure that the bull's actions were not going to return to normal. She was about to call to Corquée when he stopped and turned his horse back alongside of her.

"What's wrong? Are we there?"

His face was grim. "I wish I knew. We should be. Should have been half an hour ago."

"We're lost?"

"Not really. Just misplaced. If it was a clear day, I guarantee that we would see the Rock, standing up there as close as anything. The visibility is getting worse, though, and we might miss it. Then we'd have to camp dry and wait for morning, hoping the wind died. Not fun."

"And then if there's no water there…"

"Exactly." He slapped his gloves against the saddle peevishly. "I know it's nearby. If that Deity-bedamned wind hadn't risen. Pardon, Madam Teora. I know I shouldn't speak that way. It's so frustrating!"

By this time, the others had caught up, and the Herdsmen were gathered in the shelter of the horses. Goianor pushed forward.

"Where are we? I thought you said you could find water before nightfall!"

"Well, that proves how unpredictable life is, doesn't it?"

"I hardly feel this is a time for levity. Where are we?"

"It's not where we are, it's where we should be that's the problem."

The Priest tore the hood back from his head and glared up through the gathering darkness at the Rider. "Don't play games, boy. Have you got us lost?"

Tourantij had begun to shove his horse between the two when Barozon moved, stepping out of line and plodding away.

Teora's sudden exclamation drew the men's attention.

Corquée dropped his bantering. "Where are you going, Teora? Stop! You'll get lost!"

She managed to stop her Partner but could feel his anxiety to continue. "I don't know. He just started off. He's been acting strangely for the last quarter hour, moving off in that direction. I was about to stop you, Corquée, to ask about it."

"Well, for heaven's sake, girl, get him under control. I have enough problems with an incompetent guide and a sandstorm. I don't need you running off and getting lost." The Priest was urging his horse in front of Barozon, trying to head him off.

Teora forgot her resolve to be kind. "You'd better not get in the way. I may not be able to keep him here long, and if you're in front of him, it won't make much difference. He finds horses rather puny things."

Corquée pulled up on her other side. "Let him go. He's not stupid. If he wants to go that way, then there is something in that direction that he wants. Get out of the way, Priest, and let him have his head."

"Do you think so? What could he want?"

Corquée's grin had returned. "What do we all want?"

She grinned back and relaxed her hold on her Partner. He immediately started off, his plodding gait purposeful. The rest followed closely, keeping watch on each other in the worsening gloom and wind.

They had been going for only about five minutes when Teora felt the change. She looked up at Corquée, riding beside her. "Have we changed direction?"

"No. It's the wind starting to swirl. It's been blowing from the west, and we probably caught a gust from the south."

"What does that mean?"

"Count two hundred paces and you'll know."

With that cryptic answer he would say no more, though she could tell he was pleased about something. She could sense the swirling of the wind, coming now from one side, now the other, once seeming to come from straight up. If the Rider hadn't seemed so pleased, she would have been worried. She continued, counting.

At one hundred sixty, Barozon slowed, and his head dropped. He snuffled at the ground, then pawed tentatively. He moved on, then pawed again. Teora looked up to see Corquée jumping off his horse. Something appeared different. It seemed darker, yet she could see him clearly. Then her eyes adjusted to what she was actually seeing. Rising out of the sand behind him was a dark wall of rock. The wind had almost stopped, and she could see the cracked and broken surface quite clearly. Barozon pawed again, more vigorously.

The Rider strode up and pushed the bull's head away. "Move out, you big lug. We can do much better with a shovel." He strode to the packhorse, pulled one from under the ropes and began to dig. Barozon stood back a step and watched. After a moment, the Rider leaned down into the hole and felt around. He shook his head, and dug some more, then felt again. This time, he stood up. "Keep him out of it for a while." He walked a bit closer to the wall and started digging again.

She jumped to the ground and knelt by the hole, pushing the bull's huge nose away. Down in the bottom, she could feel the dampness. She licked her fingers gratefully. Looking up, she could see that the others were digging too, Tourantij with another shovel, the Herdsmen with whatever they could come up with, assisted enthusiastically by their dogs. Realizing that this first hole would be a long time in providing enough water for her thirsty Partner, she started another beside it.

"Not quite there." Corquée had not stopped shoveling, but he gestured with his chin towards the rock wall. "The water comes from the crack, there, trickling out of the centre of the Rock. Dig in line with that. But don't worry. I'll have one big enough for him in a moment. There should be more water closer in."

Sure enough, she could hear the change in the sound. Instead of the hissing of dry sand leaving his shovel, there was a dull thump as damp sand hit the ground. Soon, she heard a welcome gurgle each time he put his shovel into the hole. Then he stood up.

"Don't let the animals water themselves. They always put their feet in and then we have to shovel it out again. I'll get something."

She kept Barozon still while Corquée strode over and untied the canvas on the packhorse. He returned with the pot that they had eaten stew from the night before and sank it down in his hole. After a minute or so, he brought it out dripping and set it down before Barozon.

"First drink for he who deserves it most."

The bull snorted, then dipped his muzzle in and drank noisily. It was soon empty, and he nudged it towards Corquée, knocking it over in the process.

"He wants more! His majesty wants another fine wine! Coming right up, sire!" Gleefully, the Rider jammed the pot back into the sand, bowing and carrying on as he did so.

"Shouldn't you tend to your horse?"

"She knows the drill."

Teora turned to check the first hole Corquée had dug. His mare was down on her knees, her nose thrust in. She slurped a bit, then raised her head and waited, then drank again.

Farther out, the other members of the party were busy at their own holes. Tourantij was watering his horse, and the Herdsmen were taking care of the other animals. Only Goianor was not digging. He was standing beside his horse, drinking deeply from his water bottle, then pouring a liberal dose into his hand and splashing it on his face. Corquée followed her glance and raise his voice.

"Don't waste it, Priest."

The man's head turned slowly, his eyes burning at the lack of respect. "And why not?"

"Because we still might need it. This water is twice as deep in the sand as I expected. Clean water in a bottle is worth much more than dirty water in the sand that might not be there at all by morning. Don't be afraid to get your hands dirty, Goianor. Dig for yourself."

Goianor glared a moment, then turned away. Looking around, he found an empty water hole and, after a moment's thought, sank his cupped hands into it and waited, then drank. Putting her hands into her own hole, Teora felt how good it was to have them in the cool water. She was glad that this was her own hole, rather than one dug by the dogs, but the priest wouldn't want that fact drawn to his attention.

The relief of finding water carried them through the early evening, but it was still a poor night. The wind had not stopped, just lost its energy in the lee of the Rock, so the sand and dust swirled down on them from above. They had no fire, simply pitched their tents close to the wall and slipped into bed munching dry rations and drinking muddy water, shaking their clothes outside the tent. The heat of the day had gone, but Teora still felt suffocated in the closed tent and dared not open it because of the sand. She did not sleep until much later, when the air cooled.

She awoke to find the early sun shining directly on the walls of her tent, brightening every streak of dirt, accenting the gritty feeling of her sleeping robe. She hunted clean underclothing out of her pack, squirming at the thought of putting it on over her dirty body, but feeling better afterwards. She wondered if there would be enough water in the holes they had dug to rinse something out. She hoped so, in case this was the last water they would see before the mountains.

She stuck her head out of the tent to see Tourantij bent over a farther hole, wringing out his shirt. He must have heard her stirring, for he noticed her immediately.

"Good morning, Teora. Drinking water near the wall, washing farther out. We'll water the animals before we leave."

"When do we leave?"

"Don't know yet. Corquée has gone to scout around. This water your friend found is a good sign, though. We won't have to detour to the Dead Forest. Too bad you'll miss it, though. An unbelievable sight."

"What exactly is this Dead Forest? I've heard about it, but I don't believe half of what they say."

"If you heard that it's a forest of trees all made of stone, you can believe it."

"It really is?"

"Yes. All lying down, of course, and broken in many pieces. But definitely trees, and definitely stone."

"But how could such a thing be?"

"Have you ever seen coal?"

"Of course. We burn it in winter at home."

"Ever looked at it closely?"

"Not really. It's dirty and it comes in small pieces."

"Well, it doesn't come from the ground in small pieces. If you ever get a chance, check out a larger hunk. You know what it's made of?"

She looked at him a moment. "Not... trees?"

He nodded and smiled faintly. "Not big trees, but if you look closely, you will see leaves and branches and moss. All coal now, though. If trees could turn into coal, which is like soft rock..."

"Then by the same process they could turn into hard rock. I suppose so."

The camp was beginning to waken, others leaving their tents and starting their morning work. Teora smiled at Tourantij and headed for a washing hole with yesterday's clothes and a sliver of soap. As she worked, she wondered again about the soldier. How did he know so much about so many things? One answer would be a university education at the Centre. At least she had pulled a smile out of him. That was an accomplishment, especially since the incident at the Rim.

According to her companions, they never did get to the true desert. *Which is just as well, considering what we are going through.* The storm had calmed during the night and the sun brightened more as it rose through the haze of dust near the horizon, its heat evident even as they started out. There was no trail, but Teora had ceased to marvel at Corquée's navigation. If he could come this close to his destination in yesterday's conditions, she had no doubt of his ability to keep them going in normal light.

They spent the day plodding through broken country studded with brush and cactus. Occasionally, they crossed a dry watercourse, its banks and lines of driftwood mocking with hints of flowing water. When she questioned this, Corquée explained.

"There are two types of water paths out here. Some could almost be called creeks. The water flows through them, but most of the year it seeps underground. In a wet year, they flow on the surface for

92

several months. Times like these, the water is very far under. In some cases, too deep to dig for. You can tell that type because of the plants that grow along the edges: plants with very long roots.

"This other sort has no water most of the time. They only take the extra that flows over the surface of the land when there is a big storm. It can be very dangerous, because of the speed and the amount of water."

"And what about the water Barozon found?"

"That one is rather strange. It comes out of that crack and disappears into the sand about thirty paces from the rock. A few bushes grow near it, but for some reason they are very sparse and low. Something to do with the way the wind moves the sand, I suppose. It is very hard to find." He glanced with appreciation at the bull. "Your Partner has a very good nose."

"A good nose?"

The Rider seemed perplexed. "Of course. That's how animals find water. Usually, my horse does the job for me. I'm surprised that Barozon was able to notice it first. Especially with the wind angle."

"So am I. He has a terrible sense of smell."

"He does?"

Teora had to laugh. "That's what I said. He doesn't smell very well at all. It's his one failing."

"But that's impossible." Corquée sounded seriously concerned. "How do you know?"

"You must trust me to know my Partner. It is part of our training, part of our rituals. I always thought it was only tradition, but I am learning more about the practical nature of the old ways. We test our Partners on everything as they grow and keep close track of their progress." She knew a bit of pride crept into her voice. "Barozon always topped the tests, every time. He is the most perfect specimen in many generations." She paused to look ruefully at her companion.

"But his sense of smell is only average, I'm afraid. I have often thought that this was the Deity's way of reminding us that only the gods can be perfect."

She reached down and slapped the rippling shoulder in front of her leg. "It bothers me a lot more than it does him. In fact, it doesn't bother him at all, because he has no idea that he's almost perfect. As far as he's concerned, he's just him!"

93

She glanced up to catch the effect of her small joke, but it had gone completely past Corquée. Something more important was on his mind.

"But how did he find the water, then? None of the other animals noticed, and the wind was blowing away from us towards the water."

"I don't know. I thought you might have an idea. I don't think he smelled it, that's all."

The Rider shrugged. The long silence between them was underscored by the plod of their mounts and the creak of leather. Then Corquée kicked his horse and moved in front of her, his head bowed in thought. She stared after him, then shrugged to herself. *Whatever is bothering him, I'll find out in time.* She allowed herself to slip back into the hypnotic rhythm of her Partner's gait.

9.   Trapped

They camped dry that night, doling out a meagre portion of their water to the animals, less to the humans. There was little conversation: people withdrawing into themselves, saving their energies for the coming day. Teora was concerned about her Herdsmen, but they assured her that they were in good shape. The dogs seemed unaffected once the main heat of the day was past, although they moved slowly, flopping down to pant in whatever shade they could find.

By unspoken mutual consent, they rose with the first greying of dawn, ate a handful of dry food, moistened their lips from their canteens and mounted. Even Goianor needed no rousing. He stumbled out of his tent in the clothes he had worn the day before, walked straight to his horse, mounted and slouched into his saddle in mute anticipation. Again, Teora felt a trickle of sympathy for the man's obvious suffering and squelched the uncharitable thought that the one benefit of this country was its calming effect on the Priest's tongue. Radman walked over and handed the priest a bit of bread, which he received wordlessly. The Herdsman shrugged and grinned to Teora as he returned to his companions.

The day seemed even longer, the heat fiercer. At noon, they changed course, and soon Teora saw the reason. Just ahead, on this new angle, a smaller version of the Rock barred their way. Corquée led them into a break in the rock, where a large pool of shade stretched across the sand. The weak breeze that had been breathing the heat of the sand against them seemed almost cool here, and Teora slid from Barozon's back and collapsed to the ground at the base of the rock.

"Dig down a bit. It's even better."

Corquée was scraping the sand away from the stone. She copied him and the sand became cooler as she went deeper. She relaxed into her trench, her arms spread wide to allow the sweat to evaporate as much as possible. Tourantij was passing along the line of animals, hefting water bottles and listening to them as he went. He checked everyone's personal supply as well, then dug himself a spot between Teora and Corquée.

"How's the supply?"

The soldier nodded. "Not too bad, considering."

Corquée's tone sharpened. "Considering what?"

"We are moving slower than normal travelling pace and the priest is drinking twice as much water as anyone else."

Teora jumped in quickly before Corquée could react. "Is it Barozon and the Herdsmen? Should we be going faster?"

Tourantij glanced to his left, passing the question to the Rider, who choked down his anger enough to answer. "No, Teora. Don't push any faster than you have been. That could be fatal. Keep a very close eye on your Partner, but the speed that will get us the farthest is the pace that is comfortable."

"Like swimming under water."

"What?" Both Teora and Corquée turned wondering eyes to the older man.

"Swimming under water. You might think that you should swim fast, to get the farthest before your breath runs out, wouldn't you?"

Teora took a moment to absorb the thought. Having enough water to swim for any distance underneath it was a concept that had not occurred to her often. In fact, it had never entered her mind. After a moment, she nodded.

"Wrong. If you try to swim fast you have to come up much sooner, because you use up your breath faster. To go a long distance, you move slowly and keep as relaxed as you can."

Teora leaned forward to meet Corquée's amused grin. "Thank you, Ser Niverdhal, for that important piece of information."

"Yes, my friend. We are deeply in your debt. The very next time I am swimming under water, I will take your lesson into account. Very seriously."

The soldier merely raised his eyebrows. "Never take proffered knowledge lightly. Such gems as fall infrequently from my lips should be treasured up against possible need."

Teora leaned back, enjoying the momentary coolness as she touched the sweat-dampened rock. "The desert has really got to your brains today."

"As I have mentioned before, dear lady, we have not seen real desert yet."

"You mean we're going to...?" She jerked upright, then caught the joke. She looked across. No smile appeared on the craggy face, but she detected a wrinkling around his eyes. She sank back again. "Well, when we get to a real desert, you point it out to me, and I'll see if I can tell the difference."

They lapsed into companionable silence, and Teora considered how adroitly the soldier had turned the conversation away from the Priest's mistreatment of their water supply. *It must not be too serious, or he would do something about it. I hope.*

They rested through the midday heat and then continued, burning into the face of the sun as it swung westward. Teora lost sense of time as she faded from the reality of the dirt and heat into a half-sleep, which barely allowed her to keep place in her harness. It must have been much later when she was gradually roused by a sense of unease. The moment it touched her, she jolted awake with sudden guilt. *Barozon! I was supposed to be keeping watch on him.*

Leaning forward, she patted his neck, murmuring an apology to his receptive ear. He shook his head slowly but did not break stride. All senses attuned, she rode on, searching for what had awakened her.

Only a few minutes later, Corquée, who had been riding farther ahead, turned and walked his horse back towards her. He had a grim expression on his face.

"Is something wrong?"

He swung his horse around and fell in beside her. Glancing back, he leaned down and spoke in a low voice. "I don't want to alarm you, but we seem to be repeating ourselves. I thought I would know where we were by now, but we aren't. Possibly I have been fooled by our unfamiliar pace, but it's hard to tell. How are you doing?"

She considered. "I'm not sure. I got a different feeling a moment ago, and I was trying to figure it out when you rode back. If you want, let's ride on, and I'll see if I pick up something more."

The Rider glanced back again then gave her a relieved smile. "Good idea. Be sure to let me know the moment anything different happens." He glanced down at Barozon, and she knew what he meant by "different."

She tried to smile reassuringly, and he moved ahead.

It took her some time. Barozon settled down to his pace again, and she sat still, listening with every pore. After a while, she realized she was trying too hard. She relaxed, allowing herself to fall partly into the trance of the road. Only then did she get it. *Barozon is tired. He is also puzzled. He shouldn't be tired, but he is.* She waited a while, but that was all she could get. More positive, but the same message. *He shouldn't feel tired, but his legs are not moving as easily as before. Each step seems harder, somehow. What is wrong?*

When she realized she was going to get no more information, Teora whistled. Corquée turned back too eagerly.

"What is it?"

"I don't know. He's tired."

"That's all? Tired?" His disappointment was palpable.

"Not quite all. He feels tired but doesn't know why. Like it's harder to move his feet. Does that mean anything to you?"

A frown warred with an uncertain smile, which finally won, spreading across his face. "Harder to move his feet? Good!" He kneed his horse ahead, leaning down to rub Barozon behind his right ear.

"What?"

The Rider straightened, allowing his horse to fall back beside her. "I know where we are, now. It was the haze that kept us from seeing."

"Corquée, will you please tell me what this is all about? Obviously, you and Barozon know all about it, but please keep us poor mortals in mind."

The Rider's face immediately straightened, and he glanced at Barozon before he spoke. "Do not make light of the Gods, Teora."

"I meant no disrespect, I assure you. Now tell me what is causing this."

"The slope. We have started up the long slope to the pass. If that dust did not hang like a cloak in front of our eyes, we should see the white peaks of the mountains very close now. You will see. Do not worry. But it will get harder, now. Soon, the others, the normal ones, will notice it as well. We must climb, now. Let us stop here a moment."

They pulled up, and watched the others catch up. Goianor seemed barely able to drag his interest outside himself. The Herdsmen trailed in, still moving well, but not enjoying it. Tourantij was riding last, now, and still seemed alert.

"What's happening, Rider?"

"Time for more water. It will be harder from here, as we climb up to the pass."

The soldier looked around pointedly. "Climb? Do you see a mountain that I missed?"

Even the priest seemed interested in the answer.

Corquée stared proudly around the group, his eyes resting a moment on the Priest. "You will see mountains soon enough. But we should water the animals some, now. We are assured of water, probably tomorrow, and the climbing is very hard, with thirst."

Teora met Tourantij's questioning stare with an innocent smile. The soldier held her eye long enough to tell her that he knew something was going on and he wasn't sure he liked it. Then he swung off his horse and started untying a pack. The others followed suit and, after the stock was watered, the riders stretched their legs, the Herdsmen sitting on their robes on the ground, dogs panting beside them. Her people seemed tireless, but they knew how to conserve their energy.

After a brief rest, they continued in higher spirits, although soon the pace became perceptibly slower. *Knowing the reason makes a great deal of difference. Speed is not important. Distance and endurance are. Swimming under water. What a strange man.*

They slogged on, winding through sand hills and around outcroppings of rock. Teora's enthusiasm soon waned, and she tried to regain her trance. It didn't work. The thought of ending this ordeal stuck in her mind, and the idea that she must continue to endure it seemed impossible. The very concept of one more minute, let alone several more hours, of this torture was unbearable. She shifted her weight, suppressing the urge to scream, to jump down and run. Barozon snorted: disdainfully, she thought. After all, who was doing all the walking? Who had a right to complain? She kept that in mind, and it helped some.

Darkness caught them still climbing through the foothills, and they camped dry, not bothering to change their clothes or perform more than the barest necessities before falling into restless sleep.

In the morning, the heat started even earlier, and Tourantij appeared grim as he checked the water supplies. Corquée was less dismayed, although he still couldn't pin down when they would reach the water.

"There are several springs this side of the mountain, but some may be dried already. Don't worry. We will reach water today." He smiled, but Teora felt that his cheer was forced. She mounted reluctantly, and Barozon also seemed unenthused as he stepped out up the trail.

At least the weather was clearer. Piles of jagged rock closed in around them, but sometimes a higher peak peered down from the end of an empty wash. The sparse sod and grainy soil fell away and soon they were walking on bare stone or gravel. The slope began to steepen, and the heat bouncing off the walls was a force in their faces. The animals plodded forward, struggling as if against a wind, though no breeze came to cool them. The Herdsmen plugged onwards, leaning on their staves, the dogs panting in line behind. The dark one was last, and he still had the energy to nip lightly at the haunch of the dog in front of him when it slowed.

As the party penetrated further into the mountains, their thirst increased, and the sloshing of near-empty water bottles became a torture to their ears. Once, Corquée stopped at what might have been a stream, and looked searchingly at the parched gravel, mocking them with its stream-rounded curves.

"No water under that. You either see it, or you don't." He turned his horse up the trail again before the others caught up. Twice more in the morning he strayed from the trail then returned, shaking his head. They rested more frequently, whenever a large enough patch of shade appeared, but these spots became rare as the sun rose. Finally, a whistle from the rear stopped them. Teora and Corquée slouched numbly and watched the apathetic approach of their party. Tourantij brought up the rear as usual, but he was leading one of the pack animals. The one with the water.

Teora wondered what that meant, and what had gone on behind her back while she hid her senses from the discomfort of the trail. The soldier's face was grim almost to the point of anger, it seemed.

"How much longer, Rider? Where is the water you promised?"

The Rider's back stiffened into what was now a familiar pose. "Oh, we've passed several nice, cool ponds. I just like travelling this way. Can't you keep up, Soldier?"

Teora dragged the energy from somewhere, although the crack of her voice sounded weak and tired in her ears. She was gratified that it was enough to rouse her Partner, and his horns rose to a more useful level. "Stop this argument! We expect more of you than pettiness."

There was a moment of tension, then both men seemed to crumple, the fire gone. She would almost have preferred that they had the energy to disagree. "Corquée, can you give us some idea of how long this will continue?"

He shifted in the saddle, gazing around for landmarks. "As I said before, I don't know. The pace is irregular, and the water holes are more dried up than I had expected."

"We have heard these lame excuses before!" Teora was startled at the sound of the Priest's voice, after a long silence. "Have you killed us all, sacrificed to your own stupid...Ouch!"

The Priest looked down to where the tip of one long horn was pressing into his leg. One large eye glared up at him. His hand twitched on the reins, but he did not move.

"I'm sorry, Goianor, but my Partner does not appreciate my wishes being disregarded so soon after I make them known." A tinge of anger crept into her voice when she thought of how many slow paces towards water that quick action had cost out of Barozon's waning reserves. "I don't see any point in trying to second-guess our guide at this point. Unless you have some knowledge we don't?"

The Priest shook his head and reined his horse away, but his black frown told her that this discussion was not over.

Disgusted, she shook her head and turned back to Corquée and Tourantij. "Well, gentlemen?"

"There is no choice. We must go on."

"At least there is water at the top of the pass."

The soldier's face lost a bit of its stiffness "Yes, a whole, cool stream of it, flowing out of a real glacier."

"But that could well be a full day's ride from here, at this speed."

"Come on, Rider. There must be water before then. What about that great pool we swam in? It must be around here somewhere."

"We passed it an hour ago. No joking."

"Empty?"

No answer was necessary. It hadn't really been a question.

Teora looked from one to the other. "What are our options?"

Tourantij deferred to the Rider.

"At the moment, we are merely in discomfort, not in serious trouble. There are two more possibilities for water ahead. If they are also dry, then we are in trouble. We will keep going after nightfall, slow as that may have to be, as the trail gets narrower and steeper. We will not survive another day's travel in this heat. For now, we should find a spot to lie up for midday."

Teora's questioning glance received a nod from Tourantij, and she nodded as well. "Then we keep on. We cannot sit here in the direct sunlight. Let us find a rock to crawl under."

Fortunately, they found one. It wasn't big, with barely enough shade for all the animals, but at least it was shade. As she lay perfectly still, Teora felt the faintest of breezes blowing up the trail behind them, a stir of air so slow that their walking pace had negated it. She rearranged herself to take advantage of as much as she could. Only decorum kept her from hiking up her skirt to let the air play along her bare thighs. What a luxury that would be! The thought of the scandalized expression on the Priest's face made her almost want to chuckle. She was beginning to think that Corquée would be almost as upset. How much those two had in common if they were ever to discover it. *Not too likely.*

She thought about the river at the top of the pass. Running out of a glacier! That would be another new experience for her. She supposed that this was a new experience as well. Fine. She twisted in her sweaty clothes, feeling the greasy cloth stick to her skin. *As long as it isn't my last one.*

We must go on. There is no choice. We must go on. She had heard those words often on this trip. Why did they have to go on? What was forcing them? The Deity must certainly be determined to have them get somewhere. Or determined to stop them. She idly wondered which. It didn't matter as much to her now, either way. Whatever happened, one thing was certain; as long as there was a way, they would go on.

A moment later, Tourantij was bending over her, shaking her shoulder. "Time to go, Teora."

She sat up slowly, the sleep still dazing her thoughts. The heat seemed the same, but the shadows were longer. She started to shake her head, then stopped as the dull throbbing at the top of her neck exploded upward.

Her sudden wince brought a concerned look from Tourantij. "Is something the matter?"

She stumbled up, gritting her teeth. Then her sight cleared and the pain receded. "Nobody said this was going to be fun, did they?"

He still stared at her, the lines between his brows deepening. The intensity of his gaze was disturbing. "If you are injured, you must let us know, Teora."

"It's all right, Tourantij, I have a bit of a headache. A dip in a glacier stream will fix me up fine."

"It is not a joking matter. I trust you will let me know if there is a problem."

He was doing it again. What was wrong? She laid a light hand on his sleeve. "Tourantij, I will let you know if I feel worse. Thank you for your concern."

The iron melted from his face, and he nodded. "Good. We do not want to see any harm come to you."

He turned to make his usual careful check of the gear on the pack animals, and Teora mounted, as relieved as if she had escaped some danger. If she hadn't felt so dismally tired and hot, she would have worried about it.

She was also dimly aware of some kind of squabble behind her as she turned out onto the trail, but the pain in her head and the awful thought of more hours in the blazing heat pushed all other considerations aside. She was beginning to wonder if she should be concerned when the voices stopped and Corquée's mare stalked past, moving at a faster pace than she should have been. One glance at the stiff figure of the Rider told Teora most of what she needed to know.

Well, for the moment it's over, whatever it was. I'll worry about it when we reach water. If we reach water. If no water appeared, it wouldn't matter a whole lot anyway. She wondered if she should be praying. It seemed an overwhelming task, to formulate a prayer and send it with any kind of enthusiasm. Well, maybe the Deity wouldn't mind if she just sort of thought about a prayer. What would be the best prayer? Something short and to the point. How about water? Water, that was it. Water, tumbling from the mountainside in a gushing fall of clean, clear, icy torrent, the mist rolling upwards...

Teora's head snapped up, her lethargy gone. What was wrong? Barozon's head was also elevated. Something, a noise or a tremor, brought her vision upwards.

Corquée, ahead of her, was approaching a place where the mountains closed in around the trail, leaving only a single path, from which steep inclines of loose shale slanted up on either side. Unsure why, she called his name, and he reined in, looking back.

Up to the left, where the decayed remains of the ridge jutted like broken teeth from the shale slide, she saw a puff of dust. Then runnels of broken rock began to slip down the mountain, gathering speed and size as they came. Back in the dust that boiled up behind them, Teora could vaguely see a larger mass of rock move ponderously towards her, melting and changing as huge chunks broke off and bounded ahead. It only took a frozen moment for her to register this, and then her scream fled, high above the deep rumble of the slide.

103

"Corquée!"

But she was much too slow. At the first sound, his horse had spun in its own length and was already at full gallop back towards her. Barozon had just begun to turn when the horse skidded up alongside, its shoulder driving the bull around and chivvying him down the trail. He needed no urging, plunging into his ponderous gallop, the sound of his hooves swallowed by the thunder behind.

Fortunately, the party was strung out along the path and Goianor, who was next, had time to rein aside as the two beasts stampeded past. Lucky for the priest as well that the slide came no further down the trail, as he had not the wit nor speed to escape, but sat undecided, reining his horse left and right until finally the poor animal shook its head in frustration and followed the others at a skittish trot.

Teora managed to slow Barozon before he reached the packhorses, meeting the Herdsmen and dogs rushing up the path to their defence, and the whole party milled about in confusion.

"Hold!" The soldier's ringing voice brought everyone to a standstill. They all turned and looked up the path. The rumble had stopped, and a fog of disturbed earth rose from the tumbled mass of rock that plugged the pass. Slowly, their ears and eyes searching for any sign of further disturbance, the party moved back towards the slide. Teora found herself pressed into the centre of the group, Corquée and Tourantij on either side, the Herdsmen in a tight circle around them all. Back down the trail with the pack animals, the priest sat forlornly on his horse.

As they approached the smoking mass of rock, the soldier pushed his horse in front of Barozon. "Don't get too close. It may go again."

For a long while, they sat watching the dust settle, starting occasionally as smaller sections of the slide rattled into new positions.

Silence descended. The tiny group of humans and animals stood staring up at a huge mound of rubble that completely blocked the trail in front of them.

A Herdsman poked at a rock with his staff. It shifted, settled. "Well, I suppose we could climb over it."

"My friend, you could get over with no problem. My horse, on the other hand, might not find it that easy."

Teora had to agree with the Rider. "I don't believe that Barozon..."

At the mention of his name, her Partner tossed his head, snorting. Then silence returned.

Almost.

Barozon snuffed again and lowered his head. All eyes swept down from their vigilant survey of the mountainside above. A strange sound emerged from the rocks at their feet. A gurgling, swishing sound. Teora stared in disbelief, her dry tongue running over cracked lips.

There, from the heart of the slide, seeping along the bare rock of the trail, was water! Muddy water, full of dirt and debris, but water!

Barozon lowered his head and snuffled again. His huge pink tongue lapped out, touching the growing stream. Then he lowered his head to the stream and drank. Teora looked around. The horses also began drinking, each finding a small hollow where the trickles of water had gathered.

"Stop it! Stop it!" Corquée had leaped off his horse and was tearing around like a madman, kicking at loose gravel in the path.

"Stop what?"

"The water! Dam it up. Get down here and help, everyone. Don't let any escape." Before he had finished speaking, Tourantij was beside him, scraping up a low dike in front of the farthest advance of the water. The Herdsmen were quick to catch on. Teora followed, finding a spot where the precious liquid was slipping into a crack, and filling the gap with dust that turned to a cool, delicious-feeling mud in her hands. She luxuriated in the texture, patting her handiwork and letting the water splash over her wrists, then looked for another spot. There was none.

The first rush of water had subsided, the reason Corquée had been in such a hurry. Their efforts had created a shallow pool, narrow enough to step across. The water coming from under the rock was now only a trickle, seeping through the trampled mess where the animals still milled, pushing their noses into every hollow where a bit of water might still be resting. The pool might have been expanding, but it was impossible to tell. Corquée called to the Herdsmen to bring up the packhorses, and they hurriedly filled every vessel they carried with muddy water, scooping up dirt, moss, and sand in the process. Only when the pool was so low that it was impossible to scrape up any more water did they sit back and rest, watching with wary eyes as more water seeped into the reservoir.

"How did you know it wouldn't last?"

The Rider grinned at her. "I didn't. But it stands to reason. There isn't a real stream here. It was probably an underground pocket. When it comes to water, you don't take chances." He stretched his arms high and wrung his sash out, leaning back and allowing the water to run over his face and neck. "I can't believe it. Water in the middle of nowhere. It's a miracle!"

"It may be a bit of a two-edged sword, your miracle." Teora turned at the grim tone of the soldier's voice. He was staring up at the results of the landslide. They all followed his gaze.

The side of the narrow pass they had been travelling towards was even steeper now, and dark with newly exposed rock. Where the trail had been rose the slippery, unstable mound of loose shale and larger boulders. Their eyes turned back to each other.

Teora needed more information. "So, are we better off now than before, or not?"

Tourantij and Corquée exchanged a look. Their unwillingness to respond was enough answer.

"It is time for a meeting." Teora swung around again, to see Goianor taking a huge swig from his water bottle, a bottle that hung heavy in his hands. The drink seemed to strengthen him. He strode forward and stood glaring down at the rest of the party. His face was still deeply lined, and his eyes peered out from darkened sockets, but he was holding himself erect. "It is time we stopped this haring around and making decisions on the spur of the moment. We must sit down and make a careful decision what to do. Now that we have water, this should not be hard. Let us all sit and discuss our situation."

"We are sitting, Goianor. Would you care to join us?" The lazy tone did not disguise the tension in Corquée's body. Teora regarded her companions closely. The Priest's bid to regain control was badly timed, but any kind of dissension could still be fatal, and she would have to be ready to swing her weight where it would do the most good.

Fortunately, the others seemed to accept the situation. All sat regarding the Priest, who placed himself on a stone that put him above the rest of them. Two of the Herdsmen who had been leaning on a rock slipped down to sit in its shade.

Goianor looked around a moment, possibly realizing that he was the only one still in the direct sunlight, but not willing to give up his momentum or his superior position. "We must assess our situation and our resources carefully, and make our plans precisely, based on that assessment. Rider, what do you see as our major problems now?"

Corquée gazed at the Priest, seeming at a loss for words. "I...What do you mean?" His hand swept up the trail. "Isn't it obvious?"

"Exactly what I expected. What good is a guide who cannot see beyond what is obvious? I am sure that the lowest of our Herdsmen has that part figured out."

Teora sent a warning glance towards the Herdsmen, one of whom muttered something to the others, who hid their grins.

"Now, Tourantij, do you see any danger of attack of any sort?"

The soldier surveyed the surrounding hills slowly. He was not going to be played with. "I would say that, were we attacked now, we would be hard pressed to defend ourselves. This is a perfect trap. However, I have detected no threat at the moment, and neither has Spar." The dark dog was not present. Tourantij had reacted swiftly and effectively while still doing his share of the work on saving the water.

"I expect no trouble from up the hill for a while. We saw no evidence of anyone following?" His gaze swept the Herdsmen, pausing on each one, waiting for an indication. They all shook their heads. "The trail of the Magali was wiped out by the dust storm, but I have seen no evidence that whoever they fought with came this way. Unless there is some other trail nearby — although I hope there is — we have no fear of armed attack. What about animals, Corquée?"

The Rider, taking his cue, thought this time before answering. "There are always big cats in the mountains, but they are lone hunters and not likely to attack a large party. They might pick off an isolated dog, horse, or even human, but that is not likely. The wolves might be another thing."

"Wolves?"

"Yes, there are always desert wolves. The pack that ranges this area should not be at this altitude at this time of year, as they are usually still down on the plains. Later, they will follow the larger grass eaters when they retreat to the cooler heights. We have seen no sign of them, anyway." He imitated the soldier's visual check of the Herdsmen. "They usually stay away from heavily used areas, though this is not a well-travelled trail. Not that I would like to speak for a wolf pack. They are not known for careful scheduling of their movements." He sat back with a defiant "complain about that if you can" look on his face.

Tourantij regarded the group one more time. Teora lifted a hand and shoulder when his glance included her. She knew of no danger.

"We are relatively safe from attack of any sort, Goianor, and can concern ourselves with survival."

"I was coming to that. How much water do we have?"

"Less than we should have." Teora caught the bitter note in the Rider's voice, and the quick, sharp nudge the soldier gave him.

Tourantij's voice smoothed in. "That we will not know for a while. If the water stops coming now, we are somewhat better off than we were, but might waste an equivalent amount of time, or even more, getting around or over the slide. As long as the water flow continues, our margin of safety grows."

"Then we should camp here, now, though it is not late in the day. We can scout the surrounding area on foot, looking for an alternate route. If there is enough water, we can build our pool bigger. Please set up camp."

The Priest turned and walked back to his horse, taking another drink as he walked. The three that were left considered a moment. Teora raised her eyebrows at Tourantij. He nodded wryly.

"Couldn't have said it better myself. There's a notch with a flat bottom where the Priest's horse is, close enough to keep an eye on the pool. But who has the energy to go scouting?"

The Herdsmen rose to their feet in a group. Obed stepped forward. "With a bellyful of water, it's amazing how much energy I have. We'll check around, be back in about an hour."

"I suggest you wait. Scrambling around up there in the direct sun, you wouldn't keep your energy for long. We will eat an early supper, then you can go. Let's set up the tents now."

The Herdsman smiled down at Tourantij. "Aha! You didn't want us to leave you with the tents to set up. Oh, well, I tried." In mock dejection, he slouched back down the trail, his companions chuckling behind him.

The soldier shook his head. "Where did everyone suddenly get all the energy? I seem to remember a fairly tough day on the trail."

"It will not last. Once they start moving in the heat of the sun the euphoria of the water will wear off. It is best if those of us who know better keep an eye on them."

"Well, you keep an eye on us all, Rider. I, too, have little experience with the techniques of dying of thirst." The older man walked away to oversee the unloading of the horses.

Corquée grinned at Teora. "Was that a joke?"

Teora felt a bit lighthearted herself. Or maybe lightheaded. "Whatever it was, you have been given your task. Perhaps we all need a bit of watching. Especially Goianor. I thought he was on his last legs. Where did he get the energy all of a sudden?"

Corquée's mouth twisted as if he had tasted something foul. "Water."

Teora glanced up at him curiously. "That's really bothering you, isn't it?"

"Where I come from, water is a serious business and water greed is not something to be ignored as a minor personality flaw. In the desert, the man who steals water is executed. No excuses. The man who uses more than his share is turned out of the tribe. No exceptions."

"Even if he is the leader?"

"Especially the leader. Who else gives the model for us all to follow?"

She nodded. "I'll remember to be very fair with the water from now on."

He frowned down at her. "It is not a joking matter."

She stamped her foot. "By the Names of the Deity, Corquée, I wasn't joking! I believe you. I know how close we came today, and that we are not saved yet. I will be careful with the water."

"Oh. I wasn't sure. I'm not used to people who joke as much as you do."

"I see. Well, now you know. Let's build this wall of yours a bit higher, in case the water keeps up. How about some larger stones around the outside?"

10. Water

When the Herdsmen straggled in through the approaching dusk, their report was not good. There was no real trail in the vicinity. It might be possible to mount one of the ridges to the south, travel along its top, then cut back to the trail some distance to the west of the slide. The problem was a very narrow arete with a sheer fall on one side for part of its length.

Obed shook his head. "One misstep and there is no second chance. It is a path that requires the surest of foot, the steadiest of hearts."

Tourantij nodded. "Any trail that Barozon cannot follow is of no use to us."

The Herdsmen glanced at each other, and Mayna, the shorter of the two women, let out a peal of laughter. Tourantij started at her, then at the smiling faces of the other Herdsmen. Seeing his puzzlement, she stopped laughing. "Barozon can make it. We are worried about the horses!"

Another chimed in. "It is scary. V-e-r-y scary. I would not walk it with one of those huge-footed beasts pawing at my back."

Teora turned to Corquée. "It seems that the pride of your favourite animal has been threatened. What do you say?"

Instead of answering, the Rider tossed his head, long hair flying. Then he ran to his mare and, with a flip of his wrist, untied her. With only the halter for control, he sprang aboard her bare back and kicked her to a gallop, straight up the shale side of the canyon. She scrambled valiantly, sometimes sliding back, but always making headway.

"He'll bring it all down on us, the young fool!" Goianor turned and walked down the trail a safe distance.

"I suppose you shouldn't have said that, Teora." Tourantij was watching the ascent with interest.

"By the Consort's horns! I was only joking. What's got into him?"

"Perhaps we should be watching him for water euphoria, as well."

By this time, the two climbers had made it near the top of the ridge. Just as it became obvious that the horse could never make it, the Rider jumped off, clambered as far as the halter rope would reach and gave a mighty pull. The horse surged upward, scrambling to the very top of the ridge with a final heave that threatened to carry her master over the edge and down the other side.

Before she had a chance to settle, he was on her back again, lifting her up on her hind legs to paw at the darkening sky.

"Pretty impressive. Can your bull do that?"

"Are you trying to nudge me into doing something stupid, too?"

The soldier shook his head. "No, I know you wouldn't. But could Barozon climb that slope?"

She stared at the rock in front of her. "We have never done anything like that. I guess we could try."

He was immediately in front of her, one hand firmly on her chest. "Not now!"

She looked into his eyes, then down at his fingers, which were placed perhaps a bit lower than he had intended. Catching her glance, he jerked his hand back as if he had been bitten.

"No, Tourantij. Not now. Only if we have to."

"I'm sorry, madam. I didn't mean..." He turned and strode off.

"Tourantij, don't worry about that. It didn't bother me!" Teora watched him leave, unsure what to do. She was used to being touched. The group Dances involved a lot of lifting and throwing; slips of the hand, sometimes accidental, sometimes not so accidental, were common. She thought of Renelal and grinned to herself. He was too good a Dancer to slip as much as he had.

A harsh voice intruded on her thoughts. "You must watch yourself, my daughter. This is not a time to be working your talents on these men."

"Working my talents? What are you talking about?"

The Priest looked unperturbed. "It is a common thing among those whose lives have just been spared. A loosening of the moral strength. You must not take advantage of this."

"Loosening of the morals! I am not taking advantage of anyone. And what about me? Hasn't my life been spared as well?"

His intense eyes bored into her. "A lone woman on this kind of a journey is bound to be trouble. I told them this at the Haven. They disregarded my advice. Now we are paying for their lack of foresight."

Teora sputtered. What could she say? Probably nothing. Then she had an idea. "A lone woman?" She raised her voice. "Mayna, Sabba, come here a moment, will you?"

The two women arrived more quickly than she expected. They must have sensed her anger, for they ranged up on either side of her in close support. She stood there a moment, her eyes challenging him. He stared pointedly at her companions, snorted derisively and stalked off.

Teora turned and enjoyed a moment of silent communion between the three of them, filled with a rush of gratitude for the unquestioning loyalty of such a pair. She reached out a hand and gave the wiry shoulder of each a quick squeeze. She smiled, and then the three of them burst into laughter. It was loud laughter, not ladylike at all. It was probably also due to the water euphoria, but Teora didn't care. It felt great. After a while, they wound down. Sabba slapped Teora on the shoulder and went back to the harness she had been mending. Mayna wandered over to check on the pool.

Corquée chose that moment to arrive, slipping and sliding, at the bottom of the hill. It had taken him far longer to descend, since he went about it much more carefully, and he seemed a bit miffed that no one was still watching. "So do you still think my horse can't climb?"

"Corquée, no one was belittling Samira. We all know she's fantastic. I'm sure the Herdsmen were much more concerned about the pack animals and the other two riding horses. Will they be able to stay calm, if the going gets really dangerous?"

"Oh." He seemed mollified. "They should be fine. The most important quality of a good trail animal is the ability to keep calm in swamps, rivers, mountains, any type of trouble. We brought only the best." He paused a moment, uncertain, the wildness gone. "I don't want to seem impolite, Teora, but what about Barozon? How will he handle a tight situation? He is the most important one in the expedition, saving only yourself, of course, and I need to know as much as I can."

"Don't worry about him. As I've told you before…"

"Wait. Don't say it. I'm supposed to know this, right? You have told me before that his emotions are tied to yours. As long as you are not afraid, then he will not be. It's you I have to watch, right? Well, that won't be hard."

He was so pleased with himself that Teora had to smile. His grin broadened and he stood taller. At that moment, the priest strode by, his cloak flapping around him. He gave Teora a warning glance.

"We must discuss our situation further. Come."

As they followed, she dug her fingers into Corquée's wrist to stop his mincing imitation of the older man. In retaliation, the Rider swung his hip into her and knocked her off stride. She spun around, her foot

112

whistling past his ear, and he ducked, his eyebrows raised in a mock gesture of awe.

"Next time I won't try to miss!" She strode ahead, hearing his low chuckle carrying out of the dusk behind her.

The Priest seemed to have regained even more of his strength. He stood in front of the group, his jaw thrust forward.

"I have received reports from everyone, and I have made my decision. Our situation depends mostly on the water supply. If there is a great deal of water in our pond in the morning, we will stay here during the day and search further for an easier way through. If there is no water at all, or very little, we will have to risk the ridge route immediately. There is no guarantee of water before the summit, and even with this respite we will still have a difficult time. So, tonight, we will drink all we can and water the animals again. We will also put as much as we can into the water bags. No washing, I am afraid. In the morning, we will make our decision. Are there any comments? Good. In the morning, we must again brave the rigours of the trail. But, for the moment, we rest. Sleep well, my friends." With this grand pronouncement, he paraded off to his tent.

Teora looked to the two other leaders for their reaction. Corquée's was predictable. Tourantij shrugged and spoke in a low voice. "The man seems to be learning. His plan is sound. It all depends on the water."

He got to his feet, and they followed him to the pool, which now lay like a dark void in the dim path. They all knelt and drank, then brought the mounts, one by one, for their share. Then all drank again until their stomachs were uncomfortable. By the time they finished, little water remained, but a slim trickle curved its dark path from under the rubble down the hill to the pool.

In the morning, that meagre lifeline was gone, leaving a damp stain, quickly disappearing in the warming of the day. However, the pool was full again.

They stood in a semicircle, everyone bemused with the thoughts of early morning.

Tourantij broke the silence. "Isn't that always the way. You have things set up for a simple answer, and the Deity doesn't cooperate. What do you suggest now, Goianor?"

The Priest stood there. His face worked once, a sort of grimace, as if he had started to speak, then cut it off in mid-thought. Finally, he shrugged. "A reassessment is in order. What is the condition of our water?"

Corquée gave a careful answer. There was no sense of rivalry now; the right facts were crucial. "We have enough water for two days, if we use all that is here carefully. It would only be one day from here to the top of the pass in normal circumstances. We must still travel that one day. I have not seen the ridge, but the Herdsmen suggest it might take us as long as half a day to traverse it. Taking accidents and delays into account, that takes half a day more, plus some. We are then left with less than half a day to make any decisions, do any more searching."

Tourantij did not wait to be asked. "However, if we use up that half day now, we will be on the worst part of the ridge in the midday heat."

"That's right. If we are taking the ridge, we had best go now."

Goianor stepped forward. "But no decision has been made to take that ridge."

"What is the other option? If we gamble on another route and we don't find it, we will not make it!" Corquée was starting to sound frustrated.

Teora had been watching this exchange. They were now at the point where logic would become lost in a haze of emotion and power struggle. "I have a suggestion."

They all turned towards her.

"This discussion is difficult when neither Corquée nor I have seen this ridge. Why don't we walk up there to see if the animals can do it, then come back and get them? Surely that wouldn't take too long?"

Tourantij was quick to jump in. "About an hour, I would guess. And we could also use that hour to check around a bit more. The light is different in the morning, and a pass that was hidden might be visible."

They both stared at the Priest, inviting him to make the decision. After a moment, he nodded. "We will eat, then those of you who need to shall go and assess the ridge. The rest will scout for other routes. A good decision, I think." He smiled benignly at Teora.

Corquée barely waited until the priest had turned his back. "And who will sit in camp by the water and wait for us all to come back?"

Teora hit him, hard, on the shoulder, turning him to face her. "He could have heard that! What's wrong with you? There is no place for that kind of petty arguing. We could still die here!"

Corquée had the grace to look ashamed. He spoke defensively but kept his voice down. "I still get steamed when I think of him and all that water."

"Nobody says it's fair, my lad. We only have to get through here. After that, it's a whole new game." Tourantij slapped the Rider on the shoulder and strode off to eat. As he passed Teora, he gave her a nod, as if in agreement with her stand. She felt a quick glow of pleasure. It was hard to decide how to treat people in these tight situations. It seemed that she had taken the right approach this time.

11.   Clifftop

Teora panted up the last steep curve of the incline, struggling towards the expanse of blue sky up ahead. Several times she thought that they must be reaching the top, but each time she rose toward the skyline another ridge rose with her, another summit cutting off her view, just a bit higher and further. This ridge, however, was the last. As the slope leveled, she had a feeling of relief and accomplishment, replaced by a sudden thrill of fear when the now-gentle slope broke off rather suddenly in front of her.

"Teora! Get back!"

She had heard that tone before. Resisting the impulse to disobey, she shrugged and stepped back, allowing Tourantij to rush between her and the edge. When he was sure she was a ridiculously safe distance from the drop-off, the soldier walked, with very little caution, she thought, forward, and peered over.

"Not too bad here. The ridge top is wide, and the drop would not be fatal. Not to a human, anyway."

"Good. Then may I come and see it? That's what we came here for, remember?"

She could see the struggle on his face. "All right, then, but stand well behind me."

She stepped forward slowly, more to keep him from alarm than anything else, and stared down. "You're right. This is not dangerous at all if the animals remain calm. Since it's so safe, may we go farther?"

He peered along the ridge in both directions, then back to where Corquée was toiling up the hill. "All right. It's safer with only the two of us."

They walked along the rounded top of the ridge, eyes scanning the mountains nearby for other routes. Building up her courage, Teora finally spoke.

"Tourantij, I have to talk to you. It is a matter that might affect the safety of the group."

He looked down at her. "Certainly. It will be a while before our friend's inexperienced legs carry him this far. Let's move away from the edge and talk."

She placed a restraining hand on his arm and turned until her back was to the cliff. "No, Tourantij. That's what I want to talk about. We are not near the edge. There is no danger here. I am not a porcelain figurine who must be protected at all times. I am not bragging when I say I am surer of foot and balance than you or Corquée, or even most of the Herdsmen. Why do you become fearful when I come near a high place? You are not afraid of heights yourself; I can see that. What is it?"

He regarded her, stony-faced. "You are a very important part of this expedition. The most important part, I begin to suspect. It is my job to see to your security. I must protect you from all danger."

"No. That is not what I am talking about. Protect me, yes. I am very grateful for your expertise. But wipe my nose and brush every stone from my path? I think not."

His expression did not waver, nor did he meet her eye. "It is my duty and my honour to protect you."

"But you are doing that, and very well! It is this situation with heights that I cannot figure out. In other things, you are friendly, pleasant, and very logical and rational. Yet when I come near a cliff, you become very strange – angry even – and act as if I were about to fall off. It is not rational behaviour, Tourantij. If it is rational, can you explain it to me?"

He was silent.

"Is there something in your experience that makes you consider it less safe than I perceive?"

His silence stretched on, and she realized that he was not looking at her, but over her shoulder at the drop-off. As she watched, his jaw muscles clenched, and a fierce anger suffused his face. Tentatively, she touched his arm again. With a start, his eyes focused on her a moment, then stared around wildly. Grabbing her by both arms, he lifted her and spun her away from the top, running several steps before he put her down. Then he stood there, his breast heaving much more than his exertion required.

"Stay away from the edge! That is an order!"

"Teora, are you all right?" Corquée's anxious voice came from behind the soldier's back.

With a visible effort, the man controlled himself. His hands fell, seemingly of their own volition, and he breathed twice, deeply, before turning.

Teora slipped between the two. "Yes, I'm fine, Corquée. Tourantij thought I was a little too close to the edge."

The Rider took in their position in some confusion. "Too near..." He stopped as Teora's hand signaled him emphatically. "Oh. I see."

He waited a moment. When no further information was forthcoming, he shrugged. "So, what does this path look like?"

"Too dangerous."

"Not bad."

The two voices overlapped, and the Rider glanced from one speaker to the other, confused again.

"Tourantij says it's too dangerous, and I think it's fine. Why don't we go on and check the difficult parts? Then we may have something to argue about. Tourantij, would you like to lead?" She did not bother to conceal the touch of sarcasm that forced itself into her voice. The soldier, his face reddening, moved ahead up the ridge. Corquée's eloquent shrug was all he needed as he moved to take up a protective position slightly behind Teora and nearer the edge. Tourantij glanced back, noted the arrangement with a curt nod. They went on up the ridge.

Their path continued broad and easy for some distance, then began to climb steeply. As it rose, the shoulders of the ridge hunched in and the sides fell away until they walked a high, rough backbone of rock, with scree slipping down on either side. As the going became worse, Tourantij turned to check on her more and more often; tension was building in his movements. When they reached a spot where there was room to stand together, she called him back. She sat on an outcropping of the mountain, precisely in the centre of the ridge.

"What do you say, Corquée? Can the horses get over this part?"

He looked back the way they had come. "Not a problem at all, so far. How about farther along, Tourantij?"

"The top gets a bit narrower, but the sides are not as steep. What do you say, Teora? Will Barozon have trouble with this?"

"Barozon won't be the problem."

Corquée turned to frown at her. "I told you. The horses will be fine!"

Teora gazed slowly from one man to the other. "The problem isn't with the animals, is it, Tourantij?"

He stared out over the side of the drop-off to the jagged, dry peaks they must find a way through.

"So, what's the problem?" Frustration was beginning to tinge the Rider's voice. "There is something going on here. What is it?"

"The problem is Tourantij." She regarded the soldier. "Are you going to be able to watch me ride through here on Barozon?"

His head snapped around. "Surely you won't be riding him! What if he panics?"

"You haven't been listening. Or maybe you don't want to hear. Corquée?"

"She has to ride him, Tourantij. He will be calmer that way. Believe me, it is so. Why shouldn't she?"

"Will you be able to watch, Tourantij? Would it be better if you went ahead, and waited until we caught up?"

"No! It is my job to protect you, and I will be here in case something happens."

"It is my worry that you may cause something to happen. Your response is not rational, my friend. When I get near the edge, you cannot keep control. It would be best if you were not present."

"I can keep control. I must be here!"

"Would you like to practise?"

He thought a moment. "Practise?"

"Yes, practise. I will not take my Partner out on this ridge with you anywhere near us if I cannot count on you. How would you like to practise?"

The Rider's patience finally gave out. "What are you two talking about? What is he practising?"

"It is important that you understand. Tourantij has a problem – I don't know, and he can't or won't say why – with me being close to the edge of a cliff. If I get too close, he grabs me and carries me away. He has done it twice. If he were to try something like that while I was in a tight spot, on Barozon, who knows what might happen? If he cannot demonstrate proper control, I will not allow him to be present when I do this task. He refuses to let me do it without him. He must demonstrate control, or we find another path."

The Rider thought this over. "So you go over by the edge, and he sits still. Easy."

"Not easy. Especially for him. And if he rushes me, we could both go over."

"I will not do that. I will sit here and watch you."

"And if I get too close to the edge, what will you do?"

"I will call to you, and then you must stop."

"But then you must tell me to go on. Until I say I would not like to go closer to the edge. Agreed?"

Tourantij licked his lips. "Agreed." He settled himself firmly on a stone, his hands on his knees, for all the world like a man about to have several teeth pulled.

Teora glanced at Corquée. "Watch him closely. If you think he is likely to break, tell me."

The Rider regarded one, then the other. "This is serious, isn't it? You're really worried that he will lose control."

"That's right. I know it is hard to believe that such a strong man might have such a weakness. It comes from something in his past, which he has probably hidden even from himself. My training at the Temple has taught me some of this. Perhaps we can work more on it later, when we have leisure. But at the moment, there is no time. We must cope with the situation as best we can. Will you help by watching him?"

She decided not to mention that most of her training was in getting nervous animals habituated to frightening situations, and she had limited experience with humans.

Corquée regarded Tourantij curiously, as if seeing him in a new light. "Of course. If he appears about to break, I will tell you."

"Right. Are we all ready?" Two grim nods. "Here I go."

Slowly, as well balanced and relaxed as she could be, Teora stepped towards the edge. From what she could see, the drop wasn't too bad here. A lot of loose rock and several ledges that would keep a person from falling too far, too fast. Still, it wouldn't be fun to scrape down over all that.

"Stop!"

She turned back. She had hardly gone two steps and already sweat was standing on the soldier's forehead. *This isn't going to work...it has to work. He has to be able to put up with this. It isn't that hard, after all.* How could a man who had proved his courage in a hundred battles allow a simple thing like this to stymie him? *I have to find a way to encourage him.*

"You can do better, Tourantij. I'll wait here until you get used to it, then you tell me to go on."

He took several deep breaths, smoothing his hands along his pant legs. A slightly vacant look appeared in his eyes; he was performing some private relaxation ritual. Then he focused on her again.

"Go on."

She smiled. "Good. I won't go far, and you can stop me any time." She was falling into the pattern that she used when coaxing Barozon through a new move: talking to him, encouraging him, pouring out a feeling of confidence. "See, I'm watching very carefully where I step. There is no danger here; I'm a long way from the edge, and I don't have to go close at all. I can stop any time."

"Stop."

She paused and turned back to him. He didn't seem as bad this time.

"I didn't really have to stop you that time. I was just testing. Keep talking. It seems to help."

Teora faced outwards again and moved slowly, one step carefully placed and separated from the next, talking softly all the while. After a few steps, she knew that she was making progress. Calmness came over her, and she could feel the tension behind her easing. Her voice dropped down and she murmured, only loud enough that Tourantij could hear her. Slowly, she stepped towards the edge, her concentration moving outward, upward, into the void in front of her.

Still no call from behind her. They were making progress. She stepped a bit faster, still chanting her calming litany, moving towards the edge and the high open space beyond it. The glow of rightness that she now knew was the presence of the Deity filled her, lifting her up.

"See, I am walking carefully. It is very safe. There is no danger. Don't worry. It is very safe..."

"Teora, stop."

The new voice breaking in, softly but urgently, brought her back to herself.

"You've gone far enough, haven't you? Come back now." Corquée's voice held a slight note of urgency. She wondered why.

She looked at her feet. She was right at the edge of the drop-off. Two steps in front of her, a series of ledges dropped away to the bottom of a dry wash. Now that she was this close, it looked much more dangerous. Carefully, she turned around to start back.

Tourantij was half-standing, right arm outstretched towards her. Corquée had a hand on his friend's shoulder, gently restraining him.

As she came away from the edge, they both relaxed. The younger man was smiling, a mixture of triumph and relief.

"That worked well, Teora. He stayed quite calm until I called out. Was I wrong to stop you? You didn't need to go quite that close. I figured if I was worried, then that was enough for Tourantij. You don't mind that I called out, do you?"

"Not at all." She approached the soldier and placed her hand on his other shoulder. "That went well. I didn't think you could let me go that far. Maybe it wasn't as bad as you thought."

He stayed, still staring at the cliff-edge where she had been standing. Then he turned to her. "Yes. Maybe."

"So, let's go get the others. We'll make it."

"I suppose. Corquée, why don't you go back down and tell them to get ready. Have them call in the Herdsmen who are searching for other ways, and if they haven't found anything better, start them heading in this direction. Teora and I have a bit more checking around to do up here."

The Rider grinned. "Sure thing. The sooner I get off my feet and on my horse's back again, the happier I'll be. I don't know how those Herdsmen do it, walking all the time." He went cheerfully off down the mountain, whistling as he walked.

Teora had a thought. "Be careful going down. You can twist an ankle if you go too fast."

He waved his hand above his head but did not turn around. Teora watched him a moment, then returned her attention to Tourantij. He was watching her, a bemused expression flitting across his usually stern features. She did not speak, raising her eyebrows.

"You went too near the edge." It was not an accusation.

"Did I?"

"Yes. Even Corquée was worried. You must not do that to me."

"What did I do to you? I was trying to help. Didn't it work?"

He shook his head. "Oh, yes, it worked. It worked too well. When you talked, all I could hear was your voice. It seemed to be coming from all around me. I could see nothing, smell nothing, feel no rock beneath my feet. There was no more fear. I trusted you; I was not worried for you."

Teora considered this. "You were hypnotized."

"Probably. I hope so. But whatever you did, you must not do that again!"

"But it worked! You said you were not afraid anymore."

"True. But I should have been. You went too close to the edge, didn't you?"

Inwardly, Teora cursed her inadequate training. How could they have sent her out on this task with only her meager Temple lessons in all these matters? *What could I say to him? Would he catch a lie? Would it destroy the trust I have built up? Would the truth make him worse? How am I to know?* It was too late.

"Your hesitation has spoken for you. You did go too far. Answer this instead. It is much more important. Why did you do it?"

So, it would have to be the truth. The moment she decided, the relief assured her that it was the right choice. "I don't know."

"You don't know? You almost walk off a cliff and you can't tell me why?" The soldier's voice rose. "And this was supposed to reassure me that it was safe?"

Teora shrugged miserably. "I know. It sounds terrible." She swung towards him, looking earnestly up into his eyes. "I have little experience in this." She could hear her voice rising as well and fought to control it. "I have never done that sort of thing before. Something happened, something inside me, and I started to believe what I was saying. I mean, really believe it! That it was not dangerous. The thought brushed past my mind that I could walk off that edge and keep right on going, out on the air! How could I do that, Tourantij? Am I going mad? I am not a Priestess. I do not do miracles. What is wrong with me?"

Her voice rang among the rocks, fading away to a moment of silence. Then he reached out and put an arm across her shoulders and started her walking down the ridge. She glanced up, saw him looking down on her, his face softer. A grin tugged at the corner of his mouth.

"And a while ago, you were going to cure me."

She shook her head ruefully. "I guess I'd better stick to what I know. Whatever that is. Let me know if one of the animals gets a sore foot. I can handle that."

"No, no. Don't give up. You must learn to use the powers you have in you. You cannot ignore them."

"Powers? What do you mean, 'powers?' I have no magic!"

He removed his hand from her shoulder and scratched his head thoughtfully. "Well, I don't know about that. Let's look at it this way. There are several possible reasons for your strange feeling. First, you might be crazy, and you would have walked off the cliff and killed yourself." He glanced down. "That's what you are thinking, isn't it?"

"I suppose."

"Ah. The second choice is that you were trying to persuade me and got a bit carried away with your success. You still had two more steps to go. Maybe you would have stopped on your own."

"I hope that was it."

"Third possibility. That you were right."

The ridge had narrowed, and she was walking in front of him. She stopped and turned back. "Right about what?"

"Right in your feeling. Maybe you could have walked on the air."

"This isn't something to joke about!"

"Teora, I am not joking. I have seen too many things in my life to disregard any possibility. Remember, you have been Chosen to represent the Deity. How much of Her power is in you?"

"Well...I...I really don't think..."

"Then do think." He pushed her arm, steering her down the trail. "Have you felt that way before?"

She thought back, to Linea's eyes locked on hers, the bright shafts of sunlight streaming through the dimness of the inner room of the Temple.

"I gather the silence again means, yes?"

"You're right. I have felt it before. But never so strong! And that doesn't prove anything. Maybe I was crazy then, too."

"Oh, I have more faith in the Deity than that."

She stopped again, turned to him. "I didn't know that you believed."

"If you keep stopping for philosophical debate, we're going to be awfully thirsty before we hit the top of the pass."

With a sudden blast, all the weight of the journey hit Teora again. Her shoulders slumped as her stride, loose kneed, took her down over a series of rough boulders. The heat, the dust, the thirst.

"Take your own advice, girl."

"What advice?"

"Take it slowly. Get used to it. Then, when the time of trial comes, you will be prepared."

She nodded. "And will you be prepared? Now, today, when I have to ride Barozon up this ridge?"

It was his turn to shake his head ruefully. "When the time comes, I will walk close to you. You will talk to Barozon as you always do, and I will listen. You will coax us through this together, the two of us, under your spell. I will lose my fear and my self-will at the same time. It will not be an experience I will enjoy, but if it gets us through here safely, I will endure it."

Teora stopped, overcome by what he was going through. "Oh, Tourantij, I understand how hard this is for you. Please believe that I would do anything to help you. Anything!"

He stood there, so confused and vulnerable that she had to fling her arms around his neck and squeeze him tightly. For one instant, his bristly cheek against hers and the hard bulk of his chest reminded her of the times she had hugged her father in the same way. She felt instantly embarrassed, yet at the same time comforted. She released him and stepped back down the hill. He had not moved, but his expression was even more disturbed.

She laughed up at him. "Come on. We have work to do. Don't stand there like a silly boy who just had a girl kiss him for the first time." She waited until his senses seemed to be returning, then skipped down over the rocks, a sense of lightness giving her wings.

"Teora."

She paused.

"Take your own advice."

"I know. Careful on the downhills. Whatever you say, Mister General!" She saluted gravely, then stepped with exaggerated care over to the next boulder. Then, laughing, she jumped down and continued the descent. She could tell by the rattle of his gear and his muttered curses that he was following at his best speed.

12.   On and Up

They hurried down to the camp, where the rest of the party was waiting, ready to ride. Teora glanced over to the pool, but all that was left was a muddy stain on the rocks. She slapped the canvas water bag slung across Barozon's harness. Corquée must be confident of their route if he would waste precious water evaporating from the outside of the cloth to keep the inside cool. Barozon twisted his head around but couldn't quite reach the bag. Mounting, she pushed his nose away with her foot.

"You couldn't possibly be thirsty!"

"I just watered him, Teora." Ledgard's voice was concerned.

She grinned at him. "Don't worry. He's a spoiled brat. Let's get him up on that ridge and make him work for his next drink."

Corquée and Tourantij took a last check around and mounted, and the party started back down the trail to a spot where they could approach the ridge safely. Then the work began. The steel-shod hooves slipped often, and the humans gave what strength they could. Even with two of them helping each animal, soon everyone was bathed in sweat from the midmorning heat. Teora was doubly glad that Barozon was iron shod like the horses, as her own feet became bruised from contact with the jagged rocks. They paused frequently to rest whenever they found refuge in a shortening shadow, but still they all felt the urgency.

"Don't push it too hard." Corquée was standing beside his mare, allowing everyone to pass under his scrutiny. "This is only a climb. We will need all our energy when it gets dangerous on the open ridge."

"Only a climb!" Teora met the eyes of Daegal, who had been walking on the other side of Barozon's head, helping when necessary. "I hope it doesn't get difficult or anything."

They chuckled briefly, breaking off when the bull heaved himself to the edge of a particularly large boulder and poised, unsure of whether he had the balance to finish the move. They each grabbed a horn and heaved mightily, and he lunged on.

"He may be heavy, but at least he has handles attached!"

Teora had no breath to laugh again but she grinned, once more thankful for the cheerful enthusiasm of her people.

When they reached the top of the ridge, they reorganized. Upon Tourantij's insistence, Teora went first. As expected, the priest had retreated from his leadership role the moment the climb got rough. He had complied with bad grace to the suggestion that they all must dismount and walk and was still puffing up the incline when Teora set out along the ridge.

She watched Tourantij closely as they climbed, chatting to him, careful not to let her voice fall into the murmur she used on her Partner. There seemed to be no problem at first. Barozon, as she had suspected, took the ascent in his stride, staring neither to left nor right, but concentrating on the path in front as she directed him. They reached and passed the point of the earlier incident, and soon the ridge leveled off. She began to relax.

"Well, that wasn't so bad, was it?"

The soldier looked up at her. "That was the part I thought Barozon couldn't make. Now comes the bit where you have to worry about me."

She gazed ahead. The ridge remained level, but its sides narrowed even more until it seemed to be a bridge, floating above a deep chasm. One side was only a steep slope, but the other was a sheer drop with the bottom hidden behind a swelling of rock.

"Why didn't you tell me about this before?"

He, too, was staring at the fall ahead of them. "Because this is not a problem for you. Your Partner can traverse that edge easily because it is wide. It is almost level, and the rock is good here: solid, not too smooth, very little breaking away. It is what the mountain men of my country would call 'pavement'. You will have no problem as long as you remain calm. If the horses have made it this far, they should be able to make it, as well. If they are frightened, we will cover their eyes and lead them across. If we lose a horse, it is not pleasant, but not serious."

"So shall we blindfold you, and lead you across?" She spoke lightly, but could not keep her concern from showing.

He stared ahead. "That will not be necessary. I will go with you. I will lead, and you will follow closely. Will you be riding?"

"You know it is best. Do you wish me to talk us through?"

He considered this. "Perhaps you should. But you must be on your guard. If you lose yourself in your own power..." He regarded her. "I may believe in your power, but I doubt that it extends to making Barozon and me walk on the air." His attempt at a smile failed.

"Tourantij, look at me."

His eyes were wary.

"I don't have to talk you through this. You can do it yourself. It requires strength and faith. Faith in yourself, faith in me, and faith in the Deity, who will not allow us to fail." As she spoke, a belief that she had never consciously formulated built surely in her.

"I will not fail at this task. It is too important to the Deity to bring belief back to the Aerans. I begin to understand why the Choosing happened. It wasn't because of me. There are others who could have been Chosen, others with other talents, as strong as mine in their own way but, like me, not special. But since I was Chosen, I am now special. I have powers I did not have before, and my faith is stronger. I will not fail. Believe in that as you believe in Her."

The soldier mulled this over. Then he met her eyes again. "I believe in your belief. I can feel the strength of it. While I can never have that confidence, I can know it when I see it. You are right; you will not fail. I will keep that thought before me as we cross the high spot. You will not fail."

He turned and, one hand on Barozon's right horn, he led the way along the ridge.

It was an anticlimax for Teora. Barozon navigated the ridge easily, his hooves ringing out on the solid rock. Tourantij maintained a steady pace, once in a while glancing over his shoulder, but mainly scanning the route ahead and to the sides as he usually did. When they reached the broader back of the ridge that slanted down to the west, he stopped and allowed Barozon to pass him. Then Teora saw the sweat on his pale cheek, heard his shallow breathing. But he said nothing, merely walked back to bring his horse across. The rest followed without incident, Goianor being the only one to show any real fear. Still, even the priest crossed safely, and a short scramble brought them down to a faint trail, barely discernible on the rock.

"This is not the same path we were on."

Corquée glanced at Tourantij. "No, it isn't. But it is a trail, and it leads somewhere."

"Somewhere. That doesn't sound very useful, Rider." The Priest's voice sounded hoarse, and his face was grey.

Corquée shuffled his feet, his head down. "It isn't that bad. There are few ways through these mountains. There is an old storysong of my people about a higher path, which meets the main trail near the summit..."

"So, we are to trust our lives to some old men's dreams?" The Priest flapped a disgusted hand up the trail. "Lead on, Rider. If the Deity wishes us to succeed, we will. If not..."

"When will we reach the top, then?" Teora tried to change the subject, but it didn't help.

"I can't be certain. We might make the top by nightfall. Other than that, we have plenty of water for a dry camp and we hit fresh water some time in the morning, I think."

"You don't think much at all, do you?" Goianor stared belligerently at the boy, who stood uncertainly, his face flushing. Then the priest strode to his horse and swung awkwardly up into the saddle.

Teora took Corquée's arm and shook it. "It's a trail, Rider. That's what you were hired to find. I couldn't even tell if it was a trail. It's not as if the slide was your fault."

He gave her a grateful smile, but his shoulders slumped as he walked to his horse, and he did not mount with his usual flair.

Cursing the priest again, she climbed up on Barozon. "Consider what we've been through, Corquée. We're moving again!" The bull's feet clattered on the rock.

The satisfaction of moving again gave Teora a lift. She could almost forget how stiff her clothes felt, how her hair hung in greasy tatters around her face. She patted the water bag again, feeling its reassuring fullness. "Then let's get going."

A quick check to see that the rest of the party was in line, and Corquée headed out, his mare settling down to the stroll that matched Barozon's plod.

As the day progressed, they wound higher into the mountains. Sometimes they would come to a turn and the world below would open up, giving a glimpse of the barren desert to the north or south, but ahead was always upward, always more rock. They plodded on.

13. Snow

Late into the afternoon, they forced their way higher into the mountains. Teora huddled into herself, trying to ignore the heat of the sun in her face, longing for nightfall, longing for water.

For a while, it seemed to work. The sun no longer burned as hard, and she almost thought that a stirring of wind fanned her face. Then she was in shade. She opened her eyes to see, high in front of her, a hazy line of light cloud covering the face of the sun. She watched the clouds form, darkening as time passed. She called ahead to Corquée.

"Are those rain clouds?"

He grinned back. "Could be. Can you feel the air?"

Sure enough, the air had a damp feel. Her pores seemed to open, sucking in moisture.

"Listen!"

A dull rumbling sound grew from the rocks around them. As they progressed, it got louder.

Corquée grinned back, allowed Samira's step to lengthen. "Know what that is?"

"A stream?"

"No question."

Barozon's step quickened. The Rider glanced over in concern. "Don't let him stampede. He could hurt himself."

She grinned and controlled her Partner. "Don't worry, big fellow. There's plenty of water, and you'll get there soon enough."

Then they rounded a corner, and there it was. Up to their left, the water boiled down a short canyon. Far up the valley, she could see a patch of white gleaming in the shade of a mountain peak. The glacier.

Right in front of them the trail dipped into a shallow bowl, to ford the stream where the water spread out into a wider, slower flow. Barozon dropped his head to drink and Teora, on a sudden impulse, allowed herself to slide down his neck, to land flat out in the water.

Corquée was right beside her, entering the water with a huge crash. She shouted and splashed water at him. Barozon and Samira ignored this foolishness, drinking happily.

The Rider rose to his feet and splashed her back, swooshing a huge wave of water over her. Unable to respond, she tackled him, and he fell on his back, the water deep enough to close over his head momentarily. She allowed him up and they sat, laughing at each other.

"I might have expected this childish behaviour from a Rider, but I am deeply disappointed in you, Teora."

They both turned. The Priest sat his horse, leaning backward to maintain his balance as the animal drank. The other animals were filing off the trail behind him, moving quickly to their own places at the pool. Tourantij had already dismounted and was trying to hide a grin.

Corquée smiled up at the Priest. "Come on in, Goianor. The water's great. It would do you good to loosen up a bit."

The Priest's face reddened. "You forget your place, young man. Now get out of that water and see to setting up camp."

The Rider shook his head. "It's water, Goianor, water! All we need, clean and cold."

Goianor leaned forward. "I know it's water, and it's no thanks to your incompetence that we have found it. Are you refusing a direct order to do your assigned duties?"

"Ah, come on, Priest. Have some fun for once. It's water!" Corquée stood and, as he rose, he splashed two huge handfuls of water in the priest's direction.

Unfortunately, the water caught his horse full in the face, and she swung her head up sharply, catching Goianor in the nose with an audible crack. The Priest teetered in the saddle, his hands over his face. Two Herdsmen rushed to control the horse and help the injured man dismount.

Teora and Corquée made their embarrassed way out of the pool, to be met on the bank by an irate Priest. He threw off the restraining hands of the Herdsmen and strode to the Rider, as if he intended to attack him. As he approached, the Rider loomed over him and he stopped, breathing heavily, a trickle of blood seeping from his left nostril.

"You have gone too far this time, Rider. You will pay for your insolence. Tourantij!"

The soldier stepped forward.

"I want him whipped."

Tourantij, for once at a complete loss, stared at the man. "What?"

"You saw him attack me. He must be punished. Whipped."

The soldier stared at the Priest, then shook his head. "This isn't a ship at sea. I have no such authority. Besides, it was an accident. He splashed water at you."

"He has assaulted a Priest of the Deity. He must be punished!"

Teora stepped forward. "Goianor, I'm sure Corquée didn't mean to hurt you. He was just having fun."

The Rider stepped forward beside her. "That's right. I never meant to hurt you. We were splashing each other, and I only splashed your horse...."

"And with your supposedly infallible knowledge of horses, I'm sure you knew exactly what the beast would do."

"Are you saying I did it on purpose?"

Teora stepped between the two men, motioning to Daegal. Three Herdsmen quietly edged Corquée away. "He didn't do it on purpose, Goianor. We were being silly, and we both apologize. Is your nose all right?"

"Don't worry about my nose. Is anyone going to punish this villain?" The Priest regarded the half-circle of faces. The whole group stared back, astounded.

"You may all be against me, but wait till we get to the Temple at Coalantha. I will have the proper authority there!"

Corquée twisted away from Daegal's hold to turn and face the Priest. "So, when we get to the Temple, you're going to get your big, bad friends to gang up on me, are you? Well, that certainly has me shaking in my saddle!" He turned scornfully and walked to his horse to unpack his gear. After a moment, the priest turned away as well, and the Herdsmen began to set up camp.

Teora and Tourantij were left staring at each other in disbelief. The soldier shook his head. "We didn't handle that too well."

"I didn't handle that too well, you mean."

Tourantij shook his head. "No, I mean all of us."

"I never should have jumped in the water. That was irresponsible. How can I expect people to follow me, when I act like a child?"

Tourantij reached out and took her by the shoulders and shook her, ever so gently. "Teora, you're eighteen years old. You were splashing water at a friend. You did nothing wrong."

Seeing that she was unconvinced, he went on. "This problem has been brewing ever since the journey started a month and a half ago.

132

Sooner or later, those two were going to clash. Nothing you could do would stop it. I'm pleased, actually."

Her head came up. "Pleased?"

"Of course. No danger, no outsiders present and nobody got hurt...much. Couldn't have done better if I'd planned it."

"But what will happen at Coalantha?"

The soldier shrugged. "Depends on how much clout Goianor has there. It's a pretty shaky charge, and they could ignore him completely. They won't, though. They'll impose some penalty to make the point of supporting their own, no matter how stupid he acts."

"But what if he has friends there? What could they do?"

Tourantij grinned. "Don't worry, they can't whip him. They don't have any authority over him at all. Worst they can do is relieve him of his duties. They'd pay him out, and he'd have to find his own way home. But they won't do that."

"Why not?"

"Relationship between the Aerans and the Curicuiriari is too important. They won't cause a major incident over a bruised nose, no matter what Goianor says."

He turned to Teora. "Don't worry. We have water. It's all downhill from here to the coast. And don't blame yourself. You hear me?"

Forced to look up at him, she nodded. "I guess you're right."

"I'm right."

"You're always right, it seems. Don't you ever make mistakes?"

Instead of the smile she had hoped for, his face turned grim. "I'd better not."

As she turned to unfasten her gear from Barozon's harness, it occurred to Teora that the soldier was more concerned about the incident than he was letting on. He was right about one thing, though; it would be ridiculous to blame herself for the problem. But that wouldn't stop her from keeping a close watch to make sure it didn't get worse.

Supper was a silent but uneventful meal. Goianor took his plate back to his tent and did not appear for the rest of the evening. She could imagine him in there alone, reliving the incident over and over, planning his revenge. *What a horrible way to live.*

Soon, the clouds thickened, and a gentle rain began, cooling the air but making it difficult to dry the clothing they had all washed.

Teora went to bed and listened to the rain hitting the canvas over her head. It was a restful sound, and her bed warmed up until she felt comfortable. As she drowsed, the sound changed to a hissing. She vaguely wondered what that meant but was too tired to think. Later on, she roused enough to hear that the strange sound had stopped. Good.

Some time in the night, Teora woke, or half-woke from a dream that she was being smothered. A cold, damp weight was pressing against her, pushing her off her mattress. She rolled over and her face came into contact with something wet and solid. Fully awake now, she brought her hand out of her blankets and felt the object. It was the wall of the tent, but the wet canvas was stretched in a taut curve. She pushed, felt something give: harder, and there was a rushing sound and the tent was loose again. Feeling around, she discovered that the other wall had the same problem, so she repeated the routine. Intrigued, she crawled part way out of bed, fumbled open the ties at the front of the tent, and stuck her head out.

It was still dark night, but everything was lit by a strange glow. The whole camp was smothered in white. Huge downy flakes drifted everywhere in complete silence: all sound muffled. She stared around, but the air was cold, and it was too dark to see much, so she retreated to her bedroll. The hissing sound had returned as the flakes hit the bare canvas again. She lay there for a while, then fell asleep wondering what effect this was going to have on their travelling.

Twice more during the night she had to knock the accumulated snow off her tent. The third time, it only slid about halfway down. A pile was developing. If it kept snowing, she was going to have to get out and shovel the snow away. With her hands. Listening to the sound of the snow hitting the canvas, hoping it would stop, she finally fell asleep again.

When she woke, it was daylight. The canvas above her head was only bowed slightly; the snow must have stopped. She lay there, enjoying the warmth of her blankets, knowing from the nip on her cheeks that it was going to be chilly when she got up. She could hear muffled sounds of movement outside: the crack of firewood being broken, the stamping of the horses and the jingle of harness. That probably meant they would be travelling despite the snow. *That might prove interesting. I wonder what Barozon thinks about the snow. Best if I check on him.* With one regretful thought for her warm cocoon, she got up, dressed in her warmest clothes and went outside.

She stood, surveying the camp. Everything was covered in white. The larger tents showed evidence that others, too, had been roused in the night to knock the snow off. She noted with satisfaction that Goianor's huge tent had completely collapsed at one end. Served him right. She hoped it wouldn't make him too grouchy today. *If I could make a guess, travelling and camping in the snow won't be a whole lot of fun.*

Well, it was at least a change from the drought.

She pulled on her riding boots and went down to the stream to wash. When she got there, she stopped for a moment to enjoy the image.

The banks of the creek were covered in snow, puffing out over the black water. Each small rock sticking up in the stream had its mushroom cap of snow, contrasting to the dark stone underneath. Frail willow bushes stooped low over the water, each branch a stark black curve under a fuzzy white load. Wisps of steam rose from the larger open stretches. The whole scene was a study in black and white. She longed for paper and charcoal.

"You won't find it so beautiful after a few hours." Corquée crunched by her, stooped and tossed water towards his face.

Teora looked ruefully at her hands, already beginning to redden in the chill. "You won't either, if you drown yourself before breakfast."

He swiped water off his face. "This doesn't bother me much. I'd go for a swim if it was deep enough. Don't often get that much water, all in one place."

"This doesn't really worry you, then?"

"Not really. Oh, it'll be slippery on the trail this morning, but it's not that cold. I imagine it will be melted away before tomorrow. Of course, if it were to start freezing or snowing some more, then I'd be worried." He gave his usual shrug. "But we're at the top of the pass and it's midsummer. It should get better as we go lower.

"Besides, what if it doesn't? We're as prepared as we can be. Worrying at this point isn't going to help much, is it?"

She returned her version of the shrug. "Can't argue with that. What's for breakfast?" They shared a companionable chuckle at that, because breakfast hadn't changed since the trip started. The Herdsmen provided something Teora privately thought would do very well for weaning calves – a porridge made of a variety of grains, boiled up together until they were soft, then served with honey and butter. It was quite tasty and very filling, but they could have used some variety.

At least the Rider did not seem too upset by yesterday's problems. She wished she could rebound that quickly.

14.   Wolves

The snow made the footing slippery and the trail difficult to see, but with their recent memories of thirst, no one complained. A Herdsman reached down to scoop up a mouthful of cold confection, then smiled. The dogs ducked their heads frequently, tossing up bursts of snow with their noses. Going was not quick, but it was downhill, which made a great deal of difference.

They had been travelling a while when Corquée stopped. Teora, catching up with him, peered past his horse's shoulder, and shuddered. A slide had broken away part of the trail, leaving a very narrow ledge, which wound out of sight around a corner.

"It's narrow. Barozon is the widest. Can he make it?"

"Do you want me to try?"

"Not yet. Tourantij?"

The soldier slid off his horse, tested the ledge with his foot, then walked across, stamping in a few places. "Seems solid. I'll try my horse first, then Teora."

His horse had no problems, and neither did Barozon. Teora kept an eye on the soldier as she navigated the dangerous spot. He sat his horse stiffly, twisted back to watch her intently, but that was all. It was Goianor's horse, lacking an experienced hand on the reins, that put a forefoot too far to the side. The horse scrambled backwards for a tense moment, gravel flying and bounding down the rocks below the trail, the priest's hands grasping the saddle, his face a mask of terror. Finally, they made it back to solid ground. The horse stood, its sides heaving, while the rider peeled his hands from the saddle and slid shakily to the ground.

Tourantij craned his neck to see back past Barozon's bulk. "How does it feel?"

"Not good." Corquée stood surveying the trail, the Herdsmen in a semicircle behind him. "Now there's a good hunk of the trail gone."

Daegal leaned forward, then jumped down into the gap. He kicked around a bit, and chunks of rock again flew into the void. "It's solid underneath. If we had enough rocks, we could build it up better than before."

Corquée looked doubtful, but Radman nodded. "We can fix it like a rock wall. Don't worry, Rider. We do this all the time at home."

Without further comment, the Herdsmen swung into action, scouting around to find the flattest rocks, handing them down to Daegal, who placed them with expert care.

When it became obvious that they were making good progress, Tourantij nodded. "Corquée, this is an uncomfortable place to wait. Teora and I will go ahead until we find a wide spot."

"Do you want an escort?"

"No, we're better off with the Herdsmen right where they are."

"Good enough."

Tourantij turned his face to the trail, and they continued. It was not especially dangerous, but too narrow for an animal to turn around. Teora was relieved when they reached a wider spot with no further difficulties. The snow was melting now, and footing was improving. She was beginning to relax when the soldier muttered an uncharacteristic curse.

"What's wrong?"

"It's hard to tell, but those could be wolf tracks."

Peering down, she could make out clusters of round black spots melted through the snow. If they were wolf tracks, a large number of the animals had been milling around this area since last night. Instantly, her eyes scanned the nearby rocks, but nothing moved.

"This is not a good place to be if they attack. We must move on down the trail."

"What about the others?"

"If we go back, we could be caught out on that ledge, unable to turn around. We should move on. There might be no danger. Those tracks have been melting for several hours." As he started his horse forward, he murmured something about the wind. The breeze was blowing at their backs, announcing their presence down the trail ahead of them.

They wound along among the rocks, and Teora's heightened awareness showed her many places where they could be attacked: rocks a wolf could jump from, crevices where they could hide, curved stones and shadows that seemed to move.

"There."

She started, but Tourantij was only pointing to a crack in the wall of the canyon. "The animals can go in there. We can stand on the rock. Our backs will be protected, and I doubt the wolves will try a frontal assault. If they do, there's an open space in front where I can shoot them."

"One problem."

"The horns?"

"I doubt if he can fit. The horse will be fine."

"Can you back him in?"

"Probably."

The soldier pointed. "Then we'd better get to it. That was a wolf ducked behind that boulder."

Her eyes scanned the area around them, and then, as if her eyes were coming into focus, a dozen rock-grey wolves stood staring at her. Several paced forward, their heads low, testing the smell of this new prey. Barozon responded with a snort, his head low as well, stepping ahead with menace.

Tourantij hurried his horse into the shelter of the crack, and Teora exerted all her will to force her Partner backwards. It went against his very nature to retreat, and he begrudged every step. When only his hind legs were protected, the wolves closed in, and he refused to retreat farther.

"It's safer up here, Teora, and you'll be in his way down there."

She hesitated, then, accepting the logic of his words, she stood on Barozon's hump and took the soldier's offered hand. They stood, side by side, looking out at the pack that confronted them.

There were now well over a dozen animals, from white-muzzled oldsters to half-grown pups. They seemed in no hurry, pacing in plain view, some tossing the snow with their noses like the dogs did.

"What do we do? Are you going to shoot them?"

"Not yet. If they don't attack, the rest of our party will come along and they'll fade. They may trail us for a while, and we'll have to watch our dogs don't get enticed away, but that will be all.

"If they attack, it's another matter. I only have six shots, then I'll have to reload. They move very quickly, and once they get too close to Barozon, I won't be able to shoot them."

"What about your rifle?"

"Can you shoot it?"

"I never have."

"Then you hold it, hand it to me when my revolver runs out. Can you reload?"

"I don't think so."

He grinned sourly. "Then I suppose you'd better do a bit of praying. That's something you're trained for."

Feeling inadequate, she stood, holding the unfamiliar rifle, feeling its heavy menace, her own helplessness.

The wolves attacked with a rush. Five of them surged towards Barozon. The soldier's pistol roared and one wolf stumbled; another spun sideways, yelping in pain. As he was about to fire, a movement caught the corner of his eye, and he turned to confront a wolf scrambling up the rock towards him. He killed that animal, but the other attackers closed with the bull.

It was a quick and decisive battle. The speed of the bull's forward charge caught the wolves off guard, his horn sweeping the lead animal away, one steel-shod hoof crushing another's skull. The remaining wolves slipped off into the rocks, ducking Tourantij's parting shot. Then the creatures were gone, fading into the mountain as if they were never there.

His eyes scanning the battleground, the soldier shoved a new load of shells into his pistol, while Teora forced Barozon back into the protection of the rocks.

Silence, broken only by the whimpers of a wounded wolf as it dragged itself away.

"What now?"

The soldier shrugged. "At least now our friends know we're in trouble. They'll come as soon as they can. If they don't attack soon..."

His words were broken by the second rush. This time, the wolves came from more directions, with a larger group distracting Tourantij first by scrambling up the rock to attack the humans. With his attention divided, he was not able to keep the pack from closing on the bull. This time, they did not come as close. Those in front were retreating, enticing Barozon farther and farther from his niche. The soldier's pistol was empty, and he held it out to Teora, reaching for the rifle. Her cry of alarm brought him spinning around as a huge, dark wolf sprang for the bull's hind legs. With no time for the rifle, he dropped from the rock, his heavy boots catching the wolf in the lower spine with a crunching sound. His sword was out as he landed, and a mighty slash dispatched the animal.

He had not counted on the bull's battle rage. As he dropped, Teora moved as well, her body interceding between his back and the slashing horn, her hand guiding the razor tip upward. Realizing his peril, the soldier ducked, and the horn slid over them. Teora immediately pushed Barozon's head back to focus him on the remaining wolves, which closed in from all directions.

The solder leaped back to the rock, then realized that his rifle lay where Teora had dropped it, beneath the bull's feet.

"Teora! Back up here, quick!" She glanced up, saw him torn between loading his gun and holding a hand out to her. She grasped Barozon's horn, swung up on his back, then paused there.

A great rage swept through her as she stood on her Partner's back gazing down at the wolves so far below her. *They must NOT!* Ignoring the soldier's outstretched hand, she focused on the wolves, Barozon's strength flowing into her, wiping out her fear. It all became clear. The fear was gone, the anger faded, and a supreme confidence suffused her. *We are on a mission for the Deity. Nothing will stop us.*

Barozon paced regally forward and the wolves, instead of attacking, slunk back a step, then another. She gazed down at them, willing them to fear, and they cowered in the snow, ears down, tails curved under. She reached her power towards the lead wolf. The big, light-coloured female whined and rolled on her side, exposing her throat placatingly. Teora held the pack there, impressing her power on their minds.

Then claws scrabbled on the rock and a dark fury burst among the wolves. Spar rushed through the stunned pack, his teeth ripping left and right. His momentum took him straight to Barozon's feet, and he spun and fell to his protective crouch under the bull's nose, ready to attack at any moment. Not far behind came the Herdsmen, a spear-point of flashing staves, the dogs snapping and slashing under their protection. Faced with this new attack, the wolf pack broke from their trance and fled, scrambling up impossible rock walls, breaking in all directions.

Belatedly, Tourantij brought his pistol into play, and Corquée appeared in time for one shot with his rifle before the targets disappeared.

Silence descended, broken only by the heavy breathing of the dogs and the disdainful snort of Barozon. Spar broke his watchful pose, touched noses with the bull, then went to investigate the downed wolves.

Teora looked around, the golden feeling of power fading, leaving her with a sense of comfortable triumph.

"Teora, what was that?"

She glanced up at Tourantij, who was staring at her and shaking his head as he reloaded his pistol.

"What was what?"

"That. You know. I thought they were going to overrun you for sure, and suddenly they stopped and rolled over in the snow."

"I told them to."

"That was the impression I got."

"I got this feeling, Tourantij, that they had no right to distract me from my mission, that they must see that I could not be bothered. I showed them that they had to go away and leave us alone. They were about to, when the others got here and hurried them along."

Tourantij jumped down and patted Spar's head. "They did. This fellow was certainly useful."

She, too, slid down, leaving her hand resting on her Partner's neck. She chuckled. "Those poor wolves didn't know what hit them. If there's an equivalent to the Deity in the wolven religion, I imagine they thought Spar was Her Consort and that she was very angry at them!"

The soldier shrugged. "Oh, your whole group was very impressive, but it didn't seem to me like they were needed much."

She smiled up at him. "Don't tell them that."

"They already know."

The Herdsmen were chatting with each other as they checked their dogs for injuries, nodding and glancing in Teora's direction. Then they gathered and approached her, their faces beaming.

"You have walked with the Deity, Teora." A pause, while Sabba waited for her response. "We saw it."

"You did?"

Daegal smiled. "Of course. We could feel it, as well. Look at the dogs."

She turned. The animals had approached, but were exhibiting the same sort of behaviour the wolves had.

"Well, I'm glad somebody finally treats me with the respect I'm due!"

They all laughed, but Sabba remained serious. "It was more than that, Lady Teora. We all could feel Her presence."

"I know. I needed Her, and She came with her power to save us."

They all nodded. "We are sorry we were not here."

She shook Obed's shoulder. "Don't worry. You were contributing elsewhere. We had everything under control here, didn't we, Tourantij?"

The soldier smiled wryly. "Somebody had everything under control. I'm glad I got to shoot a few of them at the beginning. At least I did something!"

"Tourantij! Dropping down into that pack with nothing but your sword was the bravest thing I have ever seen."

"If I'd have known I was going to get spitted by your friend, there, I might not have jumped."

"He didn't have time to check who it was behind him. There was too much going on. I'm sure he's really grateful, now."

"As grateful as he'd have been if I was dead. You saved my life, Teora."

She grinned. "Well, it was worth it. We'd have been very embarrassed, trying to explain why Barozon skewered you."

Their laughter was cut short by scrabbling on the trail behind them.

"The Priest! We left him behind!"

Hiding their smiles, the Herdsmen turned to escort a fuming Goianor in from the trail. The Priest surveyed the scene, the red draining from his face as he took in the bodies of the wolves scattered around. His jaw worked, then finally the words came.

"Just what has been going on here?"

15.   Healing

"And I must know exactly what happened. How you felt, how the animals reacted, everything."

She threw up her hands in exasperation. "Goianor, why do we have to go through this, over and over? I told you everything." Her finger tapped out each syllable for emphasis. "Ab-so-lute-ly everything."

He sniffed, disdainfully. "My dear, you don't understand. If I am to make the report of the Presence of the Deity, I must have all the facts. You don't just make these claims wildly, you know." He shook his head, smiled patronizingly. "Oh no, it must be done properly. Go through the proper channels."

"Goianor, I am not making any claims."

The smile lost some of its animation. "But you already have. You said the power of the Deity was in you, and you sent the wolf pack away. At least you were going to, when help arrived and drove them off."

She stiffened. "Yes, I was going to send them away. And they would have gone, too. Ask Tourantij. But I'm not making some kind of claim to sainthood. I have been Chosen by the Deity for this task, and I suppose She helps me when I need it. That's all."

"My dear, I don't understand you. First you make a claim of Possession, and now you say you don't. Will you make up your mind?"

She jumped up. This was too much frustration to take sitting still. "I have made up my mind! Look, you and I are never going to communicate on this. Forget it, all right? It never happened."

"But what am I going to write in my report? Who saved you from the wolves?"

"I don't care what you write! Say you saved us, for all I care. Forget I had anything to do with it!" She stalked towards her tent, fuming.

"What are you laughing at?"

Corquée smothered his chuckles. "You, of course. You were so funny, jumping around, flapping your hands in the air to keep yourself from hitting him. Like a rooster with a string around its neck!"

She doubled up her fist. "Don't talk about roosters to me!" She swung, and he slipped sideways, the punch glancing off his shoulder.

"Oh, that was a terrible ferocious blow. Too bad you couldn't hit the side of an ox."

He caught her second blow in his palm, laughing again. She threw several more, but he caught them or dodged them, and she began to lose her breath. Then she was laughing too, her hands falling helplessly to her sides. After a moment, she stopped. "Why do I always want to fight with you? It's very undignified. We should act our ages."

"I am. How could I act any other age? If you want to take a swing at me, go ahead. As long as you miss, that is." He raised his hands, far apart. "Want to try again?" He stuck out his chin, taunting. "Come on, try one here."

She smiled, shook her head. "No hits in the face. That's the rule." She looked up at him. "At least that was always our rule. Do you have rules like that?"

He thought a minute. "Sort of, I guess. At least for playing around with your friends. But they aren't quite as nice as yours, I suspect."

"No, I suppose not. But we'll play by my rules, all right?"

He shrugged. "Whatever you say. Wanna try again?"

"No, I do not. I'm calmed down now. Thanks, by the way. A good laugh was just what I needed."

"From the look on your face, I thought you needed to hit somebody, and I thought it would be better if it was a friend."

She regarded him. "You really mean that, don't you?"

He sobered as well. "I guess so. I mean, if it was the difference between hitting me for real, and hitting him and getting into trouble, well... I guess I could take it."

She took his hand, squeezed briefly. "Thanks. I doubt it will come to that, but thanks."

"What was that all about?" They turned to see Tourantij strolling over. "I thought for a moment our young friend was going to get what he deserved. But you disappointed me, Teora. I guess your reach isn't long enough."

She felt herself blushing for some reason. Corquée answered for her.

"She was a bit angry. I thought I'd cheer her up a bit."

The soldier nodded, his eyebrows raised. "Strange idea of cheering someone up. I hope you'd do the same for me?"

The Rider glanced at his friend's big, scarred knuckles. "Somehow, I doubt it."

Tourantij also regarded his hands. "I suppose not. But seriously, Teora, what was the argument about? If I may ask."

"Oh, you can ask all right. He wants me to make a formal claim of Possession by the Deity. Like I get a medal for it, or something."

"Well, you were possessed, weren't you? That's what you said."

"Yes, but I don't want everyone to make a big deal out of it. This wasn't the first time – you know that – and it probably won't be the last, if this trip goes like it has been. It's not something I can do at will. When I need Her, the power comes, that's all. I've been Chosen to complete a task for the Deity, and She helps me when I need it, to make sure I finish the task. It's no credit to me, really. The next time I'm in trouble, I'll solve it myself. This power of the Deity is a mixed blessing, believe me."

Corquée looked concerned. "Then you don't want me to tell it at the Story Fire, either?"

She thought a moment. "I don't know. I wouldn't mind that. As long as I didn't have to be there and listen. But if Goianor gets hold of this, it will become some big ceremonial thing."

The Rider's lips twisted. "With him somehow getting most of the glory."

She nodded. "I have to admit, that's part of my aversion."

"And you don't mind Corquée getting some glory from telling it?"

"No, Tourantij, I don't. Or you, either. If you want to tell all your soldier friends that you were saved from a wolf pack by a woman who comes up to your shoulder, you go right ahead."

The soldier turned to Corquée and spoke as if she wasn't there. "Are you sure you wouldn't like to hit her back, just once, lightly?"

She raised a fist, mock-threateningly, then dropped it. "You know, before I came on this trip, I never tried to hit anybody except my brother, and that was in fun. Why all this violence now?"

Tourantij shrugged, but she felt he was trying to answer her seriously. "It's a violent world out here. You are reacting to it." Then his lip twitched upwards slightly. "So far, you haven't done any harm. Don't let it become a habit. You might let yourself go at the wrong time."

She regarded Corquée. "We had just mentioned that as you came up." She looked at the soldier a moment, then around at their camp. They had found a sheltered spot under the spreading evergreens near a brook, farther down the mountain in the growing warmth and dampness of a cedar forest.

"By the way, Tourantij, you and I have something to discuss. Corquée," she squeezed his shoulder lightly, "thanks for the help, but would you mind if I had a chat with Tourantij? It's business."

He put on an injured frown. "I suppose I can tell when I'm not wanted."

"Don't pout. It's not as if you won't see me at supper." She slapped him on the shoulder, and he ducked away, feigning pain. When he was gone, the two walked a while in silence.

"Why do I do that? I hit him again."

"You don't usually play like that?"

"With my brother, but very rarely. I'm not a violent person. What if it gets out of hand?"

He regarded her, his face seeming softer. "Teora, I don't think you're going to turn into some kind of animal, lashing out at anyone who bothers you. But you should be careful. If you have had a restriction all your life and suddenly it is lifted, there is a chance you might overdo it. Some time when your emotions aren't quite under control, you know."

"You mean I might hit someone for real?"

"The response is there in everyone, but you have it under control. Now you are relaxing that control. You have to learn to control it at the new level. Otherwise, it could get out of control."

She glanced up at him sideways as they strolled through the shade under the trees. "It's certainly nice to have an expert along when I have these problems."

"That's what I'm hired for. Violence."

"Does that bother you?"

"Not at all. It's been a large part of my life ever since I can remember. I have no use for uncontrolled violence. Bar brawls, bullies, people who go looking for a fight, that sort of thing. But it's a rough world, and if you're not prepared to deal with it, you'd better be able to hire someone who can."

They walked in silence for a while.

"Tourantij?"

"Yes?"

"You know what we have to talk about."

"Do I?"

"Come on. You're the soldier. You're supposed to be brave. You know what I mean."

He stopped, turned towards her. "Teora, one thing I've learned in all my fighting. No matter how brave anyone seems, there is always something he is afraid of."

"And this is your thing?"

"Could be. It's a part of me that I can't do anything about, and that, in itself, is a bit frightening. I lie awake some nights, worrying that some day I'll get in a situation where I have to deal with it, and I won't be able to control it."

"But if you could fix it?"

He shook his head. "I don't have much hope of that. I've tried, but..."

"You controlled it up there on that ridge the other day."

"I suppose. But I keep wondering maybe if you'd slipped or something, even a little movement, I might have lost control. I doubt if we made much progress."

She sat down on a nearby log. "You have to get rid of the source of the problem. When you have done that, getting rid of the symptoms will be much easier."

"What source?"

"Well, you didn't pick this fear up out of nowhere. Something happened to you in the past that caused this problem to start. Do you know what it was?"

He shook his head immediately. "I can't think of anything. I've been up and down mountains all my life, never worried about heights myself. It's only other people I get upset about."

"Did you ever lose anybody to a fall? A friend, a brother, something like that?"

"Not that I can recall. I've seen men fall in mountain battles, but that's only another way of getting killed, after all." His mouth twisted into that wry smile again. "I ought to be used to that."

"Then it's something deeper than that. Something you have forgotten. Made yourself forget."

He stood, paced, stilled himself. "No, I can remember everything important in my life, if I try. And I have tried. Perhaps this is just something I have to live with."

Teora could see him there, standing, peering up through the interlacing tree branches to where the first faint stars were appearing in the tattered open patches of sky. She was losing him again.

"But I could help you deal with it."

"Perhaps."

"So?"

"So what?"

"...so we agreed we would wait until we were in a secure place, and I could help you. This place is secure. We were doing fine. Why did you stop?"

He nodded thoughtfully. "It seems to me that perhaps the best time would be at the end of our journey. No, listen. I have been functioning like this for most of my life. I have always done well. I was deemed worthy of this task, to guard this important party. What if whatever you do impairs my ability to function? What if curing me reduces my drive to succeed, to do well as a soldier? No, this should wait a bit longer."

She sat and looked at him; looked and waited.

"The problem is with mountains, right? Well, we're through the main mountains. It's only rolling hills from here to the sea, then we take a ship from there, then up across more smooth country, through a very small set of mountains — hills, really — till we reach the plains of Aeru. Then it's all level. You see? We don't need to mess with this."

She fought down a surge of wonder that this tough, competent man should be pleading with her like a child reluctant to go to bed. She concentrated on keeping a firm face and waited.

"All right, there are some minor mountains. But I showed you in the last part that I could handle it. I'm getting control of the problem." He shrugged, tried to smile. "It's not going to affect us again. Thank you, Teora, but I'm sure I'll..."

"If you really don't want to do this, it's all right. I can't force you."

He was silent. Then, once more, she watched him consciously take control of himself, saying some private mantra in his head. Slowly, his breathing evened, his shoulders relaxed. His attention turned to her. "What do you want me to do?"

She expelled her breath slowly. Now, it was all changed. It had been fine, watching and feeling so superior while he fought his struggle, but now he was turning the battle over to her. Now, for the first time, she wished she had concentrated more on the rest of her training instead of only dancing. Now that she needed it, she could see its value. She tried to remember how the lesson had gone. They had tried to induce the trance in each other, with varying degrees of success. She remembered that the old priest who had been instructing had told them that it was a combination of the skill of the practitioner, the attitude of the patient, and the relationship between the two. Any one of these could make it impossible to work.

That wasn't exactly the part of the lesson she needed to remember. She needed the opening phrases. Tourantij waited for her. Mentally slapping herself awake, she pulled him down to sit opposite her, taking his shoulders and turning him to face her directly, whispering a prayer for strength to the Deity as she worked.

The action — or the prayer — started Teora's mind working again, and she slipped into the pattern of the ritual as it began to flow. She settled him comfortably on the mossy log, speaking in a low, even voice. "This technique works on my people easily because they have all been trained to it. I've never done it on a stranger, but everyone has a first time, and there is no reason why it shouldn't work. It depends on how much you want my help." She relaxed him further, moving her hands slowly around him, defining the shape and texture of the space they would occupy for the ritual, consecrating it to the Deity and making it safe and inviolable in his mind.

"All I will do is relax you, allow you to let down the guards you have put up, allow you to let the fear and horror out, let it run from you, leave you whole and clean." She moved into the second phase, breaking down the barriers within the sphere, joining their bodies and spirits with light, stroking touches of his hair, neck, shoulders and cheeks. He sat perfectly still, tense at first but, gradually, as the ritual took them both, relaxing fully. Her voice dropping, she moved into a murmured chant, manipulating her fingers in ritual sweeps in front of his eyes.

She watched his face intently now, checking for the slackness of the muscles, the slow breathing, the heavy eyelids. She continued the chant, sitting in front of him now, her hands never pausing. She could feel the resistance in him. *Just this far and no farther.*

She softened her voice, murmuring the phrases in their rhythm, working hard but trying to show no effort, only comfort, ease, happiness. Still, she could feel his reluctance. *Strength; the will of iron; never let down your guard; the only way to survival.*

Patience. She continued, building on her success, willing his release with all her power but never letting it show. Slow, easy, gentle; that was the key.

The ritual had taken her in. There was no question of remembering or not; it flowed from her. A part of her thought of the chill water of the mountain, flowing over her after the hot climb up through the crags of the desert. She thought of the cool, moist wind, wrapping her dry, tired body in its gentle caress, easing the tightness of her skin, soothing the pain in her parched throat.

And as she spoke the words of the ritual she could feel the relief building in her, filling her like a pool, waiting to spill over into him, to cool and soothe him as well. As if in a dream, she watched the other part of her mind as it watched him, noting the change in breathing, the relaxation of the shoulders, the faint and agonized *Please, no! This is the way I am. This is how I survive. Don't take this from me!*

But deeper down she heard another voice, even weaker. *Help me! Deity, take this from me!*

With a glow of hope rising in her, she centred on the smaller voice, nurturing and caressing it, bringing it out from hiding like a tiny animal to be tamed. And gradually it came, out into the sunlight, glancing around, seeing that the heat and brightness was not that bad, that the cool shade beckoned, inviting and safe, nearby.

She watched his eyes moving, faster and faster, and knew he was reliving some incident, some happening from his dreams or from his real past. His breath came quicker, and his lips were half parted. In the moment before he spoke, she knew it was coming.

Then the power of his agony hit her like the floodwater of a mountain stream, tossing her aside to float in a back eddy as it tore past her, unaffected by her presence.

"NO! Not the child! Not the cliff! No! You can't!" He was on his feet now, and she was physically cast aside as well. "No! He's so frightened...tell him! Tell him, you fool! Can't you see, he'll throw him over...tell him! Tell him something, tell him anything...I can't stop him...you have to tell him. He means it...he has no pity. Save the child, save him...I can't! I can't! I...!"

Tourantij stepped forward, his hands blindly flailing, waving at some scene in front of his eyes. His elbow caught her a glancing blow and her dazed mind started to function. *This is out of control.* Scrambling up hastily, she clapped her hands in front of his face, once, then again, harder. He gave no response, his hands continuing to wave, his body pushing forward.

Then his steps faltered, and his hands moved less and less, finally falling to his sides. He stood there, confused. She took his arm and led him back to his seat. They sat and stared at each other for a long time. Finally, he broke the silence.

"What happened? Something must have. It was like the other day up on the mountain, but much more. Did you find anything out?" He tried to grin, couldn't.

She attempted to return the smile, with little more success. "You have a scene fixed in your mind. Perhaps something that happened in the past. It has to do with someone, a child probably, falling or being pushed off a cliff. Somebody was supposed to tell something, to save the child, but he wouldn't. The story isn't clear, but it makes your actions lately very understandable. Do you remember the incident?"

As she spoke, the words had their effect on him. Once again, she could see the scene playing out in front of him. Frightened, she watched him. If he relived it without the trance, could she break him from it? *Should I have meddled with something I know so little about?*

Gradually, his eyes came back into focus. He looked at her, a long, slow stare, recognition of a sort, not just of who she was, but of what they had shared. Then his shoulders slumped, and he held his head in his hands, elbows supported by his knees. His voice seeped faintly from the middle of his being, getting stronger as he spoke.

"I remember, all right. I thought I had erased it from my mind, but it was there, wasn't it, waiting to jump on me? Yes, I remember." His head came up, his eyes seeking hers.

"But what good is it to remember? It was a horrible thing, not something that is going to help me. Won't this make it worse, now?"

"I hope not. If this terrible incident was hiding in your mind, you hadn't forgotten it, you had only put it away. It was still there, making you do the things you did. Now you must get it out of yourself, until it has no more effect on you. Not that you will be able to remove it completely. You probably shouldn't. But so that you can control your reaction to it." She stopped herself from saying, 'at least that's what they taught us at the Temple.' He needed all her confidence now. It was too late to back out.

"How do I do that?"

"Awareness of its presence is a good start. It would help if you could talk about it. The incident probably isn't as horrible as you think; it's your agonizing about it that makes it so."

He smiled now, his lip rising in a snarl. "I don't know. It was pretty bad. Who am I going to talk about it with?"

"Me."

He laughed, a sound that matched the twist of his mouth, as devoid of humour. "And give you the same problems? You don't know what you're offering."

She did know. She could pay for this with nightmares of her own. She straightened her back. "This is my place. This is the duty for which I was Chosen. The Deity's strength will allow me to bear the load." She could feel that it was true. Potency grew slowly within her as the days rolled by. "Do not worry about me. As I said before, this incident is not as bad as you fear. You have probably seen many worse ones since. But this one, for some reason, caught you where you were weakest, and has never let you go. For me, it will only be a story, no matter how terrible. Tell me."

He leaned forward, a strange satisfaction in his eyes. "All right. If you think you can handle this, then listen. We'll see if your platitudes can stand up under some real hardship." His words punched at her, and he leaned forward to deliver them.

"You think this is about a cliff. It's worse than that. Worse still for a woman to hear. Are you still game?"

She sat back, gripping the edge of her robe with both hands, as if to keep herself in place. Words would not come. She nodded.

He sat back. "All right. You want to know what happens out here in the real world. Listen to this." He began to talk in clipped sentences, more like a written report than a story.

"I was liaison for the government with a mountain tribe during the last Uprisings. No idea why they were chosen — could have been any of the tribes. But for some reason the Kings felt this tribe was important. I was only twenty, just learning, full of importance at the responsibility. Didn't like fighting that much, then. Had visions of being a diplomat. I fought alongside them – couldn't make distinctions during an attack. I'd have been a fool to go without my weapons.

"This tribe had grabbed some prisoners from the enemy – no great catch: a man, his wife, and a boy of about six years. At least, someone said they were the enemy. How could I tell? They were all the same people, to me. They were being questioned, about something, I don't know what – didn't know the dialect well enough. They beat the man around a bit. He either couldn't or wouldn't answer.

"So, they turned to the wife. Tore her clothes off, asked him the questions again. No answer. Then a soldier threw her down on the rock and raped her, right there with everyone standing around joking and cheering him on. Asked the man the question again - no answer - another soldier raped her. After four or five, they gave up on her, turned to the boy.

"A soldier was holding the boy, and the chief of the tribe asked the father the question, got no answer. The soldier pushed one step towards the cliff. He asked again. Again, no answer. He pushed him one step closer. The poor kid didn't understand, kept looking at his father with big, frightened eyes, waiting for him to make it all better. I couldn't bear it, so I watched the father. I could barely stand to look at him, either. He knew what was going to happen, but he still couldn't give the man what he wanted. Finally, the interrogator got mad, strode over, grabbed the boy and threw him out, as far as he could. He didn't make a sound, just fell out of sight."

The soldier stopped speaking, tears streaming down his face.

"And I didn't do anything. I stood there, superior, above all this, and let these savages perform this atrocity! Not that I could have done anything. I was one man, and I had my position to maintain. But I should have thought of something. Anything!

"Then the man broke. His hands were tied, but he rushed the interrogator, hit him in the back as he was turning around, and they both went over the cliff. I don't know what happened to the woman. Last I saw, she was lying there on the ground. I don't even remember what we did next. Went back to fighting, I suppose. When I told my commanding officer about it later, he just shrugged and said something about the expediencies of war, and that I'd get used to it.

"So, I got hardened up pretty quick. Learned to be a fighter. Never got to the diplomatic side of things. I never want to be responsible for that sort of 'expediency'." His face hardened. "Anybody I kill is trying to kill me and he gets his chance."

"And some day you're going to let one of them win, aren't you?" The inspiration had come from somewhere, she didn't know where, but she knew that it was true.

"What?" Her strong reaction had startled him.

"You have carried the guilt for that atrocity around with you for all these years. Sooner or later, if you let it go on, that guilt is going to hit you when you're in the middle of a fight, and you're going to decide on the spur of the moment that it would be right and just if someone got a chance to kill you. And you're going to let them."

His face and body screamed agreement, though his mouth denied it.

"Oh, I don't mean you'll do anything as stupid as falling on somebody's sword or stepping in front of a bullet. But it will start to slow you down. I don't know anything about fighting, but I do know that when I'm Dancing, if I let my attention waver a little bit at the wrong time, I could very well end up hooked or trampled. Is it any different for you?"

She had taken the right approach; he nodded. "So how do I stop this guilt you're talking about from making me let myself get killed?" Irony filled his voice, but from the accuracy of his statement, she knew that he had followed her closely. Now, he was going to have to do something on his own.

"The Deity knows, Tourantij. I'm a Dancer, not a Healer. I haven't had time to learn everything, you know."

He laughed, another humourless sound. "So, having ripped me wide open, now you tell me you never learned how to sew me up. Some doctor."

His words struck close enough to home that they stung her into sharper speech than she intended. "You know as well as I do that nobody can cure this problem except you. Stop ducking your responsibility. It's your job to see to the defence of this group. Since you're the one most effective weapon we have, it's your responsibility to get yourself in proper fighting order. This does not mean allowing some incident that happened twenty years ago, horrible as it may have been at the time, to interfere with your efficiency."

His lip twisted again, but his voice was softer. "Do I look that old?"

She gulped. "It was a number I picked out of the air."

"Hmm." His smile widened as he realized that she was truly sorry. "Don't worry. You weren't more than five years off. I should take it as

155

a compliment, I suppose. And I'm not ducking my responsibility, as I hope you won't duck yours."

"Which is the spiritual well-being of my people. Neatly put. Of course, I'll help as much as I can. Don't expect any miracles. Talking about it will help. The one thing I know for sure; don't push it back into wherever it was hiding, and don't stew over it alone. You must deal with it."

"I suppose. At least I know what the problem is, anyway." There was relief in his voice; the situation had bothered him much more than he had let show. She hoped they had discovered the real problem. Now wasn't the time to let any uncertainty creep in, however.

She stood up. "That's the attitude. Any time you want to talk about it, call on me. We've got plenty of time on the road." She grinned up at him. "In fact, I may ask you about it as part of my job of keeping track of the spiritual well-being of my flock."

He chuckled and, as they walked back towards camp, he threw his arm over her shoulders. It was a companionable gesture of thanks, and she could tell it was carefully calculated to be no more than he would intrude on any other friend, male or female.

Despite this, she felt Goianor's eyes on them as they returned to the firelight. The Priest rose, his hand outstretched towards them, a frown forming on his brow, his mouth opened to speak.

Before the words could form, Tourantij spoke in high good humour. "Goianor, take your dirty, suspicious mind and…" he continued with a suggestion that Teora, even with her extensive training in animal husbandry, found quite enlightening. A dead silence followed, broken by the freest laugh she had ever heard the soldier give. Then he squeezed her shoulder and strode off towards his tent. Unwilling to be left as the centre of attention, she followed his example.

16. Logging

They broke camp the next morning and headed down the trail, a changed group. Goianor wasn't talking to anybody. Tourantij was. He was in high spirits, slapping Corquée on the back and jesting with the Herdsmen. He seemed to take special pleasure in giving Sabba, the taller of the two women, a hard time about her dog, the only herding animal of the bunch. Teora overheard part of the conversation, when he had goaded the girl to the point of vehemently defending her dog's intelligence.

"…and she can out-think and outmaneuver any three of those other big, clumsy fighting dogs. What good are fighters, anyway? If anybody's stupid enough to put their herd in danger, a few dogs aren't going to help…. You're making fun of me, aren't you?" A further flush of anger flooded Sabba's face as his smile confirmed her suspicion. Her fist flashed out, connecting with his solar plexus with an audible *smack!*

The stocky soldier rocked back with the force of the blow and there was a frozen moment while the girl realized what she had done. Then Tourantij's laugh, loud and free as it had been last night, rolled over the campsite. He turned to confront Teora's horrified face.

"Now that was a punch. If you're ever going to hit someone, Teora, you take some lessons from her." He turned back to his victim. "She's cute…the dog, Sabba, I meant Nipha. I like her! She's cute." Laughing again, he turned and strolled away.

The Herdswoman regarded Teora helplessly. "What's wrong with him?"

Teora mirrored the look. "I guess he's … feeling better?"

"Well, if he's going to develop a sense of humour, he ought to warn a person first. I was about to take him apart."

"That would have been interesting."

The girl shrugged. "Well, he got what he deserved. 'Cute!' Huh!" She spun on her heel and walked away, snapping her fingers at her dog, who trotted obediently at her side. Teora had to admit she was a pretty little animal, with long hair that flopped over her eyes and a tail always moving. Teora didn't know whether to be amused or worried.

The trail continued downward, and the vegetation grew lush, but they were still in the mountains. Huge rocks appeared in the undergrowth from time to time, and high cliffs, fringed with bushes, stood over their path. They had just completed a narrow passage along the face of one of these crags when Tourantij called a halt.

"A good place for the noon rest. Plenty of food for the animals over there, water here." He dismounted.

It seemed a bit early to Teora, but she complied. This was, after all, not her decision. They ate a comfortable lunch, reclining on soft grass in the meadow, while the animals made good use of the same carpet for their lunch. Afterwards, while the stock continued to graze, Tourantij threw himself down beside Teora. He stayed silent awhile, and she wondered where the ebullient mood of the morning had gone.

"I'm not cured, Teora."

"I didn't think you were. How did you find out?"

"That last pitch in the trail, along the rock face. I watched you, and I could feel it all coming back again. I was sort of hoping, you know..."

"Me too. But it was too good to be true, wasn't it? After all, you have been practicing this reaction for almost twenty...pardon me...fifteen years. That much practice is not going to disappear overnight. All we have now is a hope that you can deal with it, now that the original cause is gone. How bad was it?"

"Not bad at all, but it was a very small cliff."

"But you were able to control it."

"I would have been able to control it before. It wasn't that bad."

"Maybe. But maybe it would have been much worse. You can't tell. Do you want to go back and check?"

He looked around, checking the military virtues of their position. He snapped his fingers, and the big dark dog came bounding over to him. "Can I borrow Spar for a bit?"

Daegal nodded casually.

The soldier stood. "Let's go back up the trail."

When they reached the steep spot, they repeated the exercise they had tried up on the ridge. She would walk towards the edge; he would tell her to stop. Then he would tell her to move closer. She spoke very little, following his directions and asking how he felt at times. She sought no trance this time, nothing mystic: only a training session. When it was over, they walked back down the trail, satisfied.

"That worked. I was watching your breath rate and your face. You were much less upset than before."

"I was. And I even remembered to check on Spar a few times, right in the middle of it all, to see that he was on guard. I can't let this get in the way of my duties. That's one reason this problem used to worry me. It takes my mind off my work. When we get into more dangerous territory, I have to be on duty every second. If I lose concentration at the wrong moment, it could kill us all."

"You are on the mend. Watch out for mood swings, now. I remember them warning us about that, but I didn't know what it meant until I saw you this morning. You were really mean to Sabba, you know. She had no idea you were joking. You never did before."

He rubbed his stomach ruefully. "I got the message. Man, that girl has a punch!"

"I told you when we started. Our Herdsmen are the best we have."

"And she's one of the best of them?"

"Do you have any doubt?"

He rubbed the sore spot again. "Well, she sure has some punch."

They entered the meadow and Tourantij released Spar from his vigilance. Teora noticed the priest glance up suspiciously and filed that away to be dealt with later. At one time, she would have considered it important to inform the expedition leader what was going on, but now she knew that it would only provoke some negative response, as he tried to find another way to put her under control. Or Tourantij. At the moment, she couldn't be bothered to face that sort of stupidity.

They mounted and rode on, the mountains gradually smoothing into hills, the trail winding down between them. The party started to see signs of civilization: a rough farm tucked in a sheltered angle of the hill; bare places where logs had been cut and hauled away. The trail widened after this, developing two tracks, and late in the day they caught up with the reason for the change.

Blocking their way completely, its huge wheels towering higher than Barozon's shoulder, a log-hauling wagon creaked along, its load swaying dangerously with the hollows of the road. At a whistle from Corquée, a head appeared high up at the front of the logs as the driver checked on the disturbance. Seeing them, he waved cheerfully, with a signal to wait a moment.

Sure enough, a hundred paces later the road widened further, and the wagon swung aside. They started to canter past, Teora admiring the hefty oxen pulling the great weight. She counted twelve span, trudging along in their grinding pace. They were fine beasts, heavy at the shoulder, though nowhere near her Partner's bulk. As she checked them over, her professional eye automatically checked the pace and carriage of each animal.

Then she stopped. When the front of the wagon caught up with her, she started Barozon moving again until their speeds matched. Standing on his hump, she leaped nimbly onto the high wagon seat.

"Hey, careful there, Lady. That's a long way down." The driver reached out to give her a steadying hand she didn't need. He was a stocky, dark-haired man with a wide, pleasant face. "Nice animal you've got there. Is he for sale? Available for stud?"

She laughed. "No, he's rather special, as you can tell. I wondered if you had noticed the near ox in your fourth span."

The man's smile disappeared as he concentrated on the animal she had mentioned. He then swung down off the seat, jogging forward to see the ox more closely. He reached out and laid a hand halfway down one leg, nodded, and jumped back up on the seat. "Very good eye, Lady. He's going to need a rest tomorrow. Do you think he'll finish out the day?"

"If you don't push him. It doesn't seem serious. A strained muscle?"

He grinned at her. "I agree, though I don't know how you could tell at a glance." He looked ahead at his team, then glanced at her slyly. "Of course, you Dancers have the training, don't you?"

"Oh, yes, we do." She concealed her surprise. This man worked oxen. He would know a Dancer and her Partner the moment he saw them.

"You from the Haven? I thought so. Don't see many animals like that one down on the Flat or at the local competitions. In fact, you don't see too many like that anywhere. When the Priestess made her last Rounds, her Partner wasn't up to that standard."

"As I said, he's a bit special."

"You're sure he's not available? I could use some blood like that in my stock."

"You could talk to the Temple in Coalantha. I don't make that kind of decision."

"I might do that. There are some people who owe me favours. Are you staying there long?"

"Only a few days. How soon will you get there?"

He laughed again. "I'm not going far. We're an hour from home now, even at our pace. Why don't you and your party stay overnight? We aren't permanently set up, but we can certainly take care of your stock. In fact, your animals will probably fare better than your people will."

She smiled back. "Again, not my decision. But I'll pass the message along. I would personally be pleased to talk shop with one as knowledgeable as yourself."

"Vachel Yamil, at your service." He managed a creditable bow from his sitting position, strengthening her impression that this wasn't an ordinary teamster she was dealing with. She gave her name with equal ceremony, motioned Barozon alongside and dropped onto his back. The rest of her party had already passed, and she hurried ahead to Tourantij, who was pacing the head of the logging team.

"How would you like to sleep under a roof tonight?"

He glanced back at the teamster. "What kind of roof?"

She shrugged. "Anybody with a team like this is no peasant. Especially if he can handle them alone. I'd like to talk to him. He sounds knowledgeable."

Tourantij nodded and urged his horse ahead. "I'll take your word for it. Have to ask the Priest, of course." He trotted away, leaving her to the company of the Herdsmen and dogs, the log wagon falling behind.

Not long after, the road swung out of the trees into a large, raw clearing on a slight hillside, where logs and lumber were scattered in organized piles. A huge black engine sat in the centre of a complicated series of roofs and platforms, smoke pouring from its stack; the slow rasp of a mechanized saw and the hiss of steam filled the air. A skidway full of logs lay parallel, waiting their turn to be rolled into one end of the mill, and a stream of white, newly sawn planks was carried out the other end by sweating workers. The sweet smell of crushed bark, tree resin, and fresh-cut wood filled the air, blending with the stink of hot grease and cinders.

The road swung along the upper edge of the clearing, and everyone in her party craned their heads to watch the activities as they passed.

Just out of sight of the mill, around a bend in the road, was the camp. A huge, low barn stretched along the road, with enough stabling for three teams like the one they had passed. Other sheds and buildings stood nearby, including a bountiful hay shed, a smithy, and a more substantial building for harness and other equipment.

On the other side of the road was accommodation for the human workers, on a smaller scale but impressive, nonetheless. Except for the stables, all the buildings were mounted on skids, and the whole camp could be packed up and dragged off by its teams. Bunkhouses, wash-up areas, and even a double-width dining hall were all of the same style. The clearing seemed newly slashed out of the bush.

She caught Tourantij's eye, and he rode over. "I've never seen an operation quite this big. Would you believe this was all solid forest when we came through here a few weeks ago? Whoever owns this certainly moves fast."

"He certainly does."

Tourantij turned to watch a stocky man in heavy boots stride across the clearing towards them. He wasn't tall, but his general proportions reminded Teora somewhat of Barozon: the same huge head, thick neck and shoulders, tapering off to stocky but somewhat slimmer hips. This was a man to be reckoned with, and his purposeful movements underlined the impression.

"Welcome, travellers. I don't suppose you'll be interested in buying some wood?" A laugh that was somehow familiar rang across the clearing.

On impulse, Teora took the initiative. "No, sir, we aren't. We met your brother back on the road and he was good enough to offer your hospitality for the night."

"Oh, he did, did he?" A shrewd, dark eye flashed over her. "And I suppose he wants something in return? Always has his eye open for the advantage, my little brother. Worse than a horse trader, he is." He winked at Corquée, who had just ridden over. "No insult to horse traders intended."

Corquée grinned back, and the mare danced a few steps as the laugh spread out through the surrounding forest.

"Well, if hospitality has been offered, the Yamil family is not one to back away. Step down, my friends. We don't live fancy here, but we don't starve." His voice rose again, and several of the workers who had been standing nearby moved forward to take care of their visitors' animals.

The big logger was not lacking in social graces, giving proper deference to the priest and treating Teora with the rough gentility she had noted in his brother. Satisfied that their stock was properly taken care of, he led them to the big dining hall, where long trestle tables and benches filled the room except for the spacious kitchen that took up one end of the building. He motioned them to a table that was set apart from the others.

"All we've got for a reception room, I'm afraid. There's no space for frivolities, and the men spend their leisure time in the bunkhouses. No problem with beds. We have a couple of private cabins for the gentlemen and the ladies, if your Herdsmen don't mind bunking in with the bull-cook and the flunkies."

Goianor nodded, rather taken aback by the man's overpowering character, but flattered by his deference. "I am sure that will suit us well, Master Yamil. You certainly have an amazing operation here."

"I guess so. It's for sure the biggest operation in this neck of the woods. Anybody want to look around? You came at a good time. The crew won't be in from work for a while. Unless you'd like to see the mill?"

The Priest nodded. "I would be very interested. I have some knowledge of steam engines myself, and would welcome the opportunity to see a new application."

The logger jumped to his feet. "Well, then, why don't we take a stroll up the road? Does the crew good to have the boss wander through in the last half hour of the day when they're anticipating supper. Helps their concentration." He threw back his head and laughed again, striding to the door and holding it open.

Teora watched in amazement as the Priest, his face more animated than she had ever seen it, strode back up the haul road, his hands moving as he discussed some technical matter with his host.

They returned half an hour later, perched on the now-empty wagon of the younger brother. The three of them swung off the tailgate, and a hostler took the team to be unyoked. They were chatting freely as they walked.

"...but I didn't get a chance to bargain for the bull."

163

The older man nudged his brother, speaking in a stage whisper, but winking at Teora as they approached. "Could you arrange to get a couple of heifers turned loose at the right moment?"

The smaller man laughed. "Not polite, brother of mine. The only way to get what we want is to go through the proper channels, and that's the Temple down in Coalantha. Am I right, sir?" This last was directed at Goianor.

The Priest nodded. "Out of our hands entirely, I'm afraid. Proper channels is the key here. Of course, if it were in our power..." His diplomatic smile left no doubt as to his preference.

"Not to worry. Let's hit the grub before the crew gets it all." He tossed a thumb over his shoulder towards the mob of men strolling down the road towards the cookhouse.

Supper was an experience in itself. Teora couldn't believe the amount of food that lay on the tables when they entered the dining hall. When she saw the men eating, she began to understand.

The mainstay of tonight's meal was steak. The way Teora was seated she could, without being too obvious, keep track of what the men at the next table were putting away. One man grabbed the platter as it went by and hooked off two steaks as thick as his hand and the full size of his plate. When he finished them, he called for the rest of the meal. Bowls were duly passed, and he refilled his plate completely with a variety of vegetables, emptying the juices from the steak platter over the whole thing before he shovelled it down. This was accompanied by innumerable cups of tea and slices of bread, heavily buttered.

Then dessert came. Each table was provided with one huge cake and several fruit pies. The man she was watching made some joke about not being too hungry, having eaten a big lunch. At the time, he was levering half a pie onto his plate and drowning it in heavy cream from the pitcher on the table. Many of the men were eating similar amounts. When she had time to think about it, the food was delicious as well as plentiful. She shook her head and took another forkful of pie. The crust was as flaky as any she had ever eaten.

Her host noticed the direction of her glances. "The boys eat pretty well, don't they? Well, they burn it off, I guess. You certainly don't see any of them getting fat!"

She nodded. "And it tastes great! How can you afford to feed your crew like this, so far from town?"

"I can't afford not to. These men are out here for weeks at a stretch. They work long hours, they eat, and they sleep. That's all. Eating is the most pleasure they get. Surest way to a happy camp is good food. I buy the best, hire the best cook and get the best out of my men. Any complaints, and it's the cook who goes down the road. I know it sounds tough, but that's the way to run a good camp. Look around you. Does it work?"

She had to admit that it seemed to work fine.

After the meal, the party broke into groups, with Teora and her Herdsmen discussing stock with the younger host, and Goianor and Tourantij analyzing different styles of steam engine with his older brother.

As soon as it was dark, Vachel showed them to their bunks. Teora was sharing with the other women and her packs were already there.

"There you go, Lady. If the bed's hard, turn the planks over; the other side is sometimes softer." He laughed at his joke, wished her a good rest and strolled away.

Teora's bed, which was the lowest of three bunks stacked against the wall, didn't seem that bad. The straw tick would soften the planks. With her own thin mattress over it, she would be more comfortable than during her nights on the hard ground. Early though it was, Teora fell asleep immediately.

She was awakened in the middle of the night by a loud clanging sound that went on and on. She rolled over blearily. A faint glow of dawn peered through the cabin's one small window. The blob of Mayna's face peered from the upper bunk.

"Are we supposed to be getting up?"

"I hope not." That was Sabba from farther up the bunks.

Teora groaned. "Considering how our dear Priest was getting involved in the business yesterday, I suspect he considers himself a logger, now. We'll be getting an early start this morning."

Sure enough, not more than five minutes later, a loud rapping at the door heralded the Priest's voice floating through, as cheerful as she had ever heard him. "It's daylight in the swamp, ladies. If we don't hit the chow line now, it will all be gone."

Mayna lit the oil lamp by way of reply, and footsteps moved rapidly away, accompanied by a strange sound. They regarded each other in the dim glow. "Was he actually whistling?"

Teora shook her head. "Hard to tell, since he only seems to know one note. In any case, at least he's in a good mood."

"True, but we won't be."

"Maybe breakfast will cheer you up, Sabba."

"If it's anything like supper, it might."

Yawning and stretching, they made their way to the lean-to where the few women in camp did their washing up. Then they headed to the cookshack, where they met a wave of men coming out the door. There were several jibes about the ladies of leisure finally getting out of bed. Teora smiled and let Mayna and Sabba take care of the repartee.

When the door was clear they went in, to find the rest of their party just digging into another huge meal. Platters of pancakes, fried eggs, bacon and sausage filled their table. Coffee flowed, and bowls of jam and pitchers of syrup were passed around. Goianor was drinking a last cup of coffee, leaning back in his chair and discussing with Yamil the finer points of something to do with the length of a piston stroke. Teora had never seen him so relaxed.

Stomachs almost too full to move, they complimented the cooking staff and were on the road while the sun gilded the treetops above them. Waving to the two brothers, they called out their thanks.

"See you in town tomorrow." Vachel had not given up on his plans to meet them at the Temple. The temporary logging camp was not his real home. Down on the outskirts of town, the family had a lumberyard where the older brother lived. The younger took care of their large farm nearby, where he bred and raised the livestock needed for their operation. To the last moment, he had continued his sly invitations to Teora to come and visit any time.

She had turned him down. "Too much chance of a heifer getting loose. You wouldn't want me to spoil all the planning you have been doing for your bloodlines."

"Oh, spoil them, spoil them, please! Improvisation is good for me; keeps me on my toes."

They laughed together, and she turned to the road.

It was a long day's ride to the city of Coalantha down on the coast, and they were glad they had started early. It did not hasten their trip to be stopped by three different patrols of soldiers and required to justify their presence on the road. This was one situation where the priest could not ease their way. Quite the contrary, in fact. The soldiers treated him with cold courtesy and double-checked his personal papers.

The sun was only a memory in the west when they stopped at the high stone wall, and a suspicious soldier checked them over. Teora didn't catch the conversation, but she gathered that the man was stalling. Then Goianor got impatient and started to throw his weight around, and finally the official decided to open the gate. As they passed through, a large number of guards stood by, peering at them in an unfriendly manner. On the streets, though it was early evening yet, there were few citizens about, outnumbered by the soldiers who patrolled, nowhere in groups of less than four.å

As they passed along the main street, Teora pulled up beside Tourantij. "What's going on? Is there going to be a war, or something?"

The soldier didn't seem overly concerned, although he was as watchful as he had been on the trail, and kept the party closely spaced. "Nothing to worry about, Teora. They were like this when we came south. The local lord is a nervous type. I would be, too, with Magali testing my borders. I have heard nothing to indicate that there is any threat to us. We will be minding our manners, though. Relations between the lord and the Temple are a bit delicate."

"I understand. But I still don't like it. All those soldiers look distinctly unfriendly. See how the local people avoid them."

"Very observant, Teora. I wouldn't like to live here either, but we'll only be here long enough to check in with the Temple and wait for the next ship leaving to the north."

She allowed Barozon to slide back into line and continued her observations.

At least their reception at the Temple was warm. Head Priest Dezter, a gaunt, bearded older man, welcomed Teora with an amount of deference that was on the verge of making her uncomfortable, but she suppressed the feeling. This was another part of her mission, another aspect of being Chosen. She was beginning to see that the life of the Chosen in the Haven would not have suited her at all, and she gave private thanks to the Deity for giving her an alternative. She saw to Barozon's quarters, left him in the hands of some admiring junior Priests, and went on to her own rooms, which were more sumptuous than she had ever experienced. After the sparse conditions on the trail, they were overwhelming. Fortunately, she had asked for her own attendants. The old Priest had seemed a bit taken aback at the irregularity of having Herdsmen in his temple quarters but had agreed that this was a special situation.

"It is not often that we get a Chosen travelling with such a small retinue." He shook his head. "These are hard times for us. We have fallen from the old days of glory. I fear for the future of our people. Well, we must all work our hardest to keep to the Path."

Teora had agreed, privately thinking that this Priest was perhaps a bit too far from the old days to remember them clearly. Her history lessons hadn't said anything about any recent glory.

As it was, she had attendants who were equally in awe of the hangings and furnishings of their suite. Sabba felt her bed, one of three in a small room off Teora's bedroom. "I can't sleep on that! I'll smother."

Her friend plopped down on hers. "Ooh! I like this. I'm never going back to sleeping on the ground again."

Teora gave an evil smile. "Enjoy yourselves. The next bed you sleep in will not be quite so solid."

They stared at her.

"Think. Where are we going next?" She watched realization dawn. "How are you for seasickness?"

"What's that?"

"I hope none of us finds out. I've heard it isn't fun."

They shrugged. "Well, let's not borrow trouble before it happens."

Teora thought that was a marvelous philosophy and, grabbing a piece of fruit from the bowl on the table, she threw herself full-length on her large, soft bed.

But the fun had to be paid for.

17. The Ultimate Punishment

The next morning immediately after breakfast, she was summoned before Dezter, the Head Priest. At least, it seemed like a summoning to her. It could, she supposed, have been a polite request for a meeting, but somehow it didn't sound quite like that. It could have been that the servant who brought the message was used to carrying the unquestioned orders of the priest and simply spoke that way out of habit. It could have been.

In any case, she felt a slight chill of warning and prepared herself for the meeting accordingly.

He received her, not in his office, but in a larger, more ornate room furnished for formal occasions. To accommodate her presence, a chair almost the size of the Head Priest's had been placed facing him. Goianor stood smugly at the Head Priest's shoulder. *That isn't good.* She sat down.

The Head Priest didn't spend much time with the social necessities of inquiring after her sleep. He was eager to get on with the grim business of the meeting.

"I understand there have been some irregularities on your journey here, Lady. I hope these can be explained in some way."

She regarded him with polite interest. "I don't know, sir. It was a very difficult journey, in my inexperienced opinion. I didn't notice too much that was regular about it."

Dezter stared thoughtfully at her.

She refused to acknowledge Goianor.

"I gather you have something rather important for me."

Teora was prepared for this. The leather case was in her hand. "Yes, sir. I have been instructed to present this to you."

"And why wasn't I given this last night?"

She shot a quick glance at Goianor, saw his pleasure. That was it! The Head Priest at the Haven had preferred to trust this message to her, and Goianor was upset about it. Now, he was trying to make her seem thoughtless.

"I was given specific instructions as to its presentation. Last night was neither the time nor the place. I was requested to give it to you privately…"

The older man waited, then glanced at the priest. "Priest Goianor is sufficiently trustworthy, my dear. Could I have my message, please?"

Shrugging inwardly, Teora rose. The words came easily to her, and she passed the ornate case over with the appropriate formal gestures. The Head Priest, she could see, was almost too anxious to wait for the completion of the ritual, but she pushed through to the end. Her own Head Priest had impressed upon her the serious nature of the message and the absolute necessity of following the correct procedures in order that the missive should carry its full weight. Noting the Priest's desire to cut through the ritual, she was tempted to give in. Partly through perversity, she refused. As instructed, she was insistent that he check the seals to see that nothing had been tampered with.

Finally, he had the case open. To Teora's disappointment, only one roll of parchment slid out. This was a work of art in itself, covered with stamps, seals, and other drawing, but the message was short. The Priest read it, then sighed and shook his head, although Teora could see that he was relieved. His anticipation had been so great and his reaction so strong that Teora was beginning to be curious about the letter herself. She supposed she would never know.

She was wrong.

The Priest passed the letter to Goianor, whose triumph, as he read it, was much less concealed. "This is all you hoped for."

The Head Priest shook his head again. "It was what we asked for, Goianor. I had hoped they would have another solution, one I had not considered. But they have not. Now we go through with it."

"Of course we do. This will show them. This will reaffirm the power of the Deity in this city: on this whole continent."

The Head Priest sighed. "The power of fear is not our mandate, Goianor. It is only necessary in the most extreme of circumstances." He turned back to Teora. "I should explain, Lady, as you have a further part to play in this. I assume you are familiar with the Ritual of Exclusion."

She sat up straighter. "Of course. It is part of my training. Exclusion was last used on Lord Powa in Sarajio, several years ago. I remember everyone talking about it."

He nodded, pleased at her knowledge. "We have asked the Temple in the Haven for a Ritual of Exclusion. They have sent the orders, with the suggestion that you should participate. A suggestion from the Haven is as good as an order. Will you perform the Ritual?"

Teora grimaced. It was an unpleasant task. "If it must be done. Who is the unfortunate subject?"

"Lord Kilyan."

"Kilyan?" The name sounded familiar.

"Lord Kilyan is the lord of this city. His actions towards citizens, visitors and towards the Temple itself have been most unbecoming his position. Deeds that no one would ever have dared in the days of our glory. We have tried to reason with him, tried to force him. He only laughs."

"And hires more soldiers."

The Head Priest's eyebrows rose. "Yes. He does. And we fear he has worse plans. There have already been skirmishes on the edge of the desert with Imperial troops."

Teora grunted. "If the Imperials are using Magali for their troops, I'm not sure where my sympathies lie."

This shocked the Priest, but he continued. "We must act without delay. I have prepared everything necessary in case permission was granted. He knows by now that you are here, and he could be preparing a countermove. Could you begin the preparations immediately?"

Teora thought furiously. The ritual in itself was simple, but its results could be fatal for the victim. Some people, faced with complete denial of contact with their fellows, simply gave up and died. Because of this gravity, the ritual took a certain amount of mental preparation. However, she had seen the soldiers last night. She would be ready.

"Fine. Goianor will show you the Cleansing Room and I will send for your Heralds. It will not take long, and then we can deal with our other problems."

Teora's head came up. "What other problems?"

"As I said, I have heard reports of irregularities on the trip. In one instance, I gather, a Priest was assaulted. These are serious charges, Lady."

So that was how it was going to be. "Sir, I feel it would be best to clear this up before I start the Ritual. I wouldn't like to have that hanging over me when trying to do the Deity's work. Could I speak to you? Privately?"

171

The Head Priest smiled indulgently. "Of course. I'm sure Goianor won't mind leaving us alone for a while. Perhaps you could inform Noleta that we will need the Heralds. They are prepared, but will have to be brought from their home."

Goianor nodded, smiled back and left. Teora thought a moment before beginning. It seemed more and more as if Goianor had a friend here. Not surprising, considering his authoritative ideas and the old man's love of the past. She marshalled her thoughts.

"I gather Goianor has handed you a list of complaints on how badly he has been treated."

"Not at all, not at all, my dear lady. He has simply brought to my attention the problems he has observed."

"Such as?"

"Well, to put it delicately, he feels that you have been perhaps a bit too sociable with some of the men in the party. You may not be aware of it, but this kind of thing can cause a great deal of trouble in a small group, forced together for a long period of time. He has also brought to my attention the terrible lack of ability and poor attitude of your Guide, a situation where anyone can see the danger. Those are the two worst problems."

"And have you asked anyone else about this?"

"Not yet. You are the first. Be assured there will be a full inquiry."

"And would you like my opinion now?"

"Not in detail. You are the one who asked to speak to me, you recall." He smiled indulgently again; a grandfather giving in to the wishes of a child.

This attitude, plus the unfairness of the charges, pulled Teora's fists into knots. "I don't want to get into detail either, but I can tell you one thing. Most of the problems we have had came directly from Goianor. Ask Tourantij Niverdhal, if you like."

The Priest's smile faded slightly. "I understand that Ser Niverdahl has displayed a certain incompetence, as well."

She laughed sarcastically. "Incompetence? He is the one who led the group. He is the one who can work with everyone, get all of them moving, doing their best. He even gets along with Goianor; I don't know how. And this is what it gets him. The man goes behind his back and complains about his ability. I tell you, your Priest is completely incapable of dealing with people. He thinks of nothing but his own personal power, and will sacrifice anything to maintain it."

"That is a serious charge."

"It certainly is, and I do not make it lightly. Let me tell you, the trip has not been perfect. We almost died several times. Yes, I have had to deal with the relationship between myself and the men in the group. I'm not that young and silly; I understand the problems. But it would certainly have been easier without having someone there, undermining everyone's confidence, pushing everyone around."

"I gather you don't like Priest Goianor much."

Teora threw up her hands. "Oh, I don't know. There are times when he seems fine. He is intelligent, has many good ideas. I even agree with many of his philosophies. But then he loses control and spoils it all by trying to twist everyone's arms. I tell you, at times I wonder if he's mentally stable. Oh, I know. You have never seen that side of him. With his superiors, he would never show his anger. He would go and take it out on someone else."

She paused a moment. "I don't know what you're going to do about the whole thing, and I assume you have no power to send someone else instead of him for the rest of the trip, but there is something you can do."

"And what is that?"

"Talk to him. Tell him not to push people around. Tell him he doesn't have the power to do it. If he would work to gain some respect instead of fear, he could do fine."

"I certainly will be talking to him. And to all of you. This is too important a mission to be spoiled by personality clashes. But I can't promise to make any changes."

Teora felt a sudden chill. "I hope you won't. I would be very upset if I were to find that one of my people had been removed, while Goianor stayed."

"You don't consider Goianor 'one of your people,' I gather?"

She smiled wryly. "That's one positive effect he has had on the group. Between the struggles of the trail and the struggles against the Priest, we have formed ourselves into a very tight, compatible group." She considered. "It must be hard for Goianor, watching us and knowing he's on the outside. Of course, he probably considers it part of the loneliness of leadership."

The Head Priest also smiled. "I imagine he does. You can't be a leader and be friends with everyone, you know."

Teora shot back her answer. "You don't have to be enemies either."

That left nothing more to say, and she took an abrupt leave.

When she reached the preparation room, Goianor was nowhere to be seen. *Good. At least the Head Priest listened.* A nondescript, middle-aged Priest was there with the appropriate equipment: the paint for the bull's horns, her brown garment of mourning.

While she dressed, the Heralds were brought in with their mother. Teora could immediately feel the tension. The woman was plainly upset at the situation, and it was affecting the children. The older, a girl of about ten, was trying to be brave and not doing too well. Her little brother wouldn't leave his mother's side. As she helped them dress in their costumes – black for relief, white for release – Teora tried to calm them, but could see she was having little effect. Finally, she gave up.

"Madam, this is not going to work. These children are so tense they will never be able to function. What exactly is going on?"

She received a tightlipped stare in return, but the woman's eyes shifted a moment to the Priest.

"I don't suppose we could be alone?"

The Priest smiled gravely and withdrew.

"Can you talk now? I assure you there is little danger for the children. They will be under the Deity's protection throughout the ceremony. And under my protection as well, I might add."

The woman smiled sadly, indicating Teora's stature. "Your protection? Going up there into that castle, full of vicious soldiers? I appreciate your attempt to cheer us, Lady, but we will be forced to accept our punishment, hard though it may be."

"Punishment? To be a part of a ceremony of the Deity? Parents in the Haven would be pulling strings to get their children into such an experience, even a sad one like this."

The woman's lips twisted. "We are not in the Haven, Lady. Perhaps I shouldn't speak freely, but the damage was done long ago, and I can hardly make it worse. My husband, Jalil, is a Priest here, and he is being punished for his views, which do not agree with those of Temple authorities. He has been sent on a dangerous mission to the Magali, from which he may well not return. While he is out of the way, his children are being sent into an even more dangerous situation. Should they not return either, that would suit some here very well."

"Who is responsible for this? The Head Priest?"

174

"Not Dezter. He simply sits around and dreams of his days of glory. There is a cadre of Priests at the next level who use his orders to further their own ends. My husband thought he could speak his mind, and the right of the Deity and common decency would protect him. He was foolish, I suppose, but the truth seemed important at the time. Now, it matters nothing, if only I could have my family back." The woman tried to exert control, willing the tears back.

Fury rose in Teora. "Let us get one thing straight, madam. This situation may have started with the petty politicking of Temple officials. However, it has now gone beyond that. Far beyond. You tell me that I am not at the Haven anymore. I tell you that I am Chosen. Your belief tells you what that means; wherever I go, I bring the power of the Deity with me. Your children are under the protection of the Deity and her Consort. You have little to worry about. In fact, the whole plan may backfire considerably if your enemies think you will be punished."

Her intensity was getting through, but the woman was still hesitant. Teora smiled. "You are also forgetting one detail. I am not the only one going up to that castle with your children. Come."

She led the way from the Temple, around to the stables. As they approached, laughter and a good deal of noise burst from around the corner where Barozon was quartered. As they neared, Sabba's little herding dog came pelting around the corner, tail between her legs, pulling up to a comical four-foot sliding stop at Teora's feet. She then ducked around behind Teora's legs, staring fearfully back the way she had come.

"What is going on…? Oh. I see."

She looked up to see Barozon's head sticking around the corner. "And who have you been bullying, my friend?"

Her Partner's head dropped a fraction, and his ears flicked back in a minor show of contrition. She stepped forward, the dog following closely. "I know. It was all her fault, right? She's been teasing you, hasn't she?" She rubbed behind his ears and under his chin, and his eyes half-closed.

"I have someone I want you to meet. They're going to do a job with us this morning. Come and say hello." She turned to where the woman was standing, her children tucked safely behind her. "This is my Partner, Barozon. He will be accompanying us to the Palace. Believe me, madam, your children are in no danger with him nearby. Come,

Barozon. Make acquaintance with Natanya. Forget your silly friend. You two can play later."

With a final derisive snort in the direction of the dog, the bull did as he was told, stepping forward and snuffing at the hand the little girl held out timidly. The boy wouldn't move, and said something into the folds of his mother's dress. A bit of translation was required, and finally they figured it out.

"He wants to talk to the dog?" Teora laughed out loud. "She's more your size, Akio, isn't she? Well, I suppose that will do no harm. Nipha, come here." She snapped her fingers as Sabba did and the little dog trotted over. The boy's hands went out, and immediately the dog went to him, pushing close to be petted.

"He does very well."

The mother shrugged. "He's always loved dogs."

"Perhaps we can use the dog to get him to go near Barozon." She noticed the look on the woman's face. "Oh, they joke around like that. She sleeps at his feet sometimes. No fear at all." She turned and nodded over the woman's shoulder. "Speaking of no fear at all..."

The little girl was completely engrossed in the huge bull. She was petting him, talking quietly all the while. He stood and endured it, allowing her to pull at his horns to turn his head around, and to run her fingers through the curly hair on his poll.

"Would you like to Dance with him?"

Immediately, the girl's hands went behind her back, as if caught doing something wrong. Teora repeated the question. The girl looked to her mother, who, after a moment's thought, nodded encouragingly. Teora took the girl's hand and placed her in front of the bull.

"Now, in order to Dance, first you must ask permission. Like this." She demonstrated the Invitation. Barozon's ears swung forward.

The little girl made a passable imitation, and the bull stepped towards her. She glanced up at Teora, frightened.

"Now you slide aside and, as he goes by, you jump on." Teora gave her pupil room to move, then, as the horns moved past, grabbed her under the arms and boosted her up on the hump. The girl instinctively taloned her fingers into the curly mane and sat, rigid with fear. After a moment, though, when Barozon continued to walk slowly, she began to relax, then to enjoy herself. Teora brought the bull around in a circle, then swung up to kneel behind her. She first invited Natanya to let go of the hair and hold Teora's hands, then encouraged the girl to stand. After a moment of breathless balancing, they made it, Teora holding the girl's arms rigid, her pupil steady between them.

Teora directed Barozon to move past the rest of the family, to let the girl show off. "All you have to do now is learn to manage this at a full gallop." She laughed at the nervous tightening of the small fists. "Not today. That was enough. Now we will dismount and thank our Partner for his cooperation." They did so, the girl's eyes shining as she copied Teora's every move.

There was scattered applause from the group of Herdsmen, minor Priests, and Temple workers who were watching. She leaned down and whispered, "It is customary to acknowledge the audience as well." They both bowed deeply, then the girl broke and ran to her mother for a hug. The woman met Teora's eyes, relief visible on her face.

"That one is ready for training."

"Training?"

"Yes. Doesn't she want to be a Dancer?"

The woman's smile twisted, but gentleness tempered her irony. "Lady, not every girl gets to be a Dancer, down here in the real world."

"Not even if they show real talent?"

"Not everyone gets a chance to find out."

Teora nodded grimly. Politics again. She raised her voice, until the Temple people could hear. "But once the talent has been demonstrated, it's too late. When She places her hand on a child, the Deity must not be denied. Not even a Priest would dare. It would be very bad politics." She stretched the last words out meaningfully.

"Now, young lady, let's get your brother disentangled from my Herdsman's dog. We have business to do. All four of us. Do you know the way to the Palace?"

The girl looked up at her mother, then back to Teora. She nodded firmly and dropped her mother's hand. Despite their fear and reluctance, the two children would have been forced to learn the route they would take, all the way into the throne room of the Lord.

"Good. Why don't we go back and finish dressing, and I can remind you what you have to do. Then we can come back here and see that Barozon is ready. All right?"

The little girl nodded and grasped Teora's hand firmly. Through the whole time, she had not spoken, except to Barozon. "Does she talk?"

"Continuously." The mother exhibited that strange mixture of pride and helpless dismay that parents often feel. "I'm sure once she gets loosened up a bit more, she'll be rattling on steadily."

Teora's voice dropped. "I'm not sure we'll have time for that." The other woman nodded, and they went about the business of preparing for the Ritual of Exclusion.

Considering that the task was to overthrow the powerful lord of a large city, it was an insignificant party that left the Temple and climbed the winding road to the castle, which overlooked the town from a forbidding crag. As they approached the gate, Teora understood the reason. Two small children in black and white masks. Who would dare damage such innocence? Following them, the Partner of the Deity, his curly poll and horns reddened. Innocence, followed by power. Then, directing the bull's steps with signals hidden in her ritual gestures, the Chosen, representing the people's faith in the Deity.

Watching this group approach, the guards moved restlessly, at first pushing to the front to see, then pushing to the back to get out of the way. They had no idea what to do and, in the end, they did the easiest thing: nothing. Her head high, Teora sent her forces into the Palace.

The throne room was huge, with tall pillars holding its roof out of sight up in the dim shadows. A subtle angle to the pillars accented the proportions of the throne, set high at the far end. She could make out the figure on the throne above the milling crowd of brightly dressed nobles who attended. As she moved up the long hall, they swirled in an agitated mass, finally breaking apart as the children approached the dais.

When the Heralds reached the first step, they stopped. The girl nudged her brother so that they split, each going to sit on one end of that tread. Barozon did not pause. He marched slowly and majestically up the stairs and placed his front hooves on the third one. Teora took a deep breath and moved.

With a quick running start, she vaulted up onto her Partner's back, using it as a ramp to approach the Lord on his throne. The bull had his head up, and she paused for a long moment on his hump, staring at the man below her. It was probably the first time that anyone had ever looked down upon anyone in that throne, and she could see the flash of fear on his face.

When she had made her point, she gave the signal, and Barozon lowered his head. She slipped down between his horns, to melt into the traditional posture of mourning on the floor, leaving a long silence.

The man on the throne finally spoke. "What is this silly mummery? Who do you think you are, girl, to burst in on me like this?"

She raised her voice in the ritual phrases:

> *"I am your People, in mourning that you are gone.*
> *I am your Land, in sadness that I no longer feel your step.*
> *I am your friends, who miss your presence.*
> *We mourn for you, outcast and excluded from the life of the People."*

She dropped her head again. For her, the ritual was over. It was all timing, now. She would wait for long enough, then leave. No one could tell her how long, but she would know. She was the Chosen.

He laughed, a loud, hollow sound in the echoing room. "What is all this? Where are the guards? Throw this lot out, back to the circus they came from."

No one in the room moved. Rage began to build in the man's face.

"Where are the guards? Throw them out, I say."

He stared around. Not a guard to be seen. He next turned to the nobles. "Well, you are always telling me how loyal you are. Is there no one who can remove this scum from my presence?"

General movement among the courtiers left the throne isolated. A few men hesitated, made as if to move forward, but Barozon's huge head swung around and they, too, slid back. The Lord sat alone. Silence descended again.

Then Teora started the funeral chant, low in her throat so that it could hardly be heard. As she rose, the sound built, and she paced down the long hall, her voice rising and falling in rhythm with her steps. She turned in the doorway to see a small, lonely figure shrinking on the huge throne that dwarfed him.

Barozon and the two children followed sedately out the huge doors and down through the twisted passages to the gate of the castle. This time, the guards did not hesitate. They moved away in a body, allowing Teora and her party to leave freely.

She stopped the chant as she left the gate, and they walked at a normal pace back down through the town. Now, people thronged the streets, all of them moving towards the castle or standing on the sides to watch Teora go by. There was a low buzz of talk but little else. The children's mother was waiting near the gate, and Teora gave her a quick nod. The children ran to her, she whipped off their costumes and they disappeared into the crowd.

Teora's training had prepared her for many rituals and ceremonies, but not for what to do when walking through the streets after it was all over. Everyone knew that something had happened, and all of them gave Teora and Barozon a wide berth. Alone in the bubble of their power, they strode towards the Temple.

The Head Priest was waiting for her, surrounded by his people: Priests and laity as well. "How did it go?"

She paused, the fatigue hitting her. "The ceremony went smoothly. The reactions were what I had been led to expect. The people of the town are agitated, but not seriously. There were certainly fewer soldiers on the street as I came back."

The Head Priest nodded, sedately leading her back into the Temple grounds. However, once they had entered the Temple itself, a lighter mood prevailed. While no one would allow the general public to see it, a feeling of triumph filled the space. People walked freer, voices were louder and smiles seemed everywhere.

For Teora, it was all too much. She carried with her the image of that slight figure, dwarfed by the huge throne, alone. She was aware of the effect her appearance would have on her victim. *I fervently hope that he deserved his punishment. My recent experience with this Temple leads me to believe that there are other factors to consider.* However, the deed was done, and she had other things to occupy her mind.

Mainly Corquée and his hearing before the Head Priest. She felt guilty for her part in the incident and incensed that Goianor would be able to use his friendship with the Head Priest to influence the decision.

As it turned out, she had no influence on the outcome. By the time she was ready to deal with it, the hearing had already taken place and the verdict was handed down. Corquée himself told her about it.

"It wasn't that bad, you know." He was slouched on the edge of her bed while she sat in a chair nearby. She supposed that Goianor would disapprove of the Rider's presence in her bedroom, but at this point, she couldn't care less.

"Did they listen to you?"

He grinned. "Probably not. They seemed to be very nice, but I doubt if anything I said meant a thing to them."

"What did they accuse you of?"

"Assaulting a Priest."

"And what did you say?"

"That if throwing a handful of water at his horse constituted assaulting a Priest, I guess I was guilty."

"Corquée, surely you defended yourself better than that?"

"Well, I tried. The problem was, the Head Priest kept telling me that they weren't interested in what had led up to the problem. They were only interested in the act itself and its consequences. I said if that was the case, it was pretty cut and dried. Did I splash water at him? Yes, I did. Everyone agreed. What was the big investigation about?"

"Surely they had to admit that you had provocation."

"Well, the Head Priest said that didn't really count."

Teora was disgusted. "Of course it counts. If you had good reason for what you did, surely that makes a difference. It's not as if you went out and attacked the man out of spite."

"Well, they said it didn't make any difference."

"Did you draw their attention to the fact that there doesn't seem to be any damage done? I checked his face this morning. There's no swelling, and the redness is almost gone. I doubt if he was hurt much at all."

"I never thought of that. Anyway, I said my piece and I got my punishment."

"What was that?"

"Well, I get docked some of my pay for the trip, and the incident gets noted in Temple records."

Teora eyed him suspiciously. "How much of your pay?"

He shrugged. "A sixteenth part."

Teora couldn't believe what she was hearing. "A sixteenth?" She did a quick calculation. "That's almost five day's pay!"

He shrugged again. "I guess I got off light. According to the priest they appointed for my Defender, I could have been thrown off the job completely."

"Because of Goianor?"

"Because of him."

Teora considered. "They've made a mistake, you know."

"You're telling me something I don't know?"

"Yes. I mean, they have put Goianor in a position where he cannot function as leader of this expedition."

"How have they done that?"

"Up until this point, we were all willing to put up with him in the hope that everything would work out well in the end. What they have demonstrated here is that giving in to his mad power game is useless. If you give in, he will push for more power. I, for one, have given up. I will no longer try to please him. I will base my decisions on what I believe is good for the group to make our journey go better. I will ignore anything he says that goes counter to my opinion. My Herdsmen will back me, I know that. Will you?"

He grinned. "Are you giving me a choice of following you or him?"

Teora was horrified. "No, of course not. I am suggesting that we make our decisions in some other way than by following Goianor. I would be happy to follow Tourantij, if it came to that."

"Despite his problem?"

"Corquée, is the problem serious enough to keep Tourantij from leading us?"

The Rider thought about it. "It hasn't so far."

"Right. And it won't in the future. I can guarantee it."

"So, we are going to rebel against Goianor?" His smile had a wolfish flavour that she didn't like.

"No, Corquée. We will have no rebellion. But we certainly aren't going to put up with any nonsense. Any time Goianor starts playing one of his little power games, we will bring it to his attention. After a while, I'm sure he will stop. He's not stupid, you know."

"Unfortunate. If he was, he wouldn't be such a problem."

She grinned. "Very perceptive, for a horseman."

He returned the smile. "Very charitable, for a cowgirl."

18.   Fight

They boarded the ship the next day, taking all morning at the task. With a long voyage ahead of them, it would do no good to hurry things at this point. *The Camisha* was a sturdy little two-master, broad-beamed and neatly turned out, from what Teora could gather. She had a long gangplank that led up to the deck, and when the horses were led toward it, they began to toss their heads and stamp their feet.

When Teora saw that the stock was going to have a problem, she suggested that Barozon go first, as the horses were used to him and would probably follow.

The longshoreman in charge rubbed his bushy hair. "I was sort of saving that big brute for last, hoping he'd go along with the bunch."

Teora laughed. "You've got it backwards. He's the pussycat of them all."

The old man scratched a stubbled cheek doubtfully. "Don't tell me he's got claws, too."

"No, no. I mean he'll go on board easily, and the rest will follow him."

The longshoreman looked her up and down doubtfully. He had no idea of who she was. She looked to Tourantij, standing nearby. The old man seemed happy to be referred to someone with obvious authority. His relief was short-lived.

"Whatever she says, man. It's her bull."

The dock foreman looked doubtful. "Well, shall we blindfold him, tie him and sling him in a net, or what?" His eyes still slid to the soldier for confirmation.

Teora raised her eyebrows. "Are you going to put the blindfold on? Why borrow trouble? Why not just walk him up the gangplank, there?"

A slow shake of the head. "Sounds easy, I know. But they get one foot on that hollow-sounding, bouncy plank and they balk. Happens every time. Then the trouble starts. Had a deck hand kicked through a bulkhead last year. Poor lad; never did get right better. No, I don't think it'll work."

Teora patted his arm gently. "Why don't we try it? My Partner is much better mannered than you might suppose."

"I hope so, ma'am. I hope so."

As she had predicted, Barozon strolled onto the deck of the ship like he was heading for a new pasture. If she was interested and enthused, he would be. There was an imperceptible hesitation exactly where the longshoreman said the trouble would start, but Teora was ready, and everything went without a hitch. She had made sure, again over the dock man's protests, that the horses were following close behind with Corquée's mare first, and the rest followed like calves. When all were settled in their stalls below, she walked back to the dock.

"Well, sir, how did we do?"

He was still shaking his head. "I don't know, ma'am. Lucky, I guess. I've never seen livestock move like that."

She faced him squarely, forcing him to meet her eye. "If you were to wander up to the Temple once in a while, you might understand what was going on. I have been Chosen, and my Partner is a Consort of the Deity. That's why things went so well. Don't blame luck unless you have to."

He grinned up at her, spat across the dock into the water. "I might do that. I'm pretty impressed. I guess there's things even an old hand like me can learn. Even from a pretty young thing like you."

She returned the smile but kept the warmth to a minimum. "Flattery won't do you a whole lot of good, but thank you for the compliment. Now, I have to see to my animals, and you have a lot of equipment to load."

He seemed unabashed. "Right you are, ma'am. Back to work for both of us." Despite his familiar attitude, he gave her a formal salute as he left. Then he spoiled it all by winking at her. She laughed and returned on board.

"Well, we may get rid of a few rats, this trip."

Teora looked over to the man leaning on the rail beside her, watching through the cargo hatch as the dogs familiarized themselves with the holds. He seemed similar to the other sailors, although his skin was a shade darker and his hair was black. His clothing was almost as shabby as the rest, but his lack of activity and the fact that he wore shoes must mean something.

"Is there a rat problem?"

"Oh, I wouldn't call it a problem. That's like calling winter storms a problem. More like a fact of life. You got a boat, you got rats.

Sometimes less, sometimes more. If there's less, it's like a few winter days with no storm. You take it, and thanks to the gods."

"Thanks to the Deity."

"Whatever suits you. If any god will send me fair winds, I'll name him anything he wants."

"She."

The man glanced at her. "Whatever you like. She. I'm not fussy about gods. Just wind."

Teora nodded. "Whatever you like. You concentrate on the wind, and I'll work on the religious aspect. We should do fine."

He laughed, a hard sound with little mirth. "Well, let's hope you make out better than I usually do." He turned and strode to the other side of the deck, calling to some sailors who were coiling ropes. She had no idea who she had been talking to, but he had some kind of authority, as the sailors busied themselves under his sharp eye.

She turned to scan the dock. She had half expected Vachel Yamil to show up with a scheme to get some of his heifers bred, but either they were leaving too soon, or his weight hadn't been enough to swing a deal. Too bad; she wouldn't have minded doing him a favour. Nor would Barozon, come to think of it.

They pushed away from the dock at noon, towed out to sea against the onshore breeze by a smelly little steam tug that poured grey smoke and cinders all over them. Then, to a pattering of hardened feet and a rattle of canvas, the sails spilled out of their stops on the two tall masts, and the ship heeled over and began to move of her own accord.

Teora's people were glad when the first swells of the ocean lifted their ship, and the towing hawser was dropped. This was a new experience for all the Haven group, and Teora thrilled with the others at the feeling of power generated when the prow smashed a heaving wave into lacy foam. She watched everything, trying to understand what was going on, generating a long list of questions she would find someone to answer.

That someone appeared, in the form of the officer she had talked to earlier. He was named Palani and he was the Shipmaster, whatever that meant. The sails being set, he was strolling the deck checking hatch covers and loose ropes. She waited, and he stopped courteously beside her.

"Well, you seem to have found us a good wind."

She thought a moment. "But wouldn't it be better if it was coming from behind us?"

He glanced at her, then laughed. "I suppose, if I had my choice, I would like it a point further aft, but I'm quite happy with what we have, thank you and your Deity very much."

"I thought sailing ships had to be pushed by the wind."

"The old ones, the square-riggers, did. They put up as much sail as they could, of almost any old shape, and they got pushed along. This ship isn't like that. She's a schooner, with her sails rigged along the length of the ship, see, with the front edge of the sail attached to the mast. The sails are cut so that they have a special curve that pulls the boat ahead. We can sail at a pretty good angle upwind."

Teora sort of followed. "But the wind is pushing against the side of the ship as well. Won't we slide sideways?"

"Yes, we make a certain amount of leeway. But the hull is designed to cut through the water well and we ride very deep, especially loaded like we are, so we tend to go mostly ahead. At a fair speed, as you can see."

She looked back at their wake, curling white in the dark green waves. "Yes, we certainly are. It's marvelous!"

He smiled. "Aye, it is. It's a great feeling after being on shore for so long to get back to sea again."

"I've been on shore all my life. I guess it's a bit different for me."

He regarded her strangely, as if trying to grasp such a concept. Finally, he answered, his voice tinged with pity. "I guess it must be." His eye caught something and he excused himself, shouting at a nearby sailor to help him with an incomprehensible task. Teora turned back to lean on the rail, watching the water speed past, the seagulls screaming as they hovered near her. Then, with a reluctant sigh, she turned and went down to check on the stock.

Below decks was a different matter. In the first place, the motion of the ship was less exhilarating when she couldn't see the horizon. It was also noisier. She had to assume all those creaking noises were normal and that the ship wasn't falling apart.

Barozon wasn't especially happy with the way the floor kept moving around. He had his feet planted farther apart than normal and his head wove restlessly. She stayed and talked to him, checking on the rest of the stock as she stood there. The horses were fine, having been through all this on the way south. Corquée's mare was already munching at the hay in her manger. The dogs were taking their ease in the straw of her stall, except for Nipha, who was scurrying around, nose to the deck. No question who would be a terror to the rats on board.

Two of the Herdsmen appeared, also checking on the animals. They stayed chatting for a while, but then Ledgard got a strange look on his face.

"I don't feel so great."

Teora nodded. "It's different down here. I felt much better up on deck, myself. The animals are fine. Let's get some fresh air."

The Herdsman nodded as if afraid to speak and hurried to the stairs. Out in the breeze, they felt better and stayed for some time watching the waves roll by.

Radman frowned. "Am I going to feel like that every time I go inside?"

Teora grimaced. "I gather you get over it after a while. At least, most people do. The first couple of days might be pretty unpleasant, though."

"How are you all feeling?" Teora turned at the sound of a cheerful voice. Tourantij stood there, balancing easily against the roll of the ship.

Teora grinned. "Not as well as you, obviously. What do you know about seasickness?"

He shrugged. "Not that much. Some get it, some don't. I don't unless it's really rough and I go below decks. Almost everyone gets over it sooner or later. You're better to eat a little bit of dry biscuit regularly – keep something in your stomach all the time."

"And where do we get this dry biscuit?"

"Follow me and I'll introduce you to one of the more important people on board." He turned, and Teora envied him his easy stroll down the deck. "Do you remember what Yamil said about cooking in his logging camp? That goes double at sea. A good cook makes a happy ship. I hope we have a good cook."

For the next two days, most of Teora's party had no interest in the skill of the cook. It was, in the Shipmaster's opinion, very good sailing weather. This meant plenty of wind, and that meant plenty of waves. That, in turn, meant plenty of leftovers at every meal. Teora was less affected than the others. The first morning at sea, she was able to go below and take care of the stock, although when she had finished cleaning the stalls, she was thankful to take a spell on deck in the fresh wind.

Gradually, everyone became used to the moving deck, and soon they were able to take more active interest in what was happening around them. Goianor appeared briefly from his cabin on the evening of the second day and joined them for supper on the third, although he didn't eat much. His face was pale, and Teora was torn between sympathy and the thought of how nice it would be if he were kept out of circulation for the whole of the sea voyage.

The first thing Teora did when she started to feel better was to size up the other passengers. There were only three: merchants travelling with their goods in the hold. They spent most of their time discussing commerce with the captain and keeping records in their leather-bound books. Seasoned travellers, they could sit in the heaving cabin for hours reading and writing and never turn a hair.

She had squirmed her way to comfort on the pile of rope and lay in a half-doze on the cabin top, letting the breeze cool her while the sun warmed her, a delicious half-baked sensation. As she drifted, she became aware that someone was talking on the deck just below her.

"Where did you get that tattoo?" It was Mayna's voice.

"Some port 'r other. Don't recall which. I seem to recall bein' a bit tipsy at the time. Girl I was with said it would look real pretty. Nope, don't recall the port, but I sure do recall the girl. Not half as pretty as you." It was a rough voice; one of the sailors, she supposed.

She felt guilty about listening, but too lazy to move. Besides, she should probably know if Mayna was forming some kind of liaison that might cause problems. She still felt guilty.

"Why, thank you, Yukio. You're such a smooth talker."

"I do more than talk smooth, missie."

Mayna laughed. "I'm not sure I want to find out about that."

"Oh, yes you do. Trust me."

A bit of unease crept into the girl's voice. "That would be a very poor plan."

"Don't complain until you've tried it."

"I don't think I really want to… Yukio, stop that!"

"You don't want me to stop, girlie."

A definite edge entered Mayna's voice, and Teora wondered if it was time to make her presence known. "Yes, I do. Take your hands off me!"

"Sailor, you forget your place." A new voice cut in. Daegal.

"My place? This is my place, landsman. Why don't you go back to pukin' over the rail and leave us to our little lesson."

"Take your hands off her."

"It's all right, Daegal. I can handle this."

The sailor laughed. "Well, I'm not sure about that, dearie, but I'll give you the chance to try."

A scuffling noise and several exclamations. Mayna cried out briefly, and a slap resounded. Teora flipped over and raised her head. The sailor, a stocky, baldheaded man she had noticed before, stood, his hand over his cheek. Daegal faced him in a stance that indicated his readiness, Mayna at his shoulder.

"She didn't need to do that."

Daegal shook his head. "You shouldn't have touched her. You're lucky that's all you got."

The sailor's eyes focused on the Herdsman. "This has got nothin' to do with you, landslogger. If you was to get lost right now, you might get out of this in one piece. Otherwise..." He stepped forward, intending to shoulder the lighter man aside. Daegal gave with the push, then redirected the sailor's bulk, jamming him sharply against the rail.

By this time, several other sailors had appeared, and an excited murmur came from them. The bald sailor straightened and stared at Daegal for a long, still moment. Then he started to move, circling on the deck as he talked.

"I gave it some thought, landslogger, and I decided you didn't do that by mistake." He grinned at his audience. "I decided you was lookin' for trouble and that means somebody's got to give it to you. Might as well be me."

The Herdsman also considered a moment. "I'm not looking for trouble. Neither was Mayna. You were way out of line and it seems to me you're going to get farther out, fighting with a passenger."

The watching crew muttered, but the bald sailor silenced them with a sharp gesture. "Only if you're unwillin', herder boy. But if you want to hold your head up for the rest of this trip, you won't be runnin' to the captain for protection. You looked mighty big, gettin' yourself into this. Are you goin' ta back down now?"

Daegal glanced at Mayna, who shrugged helplessly. Teora, too, was frozen. She understood the logic of the sailor's argument. If Daegal didn't fight, he would be fair game for all the little tricks and jokes that could be played on a man in an unfamiliar environment. For the moment, she could do nothing. She saw no weapons, and if it got too serious she could always step in.

Daegal seemed to come to the same conclusion. Stripping off his shirt, he stepped forward. "All right, fat boy. You get your way. For the last time."

An appreciative chuckle from the sailors. Yukio was broad, and his head sloped straight from his bald pate to his corded shoulders with no narrowing for a neck. There wasn't a strip of fat on his whole body.

The sailor smiled. "So, he's witty as well as brave. I'll do him a favour and try not to break his jaw." He circled again and Daegal joined him, moving carefully on the swooping deck. From their stances, Teora knew that the joking was over. The sailor shifted but did not attack, and Teora wondered why he was waiting. Then the ship hit a larger wave and the sailor struck. Lunging forward, he crashed chest-to-chest with his taller opponent, hooking his heel behind Daegal's leg. The Herdsman, off-balance, landed heavily on the deck. Teora gathered her legs to spring, but the sailor backed off, satisfied to play to his audience's cheers.

Daegal sprang to his feet and whipped two punches to his opponent's stomach. The sailor rocked back, the grin frozen on his face. Daegal's arms were long, and his big fists moved with lightning speed. The sailor blocked the third punch with a forearm and circled away warily, waiting for the landsman to make a mistake. Sure enough, the ship lurched, and Daegal staggered. Again the sailor attacked, swinging a muscular arm to encircle his opponent's neck.

Teora gasped, but the Herdsman's slip was a ruse. The sailor's arm circled empty air and he found himself spinning, to come up again against the rail with a shock that made the stanchions quiver.

There was no smile now, no acknowledging the support of his silent crewmembers. Yukio's head seemed to shrink into his shoulders, and he pushed himself slowly away from the rail.

Then everything happened at once. The moment the sailor attacked, Teora knew her Herdsman hadn't a chance. As the huge arms grasped Daegal around the waist and hurled him to the deck, she vaulted from the cabin top to land beside the two men.

Yukio had grasped his opponent's throat in his left hand but as he raised his right to strike, Teora laid her fingertips gently in front of his fist.

"You've proved your point, I think."

The man froze, staring at her blankly.

"Are you going to hit me?" She kept her voice calm.

Then the focus came back to his eyes, and he rose, backing away to lean on the rail, breathing heavily.

Teora glanced at Daegal, who stumbled to his feet, shaking his head. He started to speak, but she stopped him.

"I saw it all. You didn't need to let it go this far. You'd better go to your quarters. Mayna, you stay here. We have something to straighten out."

"We certainly have." Teora spun to face the new voice. Palani was standing behind her, slapping a coil of rope against his leg. The circle of sailors faded like smoke in the wind. "Yukio?"

To her surprise, the stocky sailor sighed. "I'm sorry, sir. I was just havin' a bit of fun with the girl, there, and..."

"Yukio, we do not have a 'bit of fun' with the passengers. Male or female."

"I know, sir, I know."

The officer looked grimly at the heavy coil of tarred rope in his hand. "Down. Hands on the rail."

The sailor shook his head slowly, sighed again and knelt, his hands grasping the rail, the tendons standing out with the intensity of his grip. With no ceremony, Palani stepped forward and slashed the coil five times across his naked shoulders.

Teora, shocked by the sudden brutality of the punishment, heard Mayna gasp behind her. The girl rushed from the deck, her hands to her face.

"Sorry you had to watch that, Lady. It was best to get through it quickly."

"It was good that she got to see the results of her foolishness, I suppose." Teora spoke more sharply than she intended. "My man was equally at fault. Do you expect me to mete out equal punishment?"

He worked the rope in his hands, and she winced to see a fleck of blood on one coil. "No, of course not. If Yukio was messing with the girl..."

She shook her head. "It wasn't that serious. She could have handled it. I expect better of my people than to go brawling with sailors." She grinned evilly. "I suspect he got a bit of a shock when his back hit the planks. Up until that point, he probably thought he had a chance."

"Speaking of taking chances, I don't think you should have jumped in like that."

"What would he have done? Hit me? I take worse than that at least once a month in training."

"I suppose. But if he hit you, it would have gone hard with him."

"And I'm supposed to be sympathetic?"

It was Palani's turn to grin. "You're not exactly the sweet young lady you seem, are you?"

"People keep finding that out." She gave him a moment's level stare, then turned to Yukio. "Let me see."

The sailor turned obediently. His back looked painful, with growing red welts crisscrossing the bronzed skin. In a few places, blood oozed to the surface, but the skin was broken in only one spot. She turned back to Palani.

"My people are trained to deal with injuries. Or do you have a medical man on board?"

He studied her face, then glanced at the sailor's back. "I don't think there's any problem. He can wash it with salt water. That'll clean it off, no risk of infection." He noted her wince at the idea. "It is supposed to be a punishment."

He turned to the sailor. "You all right, Yukio?"

The sailor shrugged. "Not exactly dancin' a jig, but I'll get by."

"Off you go, then. I was serious about the salt water. And then get some clean rags from the sailmaker to bind it up. You're on watch at the next bell."

"Don't worry, I'll be there."

"I know you will." The officer went to clap the man on his shoulder, then changed his mind and gently steered him around by one elbow. "Away you go."

The sailor turned back. "I really am sorry, Lady Teora."

"No harm done."

He flexed his shoulders, wincing. "Easily spoken." Then, incredibly, he grinned at her and turned away, moving slowly down the deck towards the sailors' quarters in the bow.

They stood in silence, watching him go.

"Are you satisfied?"

She glanced up at the officer. "What do you mean?"

"Do you want any more action taken?"

"Deity preserve us, no. I didn't expect anything like that in the first place. I suppose it was necessary."

He shook his head. "Oh, yes. With this lot, you can't let anything ride. Firm, fair, discipline is what keeps a ship running."

"I suppose you could call that firm."

"The fair is what counts more to Yukio."

She had a sudden thought. "But it's not up to me."

"I suppose not."

"No, Goianor will have to know all about it. Would you talk to him? You can handle it better."

"As long as you're satisfied, I have no trouble explaining it to anyone." With that cryptic comment, he turned and left her staring out over the rail, her hand shaking with the intensity of her grip.

19.   On Ship

For two more days the schooner ploughed her way northward, the wake a wide furrow stretching south towards home. The animals were restless, probably bored as well, and Teora spent her time in the hold talking to her Partner or up in the crows-nest of the foremast. She could think in terms like this, now, as her familiarity with the ship increased. From her high perch she could gaze out over the stretches of rolling water, so like the plains of the Haven when the wind swirled through the prairie grass. She could ignore the ship below her and the people crowding in on her.

Corquée was beginning to get on everyone's nerves, with his alternating spates of silent pacing and vociferous storytelling. She couldn't help but note that most of the stories had the theme of Corquée's own prowess twisted in their threads. The inactivity was getting to him, and she understood that, but it didn't help much when the bragging became obvious. Tourantij was no help, either. He oozed comfort, his soul as tuned to the days as his legs were to the roll of the ship, but he spent his time alone, staring over the rail, always to the east where the invisible shoreline waited. Once in a while she spied Sabba leaning beside him and filed that away for the future. The two were comfortable in each other's company, and that seemed to be all there was to it.

Goianor had roused himself briefly to condemn all concerned in the fight, including Teora for not coming and getting him immediately to "deal with the situation in an appropriate manner, before it got so far out of hand." The image of the priest confronting the tough, irreverent sailors and attempting to spoil their fun had emotions of hilarity and dismay fighting in Teora's imagination. While it would be satisfying to see her enemy humiliated, she could not bear to see the status of her religion humbled as a consequence.

Mayna was avoiding her and monopolizing Sabba's time as a result.

The bald sailor, Yukio, seemed to have taken an interest in her. While most of the men on board were distant but polite, he made a point of acknowledging her whenever they met. His presence fascinated her, especially his strength. As she noted the healing of his welts, she saw how broad and muscled his back was. He was not that much older than the average crewman, despite his baldness. True to the officer's comment, he was one of those who spent his time at the huge wheel in the stern, his eyes roaming from the compass to the sails, to the horizon and back to the sails again. A quiet word from him to the officer on watch, and sailors would be sent to adjust some small detail of the ropes or sails. Seeing the officer consult again with the helmsman, she surmised that he was held in high esteem for his seamanship. As he laughed and joked with his crewmates or showed the younger men some technique or piece of equipment, she saw how they looked up to him for leadership.

She mentioned this to Palani, the one person she found it easier to talk to since the fight. She was wondering if Yukio held some official post in the hierarchy of the ship.

The officer laughed ruefully. "I wish he did."

She waited, assuming more was coming.

He shook his head. "He knows more about this ship than anyone aboard. He should be my Second. But he can't control his temper. If you make him responsible for a crew to do a job, sooner or later they won't come up to his expectations. Then he starts riding them too hard. One of them will break under the pressure and there will be a fight."

"Which Yukio will win, I suppose."

"Of course. The problem is, my crew is then one sailor short until the victim recovers. If he recovers."

"How often has this happened?"

"Enough for me to see the pattern. I know if I keep him responsible for himself only, then he will keep up to his own expectations and, if not, he will take it out on himself; no harm is done to anyone, and the ship prospers."

"Very well thought out."

He bowed ironically. "Thank you for that vote of confidence, my Lady."

"Oh, I didn't mean..." Then she saw that he was teasing her and smiled at him.

He returned the smile. They stood, their backs to the rail, gazing across the deck towards the sunset as it turned the fleecy clouds on the horizon to gold. Glancing up at her companion, Teora sensed a change in him.

"What's wrong?"

His eyes stayed on the horizon a moment longer, then were off on their usual sweep of the ship. After a moment, he nodded as if satisfied and returned his attention to her. "Look out there. See that line of cloud, high up?"

"Those little curvy ones?"

"Those are the ones. They mean a storm is coming. I'm not happy about the way the glass has been dropping. We may have to run for shelter."

"Where is there shelter?"

He waved a hand to the east. "The coast is not that far away. We have been staying out of sight of land, mainly for safety. The shoreline here is rocky, with many reefs and few harbours. Those inlets that do exist are inhabited by people whose property values, one might say, are not the same as ours."

"Pirates?"

"Not really. Just very poor folk who make a living off what the sea brings them. If the sea brings us, they may consider us fair game."

"But if the storm is too strong?"

"There is a good harbour a half-watch sailing from here, if my navigation is any good." The way he spoke, Teora had little doubt of his skill. "We may have to consider the population a smaller risk."

"We won't be going ashore, then."

He shrugged. "It all depends. The storm will last a day or more. If we are well received, it would be unmannerly to refuse to visit. Unmannerly or unusual behaviour might provoke an attack as well."

She remembered the pride of the bandits back in the rocks below the Rim. "Yes, if they offer hospitality, we must accept. Might we dare to take the animals ashore? They could use the break, but I suppose we don't want to show them."

"Again, it all depends. After all, we may get there and find the place deserted. We'll play it as it goes." He scanned the sails and the horizon again. "If you will excuse me, my Lady, I should speak to the captain, now."

"Oh, I hope you didn't delay, being polite to me!"

He grinned. "Not at all, my Lady. I quite enjoyed talking to one of your group who seems willing to listen to reason. Besides, there is no rush. If we time it right, we can slip into their harbour after dark but before the storm hits. Then, by the time they notice we are on their doorstep, the weather will be too bad to arrange any surprises." Saluting her casually, he turned aft towards the captain's cabin, stopping for a chat with Yukio at the helm, a conversation full of glances and pointing toward the horizon, then towards various parts of the ship. Teora wondered how two men, one who has recently whipped the other, could be talking in such a casual, even friendly manner. She supposed that the welfare of the ship was more important than petty animosities. She had seen no sign that the sailor considered the whipping anything out of the ordinary. She shook her head, thinking what a tough man he was, in both body and spirit.

Sure enough, a moment after Palani entered the aft cabin, the captain himself came on deck, glanced briefly at the sky, and called the officer on watch to him as he approached the wheel. Again, only a few words passed around the group, and then all was action and movement. Orders were shouted. As soon as the men hit the deck, Yukio swung the carved wooden spokes of the wheel easily through his hands and the ship spun obediently onto a more easterly course. The action in the rigging continued, and she could see some of the sails becoming smaller and others being taken off and replaced by sturdier ones. Once the officers were happy with that, the crew came down and began to scurry around the deck, checking knots, adding extra ropes and generally tidying up much more than Teora had seen before. This must be a bad storm, which perhaps explained the nagging anxiety that had been building in Teora throughout the day.

During all this Captain Hamal stood to one side, watching everything but saying little. Teora confirmed her impression that, although he was the captain and the owner of the ship, he was more of a businessman, and it was actually Palani who made the sailing decisions.

Speaking of responsibilities, Teora realized that she had some questions to ask. Waiting for an opportune moment, she signaled the shipmaster. He started toward her, still checking the progress of his work crews. When he was near enough to her, he stopped, his attention still on the ship.

"Will the waves get much bigger before we reach harbour?"

"Probably."

"When we are at anchor, will the boat move around more than it is doing now?"

"I'm sure you won't be bothered a lot, my Lady." He was still not really listening.

She allowed a bit of steel to creep into her voice. "I'm not concerned for myself, Palani. It's the animals. Is there anything we can do to prepare them?"

Now she had his full attention. "Of course. Pardon me for my inattention." He grabbed a sailor passing by. "Relieve the helmsman and send him over here."

As the man hurried off, the officer grinned at her. "I'll send Yukio to help. He knows how to secure cargo as well as any, and he seems to have taken a shine to you."

She was glad that her face was in a deep sunset shadow, and her blush was disguised.

"Here, Yukio, take a rest from the wheel. We may need your best concentration later on. Go with Lady Teora and show her Herdsmen how to secure the livestock."

The sailor dipped his head, then started for the companionway. "If you will bring some of your people, my Lady, I will show them what to do. I know what must be done, but I would prefer you to handle the animals." He turned and grinned at her. "Especially that great bull of yours. I have a deep respect for that one."

She raised her eyebrows. "I hope you do. I'll get some of the Herdsmen and meet you in the stalls."

She had little trouble finding the Herdsmen, since she met a little knot of them coming to look for her.

"You should come, Teora. Barozon is getting restless. Even Corquée's mare is enough upset that the dogs are staying out of her stall."

Teora walked through the group and continued towards the stables in the hold, explaining about the storm as they followed her. However, they had to pass the Priest's cabin on the way, and he was standing in the hallway blocking their progress. His face had that stubborn set, and she knew she would either have to explain it all again or walk over him. She took the less physical alternative.

"What is all this fuss about?"

"There is a storm coming. The captain has changed course to run for shelter, and we are going to prepare the animals."

"Run for shelter. He's not going ashore!"

"I believe there is a good harbour nearby."

"But there are pirates all along this coast. We must not get near enough for them to see us. He must not do this. I will go and tell him."

The closeness of the corridor worked for Teora, now. She held her ground, knowing that he would not dare push by her with her Herdsmen backing her up. "I suppose, Priest Goianor, that the captain will appreciate your meddling with the running of his ship, especially while he is preparing for a serious storm." She paused to let that sink in a bit. "Now, if you would excuse us, the sailors are waiting for us in the hold, and we must see to the animals."

It took a moment for the priest to register the tenor of her speech. When he opened his mouth to protest at her speaking to him that way, she tried a less subtle verbal nudge.

"The storm has made my Partner very anxious, and I must go and see to him. You know what happens when either of us is upset." She stepped forward. The Herdsmen crowded close behind her, and Goianor had little choice but to slip aside into his cabin and let her pass. As she continued along the hallway, she heard chuckles behind her, and glanced back to see Sabba giving her a fists-together victory sign. Repressing the urge to grin back, she stepped out faster.

Dusk turned towards night and the ship raced northeastward ahead of a black cloud that built steadily behind her. Teora, back on deck for some fresh air after the work below, noticed the new movement of the ship. The man at the wheel was doing a lot more steering, swinging the spokes back and forth, sometimes rapidly. Every once in a while, the ship would veer around to the west as if trying to get back on her original course, the wind would rattle the loosened sails and the ship would slow. The sweating helmsman would haul her back and, after a moment, she would start to pick up speed again.

"She's got a bit of movement on her now, my Lady."

Teora turned to see Yukio looming beside her in the gloom. "Why does the helmsman let the ship turn like that? Is he new at the job?"

The man let go a burst of laughter, then stifled himself, peering anxiously to see if she was offended. Reassured, he smiled again. "No, my Lady. He is as good a man as any. It's the waves."

"They don't seem a whole lot bigger."

"Generally, they aren't. But they have changed. Do you see where they are coming from?"

Teora peered over the side, sighting against the afterglow in the sky. "From the left, I mean port, like they have been for days."

"True. Those waves are still there. What you don't see is that there is a long, deep swell under them, coming from farther aft, from the storm back there. Now, if you consider a bunch of waves running this way," he held one scarred hand in front of her, "and put another set running at a different angle," here the fingers of the other hand went on top of the first, "you get places where there's one taller wave in this set on top of another taller wave in the other set and you get a peak running sideways along the crest. Every once in a while, one of those peaks hits the port quarter. That's the corner of the stern, back there. That's what slues the boat around.

"If you hear it coming you can steer her away from it, but that changes the course and slows us down as well, so you try not to steer too far. Especially at night, there's no way to do it right every time. As a result, we go on a bit of a sleigh-ride sometimes."

"Which is why you'll be back on the wheel soon."

He grinned with pride, and something else as well. "As long as I'm talking to you, Lady, no one will bother me. It's a hard job, helming in this weather, and I'll rest as long as I can, if you don't mind."

She smiled back. "Fine with me. But I doubt that Palani will care who you are talking to, if the ship needs you."

The man rolled his shoulders experimentally, as if feeling for soreness. "I don't need the rope to remind me of that."

"Is your back all right?"

"Hah! A bit of slappin' like that? Now if you hadn't been there, Lady, or if you hadn't stepped in and finished the fight, he might have used more than what he had in his hand." The shiny head shook ruefully. "I've really got to keep from doin' things like that."

"Why do you do it?"

"Well, you gotta realize, my Lady, we were just havin' a bit of fun."

"Fun? Hitting people like that is fun?"

"Well, you gotta admit he deserved it, hornin' in when he wasn't needed."

"I don't have to admit anything of the sort. I doubt if the captain would have appreciated you messing with one of his passengers."

The sailor shifted his feet a bit. "Well, savin' your lady's pardon, but she was messin' with me a bit, too."

"I suppose she was. I've talked to her about it, and it won't happen again."

"That's too bad."

"This doesn't seem to be much of a problem to you, does it?"

"Not really, my Lady. I screwed up, I took my licks. We've all forgot about it, 'ceptin' you."

Teora gave up. "I'll do my best. It seems I'm not used to the way things go on this ship."

"Oh, this is a great ship to sail on, my Lady. Palani is a good man. The best. There's men would fight to get a berth on the ol' *Camisha*. Men have."

Teora could see his teeth gleam in the light spilling from the hatchway, and she wondered about the story behind that comment.

Then the ship lurched sideways again, wallowing in the waves with a huge banging of canvas and rattling of blocks. She was a very long time coming back on course, and several sailors moved about, setting things right again. The big man at her side removed his hand from her arm where he had steadied her and shook his head.

"I guess I'd better not wait any longer. She does that again and we might bust somethin' loose. Nice talkin' to you, my Lady." He gave her the same casual salute that the sailors all used and strolled towards the wheel. As he appeared in the dim circle of illumination thrown on the deck by the compass light, the man on duty looked up in relief.

With a grin and a jest, Yukio clasped the spokes. Then his face straightened as the concentration took over. The wheel moved less in his hands, and while the boat's course still seemed to weave among the waves, it steadied under her feet. She watched for some time, trying to see what he was doing different from the other man, but it was too subtle, and she had too little knowledge to figure it out.

After a while, she went below, searching for something to do. She wondered how they would approach the shoreline in the dark, but didn't know whether she wanted to be on deck watching or below trying to ignore the tension.

It seemed that most of the passengers felt the same way. There was a lot of movement in the common room and the talk was louder than usual. Several people noticed her appearance, and a voice rose over the din.

"What happened, Teora? The boat feels better now."

She turned to her Herdsmen, seated around a table along one curving wall. "Daegal's old friend Yukio took the wheel. Let's hope he steers as well as he fights."

Daegal glanced up at her, the shadow of a bruise still showing along his cheekbone. "If he makes this ship go easier, I don't care how he does it. I don't like it when it tips over and bangs around like that."

The others laughed good-naturedly and Teora joined in, happy that there seemed to be no lasting antagonism on either side. She was also pleased that her group felt unworried about the storm. Well, she should take her cue from them. This was a good ship handled by able men, and she would trust in them. If the crew started to look worried, time enough for her to panic.

"Does anyone know where we're going?" That was one of the merchants.

Teora turned to him. "I gather there's a safe harbour nearby. The captain thinks there's less risk there than fighting it out at sea."

Another merchant nodded sagely. "I suspect he's less worried about the risk to the ship. More likely the comfort of the cargo. That livestock won't take too much tossing around, and some of my goods are fragile, although they are packed carefully."

The third man scowled. "Not much profit in saving the stuff from getting broken just to hand it to a bunch of pirates."

The other two laughed. "Come on, Zebulon, don't worry. At this time of year, they will all be up the river harvesting the freshwater salmon runs or picking berries."

"So instead, we get massacred by the wild men."

His companions laughed again. "Surely you don't believe in that old story."

The man stared at the deck stubbornly. "I don't say I believe, but I don't say I disbelieve. There are wild ones on that jam, I'm sure of that."

Teora wasn't getting any closer to figuring out this conversation. "Excuse me, sirs, but what wild men are you talking about?"

The oldest of the three merchants smiled. "Well, my Lady, it seems to me that the only good harbour around here is at the mouth of the Ayanna River. Now, that's a safe port, all right, if the locals don't decide to clean out your holds. What my friend, here, is talking about is the Floating Island. The Log Jam."

He waited a moment for their questions, then started before they had begun. "Yes, my friends, a log jam. The Ayanna starts in the mountains to the northeast, where the rains fall, and the trees grow to quite a size. Those rains also cause a lot of flooding at various times of the year, and the trees get washed off the banks and come sailing down river. Centuries ago, no one knows how long, a bunch of them got piled up on the sand bar at the river mouth. More and more jammed into them and they formed a floating island. This island now stretches more than two days' journey upriver and seems to be growing still. A great inconvenience, since it fills the surface of the river all the way across, making navigation impossible. There are forests and cliffs along the banks, making road-building expensive. There's a whole lot of country up that valley, waiting for a way for people to get there."

"But what about the wild men you mentioned?"

"Oh, those. Well, my Lady, there is a rumour that a bunch of very primitive people actually live on the log jam. Some of the trees are so old that their centres have rotted out and can be used to grow crops in. There are holes they can fish through, and they're certainly never short of firewood!"

Teora stared at the man. Was he pulling her leg? He seemed quite serious.

"I know you don't believe me. I don't know how much of the story I believe myself. I do think that people could live on the raft, and if they are as primitive and timid as the story says, they certainly wouldn't show themselves to the type of person who lives in the town at the river mouth."

His two companions nodded seriously. "Those are the ones we have to worry about. Your animals would make a fine prize for pirates, too."

Teora spotted Tourantij, alone as usual, his chair tipped back against the wall, oblivious to the movement of the ship. He was, however, listening to the conversation.

"There's not much we can do at the moment, Teora. Once we get anchored, we're vulnerable, and we will keep a very sharp eye out. The ship has a tough crew and, with our people to strengthen it, I doubt that anyone will try to meddle with us."

"Especially since we can blow them to bits if we try."

Teora looked over at Corquée. "What will we blow them to bits with?"

"The cannons, of course."

"I haven't seen any cannons on deck."

"Not on deck. They're too heavy to keep up that high and have the ship stable. They are on the lower deck, nearer the waterline."

"Then why haven't I seen some of them?"

Tourantij smiled. "Have you got a large box in your cabin?"

"No."

"Are you sure? A long, low box with one end built against the outer wall, the hull?"

Teora thought. "Yes, but that's just my..." The realization hit her, as the laughter started. "You mean I've been sleeping on top of a cannon?"

She stood in the middle of the uproar, wondering how she was supposed to take this. Finally she grinned, then laughed along with the rest.

"I'm glad you all find our situation amusing." The harsh voice cut through the subsiding laughter, and they all turned to see Goianor standing in the doorway, his hand steadying him against the rolling of the ship. "What is so funny?" From his tone, Teora assumed that he didn't want to join in. *Why does he have to come and spoil every bit of fun we have?*

Tourantij stood up. "Nothing to worry about, Goianor. Teora had just discovered that she's been sleeping with Long Tom for a half-month and didn't know it." An appreciative chuckle filled the room.

"Sleeping with whom?"

Teora turned away from the anger and suspicion in the Priest's voice. This was getting boring.

"The cannon, Priest. The cannon under her bunk. She didn't know it was there."

"Oh. The captain did say he had to make some modifications to carry all the passengers." Teora was surprised to hear the priest chuckle. "It's a good thing we haven't needed to use the guns. She might have been a bit surprised at a crew of men rushing into her cabin in the middle of the night."

Mayna giggled. "Especially if they tossed her off the bed and ignored her afterwards."

Another roar of laughter, which Teora was forced to join. When the noise subsided, she knew it was her turn to respond. She opened her mouth, but nothing witty came out. She closed it again, then smiled.

"I hope we don't have to use the cannon, and not only for the sake of my own privacy."

There was a general murmur of assent, followed by a long silence, each person considering what the future might hold.

It was Goianor who broke the silence. "Well, if the captain says we must turn to shore, then I suppose we will turn. I cannot say I am anxious to have the boat moving around any more than it is at the moment."

He suited his words by sitting hastily as the ship lurched over another cross-wave. He ended up near the merchants, and they began a serious conversation. Watching him converse easily with these relative strangers, Teora reminded herself that, while she had seen mostly his worst side, this man had the brains and the ability to rise high in the temple hierarchy. *Amazing. And not a good comment on that hierarchy.*

They sat, talking idly or staring into space, until Teora felt the motion of the ship change. No longer the wild, rolling plunges, the huge swings to the left. Now the waves must be shorter, because the movement was jerkier. She stumbled up on deck to investigate.

She was greeted by complete darkness. For the moment, all she could see was the faint red light from the compass shining up on the helmsman's face. It was a different man, but he seemed to be having much less trouble steering.

As her eyes became accustomed to the night, she began to see the white wave-tops rushing beside her and the spray as it splashed away from the side of the ship. Over the rail, she could glimpse flashes of phosphorescence in the disturbed water.

She moved closer to the wheel, but stopped short of it, not wanting to interfere. Captain Hamal and Palani were together in one corner, eyes straining ahead and to the right.

A muttered voice spoke nearby, and a sailor materialized out of the dark, hurrying over to speak to the officers. "Land, sir. The lookout says land on the starboard bow."

"Did he say what it looked like, how close?"

"Fair close, sir, but he didn't say what it looked like. Not much, I'd guess, in this dark."

Palani spoke up. "Well, you're about to find out for yourself. Go and relieve the lookout and tell him to come down here with a good description of the land."

"Aye, sir." The sailor turned and moved quietly up the deck, then reached up somewhere and disappeared into the darkness overhead. Everyone on deck was being very quiet, whether to avoid announcing their presence or to listen for crashing surf, she couldn't tell.

She walked to the right-hand rail, peering off into the darkness, which seemed absolute. There were few stars showing, mostly covered by ragged, fast-moving clouds. Her eyes scanned the darkness, trying to find something to focus on. Suddenly, much higher and closer than she had expected, she saw the outline of a hillside against the stars. Once she knew where to look it was not hard to see. Scanning downward, she searched for a shoreline, but could see nothing. Then she noticed a white smudge in the darkness and heard a crashing sound close beside the ship.

Running back to the quarterdeck, she confronted the surprised faces of the captain and sailing master.

She stopped, embarrassed. What if she was wrong? They probably knew about the reef already. But what if she was right? That thought drove her to speak. "Do you see the rock out there?"

Instantly, both men swivelled to the rail, peering out.

"I can hear it."

"Damn that compass light in my eyes. I can't see a thing. Teora, where did you see the reef?"

"Along the side of the ship, over there." She pointed. Again, all she could see was blackness. Her embarrassment returned. "Maybe it was nothing."

"No, no, it would be a reef. We're closer inshore than I thought. Helmsman, take her a point farther west. If we run along here, we should find the river mouth. You and you," two men appeared from the shadows, "trim the sails to the new course. Quietly, now, there's no rush. The rest of you, keep your eyes and ears open." He grinned over at Teora. "We can't let the passengers get the jump on us. A copper penny to the next man who spots a reef."

Reassured, Teora walked over, stretched out her hand.

He looked at her quizzically.

"My penny?"

"Oh, your penny! Sorry, I just made the offer now. Perhaps if you were to employ those sharp eyes of yours, though…" he grinned and swept his hand towards the railing in a courtly gesture.

She stalked by him, her nose up. "I might do that. But not for your little penny. Only for the safety of the ship."

"That's as good a reason as any." He followed her to the rail.

"Reef off the starboard bow, sir." The sailor hurried up, pointing. Sure enough, white water foamed, farther away than the one Teora had seen.

"Good eyes, sailor. You'll get your money in the morning."

The sailor looked aggrieved.

"If we don't survive, man, you won't need to spend it anyway!"

The sailor slowly grinned. "I see what you mean, sir. It's not that I don't trust you. Someone might forget."

"Well, you have Lady Teora as a witness, Sook. Get back there and look again."

The sailor faded into the night, and Palani moved back to the compass light to consult a chart he had spread out nearby. Teora followed him.

"You're going to be a poor man before the night is through."

"Not if I know my navigation." He indicated the chart. "If we're where we should be, we have now passed the only two reefs in the area. The river mouth should be ahead very soon, now."

A pattering of bare feet, and a sailor appeared.

"Ah! News, I believe."

"Lookout's spotted the river mouth, sir."

"Right on schedule. Yukio, take a couple of men up to the bows. After we gybe around the point and enter the harbour, we'll come up on the wind. Start the anchor down, slow and quiet. Let it down about a fathom. Put a man in the chains with a lead-line and check the depth every boat length. When the bottom's at four fathoms, or if we lose way forward, whichever comes first, drop the hook. Don't wait for my order, just drop it and send word back to me, double time. As soon as it's set, up in the rigging and stow the sails. Twice as quiet, now. We're very near the town."

The men headed forward, and the officer gave orders for the other sailors to let the sails out, slowly and quietly. Then he walked to the rail and stood peering outward. After a few minutes, he gave a satisfied grunt. "I have it now. Two points to starboard, helmsman."

"Starboard two, sir."

"Another starboard...good...hold that course. Look." He turned Teora forward, pointed. A dim light glowed, then another, and soon she could see, scattered along where the shore might be, a series of what could be windows.

"There aren't very many of them."

"No, and that's fine. The fewer people home, the better for us."

He turned to the man at the wheel. "Pay off a few points...there, a point...there, see the end of the headland? Hold her steady...all right, gybe her around."

The ship turned away from the wind with a rattling of blocks, then came up on the new course, past the dim gleam of a spit of sand to starboard. They glided into the smooth water behind the point.

A muffled clank sounded from the bow. "Bring her up into the wind, helmsman. We'll have the anchor down in no time. You others, let's get all the canvas off her."

There was a quiet and efficient bustle as the sailor turned the wheel hard over, and the breeze freshened as it hit Teora's face from the front. Then the ship stopped moving, and the wind pushed her slowly backwards until the bow dipped as the anchor chain came taut.

Yukio approached. "The hook's well in, sir. Sandy bottom, good holding."

"Keep the chain short, take the longboat out and drop the kedge anchor off to the seaward side with a trip-line on it. I don't want to drag, but I want to be able to get out of here in a hurry."

"Right." The man turned away, grabbing the arms of two other sailors as he passed them, and the three swung a boat off the deck and lowered it overboard.

"Keep a sharp eye while you're down there. No telling who might be out snooping about, even tonight."

But the anchoring went without incident, and the boat returned. Double watches were set, and then all the action was over. No one was moving. The waves had stopped. Only the wind, shrilling through the rigging, seemed to be active. A stinging rain started to dash in on the wind, and Teora went below.

It was light and warm in the main saloon. With the motion of the ship gone, everyone seemed more relaxed.

"So here we are."

"At least the ship isn't bouncing around like it was."

"What's happening up there, Teora?"

She grinned at them. "Nothing. That's why I'm down here with you."

Soon, it was bedtime. One by one, yawning, they left for their cabins. Teora checked over her bunk before she climbed into it. For some reason it seemed quite different, now that she knew what was inside that ordinary-looking box. However, it felt the same. Tired out from the stress of the evening, she soon fell asleep.

She woke twice in the night, each time wondering whether the noise of the wind in the rigging had really increased or whether the whistling roar was part of her dreams. By dawn, all doubt was gone. The ship was starting to roll again, and out her porthole she could see the shoreline moving past. At first she thought they were under way, but then she realized that it was only the ship swinging about on her anchor chains. Mindful of the rising wind, she dressed warmer than usual and headed for the deck.

It was a grey, nasty morning. Even in the shelter of the spit of land there were waves rushing along at all angles, and the bits of spray that blew across the deck stung when they hit exposed skin. Landward, she was unimpressed by what she saw. The shacks and warehouses along the shore were formed of weathered planks and almost indistinguishable from the huge driftwood logs that lay everywhere. Following the shoreline north, her eyes were greeted by what at first seemed to be the opposite shore of the lagoon, flat and covered with low brush. Then, seeing the whitened roots and trunks sticking above the bushes at strange angles, she realized that she was looking at the beginning of the Log Jam. She stared at it for a while, but it still resembled a low shoreline with nothing moving. It was highly unlikely that a wild man would put in an appearance just for her; she grinned at herself and directed her attention back towards the town.

Nothing moved between the buildings, and the rain and flying spray made it difficult to tell if there was smoke coming from any chimneys. *Well, that's fine. The fewer people here, the better.*

She stood on deck until the wind and spray had thoroughly awakened her, then headed below to check on the animals before breakfast. Now that the ship was still, she had a feeling everyone would have a renewed appetite, so she hurried through her chores in the stables. Barozon seemed relaxed as well, and greeted her warmly. At least, she could tell it was warmly. To the untrained observer, being shoved up against the wall by a head that weighed more than her whole body might not be considered a warm welcome.

"Fine, fine, relax." She pulled his ear until he moved his head away. She stared into the nearest eye, deep and comfortable. "Feels good to be moving less, doesn't it?"

Someone had removed the extra tethers that had secured the animals, allowing them to rest more comfortably through the night, and she felt guilty. *Why didn't I think of that?* Well, to be honest, she hadn't known whether it was safe or not. *I could have asked.* To make up for her lack of attention, she rubbed her Partner down with extra care, checking his hooves, ears and nose for any signs of illness or other problems. He seemed in disgustingly good health, and she felt quite proud of him.

"You're taking all these changes very well, my lad. Travel seems to agree with you. Good thing. I have a feeling we've a bit farther to go."

20. Storm

"Not a chance in the world." Teora stamped her foot on a soggy plank. Little bits of something splashed into the sea underneath the dock and she stepped back, searching for a more solid place to stand.

"I have to agree. We can't unload the animals here." Corquée grimaced in disgust, scanning the waterfront. "How about onto the beach?"

Palani shrugged. "You can always sling them over the side and have them swim ashore. That works, but it's messy getting them back on board."

"And no way to leave in a hurry." Tourantij, too, had been looking up and down the docks, for different reasons, Teora was sure.

She glanced at the abandoned buildings nervously. "Might we have to leave in a hurry?"

The soldier, in his turn, shrugged, nodding his head towards the small group of ragged women and even more tattered children who peered fearfully out from the side of the largest building. "The men who usually live here will be back. They won't have left their families for that long. We can't expect them to be as timid."

Goianor had been standing by himself. "Why don't we go and ask them?" Without waiting for an answer, he strode over towards the women. Teora and the rest of the party watched with interest. The group huddled closer together, children disappearing behind skirts, as the priest approached. The interaction was too far away to hear what was said, but it was apparent that the women, too awed at first to speak to the robed Priest, soon saw that he meant them no harm and warmed up. Once the interview was going well, Palani started to move in that direction. Tourantij held up his hand.

"The Priest is doing well enough without our help. I'd rather we stayed in the open. There is no guarantee that the men really have left the village."

Neither Tourantij nor Palani had taken his hand off his pistol butt, and their eyes restlessly scanned their surroundings. Teora stared around as well, but nothing seemed out of place.

The rain had stopped momentarily, and the sun, peering through a low shroud of scudding mist, lit up patches of the wild shoreline. Dry, rocky outcroppings, sparsely festooned with shrubs or short grass clumps, climbed in jumbled ranks up the hillside. The houses were perched wherever there was a flat spot between the lumps of rock, constructed of any old pieces of wood that had swept up on the beach. Glass was unusual, and the scarcity of metal chimneys hinted at the primitive nature of most heating and cooking.

As Teora finished her survey, Goianor returned, dusting his hands in a businesslike fashion. He seemed quite pleased with himself. "Poor souls." He shook his head in a show of sorrow. "Hardly knew what a Priest was, let alone how to talk to one."

"Did you learn anything?" Tourantij eyed the women warily. They had moved farther out from their alley, staring with more curiosity at their strange visitors.

"Plenty, if all of it can be believed. Most of the village is away on a berry gathering trip up into the hills. These few were left behind because they couldn't walk fast enough to keep up, or because they had young children who would get in the way."

"Berry gathering?" The soldier looked skeptical.

The Priest nodded. "As I say, if you can believe them. However, berries may not be the only crop they are after. They also mentioned, quite out of the blue, something about the natives on the raft."

Goianor paused, waiting for his audience to register their surprise. "It seems the natives will also be out hunting for berries, and a raid is possible. Though what that primitive group might have that even these poor folk could want is beyond me."

"Women." Tourantij's voice was flat, emotionless, and Teora glanced at him in concern. "The only way these natives can protect themselves is to retreat into the jumble of the Log Jam when they are raided. If they go ashore for the berries, they are vulnerable. There is always a shortage of women in these pirate towns. The men go there to pick up whatever fun they can. They may even take a girl back to town with them, if they like her enough."

Teora was aghast. "How do you know this?"

"I don't. But it seems logical."

The Priest nodded. "That fills the gaps in what they told me."

"A good piece of deduction, my friends." They turned towards Palani, who had been listening, silent, up until this point.

"You mean you knew this all along? Why didn't you say something?"

Palani grinned briefly. "You were all having such a time figuring it out, I couldn't get a word in. But you're pretty close to the mark. If you notice the villagers over there, you'll see a certain number of them with darker skin and lighter-coloured hair. Those will be stolen women and their children."

"But that's horrid! Why don't they do something about it?" Teora could feel the righteous anger burning in her.

He held his hands out, palms upwards. "What are they going to do? The reason they live out on the Log Jam is because they are too primitive, too weak, to survive anywhere else. On the Jam, they are safe. It's only when they come ashore that they run into trouble."

"I still think it's awful!"

Tourantij stepped closer to her, then glanced up at the sky, which was spitting rain again. "We could spend a pleasant afternoon discussing these social problems, but we need to get back aboard. We can't bring the animals ashore and the weather doesn't look good."

The shipmaster nodded. "The wind has been backing around to the east. That's a bad sign in these parts. I need to consult with the Captain Hamal. We may decide to pull anchor immediately."

"I thought this cove was sheltered enough. We were safe last night."

"Last night's storm was just a normal westerly blow, Teora. If we get a southeasterly, it could be another piece of work entirely. Yes, I will consult with the captain."

"Yes, by all means. We must do as the captain says." Goianor was still cheerful from his success with the villagers. "Come, Teora, let us return to the boat." He stepped politely aside, and she had no real choice but to start in the direction he indicated.

As the sailors rowed them back to the ship, Teora noticed that the wind was rising. "Why is the water still flat? The waves were much higher last night."

The shipmaster scanned the sky again, to where a dark line obscured the southeastern horizon. "It's an offshore wind. There's no distance for the waves to pick up any size. That's the one reason for staying. We won't be bothered by waves in this storm. Just the wind. Of course," he looked down at her, "I don't want to frighten you, but if it's a typhoon, the wind direction will reverse itself halfway through the storm, and then we'll not be in such a good situation. Not really bad, though, especially since there are no other boats in the bay to drag their anchors down on us. Yes, all things considered, we'll probably stay put."

"I imagine your captain will have his own opinion."

The sailor turned quizzically to Goianor as if unsure how to take this intrusion. "Yes, I suppose he will."

Teora chuckled to herself. The Priest could hardly conceive of a situation where the captain of a vessel allowed one of his underlings to make such an important decision. She made eye contact with Palani. He grinned and turned to his work, giving the orders as the boat made its way alongside the ship.

Corquée was waiting for them at the rail, and no sooner had the shipmaster put a foot on deck than the Rider was beside him, murmuring a comment not meant for other ears. Palani straightened. "You think so?"

Corquée nodded firmly. "I've seen this before. Have you noticed the birds?"

Teora looked. There were no birds in sight.

Catching her eye, the Rider nodded meaningfully. "The stock below is jumpy too."

Instantly, Teora was on the alert. "Have they made any problems?"

"No, your people are down there, and everything is fine. They're just restless. They can tell."

"That there's a storm coming?"

"A big storm." He indicated Palani, who had left them, striding purposefully along the deck towards the captain, who was waiting for him at the top of the ladder up to the aft deck. "He knows too. Watch."

Sure enough, a moment later the shouting of orders raised a hum of activity on deck. "Like a stick stirring up a hornets' nest," as Tourantij put it. Teora, having assured herself that the animals were taken care of, watched with interest, the soldier explaining what was going on.

Anything that was removable from the rigging was taken off to reduce the weight and windage aloft. All the hatches were covered with an extra layer of canvas, lashed firmly around at deck level. The ship's various boats were brought inboard and tied more securely. Only the larger launch, the one they had used to go ashore that morning, was left in a position from which it could be easily swung overboard.

214

"There's enough room in that one for all of us if it comes to a normal abandon ship routine. As if any abandon ship is routine. If she runs aground or sinks, we'll probably launch the smaller ones right off the deck. If we can."

"What about the animals?"

He grimaced. "If she breaks up, they won't have much of a chance. We'll turn them loose on deck before we leave and hope some of them make it ashore. Most won't. By the time things get that bad, we'll be lucky to save ourselves."

Teora shook her head. "It doesn't go that way with me. If my Partner stays, I stay. If he goes over the side, I'll take my chances with him."

Tourantij looked at her curiously. "You really mean that, don't you?"

"Of course. I can't imagine what a storm like that must be like, but from what I've heard, I doubt if the boat will be a comfortable place to be, either. If anyone has a chance to force his way ashore through the surf, it will be Barozon. With me helping, and some assistance from the Deity, we'll make it."

"I envy you your faith, my friend."

She smiled up at him. "Perhaps faith is easy when you have lived a life like mine."

His face took on a thoughtful expression. "That would make a difference."

For a while, they leaned on the rail, watching with fascination the tall black clouds eating up the mountains to the east. The storm approached slowly, but its intensity was formidable. Lightning crackled from cloud to cloud, and once in a while a low grumble of thunder pushed its way through the whistle of the rising wind. Spray began to whip off the tops of the mounting waves and sting their cheeks. Gusts heeled the ship despite the stripped masts.

Teora huddled close against a big coil of rope that afforded her some protection and watched in awe the marshalling of the forces of nature. Slowly, the clouds rolled towards them, towering ever higher into the sky over their heads. Soon, the weak light of the sun was gone, hidden behind a swirling arm of the storm. Ashore, a hazy line of rain advanced down the mountainside towards them, then stretched out across the water.

As more rain began to mingle with the driving spray, Tourantij gently shook Teora's arm to get her attention.

"This is no place for us."

She glanced up at him, wondering. "Isn't it fantastic? How can you watch the power of the storm and not be moved to praise the Power that controls it?"

"I never looked at it that way. All I know is that it's going to get powerfully uncomfortable out here in a moment. If you want to stay out here and commune with the Deity, go ahead. I'm going to do my praying in a drier spot."

As he turned away, she took his arm, laughing. "I know. A poor time for theological debate. I get cold and wet like anyone else, you know. And I should be down with Barozon when this hits."

Supporting each other, they stumbled to the companionway and down into the relative stillness of the interior of the ship.

All the rest of the day it rained and, as night fell imperceptibly through the dimness, it continued to rain. It was a blanketing downpour of water, so strong at times that it seemed to overcome the wind, flattening the waves to oily ripples. A haze formed above the face of the sea, with the spray rising from the striking raindrops mixing with the falling water, and the surface itself was invisible from the deck of the ship. Teora went out several times, fascinated by this incredible volume of water. The third time, as she stood in the shelter of the doorway, a dark figure loomed in the dimness, splattering her with the water that sheeted off his cloak. Hearing her splutter, the man turned, revealing the dark face of the shipmaster.

"Teora! What are you doing out here?"

"Just watching the storm. Shouldn't I be here?"

"No, that's all right. There's no more danger here than anywhere else."

"Is there a lot of danger?"

The man looked down at her for a long moment, as if making a decision. "I might as well tell you, I have never experienced a rainfall like this in my life."

"That's two of us."

"Oh, you often see rain like this in tropical squalls. But they only last a few moments, then the sun comes out. This..." he swept his hand out at the deepening darkness, "this is beyond me. Maybe you ought to be asking that Deity of yours what's going on."

It was her turn to look carefully at his face. There seemed to be a serious undertone to his jests. "I'm not good at that sort of thing. If it's prayers you want, we have a perfectly good Priest along."

"So, what are you good at?"

"I don't know how to put it. Doing things, I guess. You want something done, something that needs strength and faith, then Barozon and I will take care of it. We're not much use in this sort of situation."

He grinned. "Well, it's comforting to know what I can expect, anyway."

"Are we really in any danger?"

"Not at all. The wind is strong but not hurricane force, at least, not yet. The extra anchors are holding well, and the ship is riding these puny waves easily."

"Then why are you worried?"

"I guess I shouldn't be. But this is an unknown experience for me, and that makes me want to be very careful."

"Can the rain hurt the ship? We couldn't get full and sink, or anything like that?"

He lifted his head, and a roar of laughter filled the confined space where they sheltered. "No, of course not. Oh, it will make things uncomfortable after a while, when it seeps down through the cracks and everything gets dripping wet, but that's sort of normal, for a sailor, anyway."

"Is it the river, then?"

He nodded. "I'm trying to think what might happen. The women told Goianor that they've had a lot of rain and the river is high already. If this drenching continues, the river's bound to rise more, and the Log Jam might shift. There could be more wood floating around here in a few hours. Of course, we're well out of the current over in the bay here, so not much driftwood will come our way. I will have the men keep extra watch tonight, though. I'm glad I talked to you, Teora. It always helps to talk to another inquiring mind."

"Well, if I've helped, even a bit, I'm pleased. Right now, I'm not going to see much more, and your cloak is dripping on my shoes."

"Oh, I'm sorry. Here, let me..."

As he bent down to see her feet, a fold of his cloak slapped across her arm, soaking her sleeve. "No, no, don't do anything. You'll just make it worse. Here. Make yourself small, and I'll go down the stairs."

"Companionway."

"Right. I'll go down the companionway. Whatever you call it, there isn't room for me and a large, wet sponge. Stand back."

She went down the stairs, and he followed at a decent distance, slapping the water from his clothing. She went along to the holds, but the animals had calmed, leaving nothing to do. After a serious talk about nothing in particular to Barozon, she returned to the main cabin for supper.

It was a long, boring evening. The rain cascaded down without letup, the wind howled through the rigging and the ship rode comfortably. Teora went to bed early for lack of anything else to do. She was soon deeply asleep, ignoring the water that trickled down one wall of her cabin and found its way through the floorboards to the bottom of the ship. She was vaguely aware, once, of the sound of the pumps, as the sailors laboured to bring the water level in the bilges back to normal.

It must have been late in the night that she was brought slowly awake by a dream. A dream of a low, rumbling noise that went on and on, gradually getting louder until it forced itself on her consciousness and she found herself sitting bolt upright on her bunk, listening. The sound went on, a low growling off in the distance. She tried to distinguish all the noises around her: the creaking of the ship's timbers, the shriek of the wind, the gushing of the rain; nothing had changed there. It was just that low, unceasing rumble. Hastily shoving her feet into her clammy boots, she started out of her cabin. She had slept in her clothes, so they were nicely dry, but her cloak was still damp. She put it on anyway, in case she went on deck.

The main cabin was empty; only the flicker of a lamp, swaying in its gimbals, sent the shadows fleeting back and forth along the walls and ceiling. She made her way to the deck and peered out from the cover of the doorway. She could see nothing. Aft by the wheel a dim, warm glow of light showed where the sailor on watch should have been.

As her eyes grew more accustomed to the dark, she began to make out the silhouette of the masts weaving their paths against the sky. The strange sound was much louder here, but no more distinct. As she stood, listening intently, a thud, not loud, penetrated the planks at her feet. She jumped. Had the anchors drifted? Had they hit shore? A shout sounded up forward, then an answering call. Another crash jarred the ship more distinctly this time, then all was quiet again. At least back to the normal sounds of the storm.

She had to go and see. Wrapping her cloak tightly around her, she braved the rain and wind, leaving her shelter and fighting her way along the deck, keeping away from the rail, using the side of the cabin to help her along. There was another crash, not as heavy this time, and another series of shouts from the forward part of the ship. As far as she could tell, the shouts were communication, not fear.

Coming around the corner of the forward cabin, she received the full brunt of the storm. The wind tore at her face and clothes, and the water poured at her in a steady stream. She could feel a trickle start down her back, and pulled her hood even closer around her head. Now she could see something of the activity on the foredeck. Dimly, in the light of lanterns slung in the rigging, there were men out there, leaning over the side of the ship despite the storm, pushing at something with pike poles. Once in a while a shout would rise, and the group would gather around one spot, pushing madly. Sometimes the activity would subside, but at other moments there would be one or two of the jarring crashes first. From what she could tell, it seemed that something was hitting the ship, but she had no idea other than that.

Groping her way forward but careful to stay out of the way, she made it to the spot where the bowsprit pushed out over the bow. There, where the railing was low, a tight angle was shielded on two sides by the railing and the bowsprit, and she was able to crouch in comparative shelter and watch the activities. Soon she was able to see the pattern. The sailors were watching intently. Anyone who saw something would call out, and the two on either side would run to help him. Palani was pacing back and forth across the deck: observing, calling orders, sometimes throwing his own weight on a pike handle. During one of his pacings he stopped near her, then strode forward, grabbing her shoulder, shouting.

"Who is that? Get on a pole, you lazy…wait a minute. Who is this?"

"It's me, Teora! What's going on?"

His face was close to her ear, and the shadows darkened the lines of worry in his frown. "You shouldn't be here! It's too dangerous."

"I'll stay safe. What's going on?"

He paused to survey his sailors, then his face swung close to hers. "Probably what we talked about. There are logs all over the place. If the wind was from offshore, the waves might be big enough to drive one right through us and put us on the bottom. As it is, we can usually fend them off. So far."

"How much do you think the Jam has shifted? Is that what's making that noise?"

"I don't even want to find out. We'll deal with what we have to, when it happens."

Teora could hear the tension in the man's voice and knew that he wasn't showing all his fears. She laid her hand on his, where he had braced himself against the heavy timber of the bowsprit. "She's a strong ship, Palani, with a good crew. I'm not worried."

"Then you're not as smart as I thought."

"Yes, I am. I know that if we get into real trouble, you'll let me know in time to do something for my Partner. That's all I ask. Everything outside that is in the hands of the Deity."

He smiled crookedly in the changing shadows, then a shout recalled him to his duties. "I don't think you should stay here, Teora."

"I suppose not. You don't need me to worry about, on top of all this." Slapping his shoulder, she charged past him, headed for the safety of the deckhouse before the wind and rain could drench her completely.

When she got down to the main cabin there were several people seated or wandering around, looking up fearfully every time another log crashed into the hull. Teora hurried to reassure them, keeping Palani's worries about a wind change to herself. She got them busy preparing hot coffee and drinking it. By the time they were finished, the first gleam of daylight was showing through the portholes. Her own anxiety overcame her, and she squirmed back into her wet cloak and headed up on deck.

The quiet bay had changed completely. From shore to shore it was full of wood. Small logs, bunches of branches, whole trees complete with roots. Some wood was old and rotten; some still had leaves attached. The older clumps had grass and shrubs growing on them: floating islands. This connection sent her gaze up towards where the river had been the night before. Instead of water she saw a solid stream of logs moving ponderously towards the sea. In some places it was low, in others piled high, with odd trunks and logs prickling out in all directions.

The movement drew her eyes seaward. At the bar where the mouth of the river reached the sea a huge pileup towered higher than the masts of the ship. On either side of the pile, masses of logs flowed west, pushed by the current and the violent wind. The ocean, as far as she could see in the growing light, was full of piles and bundles and bunches of wood. There, some of the floating islands looked bigger than the ship, moving on the waves in slow undulations.

Her attention was attracted closer to the ship by a mewling cry. A bedraggled wildcat, drenched and miserable, balanced on the end of a log. As she watched, the log spun and the animal, after a futile attempt to stay on top, splashed into the water. It swam to a larger clump, pulled itself up and crouched, too tired to shake the water out of its long fur. After a moment's rest it stared around, rose, and carefully started off along the logs, headed shoreward. She watched the animal's progress as it alternately crawled and swam through the mess, then lost its small body among the grey of water and sun-bleached wood. She hoped it made shore safely. Poor thing. She wondered if it had lived on the Log Jam normally, or if it had been out on a hunting trip at the wrong time.

A sudden thought spurred her up the deck to Palani at the bow. The sailors were no longer working as hard, and the jarring crashes seemed to have been replaced by a grinding noise. She approached cautiously, but there was much less action than before. She stood a moment beside the shipmaster, to be sure of attracting his attention.

"Palani, is the whole Raft breaking up?"

He regarded the river, listening to the steady roar. "I suspect so. A large amount of it will be pushed out to sea, anyway."

"What about the natives? I thought they lived there."

His face froze, then he let go a short, sharp word that she assumed was a curse. "The natives!"

"If the Jam breaks up, they'll drown, won't they?"

He thought a moment. "Maybe not. Look out to sea there. Many of those clumps are huge. Those logs have been jammed together for years. Some of those rafts may stay together for days, if there isn't another storm."

"But how will they get ashore? Isn't the wind dying down?"

"Yes, I've noticed the wind dropping. If there are people out on those logs, getting ashore may be the least of their worries."

"What do you mean?"

"I told you last night. Halfway through the storm, the wind dies. After a while it comes back from the opposite direction. In a few hours the wind is going to start pushing that tangle back onto the beach. It's going to be an amazing mess."

"But what about the ship? Will we be trapped in the bay?"

His mouth formed a grim line. "If we're lucky. When the wind starts pushing the logs against us, we could be in serious trouble. We might get crushed, we might get rolled under, we might get pushed ashore, high and dry. Who knows? This whole thing is out of my experience."

"So, what are we going to do?"

"Once the wind changes, I suppose the safest spot in the bay is against the new upwind shore, over there by the spit where the logs will be blown away from us. But I can't think of any way of getting there, with this mess in the way."

"Couldn't we sail over there? Slowly?"

He nodded thoughtfully. "Probably. But I don't know what the bottom is like. It's quite shallow, and we could run aground."

Teora waited, knowing that he wasn't really discussing anything with her, only thinking aloud. Sure enough, he straightened, his mind made up. He strode over to the sailors, gathered them together and started them raising the anchors. Soon the ship was a-hum with activity, with a few small sails pulling them away from the village towards the outer rim of the bay. Sailors with pike poles were stationed on either side of the rudder to protect it, others were in the bows, fending off the logs ahead. Palani peered from the crow's nest on the foremast, finding the best path through the mess in front of them, shouting directions to the sailor at the wheel.

Assured of the lack of danger, the other passengers were on deck with Teora, fascinated by the whole proceedings.

"The hand of the Deity is powerful!" She didn't need to turn to know who stood at the rail beside her. Goianor was staring in fascination at the roaring, tumbling stream of logs that shouldered its way, at unabated speed, past the heaped sand bar and out to the sea. "Truly a Sight that few have been honoured to see."

Teora could hear the capital letter on the word "Sight" and wondered what nonsense was going to come of this.

The Priest was musing aloud. "I wonder what this means. Is this a demonstration She has given us, to show us Her Power? Is this meant to hold us here for some purpose?"

She couldn't help but break in. "I suppose we happened to be here at this moment. Perhaps the Deity is leaving it up to us to handle the situation."

He nodded judiciously. "True. It could be a test of our resolve. Perhaps such a trial will prepare us for more difficult times to come."

Teora gave up and turned her attention out to the moving logs. A different motion caught her eye. Someone was moving along the logs! She shouted up to Palani in the rigging, pointing to the moving figure.

The officer nodded. "I saw him. He's headed this way."

"Should we send someone out to save him?"

She could hear the laughter in his voice. "I was sort of hoping he was coming to save us!"

She watched the moving figure. Sure enough, the man navigated easily along the logs, sometimes running, leaping, at others balancing with the pole he carried. Soon he was close enough that she could see his features. He was not tall, and his long, blond hair flew about his head in straggly locks. He was barefoot, dressed only in a sort of skirt, and the muscles of his arms and chest were lean and corded over prominent bones. He was slim to the point of emaciation, but he moved easily across the logs. Teora marvelled as he ran quickly across several small poles, each one too light to take his full weight, moving on to the next pole before the last one had time to sink. Then he gained the safety of a huge trunk and stood there, his chest rising and falling rapidly, resting on his staff and surveying the nearby ship.

Palani shouted a greeting, to which the native answered with a wave of his hand. Encouraged by a responding gesture, the man ran the length of the tree and, making use of a jutting root, clambered up to the level of the deck and leaped across, balancing briefly on the rail before climbing up the rigging to the crow's nest. The shipmaster greeted the man in a strange, guttural language, and soon they were conferring busily, pointing at various parts of the bay. After a while they both seemed satisfied, and Palani called new instructions down to the man at the wheel.

The ship ground slowly through the tumbling wood, making gradual progress towards the new anchorage, but they were slowing down. The logs were tighter here, and the wind was dropping. More sails were put out, but to little effect. Before the ship stopped completely, the shipmaster ordered the helmsman to swing her bow to the wind. The sailors laid out the anchors as before, and Palani started down the rigging, followed by the native.

Seen closer up, the man's skin was wrinkled and not that clean. He slouched by the tall officer, oblivious to the stares of the crew and passengers.

Palani waved a hand towards the logs. "Most of his people were ashore when the Jam started to move. The rest, he doesn't know. Some will have survived, no doubt, but there is nothing we can do to help them. You have seen how well these people move across the logs. He's more worried about the villagers. We were right about the raiding. Only the bad weather kept his people safe yesterday, and now that they have no retreat, their defences are very weak."

"How many of them are there?" Tourantij was looking shoreward, as if gauging the possibilities of attack.

The officer shrugged. "He doesn't use numbers that big. They have more than one camp, or clan. His particular family is only ten. We could take them aboard, but they would be in more danger from the storm. He would like us to come ashore and stay with them, but my crew will remain with the ship. What about you?"

Since the merchants wouldn't leave their cargoes and the Haven group could not take their animals with them, it seemed that everyone was taking their chances on the ship. Palani conveyed this to the native, who nodded, then turned without a word and hopped overboard, running lightly again across the logs towards the shore.

They all watched him go, unspeaking. The silence made Teora aware that during the man's visit the wind had dropped completely. The debris still ground against the side of the ship, underscored by the roar of the river of logs.

"What are we going to do about them?"

Palani regarded her. "We have problems of our own to deal with, first."

His head was cocked to one side as if listening, and she followed his eyes to the rigging. The wind was rising, flecks of spray streaming in over the mass of logs in the open ocean to the west.

21. High and Dry

There was little more they could do to prepare. Teora went below again to explain to Barozon what was going on. He was restless. Not really worried: more like ready for action. She attributed this to lack of exercise.

"Don't get too anxious, there, fellow. You want action, you might get more than you asked for. Swimming might be fun, but not in all those logs."

He swung his head back and forth, disbelieving.

"Don't say I didn't warn you!" She gave his hump an affectionate slap and went back on deck.

The wind was freshening rapidly and the logs in the bay were starting to move again, leaving a bit more room around the ship, but logs from the river mouth were starting to edge in their direction. If the wind continued as it was, soon the bay would be solid.

Throughout the afternoon the wind rose until it had achieved the piercing shriek of the night before. The rain began again, perhaps not the same downpour, but combined with the spray streaming across from the outer shoreline, it was difficult enough to face. Once again Teora found herself the only passenger on deck, with the calming presence of Palani to keep her company. Together they watched, fascinated, as the storm built.

While the water around the ship remained calm, held still by its blanket of wood, the shoreline of the ocean was another matter. As the afternoon progressed the waves mounted, tossing huge tree trunks up on the shore like matchsticks. Soon a barrier towered along the beach, with the weight of the logs in the water pushing the logs ashore into higher and higher mounds.

"Well, I guess we won't have to worry about the waves breaking over the spit. They seem to be building a marvelous breakwater for us."

"Is that good?"

"Probably. I'm more worried about the anchors. There's a lot of weight on the chains, because of the shifting of the wood. I had the men out trying to push the logs aside, but there's too much pressure. They couldn't budge them, and in the end, we gave up. Damn! I feel so helpless. I wish we could do something."

Teora nodded glumly. "I know how you feel. This inactivity is hard on the nerves. What will you do if the pressure gets too much for the anchor chains?"

"Nothing. We can't haul them in, and I don't want to let them go. Even if the wood piles up a lot and they drag, they'll keep us bow on to the pressure, and the ship is sturdier that way. If we turned sideways, she might crush."

Teora tried to picture it. "If the ship's bottom is curved, wouldn't she get pushed upwards, and ride on top of the logs?"

"Maybe. If there are a lot of logs low in the water, she might. If we get pushed by several high piles above the water line, it will not be good. It helps that the water is shallow here, and the high piles must also be very deep, or they wouldn't float as high. Like icebergs."

"Icebergs?"

"Yes. Huge chunks of ice that float down from the Northern Ocean in the summer. They only show a bit of their top. The rest stretches out under the water. Makes them dangerous. You can run into one before you get anywhere near the part you can see."

Teora couldn't get her mind to accept the idea of a piece of ice that big. She turned to more immediate matters. "But if some big pieces of the Log Jam float in here and run aground, won't that make it safer for us?"

"I suppose it would. Of course, it might make it more difficult to get out of here when the storm is over."

"I hadn't thought of that."

"I did. And several more possibilities, all worse. That's how I got to be shipmaster. I think of all the problems that might happen, and I have a plan to fix each one before it starts."

"You mean you can think of worse things than the ship getting crushed?"

"Oh, yes. If the logs are jammed that tight, the ship won't sink. We'll be able to stay put or walk right off the ship on the logs."

"So, what's worse?"

"Since you're a passenger, and I don't want everyone to panic, I won't go into that."

"I won't tell anyone!"

"Well, then, for your own peace of mind."

"It's worse, not knowing."

He smiled down at her. "No it isn't. You only need to know that the other nasty possibilities are, in my opinion, quite unlikely. If I told you about them, you'd lie awake all night trying to solve them. I know you well enough for that, Teora."

"I might be able to solve one for you."

He smiled, a bit grimly. "It's a poor sailor who dumps his problems on the passengers to solve."

She frowned back. "It's a poor leader who tries to keep all the problems to himself."

He stopped smiling, regarding her. "You're right. I'm going to talk to Yukio. Thanks for the idea." He grinned at her open mouth, then turned and walked out into the storm, back towards the wheel where the bald sailor was keeping watch.

Teora stood staring after him, wondering whether to be angry or flattered. *At least the conversation kept me from worrying for a while.* She stared out at the incredible mayhem of the beach and the solid packing of the wood in the bay and listened to the grinding of the logs against the hull of the ship. Nothing to do except worry. Maybe if she went below, she could forget it for a while.

Inside the hull the grinding of the wood and the protesting squeals of the ship's joints made it difficult to ignore their plight. She found the other passengers as touchy as she felt. The only comfortable spot she could find was down in the hold with Barozon and the dogs.

So, as evening fell and the whistle of the wind gradually increased, she fell into a semi-sleep in the hay next to her Partner, a dog or two curled up nearby.

She was roused several times during the night by feet pounding above her on the deck, and wondered why. *Nothing I can do to help. If they need me, they'll call me.* She let herself drift back to sleep.

As the night wore on, it seemed that the grinding of the wood against the ship's sides got louder, and the protesting creaks of the hull came more often. Again, Teora roused for a while, worried for a while, then left the problem in the hands of those more capable and drifted back to her restless sleep.

She woke slowly to the feeling of overbearing heat and soft pressure on her body. She forced her heavy eyelids open. She was lying in the straw with her back against Barozon's chest and two dogs curled up against her front. In the moment before she pushed them away she became aware of another strange sensation: silence. Sitting up, she listened. No sound of wind. The grinding and protesting of the hull had stopped. Even the roar of the moving Log Jam was gone. Now that she listened, she couldn't even hear the sound of water lapping against the hull.

All three animals groaned but otherwise ignored her as she slid from among them. Climbing the companionway to the deck, she looked out on an amazing sight. Everywhere she turned, her eye fell on a solid mass of timber. Logs, trees, rotten stumps, splintered trunks, growing bushes, every type and description of wood she could think of. It was like a forest flattened by a hurricane. Shoreward, the logs had pushed up against the houses of the town, shattering the old docks. Seaward, the windrow of timber towered above the sandspit that enclosed the bay. The mouth of the river was also crammed, although a slow movement of logs still edged towards the sea. Out on the ocean the waves moved up and down, smoothed by a blanket of wood. Islands, large and small, dotted the expanse. Some had considerable clumps of living trees growing up from them. Opposite the ship, she saw a tumbledown cabin on one of the larger islands, tiny figures moving about near it. At least some of the natives had survived the rending of their habitat.

She looked back at the ship. Completely surrounded by wood, canted over slightly to port, it seemed to be no longer connected to the water. All was completely still. The sails and ropes were all neatly tidied away. Only one sailor was visible. He was coiling a rope, his back to her.

"Where is everyone?"

He turned. "All below, Miss. It was a rough night, and Palani sent them all off watch when the wind died. Left me here to tidy her up."

She surveyed the deck again. "You have done an admirable job."

His dark face split in a jagged-toothed grin. "Thank you, Miss. I couldn't bear to sit still. Seems strange, her not moving."

"I know what you mean. It doesn't seem like a ship at all somehow. How are we going to get her out of here?"

He frowned. "I'm glad I don't have to worry about that, Miss. Unless somehow the wind moves these logs, we wait. There's no way we can move the lot. A couple of high tides might help a lot, though."

"High tides?"

He looked at her as if deciding whether she was joking. "Yes. Tides. You know, when the water goes up and down?"

"Oh, yes, of course. What is the tide at now?"

"It's low. Should be, anyway. I sure hope it is. That would mean a chance of some movement when it rises."

He returned to his work, leaving Teora with some ideas to chew over. She gazed out to the island with the house on it. Sure enough, a smudge of smoke hung over it as if someone had started a fire with damp wood. People, she counted three at least, were moving around the house, hauling chunks of wood, probably doing repairs. *It must be a very large island.* While the water around it heaved with the swells left after the storm, the island itself remained steady. Perhaps it was a bit farther from the river mouth than when she had first noticed it. She watched for several minutes, but could not see any movement.

Getting no more information there, she strolled across the deck and turned her attention inland. Every house ashore had smoke coming from the chimney. People moved about: large numbers of them. Some seemed to be doing repairs, others carrying out their errands like in any normal town. Others sat or stood around in aimless conversation. After a while it occurred to her that some of them were looking out towards the ship. Quite a few of them. As she watched, the crowd grew, and they were definitely all staring in her direction. She called to the sailor.

"What are those people ashore doing?"

"I have no idea, Miss. Cleaning up after the storm like we are, I suppose."

"No, that's not what I meant. Look at them."

The urgent note in her voice brought him next to her immediately. After a moment's observation, he muttered a curse. "I don't like this at all. I don't like all the attention from that lot."

"Should we wake someone?"

"That's for sure."

"Wait." She put a hand on his sleeve as he turned. "They're watching us. If we suddenly start running around, that might set them off."

"That's right, Miss. What should we do?"

"You stay on deck and keep working, but keep watching. See if anyone sneaking off, like they're going to circle us. I'll slip below and get Palani. He can get the rest of the crew."

The sailor grinned again. "Good planning, Miss. You done this kind of thing before?"

She made a face. "Never. But I'm learning fast on this trip."

She slipped below and knocked on the door of Palani's cabin. He was in front of her immediately, fully dressed. Either he had been already awake, or else he had slept in his clothes. "Is something wrong?"

She appraised him of the situation in as few words as possible.

"Good thinking, Teora. Go wake up your people and get them ready for trouble. I'll get the crew organized." He was off down the passageway as he finished, and she hurried to wake her group, Tourantij first.

The soldier, too, had slept at the ready; he was buckling on his weapons belt when he came to the door. He asked no questions, simply told her to have everyone meet in the main cabin.

The quick and concerned reactions of these two men gave Teora some idea of the gravity of their situation, and she hurried at her task. By the time the Haven group and the merchants were assembled, Tourantij had been on deck and conferred with the captain. He looked grim as he faced them.

"This is bad. The townsfolk have lost a lot to the storm. They need supplies, and we have them. We no longer have the ability to sail away. They can walk right out to us and take what they want."

"Could we fight?"

"There's about two hundred of them. We have twenty-five. Standard military statistics say that a well-dug-in defence can handle five to one odds. We aren't dug in well. We have good weapons and the bulwarks of the ship, but our cannons are mostly too low in the hull to shoot over the piles of wood. One of those little islands has pushed right against us like a ramp. They could walk right up it and step over the rail onto the deck."

"Well, Soldier, perhaps fighting is not our best option, then?" The rasping voice of the priest cut into the silence.

Tourantij paused before answering. "What did you have in mind?"

"When I spoke to the women on the dock, they seemed to know enough about our religion to be greatly in awe of it and of myself as Priest. Perhaps a bit of that feeling is present in the men as well. I suggest I go and talk to them."

The soldier nodded. "A good plan. We shall have to confer with the captain, but I suggest you don't go to them. They should come to us. Less vulnerable that way."

"But more confrontational."

Tourantij grinned, his eyes showing no humour. "Bargaining from strength is the trick here. We can rig a cannon to sweep that ramp with grapeshot. Stay on the ship and you'll be safe. You can bargain all you want."

The Priest nodded. "I bow to your experience in such things."

At that moment the cabin boy came panting down the stairs. "They've started out across the logs, Ser Niverdahl. Captain Hamal would like you on deck, if you please, sir."

There seemed to be no need to stay below, and the whole party filed up on deck, spreading out as they arrived. The men from the village were advancing across the logs, working their way over the tangled heap in a widely spaced line. It would take several minutes for them to approach. She also could see that the ramp Tourantij had talked about was truly a problem, with several huge logs pointing at a gentle slope right towards the centre of the deck, close enough that a man might jump across to the rail.

Tourantij's advice was unneeded on that account. Several sailors, under the charge of Yukio, were already lining a small cannon into a position where its fire would sweep the length of the ramp. However, there were several more places where the piled logs allowed access to deck level.

Sailors with rifles were scrambling to positions in the rigging. Her party stood at the foot of the main mast, her Herdsmen and their dogs ranged around her, the priest at her side. Despite these precautions, she knew that the mass of men coming across the logs towards them could fight their way on board, simply through strength of numbers. If they were willing to pay the heavy toll.

A sudden inspiration sent her sprinting towards the companionway. Ignoring the surprised shout of the Priest, she dived down and hurried along to the hold. She slapped Barozon's harness across his shoulders, the years of practice making her fingers fly. Then she led him out of his stall, placed him at the bottom of the ramp, and told him to stay. He seemed calm despite her rush, and she knew that he would be there when she needed him. She hurried back to her position on deck, offering no explanation for her absence. None was needed, as everyone's attention was riveted on the group advancing toward the base of the ramp. When the captain thought they were close enough, he stepped forward, raising his hand in a signal to halt.

"Welcome, citizens of Tanish. What can we do for you?"

The townsmen did not pause, but continued their scrambling approach.

The captain raised his voice. "I must ask you not to come too close to my ship. We are in a difficult position, and my men are nervous. We don't want any accidents."

The attackers were close enough that Teora could see some of them exchanging words, but still they came.

"I will ask you one more time to stop." Again no response, and the captain pointed to a sailor in the aft crow's nest. A rifle banged, and splinters of wood flew from the logs very close in front of the leading pirate, a tall, dark-haired man of middle age. He stopped.

"What kind of a reception is this?" Teora noted the gentility of his accent. "We came to see if you needed any help."

The captain stepped closer to the rail. "You came a bit too well armed for my peace of mind. If you wish to help, I'm sure we will be able to use many strong backs to get my ship out of this mess. We will pay well, in supplies and coin."

The pirate leader laughed. "That sounds like a lot of work to me. If the logs crush your ship, the supplies will be available to any who are there to pick them up. Salvage rights."

"There is no salvage on a ship afloat with a full crew. Especially a crew as strong as this one. We survived the storm last night. I think the worst is over."

"Perhaps, perhaps. On the other hand, you could be here a few months. You would be better to accept our help."

"I'm sure we would. Why don't you come back tomorrow when we have had time to assess the situation? I'm sure we have many things aboard which could be of use to you, should we decide to pay you in supplies for your help."

"And there are other things we could help you with as well, should we choose." The new voice brought the pirate's head around. Goianor stepped up to the rail, staring down at the line of ragged men facing him. "I talked to some of your people yesterday. It seems it has been a long time since you had the benefit of a religious leader. You have children to christen, marriages to celebrate. The Deity does not look with benevolence on the unblessed."

The pirate leader seemed at a loss for words. "Unblessed?"

"Yes, my friend. You seem well enough educated. When was the last time you received the Sacraments of Cleansing to ease your conscience and lighten your soul?"

The Priest was an imposing figure, standing at the rail, his arms outstretched and his robe shining golden in the sunlight. For a moment, Teora thought he was going to pull it off. Muttering erupted among the villagers, and several heads dropped, feet shuffled.

Then the leader laughed.

"Ease my conscience? Lighten my soul? You are a long way from the Haven and the Joined Kingdoms, Priest. Here we have done deeds that would take more than a temple service to pay for." He took a step forward. "No, I think we'll have to come aboard and see what else you have to offer." The men on the logs advanced as well.

The captain slid up beside the Priest. "As I mentioned, you are invited back tomorrow. For the moment, I suggest you stay where you are."

The pirate merely grinned, stepped forward again.

"Not another step, man!"

The pirate's smile widened at the tremor in the captain's voice. "Not even one tiny little step? You wouldn't shoot because I took just this one step, would you? And be responsible for all those nice people getting killed?" A note of gloating slid into his voice. This man was a bully, and enjoying this. "How about this little step? I'm not that much closer, am I?"

The captain glanced at Tourantij. Teora knew that the soldier had no compunction about starting the fight, no matter the outcome, but was searching his mind for an alternative. Well, she could buy him some time at least.

Running to Yukio, she grabbed his arm. "Open the hatch. Quick."

The man glanced at her; something in her voice got to him, and he sprang to obey. Another sailor, seeing what was going on, rushed to help, and Teora thanked the Deity for the well-trained crew, because she could hear hoof-beats on the ramp. The cover slid back barely in time and Barozon charged onto the deck, his horns swinging from side to side as he scanned his new surroundings.

Where are they? Who is making you afraid? Is it these?

The sailors scrambled to the side as Teora swung astride her Partner, knees guiding him toward the rail. The captain and Priest fell back as the bull shot between them, cleared the railing and landed, cat-foot, on the logs of the ramp. Teora, rising to her knees, glared down on the startled men below.

She pitched her voice to carry through the sudden silence. "Perhaps there are other things on this ship that you would not be so anxious to meddle with. The Deity protects all on board, and woe to any who would cross Her!"

The leading group of pirates hesitated and started to slide backwards. Their chief, left suddenly on his own, roared at his men.

"Where are you going, you craven beasts? It's nothing but a bull. A lot of good he'll do them, sliding around on these logs. He'll just get in the way. He'll look much better on a spit over the fire tonight."

This man is the one. He is the only one who could rally this mob to attack. If he was gone...

The though had barely formed when her Partner's back heaved beneath her, and they were storming down the trunk of a huge tree, straight at the pirate chief. Her Herdsmen were close behind, vaulting the rail lightly, their staves held for balance as the Raftsman had done.

The astounded pirate chief waited until it was too late, then raised his sword. His men stumbled in a mob behind him, and he had nowhere to go.

"Don't even consider it." Teora leaned over the lowered horns of her Partner, the anger growing in her. "You had it in your power to help your people. We would have given, and freely. Instead, you would choose to kill, to destroy, to have your own people die. I am not charitable, but the Deity is wise. I do not see that you have any worth, but the Deity is merciful. Lay down your sword and come with me. The Deity grants that you may talk to her Priest. Come."

Staring into his eyes, willing him to obey, she started the delicate task of turning the huge bull on the narrow platform. However, the moment her eyes broke contact with his, and the bull's head turned away, the man screamed and dove forward, sword lancing towards the exposed neck.

For a frozen moment, Teora could do nothing. Then, with graceful and deceptive speed, the huge head swung back. The sword clattered aside from a sweeping horn, and the bull lunged. The sharp horn tip entered the man's stomach, curving up into his chest. Then the sweeping movement of the head lifted him from his feet, and his body flew in a smooth arc down from the ramp, to crash in an ungainly heap on the logs below.

Barozon snorted and stepped forward down the logs. The men in front of him scrambled to get away, the lucky ones sliding down the sides of the ramp. Teora felt the rage boiling in her.

They have tried to kill him! They have attacked the Consort of the Deity!

She could feel the answering rage in the bull.

They have made Her angry. They must be gored and trampled.

Teora struggled with herself. *This must not happen!*

"NO!"

The single word was torn from her. Barozon slid to a stop, balancing precariously on the top log. The men froze in their postures of flight, their necks craning backwards, watching for death storming down behind them.

Teora found her normal voice again. "No. You shall not flee. You shall stay. You have threatened the Chosen of the Deity. Do you know what that means? You have stood and watched one of your own attack the Consort of the Deity. He has paid the price. Do you know that you must pay also?"

The men were turning to face her, mesmerized, unable to pull away.

"You who think you are leaders. Now you know of the price the leader must pay when things go wrong. Come to me and find out if you have it in you to pay. Come forward."

Somehow, three men were drawn from the group. They approached her in terror, their legs shaking, their hands before their faces, but their feet moving them forward. She stopped them with a gesture.

"You three will do. Take them." The Herdsmen darted forward along a lower log and the pirates, relieved to be in human hands, willingly allowed themselves to be pulled towards the ship.

Teora moved Barozon forward another step. She raised herself to her feet to survey the men, still frozen on the logs around the ship. "The rest of you," she held them a moment, then made a graceful sweep of her hand, "may go to your homes. Take that with you and give it a decent burial, out of respect to yourselves. I think you could find a better leader."

This time she stayed facing them until the ragged group, carrying the body of their leader, staggered over the logs towards shore. Then she pivoted her mount and brought him back up the log to the ship.

By this time, she had begun to cool down. The gap between the last log and the ship's rail seemed cavernous, but she fought down her fear and Barozon leaped it handily, his steel-shod feet gouging the deck as he landed. For a moment she sat there, looking around at everyone. They stared at her in silence. She didn't know what to do. She slid down from her Partner's back, her hand brushing his horn in the habitual gesture. It came away sticky, and she realized with horror that blood ran down to the base of the horn and stained the curls over his eye. She gazed at her gory hand and her knees began to weaken. *What have I done? The Consort has killed.* What would be the result of her rash action?

22.   Ritual of Cleansing

A timid hand touched her shoulder. "Lady, there is a ritual…"

She swung at the rasping voice. Goianor bowed his head humbly before her. *What does he want?*

"A ritual, Lady. It is very important." His head came up, and his hand gestured towards the horn, the blood.

"A ritual?"

"A cleansing, Lady. For the soul and the spirit. A death is a terrible thing, even when necessary."

"Necessary." She clung to the word.

"Of course. But still the ritual. Come. Your women will bring you fresh clothing. We will have the salt and the fresh water and the fire brought to us. Come and sit."

It was a tempting thought. Her knees weren't going to hold her up much longer. Sabba took her arm to lead her away. Feebly she motioned to Barozon, to his face.

"The blood must stay until it is cleansed. Come, let your woman help you to a seat."

This extra solicitude brought her back to her senses. Commanding Barozon to stay, she straightened and marched to the offered coil of rope, aware that everyone on the deck was gaping at her. Before she sat, she turned and looked back. Barozon stood, motionless, the blood staining his beautiful head.

But his neck was arched, and he regarded the surrounding humans in cool disdain.

I am strong. I will protect you all. You may rest.

She smiled weakly and turned away.

The ritual steadied her. The soothing words the priest intoned in as gentle a voice as he could, his sure touch as he bathed her hands, holding them in his for a long moment and staring deep into her eyes, made her realize her basic need for someone who would take responsibility, to assure her that all was well. She glanced down at his long, slender fingers and was reminded of her father's hands. She felt a sudden rush of closeness. *After all, here is the only one who understands what I am going through.*

She was going through some kind of change. These occurrences were not normal. She was developing a power over which she had little control. *I need help. I need someone who knows what is going on.* As she sprinkled salt on the bloody deck and helped rinse the red from her Partner's poll, she felt the tension ease from her body.

When the cleansing was complete, she began to lead Barozon back towards the ramp, but was stopped by some commotion up the deck.

It was the native from the morning before. Had it only been a day?

It must be the same one, but more bedraggled, with a bit of rag twisted around his head, showing a dark stain near one temple. He wanted to come aboard, balancing on the ship's rail, jabbering and gesticulating, but the sailors refused him, and two of her Herdsmen stood nearby with their staves ready. Barozon turned with her, and the native went silent, staring at the bull in fascination. Then, without leaving the rail, he went to his knees and bowed his head deeply towards Teora.

"I don't think he means any harm. Let him aboard, Yukio. That is," *I don't have the right to give orders here,* "unless the captain has given any instructions...?"

The sailors sprang aside, and the native, after an uncertain pause, leaped down to the deck. Again he stopped as if, having unexpectedly reached his objective, he wasn't sure how to proceed.

"What does he want, Yukio?"

"I don't know, Lady Teora. Let's see where he goes."

They waited and watched. Where he was going, apparently, was straight to Teora. Slowly and respectfully, he paced forward. Yukio motioned to the two Herdsmen, and they closed in on either side, escorting the man to her. She slid back against Barozon's shoulder, protected by his left horn, and watched the approach.

When the native was close enough but not too close, he knelt again, bowing his body to the deck then gazing up at her. *It must be uncomfortable down there on those hard planks.* She motioned him up. He smiled and arose, stepping closer. Barozon glanced at him without comment. He couldn't be dangerous.

"What can we do for you?"

At her speech, the native nodded vigorously and launched into a string of babble. It was full of hand motions that gave her some idea of what he meant, but not enough. It had to do with her, with him, with the Log Jam, with something ashore, and most definitely, (she shuddered at the graphic detail) with the slain pirate leader. When the man had finished, he stopped and eyed her expectantly. Helplessly, she gazed around at the blank faces nearby. No one had any idea. Then her eye fell on Goianor. He shrugged and smiled.

"The man seems to be thanking you on behalf of his people for something, probably the removal of their greatest enemy. He was very impressed at your power. If I had to guess, I would suggest he is offering himself and his tribe to come under your protection. It could be a dangerous act, but one fraught with possibility. We are not in the business of creating personal cults. However, if these people could be guided in the proper channels of worship, they could be an addition, humble thought they may be, to the Deity's herds."

"And an enclave halfway between Aeru and the Haven, at the mouth of a newly-navigable river, wouldn't do the Temple's influence any harm either."

They both turned to see Palani standing in the companionway, grinning at them. The shipmaster stepped forward.

"I am impressed, Priest, at your understanding of what the man is saying. You caught most of it." He turned to the native and spoke a few words. The man's face relaxed, his smile widened, and he nodded cheerfully.

"I have told him that you have received his message, nothing more. He seems to want little else at the moment. Do you have anything else you wish to tell him?"

He was facing Goianor, but to Teora's surprise, the priest turned to her. "What do you think, Chosen of the Deity? Are you willing to take this burden upon yourself?"

"I don't know. We have a mission; we can't stay here long enough to deal with this. What would you advise?"

The shipmaster laughed and gestured out at the clogged sea around them. "You have a certain amount of time."

Goianor nodded. "We can meet with these people, at least. Surely, they are in need, since their refuge is gone. This is a key moment, when we have the upper hand over their tormentors. If we could establish them temporarily under our protection, we could send them the help they need when we reach home."

Teora was following the Priest's train of thought. "We should talk to the captain and the merchants as well. There are opportunities here for all. If we can make the townspeople realize what is likely to happen in the future, we might be able to get them interested in something other than piracy and plunder."

Goianor nodded again. "Yes, I'm sure they follow this life in part because no other option is given. There will be good people among them. With the proper leadership, who knows what they could accomplish?"

Two weeks ago, Teora would have been surprised to hear these words from the Priest, but now she understood their basic wisdom. *Even if he is only interested in the power of the Temple, it is still reasonable to use the local people, and if it were to their benefit, well...*

She looked at the Priest, a jumble coming clear in her mind. A new town, a new set of converts to the Deity. A new Temple? A new Head Priest? She doubted if he was the right man for the job. But who knew what contacts he had in Aeru? He had been on very friendly terms with the Head Priest back at Coalantha.

While these thoughts were lining themselves up in her head, Palani was translating to the native. The man was nodding so violently that Teora hoped he wouldn't do himself injury. She had a brief thought that here was someone else who might personally benefit from this new situation, but dismissed the thought as being unworthy and cynical. *If there is change, someone has to benefit. We will have to see that if this man gains power, he is the right man to use it.*

Palani finished. The native turned to go, then hesitated and turned back. This time there was no doubt about what he wanted. Teora nodded and edged Barozon forward. The native approached gingerly. Barozon swung his head towards the man and snorted lightly, taking in his scent. The man flinched but held his ground and leaned forward to tentatively touch the sharp left horn, newly cleansed, and then to gently stroke the bull's head. Barozon's eyes closed briefly, a sign of acceptance, and she smiled encouragement. The native nodded deeply, almost another bow, and stepped back.

Turning to Palani, he said a few words, sounding very respectful. Then, with a further bow to Teora directly, he spun and leaped to the rail and was off, jogging across the logs easily, this time headed toward the seashore, where the island with the cabin had stranded itself.

Goianor rubbed his hands together. "That was well done, Teora. Now if we can make as much progress with the people in the town."

He stopped and regarded Barozon, speculatively. "I don't suppose we could get him ashore?"

She considered. "He could make it easily as long as the logs didn't shift. What if he went in a hole and we couldn't get him out?"

Goianor's eyes went to the shipmaster. Palani thought a moment.

"We should be able to check the logs out. I'm sure Tzevi," he nodded towards the departing native, "will be able to help in that respect. He'll be back tomorrow."

Goianor nodded, then turned to Teora. "It is your choice, of course. If you think it is too dangerous, there is no question of proceeding. However, I am considering the effect on our talks if you were there. The two of you."

Teora was unaccustomed to this respectful attitude from the Priest and was also torn by Barozon's need to get ashore and get some exercise. Her own need as well. "Why don't we check over the way ashore in the morning? If we all feel it is safe, we'll do it. Otherwise, I'll come along by myself. For whatever good it will do."

Both men smiled at her, and she wondered what the joke was.

"After what happened today, it will do more than a lot of good. I imagine those people ashore are just about as frightened of you as they are of your Partner." Palani turned and started off along the deck, signaling a nearby sailor to accompany him, and she knew he was back to his real responsibility: the ship.

Goianor touched her elbow. "He is right, Teora. We have come to a crux of our journey, not one which we expected, but one which could be of great help in our quest. However, there is more than that to be considered in today's events. You and I must talk. After you have seen to Barozon, of course."

It was the first time he had ever referred to the bull by his name. Before this, it had always been 'Your Partner' or 'The Consort'. She wondered what had brought about the change, and what she should now be wary of. Then she dismissed that as another too-cynical thought. If the priest was going to treat her better, maybe she could use the new attitude to smooth out the problems in their company.

She mused on this as she allowed Barozon one longing sniff at the shoreline, then led him down the ramp, back to his stall.

When she returned to the deck there were a lot of people around, but no one noticed her. She endured it a moment, then went to

Tourantij and Corquée, who were standing by the rail, looking out to sea. She slid between them. They did not move.

"So suddenly I'm a ghost, and you can't see me?"

Both men relaxed; Corquée grinned. "We weren't sure if you would be talking to us mortals again."

"Mortals? What are you talking about?"

"Lady, when the gods walk among us, we mere humans often don't know quite how to react."

She turned to the soldier. "What do you mean, the gods walking among us? And what's this 'Lady' business?"

He shrugged, then glanced over her head at Corquée. "She's back to normal."

Corquée grinned. "If she hits me, we'll know for sure."

She stamped her foot like an angry bull. "I certainly am going to hit someone if I don't get a straight answer."

The Rider grinned even wider. He laughed, but she could hear a note of hysterical relief in his voice. "She doesn't know. Tell her, Tourantij."

She glared at the soldier, who was smiling also. Then he sobered.

"Teora, you really don't know what you did?"

She held her hands out helplessly. "I guess. I got into one of my states and took Barozon down and confronted that man. It was really horrible that he got killed, but he was the leader. Without him, they weren't that brave."

"He was a brave man, no doubt about it, but a twisted one. His death will be a burden to no one. No, that was a good deed, Teora, and I hope you feel no guilt."

"Not much. The cleansing ritual helped. But I still see that horn slicing into him. I'll probably be seeing that in my dreams for the rest of my life."

The soldier nodded. "It's the same with me. My first killing is still with me, no matter how many others come in between."

"Oh." Her knees were feeling funny again.

"Are you all right, Teora?"

"I'm not sure. What really happened to me?" She reached out and grabbed the rail, tightening her grip on the firm, warm wood, feeling the smooth hardness against her palms. She stood there a moment, then didn't know whether she was pleased or not to hear the Priest's voice.

"What is going on, Teora? Is there a problem?"

"We were just talking, and she turned pale." Tourantij sounded worried, too.

"What were you talking about?"

"Oh. We were telling her about...you know..." Dimly, Teora was surprised to hear at a loss for words.

"You were telling her what happened this morning. I suspect that she hasn't had time to think about that herself, to get it straight in her head. It's very difficult, you know, being used by the Deity. It isn't something that we learn naturally, like walking or swimming. It takes a lot of getting used to. Would you like to come and sit down, Teora?" He took her hand from the rail, and she was struck again at how much the Priest's hand resembled her father's. She looked up at him.

His face was all solicitude. He seemed to be playing no games, making no points against her two friends. *He knows what I'm going through.* She allowed herself to be led to a nearby bench, where Mayna brought her a cool drink. Goianor sat beside her like a mother hen, and the other two hovered close in concern. It was these unnatural attitudes that brought her around the most. She shook herself, sat straighter.

"All right. Something happened. I'm not sure of the details, but that doesn't matter. It happened. It has happened before, but not that much, with all those people watching. I'm not any different. At least not very. I'm getting used to it already, see?" She smiled and held out her hand. It wasn't shaking much. "So don't treat me like I'm made of porcelain. Let's return to the real job, which is getting us out of here as quickly as we can. And also getting these people on shore organized as much as possible."

Everyone seemed relieved, Goianor less than the others. "Quite right, Teora. The captain has been speaking with the three townsmen you selected — or who came forward themselves, if you like — trying to figure out a way of settling them down with the natives. Things are going to change around here, you know."

"I suppose."

"No, I mean in a big way. They tell us that, except for the pileup at the mouth of the river, the Log Jam is completely clear. That means the river is now navigable, probably for a long way. This means water transportation into an area previously inaccessible."

"You mean this is going to become an important seaport?"

"A real boom town. And no shortage of wood to build the new houses."

She glanced at the Priest. *Yes, he made a joke.* He seemed so pleased with himself that she couldn't help but smile back.

"But these people have no experience with that sort of thing. They'll get pushed away, used, abused. The natives will have it bad, of course, but I doubt if the townspeople will fare much better."

The Priest nodded. "It's too bad they lost such a strong leader. No, I take that back. He wouldn't have been good for them. He would have kept all the power to himself and shrugged them off when he didn't need them anymore."

"These people will need leadership."

"Well, there are the three leaders here now. We'll have to see. After all it isn't our problem at the moment. We still have our mission."

The importance of her journey had faded, but now it came back to her.

"Yes. How are we going to get moving again?" She regarded the faces around her.

Tourantij tossed his hands up. "Once the logs disperse a bit, we might be able to find a way out of here. Especially if the villagers are willing to help. If not, we could always head up the new river and go overland to Aeru. That route needs exploring, and we could do two jobs at once. We aren't that far, now, and the livestock would appreciate it."

"Barozon certainly would. You mean we could walk the rest of the way?"

Corquée nodded. "There is a trail. I know the song."

She glanced at Goianor. "Well, it's certainly something to think about."

They all nodded as if she had made a decision. *But I haven't. I was just...*

The talk ran on, moving to provisions, safety, and routes, until she felt distinctly left out.

* * *

244

Later that evening, Teora entered the main cabin and stopped in the doorway. The room, as usual, was crowded. The merchants were at their normal table. Tourantij was chatting with Corquée and two of the Herdsmen. Two more of her people were lounging in a corner tossing the pieces of a set of Bones. By their laughter, she could tell that no serious fortune telling was going on.

She entered to a momentary lull in the conversation, then the noise resumed, louder than before. After a brief moment of uncertainty, she shrugged it off. Out of good manners, she passed the merchant's table first, giving them a polite greeting. They all responded in a like manner.

There followed an awkward pause. They all seemed to be waiting for her to say something, she couldn't think what. Unable to find a polite way to leave, she was stranded there, gaping like a fool. Then Zebulon, the eldest of the three, covered smoothly and started a conversation about the possibility of their getting out of the bay soon. Since no one had any idea of the answer to that question, the subject wound down quickly, but she had time to develop a comfortable exit line.

With her friends at the next table, however, it happened all over again. She stood, regarding them. Their conversation came to an abrupt end, and they all looked at her. *This is getting boring.* She slapped her forehead theatrically, stretched her hands up in exasperation. "What is going on here? Do you all need something to stare at? Don't I get to sit down?"

With a hurried denial, everyone slid around on the bench to make room for her. Too much room.

"So, I need half the bench? Or are you afraid I'll contaminate you? What's got into you all?"

Daegal grinned in relief. "Same old Teora, I guess."

"Why wouldn't it be?"

Corquée took up the challenge, glancing around the table. "Why should anything change? I mean, I have friends who fly all the time. Only thing different, they were born with feathers. Not huge bloody horns.... I mean huge horns..." He stopped in confusion. "I mean..."

She slapped his shoulder. "Oh, I know what you mean. Don't worry about it. It was just something that happened, and it's all right now. And I didn't fly."

"Oh, no, of course you didn't. That huge bull of yours left the deck three horse-lengths from the rail, from a standing start, and landed on a log the same distance from the ship. Not a big log. And you think everything's normal?"

She appealed to the rest. "Come on. You know we didn't jump that far, and we had plenty of room to take a run at it. We practise jumps all the time. At least we used to, before we got cooped up in this dratted ship." She looked from face to face.

"Tourantij, you have a practiced eye. Tell them."

The soldier shook his head slowly. "I don't know, Teora. I've never seen a bull jump like that."

She turned to Daegal. "You have. You've seen us work. You know what Barozon can do."

The Herdsman nodded. "Oh, the bulls can all jump, no question of that. Take Leathad, for example. Long and rangy. Lighter'n most. Fast runner. Now, he could really jump." He nodded again. "Barozon, on the other hand, is a mighty heavy boy. Lotta weight to move around. Not that it isn't all muscle, but you don't somehow expect him to be able to jump very far. Isn't exactly natural."

Teora's voice rose with cutting criticism. "Well, I guess you don't somehow expect him to fly, either, do you? That's not exactly natural!"

There was dead silence; the whole room was listening.

Tourantij cleared his throat. "You see, Teora, that's the point. It isn't natural. But what you did to those men. You had them like you had the wolves. They were stopping and stepping forward and stopping, like you told them. Oh, sure, you did it to that pack of wolves, but two hundred nasty pirates?"

"Right. I knew you had control over animals, but I never heard of anyone who could do it to people. Especially that many."

Teora was relieved at Corquée's matter-of-fact attitude. "Thanks, Corquée. Tell them it's a talent some people have, it's normal."

"Well, I wouldn't go that far. Natural it may be, in some instances. Certainly not every-day-on-the-trail normal."

"Some help you are." She frowned at them. "So, you've decided I'm some kind of a freak?"

The soldier leaned forward, his rough hands flat on the table in front of him. "No, Teora. Not at all. But when someone you know does something completely...well, out of the normal like that, you have

246

trouble calling them buddy and slapping them on the back, you know?"

She nodded, glumly. "I suppose." She tried to find somewhere to direct her eyes.

Then a rattle in the corner signaled a return to the game, and the merchants' voices rose as well. Tourantij started a conversation with Corquée about fodder for the animals for their extended stay. She knew she should be taking part, but she was too depressed. After a moment she stood up and slipped away. It seemed that no one noticed her go, but it also seemed that the conversation got louder as she went down the hallway to her cabin. Maybe it was just her imagination.

When the knock came, she had been sitting on the side of her bunk, staring at nothing, for a long time. The knock came again, a gentle rapping on the door.

"Who is it?"

"Goianor. May I come in?"

Goianor? The Priest had never entered her cabin before. She caught herself glancing around to see if it was tidy. With a snort of self-aware laughter, she got up and opened the door. He stood there, waiting.

"Oh...yes, please come in."

He entered, took the bench she offered him. Having nothing else to do, she sat again on the side of the bunk. He was watching her, a pleasant look, not really a smile, on his face.

Finally he spoke. "You are beginning to realize, now, aren't you?"

She stared at him.

"I heard the conversation back there, in the cabin."

"Oh." She did know what he meant.

"It becomes lonely, at times."

"They'll be back to normal soon. It takes getting used to, that's all."

He smiled wryly, a single slow shake of his head. "Do you think they will?"

"Friends change. You get used to them, if they're true friends you don't let it bother you."

"But relationships also change. It is not every day that one discovers one's friend is a worker of miracles. I do not know if the relationship can ever go back to what it was, after such a revelation."

"I don't work miracles."

"Don't you?"

"No."

"Teora, we were outnumbered ten to one. My diplomacy almost worked, but it did not. I admit that. If they had attacked, many people would have died. Now, I am not so naive as to think you and your Partner flew over that rail. I have been briefed comprehensively on the qualities of you two as a team. I am beginning to believe, though I do not begin to comprehend, the nature of your relationship. I had been told how he reacts when you are upset. Now I see the power of that bond. It enables him to perform far beyond his usual ability.

"It is not that physical aspect of the events which I speak of. It is the metaphysical. For example, when you called to those men to stop, they were being chased by a huge, raging animal and it was astounding that they would actually stop. However, it was possible that they were so frightened of you, and so desperate, that they would obey. That is what everyone on the ship saw. They did not see what I saw.

"It was the men on the other side of the ship who drew my attention. They ran when the others did, they stopped when the others did, they showed the identical fear. Yet those men were down on the logs, Teora. They could not see you; they could not see what you did. They could hardly have even heard your voice. Yet they were as much in your command as the first man in front of Barozon's horns. Think about that."

The Priest had been leaning forward as he spoke, and now he sat back watching her intently.

She thought, as he had asked. "I didn't know that."

"Most of the others don't, either, except perhaps Palani. The shipmaster is a most remarkable man, in case you didn't notice. Ah, but you have noticed."

"I supposed."

"He is the only one who has taken your change in stride. The rest only saw the great leap, the control of those in sight. For them it is enough. For me, I know more, and I have enough as well. Is it enough for you, Teora? Or will you still deny your powers?"

She sat, helpless. "I don't know. It all seemed natural at the time. Something needed doing, no one else could do it so I did it as best I could. Who could do more?"

He smiled. "No one could do more. The point is, no normal mortal could do anything close. Are you ready to accept that it was the Deity, moving in you, giving you powers that are not of this world?"

"Me? The power of the Deity? I always knew that She helped me, gave me strength, that my faith kept me going. But that was in the normal, everyday sense. Anyone who has faith can feel that. This is…this is…"

"Quite different. I know. It is very difficult to accept when it really happens, that one has been Chosen. Oh, certainly, the original ceremony is marvelous, and it feels warm and wonderful to be accepted. This is a harsher reality."

She regarded the older man curiously. "Have you ever experienced this?"

His hands went up in mock horror. "Me? Oh, no. I'm just a Priest, doing the best he can for his Temple and his religion." A faraway look came over his face, softening it. "Oh, I have felt the Choosing, once, long ago, at my own Ceremony of Acceptance. And again, faint shadows of it, when a hint of Her grace has touched some deed of mine."

He shook his head, and she could see sorrow in his eyes. "But never again like that first time. And never like you have." He gazed up at her. "I don't know whether to envy you or not. It is a wonderful thing, I am sure, and one that I aspired mightily to when I was younger. But I have seen the responsibilities that go with it, and now I would not wish it on one as young as yourself.

"My role must be to help you. This is a thing that will happen, whether we want it or not. We must make sure it is a good thing, a task in which I am sure the Deity will aid us. In fact, perhaps I am presumptuous in even assuming that I can affect that part of it."

He glanced skyward with that wry smile, as if he were referring to an old but sympathetic friend. *I wonder if I will ever feel that familiar with my God.*

"What I can do, Teora, in my own small way, is to make this as easy for you as I can. The situation could be difficult for you, and you need only to remember that I am here. It is not necessary, or even desirable, that you lean on me. Some of this you must endure alone. But if you need to talk to someone, need advice, I am here to give what I can. For example, I can warn you right now about Palani."

"Palani? But you just said…"

"Exactly. He is the only one who is taking your changes in stride. This means that he will be the only one treating you normally. There will be a great temptation to spend a lot of time with him. You must remember that he has his own agenda. His goals are not our goals. Therefore, from the point of view of our mission, he could be a distraction, and thus a danger. On the other hand, he could be a good balance for you when you are feeling left out. I only wish you to be aware of the possible outcomes. I would not presume to tell you how to act."

He smiled. "But I have talked enough, and perhaps you would like to be alone. Should I go now?"

It sank in that he was asking her permission, and she nodded. "Yes...ah... thank you, Priest Goianor, for your insight. You have given me much to think about. I will keep in mind your offer." She smiled, one side of her mouth only. "I have no doubts that I am going to be in need of advice sooner or later."

He rose with her and bowed formally, but his smile was a warmer one than she had ever seen on that stern face before. Without another word he left, pulling the cabin door shut softly behind him.

Teora sat on her bunk again, her head spinning. This was a side of the priest she had never seen. Oh, certainly, she had heard echoes of his old, self-centred persona there; she could pick out the references to power and politics. These were so ingrained that they would slant anything he did or said. No doubt his words held a lot of wisdom. And if she was going to have problems with the rest of the group...

Drat them! Can't they just see me as they did before? No, I suppose they can't. And his warning about Palani. Now, that was nonsense. Or was it? I talk with him a lot. And now, if the others are difficult and he isn't? Maybe the priest is right. At least he promised not to meddle with me. That's a change from a few weeks ago. Perhaps there is good in the Priest. She thought of how she had felt when the others, her friends, had been awkward with her when she needed friendly companionship. *Maybe that lonely, hollow ache is something you learn to live with. Maybe that's what turns you into someone like Goianor.* She tried to picture herself after another twenty years of power, leadership and responsibility, trying to deal with a free spirit like Corquée. *Surely I would be able to do better than the priest has.*

She wondered what life would be like in thirty years. Her Partner would be long dead. She had always known this, but it would be hard to imagine life without him. Her place in the Haven would be gone.

She would have to develop other channels, other avenues, other powers. Other friends. Surely she would have her own network of powerful friends by that time. She thought of her mother. How naive she had been. How many influential friends her mother had, how their long discussions must have been much more than the boring gossip they seemed.

She lay back on her bed, thinking. It was not too early to start. The Priest, for example. He was offering...not really friendship, but some sort of association. He was a powerful man in his own milieu. She would be foolish to spurn him simply because of his personal problems. How about Corquée? Would a contact among the Horse People be valuable to her? And Tourantij. *There is something in his past, something in his family, that gives him more than casual importance in Joined Kingdoms politics.*

She rolled to her other side. It was terrible to consider her friends only for what good they might be to her in the future. *Can't you just have friends because they're people you like? Maybe thinking like this is what turns you into someone like Goianor.* She tried to picture him of an evening, sitting around with his friends. *Does he have any? I hope so. I wonder what they would talk about. Power and politics, I'm sure. I hope I'll never be like that.*

Her mind turned to her journey. What would happen at the end? Would she be any use to the people of Aeru? *Surely I will. Why else would the Deity take this much trouble with me?*

Questions with no answers spun through her brain over and over, until finally, restlessly, she slept.

23. The Leaderless

"So, he's just going to jump that again, is he?" Corquée's voice held equal parts humour and awe. "Can he do it when he's not mad?"

Getting off the ship was going to be much easier this time. The sailors had removed a section of the rail, and the only obstacle was the gap between the ship's side and the sloping logs.

Teora glanced disdainfully down from her perch. "He can jump it any time he wants. Besides, he wasn't angry. I was."

"Is there a message there for me?"

She grinned. "Probably." *At least Corquée is willing to joke with me this morning.*

"Are we ready to go?" Goianor stepped out of the companionway, moving heavily in his ceremonial robe and headdress. He regarded the party assembled on deck. The merchants had decided to join them to spy out the advantages. Teora's full group was coming, bringing Spar as well. He was in his usual position close to Barozon's left front hoof, lolling on the steaming deck in the warmth of the sunlight. Four Herdsmen were already spread out among the logs, checking the area. Palani was going along to represent the ship and to act as interpreter. Tzevi waited to guide them: better dressed than usual, with wispy feathers scattered in his hair.

Seeing everyone was prepared, the priest nodded to Teora. "I suppose you should go first. No one wants to be in front of the Consort when he takes a run at that gap."

She couldn't help but smile back. Taking a moment to prepare her Partner, she gathered him in, then launched him at the gap. He cleared it easily, landing on the end of the top log and trotting down it to the main mass of wood, where they stopped to await the guidance of Tzevi. The others filed down more sedately. As Tzevi passed Barozon, he grinned up at Teora and spoke several quick, reassuring words.

"If you are trying to make me feel better, thanks." She gestured towards Barozon, and the native reached out and respectfully patted the thick base of the horn. She tossed a hand towards shore. "Find us a good path."

He understood and started out. They had scouted out an easy path, following the flattest and largest logs, avoiding the pricklier brush piles and higher humps of gathered wood. She gave Barozon his head and he followed Tzevi closely.

Several times the bull refused to proceed. Each time their guide came back and, after checking the logs again, turned aside to find an alternate route. Once they reached what seemed to be a dead end. Teora got down to walk the logs as well. They seemed the same as all the others, but if her Partner refused to place a hoof there, she wouldn't force the issue.

The native considered, jumping several times off the offending log, then nodding in agreement. Then he stepped to the next log and jumped on it. He jumped harder, then turned to Teora and said something which obviously meant "This one's fine."

She nodded and made a jumping motion. He nodded hugely, smiled, and made a larger jumping motion. Then he turned to Barozon and gestured the bull to come ahead. Her Partner immediately made the leap, stopping on the safe logs to glance back at her with a "why aren't you coming?" look. She laughed and took a running start, leaped to his rump from a convenient log and plopped herself into riding position. "Let's go!"

A large party of townspeople waited on the beach. Nearing the crowd, she slowed down to let her group arrange themselves around her. At a gesture from Tourantij, the Herdsmen fanned out ahead, and they all moved to the shore, winding through the farthest logs and out onto the clear beach.

Immediately Barozon's head came up and his feet began to lift. The urge to run spread like fire through Teora's legs and up to her head. With an effort she held it down. "Not quite yet, my friend. Business first."

She kept her Partner under close control as Goianor moved up beside her. Their eyes met, and then the priest started forward. She kept Barozon's nose behind the Priest's shoulder as they approached the delegation waiting for them.

It wasn't much of a delegation. More like a mob. As they came closer, Goianor's voice drifted softly back to her, though his lips maintained their stern, formal mask. "Where are the leaders?"

From her higher vantage point, she could see what he meant. The men, about thirty of the ragged crew she had routed the day before, stood in random clumps in the centre. In a great half-moon around them an assortment of women, children and older folk stood, staring. Near the seaward end of the crowd, a smaller bunch of people milled uncertainly. These were even more poorly dressed than the townsfolk, and Teora decided they must be the remnants of the tribe from the Log Jam.

Goianor stopped. "Best if we let them decide."

The group of men shifted uncertainly. Goianor stood waiting in a patient pose. Gradually three of the men were pushed forward, probably the ones she had captured the day before, and these reluctantly stepped out to meet the Priest. Palani moved ahead to interpret for the natives, and Teora maintained her supporting position. The village men's pace slowed as they neared this small group, grinding to an uncertain halt before they were close enough to talk comfortably. Watching them, Teora suddenly realized what was wrong. She spoke conversationally to the Priest.

"They're terrified."

He nodded. "Let them stay that way. Do them good." He turned slightly towards Palani. "Will they understand me?"

"Of course. It's the natives who might not."

"Good." But the priest did not start talking. Instead, he motioned commandingly, and the men moved forward again. When they again slowed, he motioned them to stop, then stepped forward himself. Teora stayed put this time. None of them was close enough to reach the priest before Barozon or Spar could interfere, and there was no sign of any guns or other weapons.

"Who is your leader?"

A general nudging and hiding behind each other brought no candidate forward.

"So, the man who got you into all this trouble was the only authority here?"

There were several relieved nods, glad to lay the blame elsewhere.

The Priest nodded himself, once, slowly. "This is good. I will talk to you all, then. I will speak to you with the Voice of the Deity, as Her Chosen acted yesterday as the Deity's Hand." He paused for effect, and the crowd shivered.

"You are a poor folk, with a poor living. Still, that does not excuse you from the consequences of your actions. Scavenging and salvage is one thing. Direct piracy is a different matter. An attack on the Consort of the Deity is unheard of!"

He raised his hands, as if to stop their arguments. "I know, the one who performed the act has been punished. The Deity knows that none

254

of you actually did the deed. But he was one of you. Your leader, even. You chose him," his voice rose, and his right hand pointed, swept the crowd, "and each one of you shares the responsibility for his sacrilege!"

Everyone tried to hide behind everyone else in a slow shuffle. The Priest held his position until they settled, fixing the last movement with a fierce eye.

"You have learned how such blasphemy is rewarded!" Then he relaxed, lowering his hand. "But you have much to learn about the Deity. You must learn that she also has a forgiving side. The sharp horns of her Consort are balanced by the soft skin of her newborn Calf. The Deity is not unforgiving. She understands the weaknesses of mortals. If you come to her in true penance, she will not turn you away."

The Priest smiled, turning with a swirl of his cloak to sit on the end of a large log nearby. "Come, my people. Come and talk with me. Learn of the Deity, Her power and Her gentleness. Teach me of your needs, your desires. You will see that She will not leave you helpless in the face of this great disaster."

The leaders moved forward hesitantly, the crowd following even more slowly.

What an acting job. What crowd control. I wonder if I'll ever be able to do that. Teora patted Barozon's neck. *Or if I ever want to.*

As the leaders of the group began to press forward, speaking at first haltingly, then faster and with more enthusiasm, she lost track of what any individual was saying and began to scan her immediate surroundings.

Her eye was caught by the small group of natives, huddled forlornly together. Checking to see that Goianor had the situation well in hand, she nudged Barozon towards the tattered group. They were mostly women, with a few men of varying ages and three or four young children rounding out their number at about twenty. Tzevi was the only one who did not shrink back as she approached. Instead, he stepped forward, greeting her gravely with his neck-stretching bow.

She made a polite gesture in return, drawing a brief silence. What could she say that he could understand? Well, he had communicated with his hands yesterday.

"Is this all that remains of your people?"

He seemed to understand her large, slow gestures, and responded in kind. He made her understand that many of his people, perhaps three times this number, were still gathering their belongings together from the remnants of their homes. Another twenty or so were missing; four were known to be dead. She nodded in sympathy, making the sign for Blessing the Departed as she did so. To her surprise, he repeated the sign, as did several of his people.

Intrigued, she tried to question him about his religion, putting in as many of her own symbols as she could. Several were familiar to him. He responded with some of his own. Most of them were strange, but a few were similar to those used by the Deity's Priests. Perhaps this man was the spiritual leader of the natives, rather than, or perhaps as well as, their political leader. After a moment they ran out of mutually understood signs, and stood in silence, smiling at each other with newfound understanding.

A general movement in the larger group drew Teora's attention. The audience finished, Goianor was rising from his impromptu throne and starting her way. She turned Barozon to face him.

"And what of these others, Chosen of the Deity?"

She understood the reason for the formality, but stepped closer to explain more quickly what she had discovered. The Priest raised his eyebrows skeptically, but a quick exchange with the native, assisted by Palani's translations, convinced him as well.

He turned and spoke quietly to the others of his party. "This is an interesting situation. It seems that the natives have a rudimentary grasp of our creed, and probably follow it more faithfully than the townspeople."

"A balance of power, Priest Goianor?"

The Priest smiled. "As usual, Ser Niverdhal, you grasp the political niceties. Yes, I see a possibility here. The townspeople have the power of numbers and civilization. The natives have the possible advantage of their religious faith. Their leader's obvious comfort with the Consort and his Partner has raised the man's status considerably in the eyes of his former enemies. Since we must leave here soon, this is perhaps the best that can be achieved."

Tourantij pursed his lips. "I can't see such a delicate balance lasting. The natives are too primitive, have too many years of powerlessness behind them. As soon as the memory of Teora's support begins to fade..."

The Priest nodded. "True. The ascendance of any leader of quality among the townsfolk would be the deciding factor. But I do not see any such person in their group. And while we must leave soon, we must also send Temple representatives back immediately."

The soldier grinned. "Consolidate your gains before they slip away."

The Priest nodded, missing the humour. "Exactly." He glanced around, noting the position of the ship, and Teora knew what he was thinking. The main competition for power in this new place would be the merchants. Goianor was torn between leaving quickly, to get back before the merchants had a chance to bring more of their own support, and staying to see that they didn't set up their own power base. She had only an academic interest in this question, and she was losing that interest. Barozon shuffled beneath her, and she calmed him automatically.

However, the priest had noticed. He smiled up at her. "Well, you have your wish. You are ashore. I am certain your Partner could use some exercise, and these people would be grateful for some entertainment." The smile hardened. "They would also benefit from a demonstration of power."

Teora shrugged, then grinned. Barozon's feet began to shift as her mood reached him. She was going to Dance; if Goianor could use it to his advantage, good. It was enough to feel her Partner's muscles rolling under her, gathering speed along the path. As they warmed up, she turned in a wide circle, searching for space to work. The only spot with good footing was in the middle of the townsfolk. They scattered as Barozon's bulk moved towards them. Vaulting to the ground, she sent him circling, defining their space. Then she began her training routines. Nothing special, nothing exacting. They had been cooped up aboard ship too long, and she wanted everything to go smoothly.

They soared through the patterns, and she allowed their tempo to increase gradually. She began to feel the exhilaration grow as her Partner's movements began to blend more precisely with hers. She moved into one of her performance routines, giving it all the feeling and grace that she would have on a Games Day with thousands watching. Without knowing how she knew, she was aware that she was performing above her usual standard. Barozon's speed was faster, his footing surer. His back felt as wide and flat as the main street in the Haven, and she flipped and rolled down its length as easily as she could have walked that street.

As the routine finished, she brought her Partner through his final turns, adding a double rollout to her dismount, knowing that she would land it perfectly. Her feet hit the ground precisely, and she held her pose, waiting in a pure cone of silence, as the dust settled slowly away from her. For a moment she was disoriented. Instead of the roar of applause she half-expected, she heard a scattering of enthusiastic handclaps, a whoop from Corquée, and the high laughter of children.

Coming back to reality, she became aware of her audience. The faces were universally awed and delighted, especially those of the natives. She bowed formally to them and was pleased to note their correct response. *Well, that will help Goianor's plans.*

Relaxing, she walked over to her friends. Tourantij was grinning broadly, Corquée was still bouncing. Palani was standing still, his jaw agape. He came to himself and snapped his mouth shut as she neared. The merchants seemed suitably impressed; Goianor looked smugly satisfied.

"Is that what you had in mind?"

The Priest nodded. "Much more than I had hoped for, Dancer. I begin to understand your reputation even better."

Palani pulled himself together to speak. "I don't know much about animals, but I didn't think you could do things like that."

Corquée slapped him on the shoulder. "You can't. No one else can. Just Teora."

The Priest spoke to the shipmaster, but loud enough that all could hear. "Do you begin to understand what it means to be Chosen of the Deity? Even Teora, talented though she is, could not achieve such artistry without Her help. Even Barozon, penultimate of his breed, could not be so nimble, were he not Consort of the Deity." His voice took on a fuller tone. "I give Praise to the Deity. May her works be many, may Her people be fruitful, may Her Herds multiply."

The murmur of responses was enthusiastic from those who knew what to say, and dutifully awed from those who wished they did. Tzevi's voice rose above the rest, and Teora could again see the eyes of the townsfolk turning to him. She hoped he could carry it off, small, ragged man that he was. She wished somehow she could help him.

But she had done her best. *Whatever happens here is outside my power. At least, I think it is.*

On their way back to the ship, the priest took advantage of the spread of the party to speak to her privately. "You realize that we must leave immediately."

"I thought we might."

"Yes. It seems it is faster to go by land than by sea from here. It is a more rugged journey, but worth the trouble. We must move while the merchants are trapped."

"Why don't they travel overland themselves?"

"They are not politicians. The prospect of power does not tempt them enough that they will leave their goods. They are more of an incidental threat, here."

"Aren't you worried about what they might do, left here with nothing else to worry about?"

"To some degree. If one of them is unscrupulous enough, he could use these poor souls to create a very dangerous power base. That is why I want your help."

"My help?"

The Priest smiled a bit. "Yes, Chosen. You have power that perhaps you have not realized. If you were, for example, to ask someone to keep an eye on the merchants, and to make sure nothing untoward happens..."

"Palani?"

"One possible choice."

"Why would he listen to me?"

The Priest shrugged. "I could give you any number of reasons, Teora, but the best one is the one you think up yourself."

She regarded him. "Is this some kind of a challenge?"

He smiled again, nodded. "You are perceptive. Yes, I have decided that you must develop political skill to go along with your growing religious power. If you could do that, your potential would be greatly enhanced." He paused to wait while she joined him on the next log. "Not that your potential is not great, as it is. I simply feel that you might find my greater political experience useful."

She thought a moment. Her first response had been to reject his casual assumption that he could take over her life in any way. But since the attack on the ship, she needed his experience in these matters. Making up her mind in that instant, she smiled over at him.

"I will accept your challenge. I will find some reason for Palani to watch the merchants."

She stopped to mount Barozon for his final climb to the ship's rail and the priest followed, a satisfied smile creasing his face.

24.   The Dusty Road Again

It was necessary to find her opportunity sooner than she had expected. At supper, Goianor announced his plans to leave the next day. He was immediately immersed with Corquée and Tourantij in a discussion of routes, ways, and means. Feeling pressured by the short time frame, Teora wandered up to the deck to think. How was she going to slip something as important as this into a casual conversation? But Palani was there ahead of her, leaning on the rail, staring at the logs that imprisoned his ship. Hoping for inspiration, she joined him.

"Going to clear a path with the power of your stare?"

He smiled but did not turn away from his study. "Sort of. I can see several weak points. If we were to hire some of the village men with poles and boats and start at the outer end where the logs are loose, we could work an open lane for the ship in a few days."

"Using some of the natives for their knowledge?"

He smiled down at her. "They seem to have become your special charges."

"They need me. Their home has been destroyed."

"No argument. I just wonder how you're going to protect them, if you're leaving so quickly. Is one of your people staying?"

She shook her head. "We have only enough in our party to complete our mission. My Herdsmen are not religious leaders, and the other three are needed. Come to think of it, we aren't too worried about them after the ship leaves. It is while you are here that the danger lies."

"The merchants? I know them well. They are not political opportunists. Nor is Captain Hamal."

"Perhaps not. Still, that is the danger we see."

He was silent, and after a moment she looked up at him, deciding to take the chance. So much for diplomacy.

"What would it take to get you to watch out for them?"

He grinned down at her. "Have you thought of just asking me?"

She was stunned. For a moment she had nothing to say. Finally she stumbled, "Just like that? Why?"

He laughed. "Don't worry, Teora. I'm not falling under your spell, willing to do anything you ask without a thought of my own."

Her smile was full of relief, but then she felt herself blushing. "I admit the thought did flash through my mind, although I know it shouldn't have."

"I'm much too old for that sort of thing, and my wife wouldn't approve." Then he sobered. "But I will answer your question. I will do what you ask, and simply because you ask it. I remember the first day on the ship. You said that we should pay more attention to the spiritual part of our lives. At the time, I thought it was rather naive of you. I have since seen the effect your belief has had on you. I have seen the power growing in you, and I have had a change of attitude." He grinned to lighten the mood.

"Others might say I'm hedging my bets, but anything I can do to help you will be done for spiritual reasons. Besides, I always did have a weakness for the underdog. The people ashore here, all of them, would benefit from some good leadership, and the Temple has a better chance of giving them that." He looked around. "Unless, of course, they send your Priest back."

Teora was startled to find herself jumping to Goianor's defence. "Oh, he has his problems. But he is very adept at political maneuvering. He could handle this."

"Do you really think so?"

She thought a moment, then sighed. "No, not really. Well maybe. He has little trouble dealing with people he can order around. Or with his superiors. It's only people who threaten him that set him off."

"And no one might do that for quite a while around here. I see your point. Anyway, I will keep an eye on things while we are here, not for your Priest, but for you and for the good of those who need it."

"And for the good of your own soul."

He grinned. "Why not? I could always use some credit in that area."

The next morning, she found a quick moment to give Goianor the gist of the conversation. He nodded, satisfied.

"Your power grows, Teora. I could not have persuaded him so easily. Now what he does is good for us, good for the people ashore, and good for himself as well. It is a happy solution you have created. Well done."

She returned to her preparations in a glow of pride. She packed her two bundles and brought Barozon on deck.

Following the Consort's leadership, the horses negotiated the frightening span of the gangplank the sailors had improvised and began picking their way across the logs. Since Barozon outweighed them considerably, there was no worry about them safely following his path from the day before.

Soon Teora's party was assembled on the beach. Many of the ship's company had come to see them off. The townsfolk were all there, as well as the natives. In the milling press of people, Teora found herself next to the bald sailor. He caught her sleeve casually and slipped something into her hand.

"In case you get caught without your big friend, here."

She held it up. It was a dagger, a beautifully etched sliver of metal with a razor edge and a carved ivory handle. His gesture indicated that the fine leather straps on the sheath could be used to attach it to various concealed places on her body. She laughed nervously, then laid a hand on his arm. "I don't know what to do with it, Yukio, but it's very beautiful. Where did it come from?"

He ducked his head, blushing. "I bought the blade. The handle's my own work."

She saw the fine craftsmanship with new appreciation. "Well, I still think it's beautiful, and I will always remember that you gave it to me." She reached out and squeezed his roughened hand.

He smiled and reddened further, then nodded a brief farewell and shrugged his way through the crowd. When she swung up on Barozon, the sailor's bulky figure was trudging over the logs back to the ship.

Palani had a gift for her as well, a beautiful piece of silk, deep blue, shot with a green tinge that seemed to move as the light played on it. "For you to remember the sea."

She held it against her face, liking the cool smoothness. "It's beautiful!" She thought a moment, then grinned down at him. "Won't your wife mind?"

He grinned back. "Not her colours. I bought it a while ago. Couldn't resist it, then didn't know what to do with it. You can see why I'm not a merchant. Very poor business practice."

"And you were saving it for a special occasion. Thank you so much." On impulse, she leaned down from her riding harness and kissed him lightly on the cheek. As she sat back upright, she noticed

Corquée, already mounted, watching her seriously. She grinned and winked at him, then returned her attention to the sailor.

"And don't let your wife know you've been giving gifts to young girls." She let her voice carry a bit, and several people nearby laughed.

Palani raised a hand in farewell. He spoke softly, but she could read his lips as he turned away. "Don't worry." She nodded her thanks.

Corquée pushed his horse up beside her, his demeanour cheerful. "Enticing older men for their riches now, are you?"

She finished stowing the cloth in her luggage, then swung the pack against his shoulder as she tucked it away. "Yep. Got 'em all waiting in line to give me precious gifts. When are you going to be old enough?"

His lip curled in an exaggerated snarl, and he turned towards his position at the front of the line, his mare's hooves dancing a step. She could tell by the set of his shoulders how good he must feel, back in his position of responsibility again after these inactive weeks. She realized with a twinge of guilt that she had been ignoring him. No doubt that would change, now.

She was smiling softly to herself as Goianor mounted, then spoke a ritual phrase or two. Tzevi slipped to the front of the crowd and responded with phrases of his own, some of them correct, some rather strange, but no one outside her party could tell the difference.

Then Goianor signaled, and Corquée started off. As she passed Tzevi, he bowed, then reached up with a rough bundle in his hand. Mindful of his need for status, she stopped Barozon and took the gift with ceremony, touching his shoulder with her hand and inviting him to pay his respects to her Partner. She could see the crowd's awed response at such familiarity, and the childlike pleasure on the native's face. When she would have opened the package, he stopped her, indicating that some mystery was involved, that she should open it privately. She nodded, playing along, and he smiled hugely, making his deep bow as she departed.

Smiling in return, she followed the Priest's upright form out along the riverbank, her Herdsmen lining out behind her, their dogs ranging happily on either side.

It was good to be moving again, even if her path was closely hemmed in by trees. They were bigger trees than she had ever seen, with deeply scored bark and thick, sharply angled branches. Tangled underbrush filled the spaces between the trunks, and a myriad of shrill voices showed where the birds and insects went about their tiny lives. Used to the open plains, she felt choked in by the lack of view, but fascinated by the hundreds of life forms the river water supported. The trail was narrow, winding through the trees, ducking mud holes and fallen trunks.

She was still holding the native leader's present in her hand. *Surely this is a private enough spot to open it.* Wondering what the mystery was, she hefted the package. It felt long and heavy. Slowly she pulled back the wrappings. When the object was completely exposed, she gave a whoop of laughter, then glanced around quickly to see if anyone had noticed.

Now she understood the native's caution of privacy, and she appreciated his perception. Her present was a large beach pebble, worn and sanded smooth by the action of the water. However, in this case the random actions of the waves had sculpted the rock into something uncannily representing an intimate part of a bull's anatomy. She giggled as she wrapped it up, imagining the reaction of her companions to such a gift. Goianor would probably understand. All the Dancers had been shown, in a secret room in the Temple, a series of ancient fertility symbols, many of which were as crude and graphic as the one she held. Tourantij would be embarrassed, and she was beginning to think that Corquée would be so offended that he wouldn't talk to her for a week. Very strange. She was going to have to be careful what she said and did when she met his people. She tucked the charm safely away and paid attention to where they were going.

Soon the trail skirted a swampy area, climbing along the side of the river valley. Only a short distance from the life-giving water the trees faded out, leaving short desert scrub with tufted grass. From this higher perspective she could see the river winding up ahead, its newly scarred banks piled with driftwood. As far as the eye could see, this watercourse had been plugged from bank to bank with logs. No more. Now the freed waters, still streaked with brown bleeding from the freshly torn sandbars, rippled in the sunlight, dashing around corners, twisting over shallows, tumbling and tearing at the scattered pieces of wood and floating islands that remained.

As the day wore on the banks closed, gradually choking in the wide, lush riverbanks until Barozon's metal shoes were clattering more and more over bare rock, and Teora could look straight down past his left shoulder to see the water racing a few lengths below.

With a start, she remembered Tourantij's problem, and glanced around to see if he was reacting. She was vaguely disappointed to see him up ahead, riding behind Corquée, chatting freely. He glanced back, saw her watching him and waved briefly, then continued to ignore her.

Well, that's progress, I suppose. Perhaps he's cured. I'll have to talk to him about it.

Later in the day the banks of the river lowered again, and soon they dismounted to water the animals where a long spit slanted out downstream from the bank. The surface of the gravel was slashed and scored as if a huge battle had taken place. Even this far from the ocean the river had recently been covered with wood.

They camped in a nearby grove of trees, the same variety as the larger ones near the coast but lacking the advantage of lush soil. The undergrowth was much thinner as well, and the insects that had been bothering everyone were blown away by a dry breeze coming from inland, ahead of them.

Tired from the unaccustomed exercise, the whole camp was quiet before the sky was completely dark. For a while Teora lay, feeling the strangeness of sleeping in the open again, in her tent, where the walls moved but the floor stayed still. Then the sighing of the wind in the leaves blended in her memory with the rushing of water against the side of the ship and she slept deeply.

* * *

The next afternoon they forded the river soon after eating lunch. They found a wide, easy crossing, with the water hardly reaching past the horses' knees. She persuaded Corquée to let them stop in the middle, and dismounted to let Barozon have a good splash. She stood, waist-deep in the cool water with her packs over her shoulder while Corquée looked on, dry and amused, from his saddle.

"What is the trail like from here? Any really dangerous spots?"

"None that I know of. I have never approached Aeru from this direction, but I know that the land gets drier and drier as we go north. There is a small range of mountains, but only narrow streams."

Teora grimaced. "I'm not interested in another desert."

He grinned in sympathy. "No deserts like that one. If the song is right, I'm sure we will camp with water every night."

She turned to him. He had spoken of this before. "Song?"

The Rider nodded. "For my people, every trail has a song. Each day's travel has a verse. We learn these songs from childhood. That way, everyone in the tribe knows all the paths of our territory. The better educated know all the main trails of the Joined Kingdoms. You should hear the one about the high road through the old Emperor's City. Quite amusing. The Curicuiriari don't have much use for big buildings, as you might imagine."

Teora considered this as she rode along, her damp shirt drying quickly in the heat of the afternoon. Her thoughts sent her to Tourantij, and she pushed Barozon alongside the soldier's horse. "Tell me, how do the Riders get along with our people, you know, the Aerans?"

"Oh, quite well, especially lately. In the old days, they held apart. The Herdsmen on the ground, the Riders on their horses. If the Aerans needed any riding done, they would hire a Rider or two."

"But that is changing?"

"Yes. Even people like Goianor have learned to ride. Some of the younger Aerans find it quite romantic to sweep across the range on a galloping horse. Also quite convenient. They spend less time travelling to the parties, and more time enjoying themselves."

"Do I detect a note of censure?"

He glanced over at her. "I don't want to offend, but yes, you do. Those youngsters would do a lot better learning the ways of their people instead of galloping off all over the place."

"I'm not offended. I have been sent to help these people, and any information you have will aid me. Is this a problem? Do they drink too much, or fight or steal?"

"Not much. I know all young folk will race around some. But this group doesn't seem to be settling down. And that could be a problem."

"Why?"

"Because they aren't running the ranches. The work is being done more and more by the Riders. At the moment, the Horse People are only hired workers. But I see a time in the future when, if the Aeran young folk have not learned to be ranchers, the Riders will be taking their places, making their decisions for them. After that, it is only a matter of time."

"Until the Aerans start losing their ranches."

He nodded. "And the Riders start taking them over. That would be a shame. It would not be good for the Riders, either. Their culture would not survive the transition."

"But there is change everywhere. Cultures, like people, must adapt to survive. Think of what is happening back in the Joined Kingdoms. With the new steam ships, the old sailing navies are hopelessly outclassed. We even notice it, protected as we are in the Haven. After all, here I am, aren't I?"

The soldier nodded. "Yes, here you are. What are going to do when you get to Aeru?"

She considered a moment. "I'm not completely sure. First thing, I know, is to arrange a breeding program for Barozon. They'll only have to check their Heritage Charts, look at their bloodlines, to know where to place him. From what I gather, even a random breeding would be better than what they have."

He stared up at her, and she wondered whether his exaggerated shock was completely feigned. "The famous breeding techniques of the Haven have fallen so far?"

She answered lightly. "In any random act, the Deity has a better chance to do Her will."

He nodded, laughing. "I know when I've overstepped the mark. You don't have to quote Scriptures at me."

Teora had a sudden thought. "How long have you lived in Aeru?"

"I didn't live there. I was in Aeru when this job came up, and they asked me to take it. I was there for another reason completely."

She waited, unwilling to pry.

"The Magali. Their power is growing in the north and west. Since Aeru has no real army, they wanted me to give them some ideas."

"What about the Curicuiriari? Wouldn't they fight if the Magali attacked?"

"Yes, but it wouldn't do the Aerans much good. The Riders are good fighters, but they are too mobile. Their technique is to hit and retreat, hit and retreat, drawing their enemy out over the plains, then rushing in from the side to harass the strung-out armies, cut their supply lines. Many an invading army has found itself lost and hungry in the plains, soon to be cut to pieces by the Riders."

Teora shuddered. "I see. But it wouldn't help the Aerans, because they have to stay in one place."

"Exactly." He rode a while in silence.

"The answer to your question is that I was there for about three months."

"Long enough to get a feel for their situation?"

"If you mean, do I have the solution to their problems, no I don't. But I was there long enough to know a bit about how things are done."

"Good. Will you advise me?"

The soldier turned in his saddle, stared at her. "Advise you?"

She snorted in frustration. "Yes, Tourantij. Don't be modest. You have many years of experience with this sort of thing. I have almost none. As we have seen from Goianor, I cannot depend on the Priesthood for information. Nor should I. If they are the problem, I must treat information I get from them very cautiously. An outside viewpoint would be very helpful. If you wish, I'm sure I can arrange for you to be paid as a sort of advisor or something. It will have to be unofficial, though, and you will have to wait till we get back to the Haven to get paid. I doubt if the Aeran Priesthood would like the idea."

He threw back his head and laughed. "Much as they like me, I doubt if they want me prying into their affairs. No, Teora, I will not need pay. I would be pleased to help you in any way I can. No one will be suspicious, since I will be waiting for the job of returning you to the Haven when and if you finish here."

She nodded, satisfied. "I will be talking to you more often, then. I need to get ready for the task ahead."

They rode along the riverbank for the next two days, and Teora's eyes kept wandering off to the east. She could see nothing because of the trees along the river. And she wasn't the only one. As it had done in the desert near the Rock, Barozon's head kept swinging off line, and only the river at his side kept him from angling to the right. Finally, she whistled and flagged Corquée down. He waited patiently until she came up to him.

"What's off to the east there, on the other side of the river?"

"Nothing special. More dry land, I guess, and the mountains farther east."

"Are you sure?"

His eyes took on a vacant look, and his lips moved soundlessly. Then he shook his head. "The song has nothing about the other side of the river. Just that the trees are bigger here. At least that checks out."

She told him about the pull and Barozon's reaction. Immediately he stepped his horse out of line. "I could do a bit of scouting." He jogged back for a word with Tourantij, then splashed across the river and up the bank and disappeared into the greenery on the other side.

He did not return for so long that Teora was beginning to worry. Finally, late in the afternoon, a splashing in the river ahead told them that the Rider was approaching. He passed the Herdsmen and shouted cheerful instructions as to how far the evening's camping spot would be, then joined Teora again.

"Well, I assume you found something interesting, or you wouldn't have been gone that long."

His eyes were puzzled. "Interesting! Certainly. I had no idea it was there, and I wonder if anyone else did, either."

"What was there?"

"All that grassland."

"Grassland? Come on, Rider. Give me the whole story."

"On the other side of the river there is a huge expanse of grassland. As fertile as Aeru, easily. It reaches all along the side of the mountain range, there, and runs off to the south, out of sight. I rode into it until I got up onto a little hill. Farther south, it seems to get smoother and drier, with no green showing. Not surprising for this time of year.

"But the west slope of the mountain is quite amazing. There is scattered forest, and the grass is still green in the openings between the trees. I didn't get close enough to get a good view, because it was time to return to the group."

"You mean that there is a bunch of good grazing land, right over there?"

"Yes. Near the river and up the foothills it would be fine for the cattle. The land to the south would be good for my people. Very open and level. I don't know why the Aerans didn't stop here. They must have passed close by on their way north."

As they ate supper that night, Teora had the Rider recount his experience to the rest of the company. This time Goianor had the answer.

"The Aerans on the Great Trek passed to the east of that mountain range. I know from our history that they found a great desert there and almost perished from lack of water. It was only because they met some of the Curicuiriari who showed them water holes that their Herd survived. It was the beginning of the long friendship we have had with the Riders. But it is ironic to note that, had they passed a few miles to the west, they would have missed that terrible time."

Teora was scratching aimless patterns in the ground with a stick. "And they might have stayed there and not met the Curicuiriari at all. And they would have been closer to the Haven and might not have become cut off."

Tourantij nodded. "The town at the mouth of the river might have become more important, as well. A lot of things might have been different. On the other hand, those things could still come to pass."

Teora's head jerked up. "What do you mean?"

"You should be telling us. You're the one who sent the Rider out."

Teora paused a moment to listen to her feelings. "I don't know. Now that my curiosity is satisfied, the pull I felt is gone. It's as if the Deity wanted us to know the land was there and now we can go on. It's something that will have to be investigated at another time."

The others nodded, satisfied, and the subject was dropped. However, Teora stretched her sleeping robe under a tree, and late into the night her thoughts swirled with possibilities.

25.   The Ultimate Enemy

Three days later the trail left the river and wound over some low hills: hot, dry and unwelcoming. Then it looped down into another valley, with more trees reaching out to meet them with welcoming shade. The sunlight falling through the leaves left a cool, dappled, pattern on the trail, and Teora's dry skin felt soothed by the moist air.

She was jolted from her pleasant doze by a scream that tore out of the woods to their left. Corquée plunged among the trees, two of her Herdsmen behind him. Spar and another dog raced ahead. Tourantij, one hand on his pistol butt, controlled his dancing horse with the other hand, his eyes scanning the greenery in all directions.

The scream came again, high and frightened, the cry of a child in terror. Without her conscious command, Barozon jerked his head to the left and surged his ponderous weight forward. The Herdsmen who had clustered around him split apart in consternation, then stumbled in his wake as he picked up speed, dashing small saplings out of his way, whipping Teora's face with leaves.

Then she could see again. Barozon had halted at the edge of a rough clearing. Right in front of them a massive brown form was hunched down in the undergrowth. It reared up, head high, massive paws spread: a bear. Its broad head rose higher than Corquée as he and Samira danced aside from their headlong charge. The animal's snout swung, questing, and Teora could see a small, huddled form at its feet, a bright blue shirt stained with blood.

The bear dropped to all fours, circling to a defensive posture behind its victim, cruel jaws opening. As Samira pranced in again, the bear dashed forward, stopping when the horse retreated, and the dogs made quick rushes from either side. Again the bear turned to its prey, jaws closing on flesh, and Corquée charged, not directly, but swinging past at a gallop.

Teora could not see what he did, but when his horse pulled up and pivoted, a rope stretched taut from the bear's neck to the twin saddle horns, jerking the beast off balance and away from the torn creature it had attacked. The bear regained its balance with frightening speed, lunging back against the rope, but the horse stood stiff-legged, and the rope held firm.

Corquée rose in his stirrups and shouted frantically at the child. "Run! I can't hold him. Run!"

A blonde head came up, blood glistening in the sunlight. Hands outstretched to either side helplessly.

"I can't see!"

"Run anyway. Run away!"

The figure rose, stumbled two steps and fell heavily. The motion attracted the bear, and it surged forward. The horse jumped sideways, pulling the bear off balance again. The creature rose to its full height once more, staring along the drooping rope towards the man and horse.

Corquée said something in a quiet voice, probably a curse. The bear was figuring out what was going on. She had heard the Rider's stories about lassoing bears, but knew that several riders were needed. In a moment this bear would stop fighting the pull of the rope and attack the horse and rider.

Before the bear could move, Corquée was shifting again, ducking his horse behind the only tree in the clearing, then pulling to the side. When the bear charged, the horse pulled back, and the great beast came up hard against the rope, jerked sideways towards the tree. The bear, growling fiercely now, lunged again and again, each time stopped by the rope. The tree, only a sapling, bowed beneath the strain, and Teora could see the trunk bending as the roots began to give.

The bear, realizing the futility of its attack, turned to snap at the rope, but Corquée was ready, setting the horse backwards so that the bear was jerked off balance again.

Again the bear changed its attack, heading for its original victim, stretched motionless in the brush. This time the pull of the lasso could only move the bear towards the child, and Teora could see Corquée frantically trying to back his horse through a screen of brush, unable to tighten the rope fast enough.

Then Tourantij was there, between the charging fury of the animal and its helpless victim. The big pistol in his hand barked repeatedly, but the bear bored forward. Then the pistol clicked, its bullets expired, and the soldier braced himself for the impact of the charging giant, his raised sword puny against the claws of the beast.

All this had happened in moments, and Teora had no time to think. Then she was aware of an immense force building beneath her. It was an emotion that she had never felt from Barozon before, a surge of outrage and uncontrolled anger. *Enemy! Attack! Gore!* To her horror, the bull bolted forward. Nothing she could do could stop him in his headlong charge towards the raking claws of his hereditary enemy.

For a frozen moment she held the whole scene in her mind: the bloody child on the ground, Tourantij standing bravely in front of the bear. Then her eye caught another movement. A lithe black form was creeping up on the bear's right side, legs bunched to spring.

"Spar!" She screamed the name with all her being, her sweeping arm throwing the dog forward into roaring death.

Obediently he sprang, straight to the bear's throat, but too slow. The massive left paw swung, and the dog's body flipped the air.

But it was all she needed. The swing of the bear's paw had opened its left flank to the charging bull. The points pierced the rib cage, and the bull's forward momentum plunged them deep. However, the great weight of the bear stopped her mount's charge dead, and Teora was for once in her life thrown from her seat, her face driven into the harsh fur of the bear's hump, its rank smell burning her nostrils.

The animal grunted in pain and tried to turn, but its legs folded under, and Barozon bore in and down, pinning it to the ground. Teora jumped free, ran a few steps, and turned helplessly. She could feel bodies around her as her Herdsmen rushed to bring their staves to her protection, but she shoved them aside so she could see.

The bear roared and squirmed, heaving mightily to get its great claws to purchase on its enemy, but the horns were too deeply imbedded. The bull's hooves churned the undergrowth as he maintained his force, and the two entangled beasts plunged across the clearing, bellowing. Then Tourantij was standing at the bear's head, thumbing new shells into his gun, his firing a continuous roll of thunder.

A hush descended on the clearing. The bear was unmoving. Barozon, too, was still, his flanks heaving with laboured breath. For a moment he held his pressure, then, warily, he drew back, the horns making a horrible sucking sound as they withdrew from the deep wounds. The bear's body moved, but only to slump to the forest floor.

Barozon raised his head, the dark blood running down his face, and turned to blast a challenge to the world around him. *We have destroyed the foe!* Teora could feel his triumphal anger, his arrogant pride, as his enemy lay dead before him. She ran to him, throwing her arms around his neck, feeling the strength flow into her. At that moment, the two of them stood firm against the world. *Nothing can stop us. No one can stand in our way.* She stared around in challenge.

No response. Everyone in the clearing was moving slowly, as if returning from sleep. Corquée had tossed his rope aside and kneed his horse towards the edge of the clearing, pacing its perimeter, eyes alert. Tourantij bent over the child, reaching gingerly to separate the long, blonde locks that fell forward, glistening with blood. A stir in the grass nearby, and Spar dragged himself forward, his nose pushing at the soldier's hands.

Teora's strange mood left her. She strode forward, concerned for the injured child.

Tourantij's gentle fingers divided the strands of hair. A large piece of the scalp had been torn loose and hung forward in a flap. Careful not to touch the inner flesh, she pulled it back into place while the soldier pushed the hair aside.

The child's head came up: a girl. Her face was bloody but unmarked. Using the tail of her shirt, Teora sponged the blood away.

"You can open your eyes, now." She was unsure if the girl was even conscious, but the eyelids twitched.

"I can't see." It was a low moan.

"Of course not. You have your eyes closed." Teora touched away a few more stains gently. "There's nothing wrong with your face. Open up."

The eyelids flickered, then opened slightly, half revealing the pupils, and again Teora wondered if the victim were fully conscious yet. Then the eyes opened fully, large and pale blue, heavy lidded, pupils wide and unfocussed.

Then awareness returned. "I can see!"

"Yes, you can. Did the bear hurt you anywhere else?"

A thoughtful look spread over the face. "I don't think so. I dropped down and curled up dead, like you do when a grizzly attacks."

The eyes flew open again. "Amand! Where's Amand?"

Teora's eyes met the soldier's. "There's someone else?"

"Amand. He fell off his horse when the bear attacked." The movements of the girl's head threatened to dislodge the rough bandage that Tourantij was applying.

"Calmly, now. We'll find him. Where was he?"

The girl gazed around more slowly, now, waved a hand weakly. "We came in from the north-west, and the bear came from over there. His horse turned back, but he was falling off. I reached to help him,

275

but my horse went the other way, and I hit the ground over there..."
Her eyes suddenly took in the body of the bear. A shudder ran through her, and her eyelids half-closed again. Then she went completely limp and slipped to the ground.

Tourantij grinned. "Now she faints."

Teora regarded him in disgust. "The reality of it all just hit, for the Deity's sake. What do you expect?"

The soldier grinned again and cocked his head to one side. "Strong language!" He called to where Corquée still circled the clearing. "Search for someone else. Fell off his horse." His arm swung northward.

Immediately the Rider's eyes scanned the ground in that direction, and the Herdsmen spread into their search pattern, the dogs ranging ahead. If there was another victim, they would find him.

A crashing in the bushes drew their attention, but it was only Goianor, sweating and batting at the leaves as his horse pushed through the spindly trees that edged the clearing. He entered, then took in the scene: the dead bear, the bull's gory horns. Then his eyes centred on Teora, and she could see the colour build in his face. He swung down from his horse and strode towards her, his finger pointing, hand shaking with building rage.

"You have allowed the Consort to fight? You have gone out of your way to attack the most dangerous animal in the world? What is wrong with you?"

Teora tried to find something reasonable to say.

Tourantij merely glanced up at the Priest. "It was attacking the girl. The bull sustained no injury."

The Priest's face drained of colour as his rage mounted. "That is beside the point. You have endangered our whole mission, and for what? To save some brat who shouldn't be out here alone in the first place?"

Teora felt herself rising to her feet as the rage overtook her. As she faced the Priest, she could see the anger drain from his face, replaced by stark terror. This gave her a good feeling, and she stepped forward. The bushes crunched beside her, and a huge, blood-encrusted horn slid up beside her shoulder. The Priest took a hesitant step backwards, but his heel caught, and he teetered, unable to flee.

Then the rational side of Teora's mind took over. Remembering Barozon's reaction to her anger, she hastily curbed her emotions. After a moment she spoke, as coldly as she could.

"It is the Bull's task to defend the Herd. I don't need to tell you that, Priest. It was not only the 'brat' that needed defending. The animal was about to attack Tourantij, and the Rider and his horse were in danger as well."

The Priest took a moment to regain his balance and his breath. "But you must never endanger a breeding animal of that quality. They are always completely protected!"

She considered. "Perhaps that is one of your problems at Aeru. Perhaps you have protected your breeding animals too successfully and have bred out any strain of spirit."

She stepped forward, spoke more confidentially. "Besides, I felt the Deity's power in me. Perhaps more strongly than ever before. It had to be the right thing to do."

The Priest considered this, nodded, and she knew she had given him a way to back out of the conflict.

"I see. Very well, then." His head came up. "You should speak to your people. It was not good discipline for them to all rush off and leave me alone on the path."

She nodded, turned to Tourantij to hide her smile.

His face stony calm, he answered for her. "I will speak to them."

The Priest in turn nodded. Then another thought struck him. "Was it not irresponsible of the Rider to leave us so quickly, when trouble was near." It was not a question. Teora couldn't believe how quickly this man tried to turn any situation to his advantage. She bit back an angry retort, her hand soothing Barozon's shoulder.

"I think not." Tourantij's voice was still in complete control. "The outrider investigates danger. Our advance party of Rider, Herdsmen and dogs was appropriate."

The calm, matter-of-fact tone of voice was exactly what would sway the Priest, and she hid her smile again as Goianor nodded and went to his horse.

Teora felt a nudge at her ankle. Spar lay gazing up at her, his ears half up, an embarrassed wrinkle to his forehead. When she turned to him, he tried to rise, but his right front leg refused to function and he fell, whimpering. She knelt by him, her fingers exploring his leg and body. Along his right ribs they came away bloody. Four long gouges

277

showed where the bear's claws had raked, but the bones underneath rebounded firmly to her pressure. The right front leg moved loosely; the bone was snapped up near the shoulder joint.

"It must have taken much of the force of the blow."

Tourantij rested his hand on the dog's head. "He attacked without fear. Right into the bear's face."

She looked straight into the soldier's eyes. "So did you."

He shrugged uncomfortably, glanced towards the blonde head, where he still held the bandage. "I didn't have much choice."

"Neither did Spar. I sent him."

"I heard you call his name."

"It was more than that. I sent him as surely as you pulled the trigger of your gun."

The soldier stared deep into the dog's patient, trusting eyes. "My bullets don't go half so willingly."

A shout brought their heads around. Daegal and Mayna were carrying a limp form into the clearing. The others followed, leading two fine, long-legged horses.

"Amand!"

Only Teora's firm hand on her shoulder kept the girl from starting up.

"Steady there, young lady. We'll see what's wrong with him."

The two Herdsmen laid their burden down. "A lump on his head the size of his fist is all. He'll come round soon."

The girl laid her bloodied hand on the dark hair of her friend. "He's still breathing."

Teora rolled back an eyelid, then took a bit of the neck muscle between her fingers, pinching. The patient groaned and moved away from the pain. "He's coming to already. Give him a while."

The girl's heavy eyelids rose fully as she stared into Teora's eyes. Satisfied with the truth she saw there, she bent again to stroke her friend's hair.

Someone needed to make a decision. Teora considered the three injured, then raised her eyebrows at Tourantij. "I don't really want to move anyone."

The soldier scanned the clearing. "It looks like a good place to camp. Corquée?"

278

The Rider, too, glanced around. "Give me a moment." He walked around the clearing, his eyes to the ground. Then he went over to the dead bear and investigated it thoroughly, opening its mouth, feeling its paws.

A derisive snort exploded behind Teora, and she half-turned to see the priest standing there, a sneer on his face. "We will now make our camping decisions based on the rituals and prognostications of a savage. Now, perhaps he will read the entrails."

The Rider, oblivious to this sniping, continued his inspection, cutting with his knife, not ignoring the bear's more intimate areas. Finally, he straightened.

"These two rode in from the north. The bear met them there, near the south edge of the clearing. Is this not so?"

The blonde girl glanced up from her friend long enough to agree.

"Good." The Rider turned to the Herdsmen, pointed south. "If you would, check in that direction. Not farther than twenty paces, I would guess, and tell me what you find."

The Herdsmen jogged off, and a moment later there came a shout. "A dead steer. Covered with sticks and brush."

Corquée nodded, turned to the others. "If we drag the two carcasses far enough away, it will be safe to camp here."

The Priest sighed, loudly. "And on what evidence do you make this confident decision?"

The Rider's face flushed, and Teora put a hand on his arm.

"How did you know there would be a carcass there?"

Corquée's face cleared at this honest questioning. "This is an old bear, a male. He is missing two front claws and his teeth are poor. He will be new to this area, probably driven out of his old territory by a younger male. These two were probably looking for the steer?"

The bandaged head nodded.

"And they were about to ride right over it. The bear was defending his kill, a rare kill that he would be desperate to keep We were coming along the trail in the other direction, making plenty of noise. Trapped between the two parties, he attacked at the weakest point. He is a male, so there will be no other bears in the area. It is safe to camp. As safe as anywhere else, I suppose. Is that enough for you, Priest Goianor?"

279

The Priest glared up at the Rider, registering the challenge. Then he regarded the uncompromising faces around. "Quite enough, Rider. I congratulate you on your abilities. If, of course, this story you tell is true. If, on the other hand, a whole herd of bears attacks us in the night, it will be too late to say, 'I told you so'." But a smile softened the Priest's lips, and while it did not reach his eyes, it was enough to take the sting from his words. Corquée nodded as if accepting an apology and went to arrange harness to drag the bear away. Tourantij and Teora turned to their patients.

The dark-haired boy was still not completely conscious, moving and mumbling. Spar was lying on his side, as comfortable as possible. Nipha got in the way, licking industriously at his wounds, while Sabba wrapped the broken leg in a splint. The Herdsmen were fussing over Barozon, cleaning and grooming him. He accepted their attention with regal dignity. Teora and Tourantij turned their attention to the girl.

"I have to put this back together." The soldier spoke with quiet confidence as he dug in his pack.

Caring for the wounded would be one of his abilities.

Soon a fire was blazing, and water was boiling in a cooking pot. Into it Tourantij dropped various metal instruments, checking his pocket watch as he did so.

"Ten minutes will be enough to make them sterile."

Teora looked at him questioningly.

"Do you follow medicine at all?"

"Only bruises and sprains. I have been known to take the odd fall in training."

The soldier took out a razor and began to shave the hair away from the tear in the girl's scalp. "It has been pretty well proven, at least to my satisfaction, that anything that touches a wound must be kept in boiling water for at least ten minutes. If you do this, there is a much better chance that the wound will not go septic. For this young lady here, if we can reattach the scalp, there is a chance that the hair will grow back normally. She will have a short scar here, where the tear comes down onto her forehead, but the rest will be hidden in all that beautiful hair, and that beautiful face will remain ...beautiful."

This jibe brought the first smile to the girl's face. Tourantij's tone was teasing, but his comment was accurate. Her face was comely enough, with smooth, fair skin, strong cheekbones, and a rounded but firm chin. Her eyes, large and heavy-lidded, drew all attention in any case. Teora could see that in a few years this one would be cutting a swathe through the local young men, scar or no scar.

Before Tourantij would allow them to start, both he and Teora washed their hands more thoroughly than Teora had ever done before in her life. Then he took a flask of alcohol from his saddlebag and proceeded to clean the wound and the area around it. By this time the instruments were ready, and the soldier had prepared the wound to his satisfaction, snipping off ragged bits of flesh and picking out any foreign matter. Then, using linen thread that he took from a tightly wrapped envelope in his pack, he stitched the tattered lips of the wound back together.

It was a laborious process. Their patient bore the prick of the needle mutely, answering their questions in monosyllables. Soon she started to shake, and a Herdsman brought a blanket to warm her. While they sat working, the camp rose around them, and soon the smell of cooking food broke across their concentration.

Tourantij glanced across at Teora, then put the needle down, stretching his cramped fingers. "I can't stop and contaminate my hands. Have something to eat. I don't need you anymore."

He craned his neck down to face his patient. "How about you, youngster? You up for a bite? Oops, bad joke." He stared at the girl, raising his eyebrows and waiting until she returned his smile. "Good. You are an amazingly patient patient. Good thing you can't see the mess I'm making up here. You'd make me take it out and do it over...No, none of that, now." The girl's face had started to crumple. "You have to be tough."

Teora joined in. "I guess you've figured out by now that you haven't had very good luck today. First the bear, and now him. I don't know which of the two I'd rather have pawing around at my head."

She had just been rewarded by the return of the smile when she looked up to see the stunned faces of several of the party staring at her. She waved her hand dismissively. "Oh, stop gawking. The sooner she starts talking about this, the sooner she'll start getting over it. If you make it into some horrible, hidden thing, she won't. Go get us some food. And check the young fellow over there. I think he's finally coming back to us...Don't move your head! You want a needle installed up there permanently?" This last was to the patient, who had started in concern.

Sure enough, the boy beside them had opened his eyes, staring uncomprehendingly at the sky. Mayna leaned over him, speaking his name softly. Slowly, his eyes began to clear. He put a hand to the bandage and lay still. Then his eyes closed again, and a moan slid from his lips.

"Hastar."

Tourantij laughed softly. "Now isn't that sweet. The first word out of his mouth. A bit young to be in love, aren't they? You'd better speak to him, Hastar. But don't wiggle."

The girl had turned her head toward her friend, but she twisted further to glare at the soldier. "He's my brother, if you must know. We have different mothers, so we look different." Her gaze left him disdainfully and centred on her brother again. "It's all right, Amand. I'm fine...No, no, I really am. The bear just scratched me, and they're patching up the wound. You lie there for a while, and we'll have supper in a moment...Oops. Now see what you did."

The sudden motion of trying to sit up had been a mistake, and the boy vomited. Mayna was alert and turned his head aside. He looked sheepish when he had finished.

Tourantij laughed easily. "Don't worry about it. That's normal when you get hit on the head. I know. It happened to me, when I got grazed by a bullet." He lifted the hair above his ear, revealing a fine white line along his scalp.

The boy seemed more comfortable, then puzzled. "What happened, Hastar?"

The girl shrugged. "When the bear attacked, your horse took off and ran you into a tree. He got ahold of me, but these people heard the screams and came and killed him. Actually, the bull killed him." Her eyes turned to Tourantij. "That must be some kind of bull. Is he yours?"

"Not me. He belongs to Teora, here. Or she belongs to him. I haven't quite figured out which, yet."

Teora grimaced inwardly as the children's admiring eyes turned to her. The soldier had been more accurate than he thought. She still didn't know who had been in control during that final charge.

"Oh." There was a world of wonder and awe in the single word. Teora uncomfortably changed the subject.

"You were chasing the steer. One of your father's?"

The girl talked on, wincing occasionally as Tourantij finished his stitching. "Yes, and one of our finest stock. He turned up missing last night, and we set off first thing this morning to chase him down. We saw no sign of trouble, right up until the bear jumped us. Your Rider is right. There should be no bears in this area."

The soldier smiled. "You think so."

"Oh, yes. We always know where the bears are. It is important to our Herd to be aware of the dangers. Father says that Amand and I are the best bear trackers he's ever had. Except for Oren, who taught us a lot. We know all about them. But not this one. He must be from farther south, in the mountains. There are a lot of brown ones down there."

"I thought all grizzlies were brown."

"No, they range from blonde to almost black, except for the lighter part on the ends of the hairs. This one looks like the southern ones."

She spoke with such confidence that Teora was amused. "And you know all this for sure."

The dark-haired boy rose on one elbow. "She sure does. She isn't bragging. Hastar's the smartest one of all of us. If she says she knows, then she does. She doesn't have to make things up."

It was the girl's turn to search for a change of subject. As Corquée returned from dragging the bear's carcass away, she watched him coiling up his rope. "Did your Rider really rope a grizzly all alone? That's either very brave or very stupid."

"He did it to save your life. You choose."

Hastar winced, then regarded the Rider again. "Good point. He's handsome, isn't he?"

Her brother stared at her in horror. "Hastar! Mind your manners."

She grinned at him. "Well, he is, isn't he? Broad shoulders, lean hips. A perfect Rider. Why would it be rude to say so?"

The boy tossed his hands in disgust, and Teora revised the time frame to a few months. Maybe it was starting already. Boys of this age had no idea what their older sisters were talking about.

"So, you think he's a perfect Rider, do you?"

"Sure. Don't you?"

"I don't know. He's the only Rider I ever met."

The girl regarded her in pity. "You should see them. They all ride beautiful horses, and their saddles are so fancy, all silver and fringes. And they have such deep, romantic eyes!"

Amand made a sound of disgust, and Teora laughed. "You'd better not tell Corquée that. He'd never be able to look you in the face again."

The girl's face twisted. "Corquée? Corquée son of Awane?"

"Yes. Do you know him?"

"Oh, Deity be sweet. Corquée, Awane's son. I've been saved from a ravening beast by Corquée, son of Awane." She rolled the name on her tongue and clasped her hands together. "I think I'm going to die."

"Don't even consider it, after all the trouble we went to keep you alive. How do you know about Corquée?"

"Oh, everyone knows that story. How he gave up his inheritance to save his sister's honour, and had to take on a dangerous journey to regain his status in the tribe, and how he died in foreign lands, never to return..." The girl moved her eyes to follow her subject's movements. "...but I guess he didn't die, did he? Is he coming back to Aeru?"

"That's where we're headed."

The girl fairly bounced, and Teora had to hold her shoulders to keep her in her seat. "He's coming back, and I met him, and he saved my life. How romantic! I could almost forgive that bear. If your friend was a bit gentler, sticking that needle into my head."

Tourantij grimaced as if the pain was his own, and Teora laughed. "He's remembering that he was the one who stood between you and the bear at the last moment. A little more gratitude is in order."

Hastar was immediately contrite, turning and placing her hand on the soldier's knee, gazing into his face for the first time. "I'm sorry. Were you the one with the gun? I couldn't see, you know, but when I heard that gun go off and the shots so quickly spaced, well, I felt a little bit of hope, you know. I thought, 'If there's someone here who shoots a gun that well, then maybe, I might just live through this'."

Tourantij snorted. "You were thinking all that, while you were lying there with so much blood in your eyes that you couldn't see."

"I certainly was. There is time for a whole lot of things to go through your head when something awful is happening. I remember thinking, as that bear was tearing at me, that I was sorry I hadn't finished the stitchery that Mother gave me to do, and now I'd never have a chance, and how upset she would be that I'd gone out riding, and how angry she'd be that I would never finish it, and all because I went riding instead of doing my stitchery, and how disappointed Mother was that I liked to ride instead of doing needlework, and now I guess I'll have to learn needlework, because a bear mauled me, and I'll never be pretty, and I'll never get a husband, and she'll say she told me not to like riding, and ..."

Teora took the girl in her arms, shutting off the gush of emotion. "It's all right. Your mother will be happy to see you, stitchery or not. And Tourantij says you'll be fine, with just a little scar that no one will ever notice. Not with big, beautiful eyes like you have. At least that's what he says. I don't notice things like that in a girl. I think you look just fine," she patted the girl's heaving shoulder, while Amand held her hand helplessly, "but it takes a man to notice that sort of thing."

Hastar quieted, and Teora signaled Tourantij to continue his work. He was almost finished now, his stitching a neat row of dark lines along the slim red wound that wandered across the girl's head.

"Speaking of stitchery, Tourantij has done an amazing job here. Your head resembles one of the maps back at the Haven."

"The Haven? You're from the Haven?"

"Where do you think we're from? I thought you knew Corquée's story."

"Of course, but I didn't believe that much of it. I mean, most of us girls weren't sure he even existed. I'm not sure that the Haven exists...I mean, I guess it must, now, since that's where you're from, but I mean before, I didn't know what to believe, and what not...if you know what I mean..."

Teora patted the girl's shoulder comfortingly. "I know. It's rather strange to have the characters from a story suddenly drop in on you. It will be very upsetting, I'm sure, to find out that we are real people, and we eat, and sleep, and sneeze, and do all sorts of other normal things."

At this moment Tourantij finished his work. "There you go, my girl. Seventy-three stitches. I've never done a job that big. You were an excellent patient. I've had big, tough, soldiers who wiggled more than you when I put the needle in."

Hastar shrugged, moving her head experimentally. "I don't know. It hurt, I guess, but nothing near what the bear did." She turned to face the soldier. "I guess if I had a choice, I'd rather have you pawing at my head." Impulsively, she threw her arms around the surprised

285

Soldier's neck and held him tightly. "If it weren't for you, I'd be dead, wouldn't I?"

Tourantij held her awkwardly, unsure of what do. Teora touched his hand reassuringly, nodding to him to keep holding the girl. The dark-haired boy sat uncertainly, patting his sister's shoulder. Teora spoke softly to him.

"She's just been through a terrifying experience. She needs someone to hold on to right now. She'll be fine in a moment. How's your head feeling?"

The boy's hand went to the bandage again. "Not too great. It hurts."

"And so it should. You did bang that tree very hard. You are going to have to train your horse to duck the trees a bit better."

"The horse! He isn't mine. He's Father's. How is he? Is he hurt?"

"No, he isn't hurt. Both your horses came back after you fell off, even with the bear around. Those are very loyal horses."

The boy seemed relieved. "Father sent us out on two of his best mounts in case we had a long way to go."

"I thought you Aerans herded on foot."

The boy immediately became uncomfortable, more than such an innocent comment might warrant. "Oh, we do. We herd on foot all the time. We obey all of the proper strictures. It's just that for longer journeys like this we take the horses, because it's, well, easier, and better. You know..." His eyes pleaded for understanding, and she filed this point away for further thought. *There must be some social conflict here, to have the boy upset over such a simple thing.*

"Of course I understand. See, even our Priest rides, when it is necessary for such a long journey as he has taken."

The boy was considerably relieved at this news. "Oh. You don't mind, then?"

She thought before she spoke. "I don't mind. It isn't for me to say. I'm sure your father knows what's best." *Time to file that away.* "Our Herdsmen don't ride. You should talk to them."

The boy's eyes covered the camp, taking in the lanky figures walking or lounging about. "Those are real Herdsmen from the Haven?"

"In the flesh."

The boy was speechless, staring. "I'm a herdsman, myself."

"Without the capital H, I suspect."

"Of course. You don't get to be a real Herdsman till you're old."

"You don't? How old?"

"Well, older than the man who fixed Hastar's head. About as old as your Priest, I guess. How come your Herdsmen are so young?"

This sounded like something important, but Teora did not want to make any judgments until she had more information. "I don't know. Maybe they started early."

The boy nodded doubtfully.

"So how far are we from your Herd?"

Amand brightened. Here he was on sure ground. "We rode south for half a day, then along the river for two hours. I could find my way back any time, day or night."

"Oh, could you? Are you a good guide, then?"

"Oh, nothing like your famous Corquée. But I do all right. I'm only eleven, you know, but I already go with the Herd to the Mountain Pastures in the summer."

"And your sister?"

"Oh, she doesn't go. Mother wants her to stay home and learn to be a lady."

"And what does Hastar want?"

The small face wrinkled. "I'm not sure, now that you mention it. Part of her wants to be off riding with me, but I know she likes to dress up for parties. Don't let all that stuff about stitchery mean anything to you. She's the best needle worker of all the girls in the Southeast Pastures."

The boy's face lifted earnestly. "She's the best at whatever they do. The girls, I mean. Actually, there's not too many boys can beat her at most stuff. Only the ones that are bigger and stronger. If it takes brains, she'll win every time."

"How about you?"

"Oh, I'm not that smart. But I do fine." He chuckled quietly. "If you have a sister like that, they don't notice you much. Which means you get to do what you like a lot of the time."

"And go on expeditions with your sister."

"Right. This one was great until that bear came charging out of the brush. I'm starting to remember, you know, and it's all coming back to me. If Hastar hadn't pushed me back into the saddle I'd have gone off right in front of that bear. She saved my life, you know."

Teora ruffled the dark hair. "Yes, it's quite possible she did. You won't forget that, now, in a couple of months when you get the urge to play some trick on her."

The calm, dark eyes looked straight into hers. "I probably will forget, you know. I mean, temporarily. You can't let something like that interfere with your basic relationship with your sister. You don't want me to stop being a normal brother because of this?"

Teora gave a shout of laughter and slapped him on the shoulder. "Sounds like my brother back home. Except with bigger words. Where did you learn to talk like that?"

The boy put a hand over his mouth and hunched his shoulders in mock dismay. "Oops! Was I doing that again? Mother says I have to talk like normal people, or they will consider me stuck up. Did I sound stuck up to you?"

"No, you just sounded like an adult. Does your mother talk to you like that all the time?"

Amand nodded, and his friendly smile lit up his face. "Yep. Hastar, too. I mean, it's really my mother, not Hastar's. Hers died when she was too young to remember, so Hastar calls my mother, 'Mother.' If you get what I mean."

Teora nodded. "Sounds logical. Now, if you've had enough to eat, let's see about finding you a place to sleep. I guess you'll want to stay near Hastar, will you?"

"Sure. We've got our bedrolls on the saddles. We throw them down any old place. The weather's great, and we love sleeping outside."

"That's fine, but I want you to keep an eye on her. She's had a pretty bad time and she might have a reaction later on. Also, her wound might start to bother her. Don't be afraid to wake me up in the night if there's any problem."

"Sure." The boy groaned as he got to his feet, putting his hand to his head and smiling wryly down at her. "Still not quite straight myself."

"Well, you let me know if your head feels funny, too."

"Sure." Amand sauntered away slowly, his eyes taking in the rest of the camp.

26.   On the Trail

"What are you smiling about?"

Tourantij turned towards Teora, bemused, then his eyes came into focus. "Was I smiling?"

"Most definitely. Not a large smile, but a definite upward curve to the lips. I'm sorry. Did I interrupt a daydream?"

"Not really." He lounged in the saddle, his eyes on the trail ahead.

"You've been smiling a lot lately."

"Have I? Life of the party am I, these days?"

"No, that's not what I mean. I've noticed that you're more...relaxed. You joke with the others more. Plus, you had another blowup with Sabba yesterday. You do tease her unmercifully, you know."

"I can't help it. She reminds me of my younger sister."

"There! You smiled again!" Teora had never seen the stiff Soldier in such a pensive mood. "Tell me about your sister."

He shrugged. "She's ten years younger than me. She still lives at home with my parents. She's pretty, she's smart and I don't see her much. I used to tease her a bit, I guess."

Teora grinned wryly. "Keep in mind that Sabba isn't looking for a brother to tease her."

"What do you mean?"

"Tourantij!"

His eyes rolled skyward. "All right. I'll be good." Then his face turned serious, and he met her glance. "Two months ago, if someone had told me I'd be hearing personal advice from a girl your age, I'd have laughed in his face. If I thought I'd be taking it, I'd have given him my pistol and begged to be put out of my misery."

"What advice?"

"Don't try politics with me. That was a very astute comment you made. You never cease to amaze me."

Teora thought back over the problem that had been troubling her. "I guess I'd better not cease to be amazing."

He caught her tone change and matched it. "What do you mean by that? You don't sound too happy."

"I'm not. Oh, I'm not unhappy, you realize, more worried."

"What to do at Aeru?"

"That's only part of it. It's this new power I have. I mean, I definitely do have a power, don't I? You don't think I'm imagining it?"

He gave that the serious thought it deserved before he answered, stretching his words. "I'm not religious, Teora. I'm not the one to ask."

"Maybe that's who I should ask. Someone who will give me an unbiased view."

He nodded. "In that case yes, you have some kind of power. Whether it is the Deity manifesting Herself, as Goianor thinks, or simply the amazing rapport with animals and people that Corquée seems to take for granted, it is a power and it seems to be growing."

"Thank you." She glanced up at him. "I didn't ask you to brag about it, you know."

"I know."

"I have to know about it. Then I can act accordingly. If I have power, then with power comes responsibility to control it and use it for the right purposes.

"It's quite unfair, you know, to give such power to someone so young and inexperienced. Why, think of the mistakes I might make, if I got angry at someone or if I fell in love. Couldn't my power be completely misused? Why doesn't the Deity give the power to someone older, someone with experience? Goianor, for example. He's spent decades in Her service. Years of studying and praying and all those things. He would know how to use the power for Her purposes. Not me. What experience do I have?"

The soldier's eyes became thoughtful. "Goianor? Having real power?"

"I see what you mean."

"Maybe the Deity isn't stupid after all."

"Tourantij! That's sacrilege!"

He grinned. "You inferred that the Deity might be making a mistake. I contradicted you. No sacrilege on my part."

"But you are inferring that it might be on mine. To suggest that the Deity might make mistakes."

"Not that the Deity cares about my opinion, but I think She chose rather well."

"Of course, She cares about your opinion!"

"Is that directly from Herself, or are you standing up for me as a friend?"

"Of course I don't..." then she caught on. "Has Sabba hit you today?"

"No."

"That explains it. You need to be put in your place." Then she sobered again. "But thank you for putting me in mine. I will continue to be concerned about doing the right thing, but I will not worry so much."

"If it's the Deity's power, She has some responsibility for seeing that it gets used right."

"But what if She's testing me, and I fail?"

"From what little was drilled into me in Scripture School when I was young, I doubt the Deity works that way. Being Chosen, surely you have already passed all the tests you need."

"I hope so." They rode on in silence, but Teora felt better. She glanced at her companion now and again, but the smiles were gone, and he was serious, checking their route and its surroundings with his habitual wariness.

They were moving through dry country again, although nothing like the deserts farther south. To Teora's experienced eye, the vegetation was not quite good enough to support a Herd. Maybe in a good year. There seemed to be enough watercourses, but poor grazing would spread the stock far apart. And if there were more bears like that one around...she gave a brief shudder. Something in this land set her teeth on edge. It seemed more than the memory of the bear.

"Is Aeru like this?"

Tourantij gazed around. "Sort of. Less exposed dry soil, more prairie grass, fewer shrubs and cactus."

"How do they manage their Herds?"

"Ask someone more experienced. Like Hastar."

"I'm not sure I'll get straight answers." She pulled Barozon to the side, letting the rest of the troop pass her until the Herdsmen and pack animals came strolling by. Amand was leading Hastar's horse, but the girl was looking much brighter. Barozon swung into step beside them.

"How are you feeling?"

The girl put a hand to her head. Teora had put a new bandage on that morning, and there was little seepage from the wound. "Still a bit dizzy at times, but I'm less weak."

"Good. Can you tell me about this land we're riding through? Do you herd cattle here?"

"Not often. It's too dry. The Herd has to spread too far, and we can't keep track of them."

Teora nodded. "That's what I thought. Then there's better pasture nearer your home."

"Oh, yes, much. That's why we couldn't figure out why that dumb steer wandered this way so far." She grinned. "Maybe he was bear hunting."

Teora raised her eyebrows. The child was rebounding quickly. *If there are more like this one in Aeru, how can there be any problems?* "I guess he found one."

"Or it found him. Either way, it was a waste."

"You ride very well."

The girl shot her a suspicious glance. "Thank you. So do you."

Teora grinned. "I had better. It's my life."

"Mine too." Hastar's eyes closed, then opened quickly, as if to catch Teora's unguarded expression.

"You ride all the time?"

"Most of the time. Amand and I are always on the outskirts of the Herd, much too far for walking."

"But your Herdsmen walk."

"Of course. Always. They always walk. That's the rule." Teora could see the girl search out Goianor's bulk, on his horse far up the line.

"Is that a problem?"

"What do you mean?" The light blue eyes were big and innocent.

"Obviously there's something wrong about it, or you wouldn't be forceful about it, and worried that the priest might hear."

The girl glanced across at her brother. He shrugged, and she continued. "Well, you see, Father has had some trouble with the Temple authorities about his methods. It's part of the reason we have our Herds this far south. The grass isn't quite as good, but they don't bother us so much."

292

Teora waited, but nothing more was forthcoming. "What do they bother you about?"

"Well...Father doesn't agree exactly with the way they do things. He says there should be more Herdsmen and fewer untrained boys helping with the herds. It's difficult to get trained Herdsmen, so Father has to use other methods."

"Such as?"

Hastar met her brother's eyes, and something in them shut her mouth firmly.

"I'm not asking you to give up family secrets. What have the Temple authorities been after him about?"

"Well, they think he shouldn't use the Riders as much as he does."

"Corquée's people."

"Yes. There are always a few of the younger ones around, the ones with no Remudas of their own. Father hires them. They can use the money, and we need the help. One taught me to ride and sold Father these horses. I don't know if he's a relative of Corquée's or not. They have a very complex system of relations all based on who your mother is, and I never did get it straight. It probably comes from the old days, when they didn't know that sex caused babies. The only person you really knew was related to you was your sister's child."

Teora glanced quizzically at the youngster beside her. "Where did you pick up that idea?"

Hastar shrugged, grinned. "Oh, I ask questions. Often I get funny looks, but sometimes I get a straight answer."

"So, your straight answer to me is that your father gets in trouble because he's not following the rules. Why does he use Riders instead of Herdsmen? They can't all be so old as to be useless."

"It isn't financially effective."

"Pardon me?"

"It costs too much. Father can hire two Riders with their horses for what he has to pay the Temple for one Herdsman."

"He has to pay the Temple?"

"Of course."

"What does he pay the Herdsman?"

"Nothing. Well, room and board and equipment, and that sort."

"But the rest of the money goes to the Temple."

"Yes."

Teora was silent, considering this. The thought of an independent lot like her Herdsmen consenting to have the Temple collect their wages brought a smile to her lips.

"What's so funny?"

She shook her head, indicated the Herdsmen walking ahead of them. "My people don't work like that."

Hastar stared around uncomfortably, then up at Teora. "I've been meaning to ask..."

"Yes?"

"Well, those two women. What do they do? I mean, they don't seem to be with any of the men, and they don't really attend you. Why are they here?" The girl's face reddened, and she glanced at her brother, who stared back at her innocently. "Or is that a stupid question?"

Teora took this all in and laughed. "No, that's not why they are here. They are Herdsmen, like the men. We brought our best people, and they qualified."

"Women? Herdsmen? Are you sure?"

Teora smiled gently. "I'm not likely to make a mistake about something like that, am I?"

"Oh, no. Of course not. I'm sorry."

The girl was silent for a long time, and Teora could guess what she was thinking. *The Herdsmen in Aeru are restricted to men who have served a very long apprenticeship. I wonder what the criteria are.* At the Haven, a childhood spent with the Herd, a strong physique and a superb rapport with the animals was all that was required. On-the-job training continued all their lives. Of course, the six she had brought went well beyond the basic abilities. When they were too old to Herd they would become Herd managers or take on other responsible positions. Some might, with the right backing, start a new Herd or take over an older one. It seemed this was not the pattern in Aeru.

She wondered what other differences she would find. Innovation was not encouraged, if the girl had her story straight. She gazed around at the sere countryside, and the feeling of wrongness persisted. Something chewed at the edges of her mind, nagging for a solution.

"How much longer to your Herd?"

"Another two hours at a horse's pace. A bit longer at this speed."

"And the climate will change that much in that short distance?"

"Yes, it's interesting, isn't it? Father says it's the rain shadow of the mountain." She pointed ahead. "See that bare, rocky shoulder to the west? We have to go around there. Many times when it's raining at home, it's dry here. Watch the clouds. They come over the top of the mountain like they're going to cover the sun, but they seem to evaporate in the dry wind that rushes up the mountain."

Amand tugged at his sister's sleeve, whispered to her. She laughed, a bit self-consciously. "I'm not boring her. She's interested. Aren't you, Teora?"

Teora laughed as well. "What I'm really interested in is how someone as young as you learned so much science. Did you go to the Temple school?"

The girl shook her head in scorn, then stopped and raised a shaking hand to the bandage. "Ooh. Shouldn't have done that. No, we didn't go to that old school. They don't teach girls anything, anyway. Father says that we live too far away for day school, and he's not having any children of his under that influence for a full five days a week."

Another brotherly tug on her sleeve. "Ooh, again. I guess I shouldn't have said that."

"We have fine schools in the Haven, and the girls and the boys learn the same things. I don't know what you have here, but I won't repeat anything."

"Thanks. It must be the fever. I'm not usually indiscreet."

Teora grinned and they rode in companionable silence for a while.

"Where do you go to school?"

"At home. Mostly Mother. She has lots of books. Sometimes Father, or someone else who is visiting. We listen a lot when the adults talk. They never send us away."

Teora nodded. "I trained with my father, too. I'm going to be interested to meet your family."

"It won't be long, now." The two children looked ahead, their eyes bright. Strong as they may have been in standing up to their ordeal, they would be happy to be home safe again.

27.   The Herds of Carlin Wynn

Sure enough, as they rounded the shoulder of the mountain the short clumps of grass began to grow closer together and the cactus thinned out. Soon cattle appeared, small dots spread over the landscape. Teora regarded them closely, but if she was expecting any dramatic symptoms, she was disappointed. The animals were healthy enough and moved placidly about their bovine business in a normal, if not enthused, fashion.

Her hope that her strange feeling was caused by the danger of the journey seemed to be dashed as well. Now that she was here, she expected a release of the tension building inside her, but it did not come. In fact, the emotion was beginning to take on new dimensions. At least that was how it felt. She tried to analyze what was going on in her head, but the new touches were too subtle to pin down exactly what they meant.

She soon gave up on her analysis and returned to a scan of the Land.

In the foreground, inundations of the landscape too gentle to be called hills were covered by a mixture of open grassland and scattered clumps of trees. Here and there widespread gleams of white spoke of homes and other structures. Off in the hazy distance she could discern a larger group of buildings that must be the main city and Temple. Farther to the west the plains swooped up to into high ridges, mounting to snowcapped peaks at the horizon.

"So that's Aeru."

Corquée looked down from his horse. "That's the part your people hold." His hand swept to the north and east where the plains stretched, a level sea of grass, into the haze of the distance. "That's my home."

He stretched in the saddle, his hands high above his head. "Ah, it's good to see the prairies again."

"Glad to be home?"

"Oh, yes." He shook his head. "When I left, if I had known..."

"You wouldn't have come."

"Oh, no. I wouldn't have missed it for anything. But I wouldn't have been so stupidly happy about being chosen for the job, that's for sure."

"I suppose your family will be happy to see you."

He grinned. "I suppose they will. Especially my sister."

She smiled back. "She's a favourite, is she?"

"Not any more than anyone else. But now she can get married."

"What do you mean?"

"It's too complicated to explain. There were some problems, and this job was the solution to them. Now that I'm back, she can go ahead. She's been pretty anxious, I imagine."

"Especially since there were rumours that you were dead."

"What? Oh, you mean her." His head tossed towards where Hastar was riding beside her brother, slumped wearily in the saddle. Her flush showed the fever was returning, and Teora was glad that she would soon be home. "That's kids' stories. They didn't expect us back much before this. We're well within the month leeway."

"Any time within a month is fine?"

"Well, on a journey that long it isn't unusual to be a week or two off in either direction."

"I don't think I'd like to have it that uncertain."

He shrugged. "You get used to it. There's no point in worrying if someone isn't back right on time. Usually some simple explanation like a lame horse, and if it isn't, what can you do anyway?"

She shook her head. "Well, I guess they'll be glad to see you."

He met her eye, then tossed his head proudly, like his horse often did. "Oh, yes, they will."

A sharp whistle broke into their conversation. Tourantij's head went up on the alert, but Hastar put two fingers to her mouth and answered. Soon they spied a figure hurrying out of a hollow in the rolling landscape. It was a middle-aged man, dressed roughly, a staff in his hand. He slowed to a walk as he approached the group. Then, spying Hastar, he sprinted forward.

"Hastar! What happened to you? Are you all right?" Ignoring the rest of the party, he charged up to her horse, one hand on her knee, the other reaching towards her head.

She laughed and put both hands to the bandage. "I had an argument with a grizzly over that steer. He won, I guess. Don't worry, Oren. I'm all still there."

The man turned his attention to Amand. "And you! I suppose you got home with everything intact as well?"

Amand saluted casually. "Nothing but a bump on the head. My quarrel was with a tree. It definitely came out on top."

The man's shoulders slumped with relief, then straightened. "I'm sorry. I should remember my manners. Who are your companions?"

Hastar gestured. "They're the group from the Haven. That's Corquée, the Rider, over there. This is Teora. She's a Dancer, and this is Barozon, her Partner. He's the one who won the fight with the bear. The others..."

Teora filled in the gaps. "You might know the leader of our group, Priest Goianor from your Temple. This is Tourantij Niverdahl, and the rest are my Herdsmen."

Hastar nodded her gratitude at Teora, then winced. "And this is Oren, one of my Father's Herdsmen. Where is Father, right now?"

"He's somewhere around the hacienda. He'd never let on, but he was worried about you. You know how he paces around. We were expecting you last night, this morning at the latest. You'd better go right in and don't waste time chatting with me. Come on." He strode off at a ground-eating pace, and Barozon was forced to lengthen his stride to keep up.

"I don't know what the fuss is. One extra day is nothing new. A lost horseshoe could make that happen." Despite her casual words, the girl nudged her horse into a faster walk.

Then Tourantij's horse was pacing beside her "Don't you even think of rolling in there at a gallop, my girl. With that fever, you might end up a heap in the dust. That wouldn't be much of an entrance, would it?"

"Oh, I don't know. It might be quite romantic." But the unnatural flush on her cheek belied her cockiness and she held her pace.

They rounded another low shoulder of the mountain, and there in front of them was the Wynn hacienda. It stood on low tableland at the foot of the hill. The house itself was not large but it was well protected against the elements. Narrow windows were set into thick walls, and a roof of corrugated metal was laid over thick adobe. The yard was surrounded by a scattering of outbuildings, calving sheds, barns, and various corrals, the light colour of the poles attesting to the newness of their construction. A general air of bustle filled the yard despite the heat of the afternoon.

Oren opened a small back gate, and Hastar and Amand proudly led Teora's party into the main yard. Then an uproar broke out, and a man rushed from one of the barns, striding towards them. Before Teora could get more than the vague impression of a rangy body and a long, handsome face, the man had reached up and brought Hastar out of the saddle as easily and gently as if he were lifting a kitten. He held her cradled in his arms, peering intently at her eyes. After a long, shocked silence, his shoulders relaxed. She squirmed gently, and he set her on the ground and knelt in front of her, still holding her by the elbows.

"Father, it's all right. I'm…"

"No, you aren't. You have a fever. That bear's claws weren't clean." He raised his head and shouted. "Adimé! Adimé, come quickly!"

A tall, dark-haired woman, moving with stately grace for all her speed, swept through the group of ranch people who now crowded round. They made way for her, and she reached the two quickly.

"Now Carlin. Don't be precipitous. The girl's still on her feet or would be if you'd let her. We have guests." She smoothly slipped the girl out of her father's grip and turned him to face the mounted party. "Amand, I see you have done yourself damage as well. Come and let me look."

Teora had been taking this all in as well as she could. There seemed to be a whole lot going on, here.

Amand grinned at her as he turned to dismount. "He does that sometimes. I don't know how he knows, but he does. Don't worry. Mother always gets him calmed down." The boy kicked his leg across the horse's back and lowered himself gently to the ground, then walked carefully over to his mother. Despite his nonchalance, his head must still be hurting.

The man on the ground regarded his guests. He stepped forward, about to speak. Then he froze, and Teora wondered what was wrong. At first, she thought he was looking at her, but a stiffening of her Partner's muscles changed her mind.

The man and bull stared at each other. The bull's head was up, his nostrils wide. Their eyes held, a challenge passing between them. Then the moment passed, and the man strode forward, a beaming smile suffusing his face.

"You have come, you have come. I knew it! Oh, aren't you a beauty. Such a beauty!" He approached Barozon directly as no stranger should have, running his hand over the bull's nose, then stroking his neck, running his hands down one foreleg, murmuring appreciatively all the while. Then he straightened and looked directly at Teora.

"And you are his Partner, the Chosen of the Deity. Welcome, my Lady. Both of you are more than I had hoped for, dreamed of. He is…he is…" The man's hands described caressing arcs in the air, comically trying to make up for his lack of speech.

"I know. I think he's pretty special myself."

Carlin stared in her face again, then laughed. "Exactly. Couldn't have put it better. When overstatement won't suffice, understatement does admirably. Come, come. Get down and bring your party in. You are three times welcome: more than that." He bustled her off her harness, and with a lingering pat at Barozon's shoulder, moved to the rest of her party.

"You will be Corquée, the one the girls are making the songs about." He slapped the Rider's shoulder. "Oh, your Homecoming will be joyous. Your Remuda will grow, lad, will grow faster than any other! No, I do not joke!"

The Rider, blushing with embarrassment, ducked his head in negation.

"Nonsense, my boy. If I had a daughter the right age, I'd be first in line. If I had a horse worthy, of course." With another slap on the shoulder, he moved on.

"And you will be the famous Tourantij Niverdahl, the Lion of the Mountains. Oh, I wasn't there when they sent you off. They don't consult me much, away down here in the foothills. I doubt if they even know whom it was they hired. But I knew. You've done a good job, man. I know it wasn't easy." He shook the soldier's hand vigorously. "Thank you from the bottom of my heart."

There was a pause, as the man reached Goianor, who had just dismounted and stood inflexibly, his eyes narrow.

"Priest Goianor, you and I haven't always seen eye to eye, but I find it easy to forget that at this moment. You have succeeded beyond our wildest imaginings. Well done. I salute you."

Teora could see the Priest's stiffness dissolving. "I wish I had your optimism, Carlin Wynn, but thank you."

"Oh, I know they didn't send the Priestess. I said they wouldn't. But how could we know that they had this waiting on the side?" He had returned to Barozon, who leaned in to enjoy the man's attentions.

"My Lady, if your qualities are anything like your Partner's, and how could they not be?" He paused for another glance into the bull's eyes. "You are something special yourself. Whatever you have done for my daughter and son, I thank you doubly, but I tell you, had you come without them, I would have found solace in your coming. Such a beast!"

He turned to Goianor and spoke wistfully. "I suppose you'll be having him well guarded tonight?"

The Priest's demeanour unbent a bit more. He almost smiled. "I am afraid so, Carlin. You will have to take your plea to the Temple like everyone else. I am sure you will get your fair allotment."

A chill hardened the deep blue eyes. "Just be sure that I do."

Teora stepped forward, ignoring the Priest's restraining hand. "Carlin. Fair or not, for your daughter's sake, you will get an allotment."

The man's expressive eyebrows rose. "Hastar? What has she done?"

Teora considered. "Nothing, I suppose. It's what she is. Her potential... I don't know."

He nodded understandingly. "I know. I feel the same way. But I'm her father. I'm supposed to. It's nice to hear it from someone like you, though."

His voice rose again, in a cry that they were to hear many times in that house. "Adimé, Adimé!"

"I'm right here, my lord and master."

"Don't make fun of me in front of strangers. See to the company, please. I have to make sure our most important guest is comfortable." Without looking back, he laid a hand on Barozon's shoulder. The bull turned easily and followed the man towards a nearby pasture.

Teora's regard was distracted by the Priest's voice in her ear. "Two of our Herdsmen with Barozon at all times. No matter what."

She turned, her mouth open to question.

"This is politics, Teora, and I know you don't like it, but please, handle it my way. There can be no hint of favouritism, no matter what our feelings in the matter. Things are very tense in Aeru, and we must give no cause for further difficulty. If he were my best friend, I would do the same."

Daegal and Sabba had heard this conversation, and Teora motioned them to follow. For once, she believed the Priest. *My real task has started. The easy camaraderie of the trail is over.*

Politics had begun.

"Will you come in and sit down, or have you been sitting too long already, today?" The lady of the house swept her hand across the horizon. "Perhaps you would like to see our hacienda?"

Teora flexed her legs experimentally. "I could do with a stretch, and I would love to see the ranch. It seems a pleasant place." Now she had it. Her strange feeling of tension had been slowly dropping. In this hacienda, all was peaceful.

"I hope you will forgive me, but I must see to Hastar and Amand. Oren will show you around. If you end up at the west paddock, I'm sure you will find my husband there, still gazing on your Partner like a lovesick youth." Although the woman's face held only a pleasant smile, a sparkle lurked in the dark grey eyes, and Teora suspected a deep well of feeling in the calm, graceful body.

"We wouldn't keep you when your children need you. Oren has proved a good guide. I'm sure he will continue."

The woman smiled and turned to her family, and the Haven group set off on a tour of the grounds. There was little more to be seen than her first impressions had shown her, but Teora was more interested in the quality and condition of the stock. This was her first chance to observe the Herds she had come so far to aid. This was her first chance to guess what her job would be and whether she would be successful.

28. Marriage

Once again, she found nothing of interest. The Wynn stock would have done any Herd master at the Haven proud. They tended to be light, agile creatures, and she could see a place for Barozon's hefty traits in the breeding program. As she continued the familiar activities of inspection and analysis of breeding stock, she was lulled into a more comfortable mood, and the edge that had been grating at her nerves disappeared. *I wonder what that was all about. I've never felt that way before. I hope the people of Aeru don't feel that way. Not every day of their lives.*

However, the feeling was gone, and she couldn't help but enjoy herself and admire the skill and artistry of the construction, the careful tending of the stock. Carlin Wynn was a superior Herd Leader.

When the tour was finished, Teora entered the main house, which was cool and bare inside. She found Adimé waiting in the main living room, where a few pieces of beautiful furniture decorated expanses of polished floor. Here and there, hangings and rugs made bright splashes in the dimness. But there was no clutter, none of the bric-a-brac that accumulates over the years.

"Is this a new house?"

"It is a whole new Hacienda. Three years ago. We moved here for...shall we say political reasons."

"Hastar did mention something about it."

"I hope she has not been speaking out of turn."

"I was gathering information. I have a task to perform here, and I want to do the best I can. She was helping me."

Adimé laughed. "And how could she evade your questions?"

Teora's cheeks warmed. "I hope you don't think I was taking advantage of her situation. I only want to do what is the best for Aeru."

The woman regarded her, head tilted to one side. "Strange that you should be so accommodating."

"What do you mean?"

"Oh, nothing. Everyone has been speculating on the great saviour that the priest would bring us. And then we get you." She smiled, a slow, pleasant expression. "Not that I mean to insult you, but you are nothing like what they expect. That will be good for them. If you are strong enough."

"Strong enough?"

"Politics."

Teora grimaced. "Yes, I know all about that. Goianor has reminded me."

"Trust Goianor to remember. He lives and breathes politics."

"Do you know him well?"

"He is my aunt's brother-in-law. If we were Riders, we would be close relations."

Teora took this in. "So do you agree, on...political matters?"

The smile came again, not as pleasant this time. "As a matter of principle, no. Every time."

Teora waved her hand around at the new house. "So all this...?"

"Correct. My husband is too outspoken, and too often right. We are better off out of sight, down here. And we can raise our children as we like."

Teora took the leather chair she was offered. It was softer than it looked, and she sank gratefully into it. A child brought her a cool drink; she sipped it, curious.

"Cactus apple juice. Do you like it?"

"Very refreshing. Especially when I've had nothing but water for days."

"Ah, yes. It has been a rough trip?"

Teora closed her eyes. "Ambush, storm, wild animals, desert: the usual travel odds and ends."

Adimé laughed. "You take everything so well."

"Not much choice, really. What good would complaining do?" She scanned the room, again noticing the quality of the furnishings. "So, what makes the daughter of a wealthy, powerful family marry a rebel and go to live on the outskirts of civilization?"

"Ah, that's a long story." The woman sat as well, arranging her long skirt about her with a graceful flick of her wrist.

"I knew Carlin before. Not well, but everyone knows everyone here. I liked him, but he married his sweetheart, Ilana. She was blonde and beautiful and intelligent, everything a man could want. He was growing in power and maturity. For a while, she kept him from making any mistakes.

304

"Then Hastar was born, and Ilana had a very rough time of it. She never recovered. When she died, she left him with a baby daughter and a broken heart.

"Now you must realize what kind of man this is. He had no mother for Hastar, so he went out and found one. Me. He chose the best he could find, and I was flattered. At first I was only tending her, but I had my suspicions, and sure enough, soon he asked me to marry him.

"I knew it could be a mistake. People told me so, in no uncertain terms. But I thought I knew him better. When I had Amand, I knew my risk had paid off. He treats my son the same as Ilana's daughter. His children are his life. Since then, I have been a good wife to him, although perhaps not as successful at keeping him out of trouble. And I have raised and educated the two children as best I can."

"Educated! I never heard such vocabularies."

"Oh, they are showing off. I have to remind them once in a while to keep it under control. Why use a big word when a simpler one is more correct?"

"It must have been hard, trying to fill the shoes of the first wife he loved so much."

"I have never tried. I am myself, not her. He may remember her all he wishes. How could he not? But I am here, and between us we are forging a life. A good life, with good children. It is here and now, and we are together."

"But why was he worried? Hastar told me she was only a few hours late. It sounded as if he knew about the bear. How could that have been?"

The woman laughed. "If anyone else was asking, I would say you were mistaken. They were trailing a steer, bears kill steers, he guessed...you can imagine the evasions.

"But you know that isn't what happened. He has been upset since yesterday afternoon. I won't say he has visions, but sometimes, when it is important, he just knows. He has done it before. He will drop everything and grab his hat and leave. Straight to where someone is in trouble. Sometimes he is too late, sometimes he can't do anything when he gets there, but he always knows. Do you believe what I am telling you?"

"A month ago, I wouldn't have been so sure. Why didn't he go this time? He must have known right away when it happened."

"That was strange, wasn't it? He kept saying 'She's all right. It was a bear, but she's all right.' Then he would pace some more. Drove us all crazy, having him do that, hour after hour. Especially me, when I was the only one who could guess what he was talking about."

"How are the children now?"

"Amand is fine. He's itching to get out of bed, but I told him he must rest, so he's reading a book. Hastar is not as well. The fever persists, and there are a few hot, red places on her scalp. I have drained two of the worst of them, and it seemed to help. Your soldier friend must have had a tough job cleaning the wound, considering how it was made."

The woman gave a quick shudder, then went on with a determined smile. "His sewing technique is not tidy, but we must not complain. He was most careful where the scar will show."

"Do you think the hair will grow back?"

"We won't know until it grows, will we? What does it matter, in the end? She has been returned to us alive, and that is what counts. I am happy that you came along when she needed you. The Deity must have been watching out for her."

The woman was shaking, and Teora reached out to clasp her hand. "I think She was. I have never felt such a strong reaction from Barozon. It might have been the bear, but even at that. He was absolutely sure that he was going to rescue her. Nothing could have stopped him, not even me."

After a moment Adimé's grip relaxed, and she smiled ruefully at Teora. "I was trying to be strong, but it is hard."

Teora smiled warmly, and squeezed the fingers she held, noticing the slim strength in them. "Tell me something about your husband. Was he a Dancer?"

"Oh, yes, very much so. 'Brilliant but erratic,' they called him. It depended on how he was getting along with his Partner."

"Getting along?"

"They used to fight sometimes."

"You can't fight with your Partner!" Teora fought to keep her voice calm.

The woman smiled. "And a man doesn't fight with a full-grown bull, either. But they did. When they were at odds, their performances were terrible. And then, once they got it settled, everything was wonderful, and they could Dance like the wind."

"Does he always deal with bulls like he did with Barozon?"

"Yes, it's very strange. He has this thing with them. Sometimes he can handle them like calves. Then sometimes he meets one that he doesn't like, and he can't get anywhere near it without the animal going wild. He challenges them, or something."

"That's what I felt today. Like a challenge, but then an acceptance. I don't know who accepted whom, though. Barozon went with him like an unweaned calf."

"As long as they have it worked out, I suppose we shouldn't complain."

The two women laughed comfortably together, dropping their handclasp and sitting back in their chairs. There was a long moment of silence, broken by a deep sigh.

"I must get up and get supper organized for all these important guests." As she stood, she impulsively grasped Teora's hand again.

"Thank you again for saving Hastar. She isn't my daughter, but I've been looking after her since she was six months old, and I couldn't love her more."

Teora smiled. "I've only known her for two days, and I've already promised your husband to risk the displeasure of the Temple for her sake. That girl is going somewhere in her life."

The mother's face lit up. "It could be. It very well could be." Then she turned, businesslike, and bustled into the kitchen. Teora sipped the last of her drink, then hoisted herself out of the soft chair to go in search of the subject of their conversation.

Hastar was propped up in her bed, very still, her eyes half-closed. Her head was capped by a fresh bandage, but her colour was better and her breathing was soft and even. As Teora turned to leave, her eyes opened. "Oh, it's you, Teora. Come in."

"No, you're tired. I can come back later."

"I'm not tired, I'm bored. I'm only staying here because Mother says I must. Come and talk to me."

It was the kind of order an invalid can get away with. Teora sat on the edge of the bed, taking the girl's hand. It felt cool and slightly damp, a good sign.

"What's Corquée like? I mean, you've been travelling with him for weeks, now, and you must have seen him in all sorts of moods."

Teora smiled wryly. "I've seen him in lots of situations, all right. Why are you interested?"

"Well, you know, it was great to have him save me, and all that, and I'd heard the stories about him, but he's not like I thought he would be. Of course he's tall and handsome, and all that, but he's not like my picture of a hero. He's much nicer, and softer, and...realer, I guess."

"I doubt if he considers himself as a hero, Hastar. He has doubts and fears like the rest of us."

"Oh, I know. All that about his sister. That must be hard on him."

"What about his sister? I knew about some kind of trouble, but I didn't want to ask him."

"Oh, his sister got herself into a very delicate situation. She managed to fall in love with this fellow, and she got pregnant."

"Oh, I see."

"I doubt if you do. You see, Corquée didn't know, and he was away. He didn't give the horse."

"What's all this about giving horses? Your father mentioned it to Corquée, and he went all red."

"That's the way they work. When a man is interested in having his sister marry someone, he gives him a horse. If the prospective husband accepts the horse, they sleep together. If the girl gets pregnant, then they can marry if they like. They don't always, of course, because some fellows get a lot of horses. That's how they build up their Remudas."

"Remuda. That's like a Herd of horses?"

"Right. And now that Corquée is home and a hero, he'll be getting horses from all over. Then he'll be rich, and he'll be able to marry whomever he chooses."

"But what was the problem with the sister?"

"Well, Corquée was on a mission – to scout the Magali, I think – and she wouldn't wait for Corquée to get back, and she went with the fellow she was in love with and got pregnant. But because her brother hadn't given him a horse, it wasn't official. That meant, technically, the father of the baby was someone else, so she couldn't marry the real father until the baby was born, and then Corquée could give the fellow a horse, and then they could sleep together, and as soon as she got pregnant again, they could get married."

"But by then Corquée was away again on this latest trip. He couldn't give the horse, and they couldn't start the whole thing?"

"That's right. Isn't it all delightfully complex?"

Teora shook her head. "Sounds awfully mixed up to me. Surely, since everybody knew, they could have pretended that Corquée had given the horse, or something."

Hastar shook her head carefully. "No, no. The Riders are very fussy about that sort of thing. They have so much pride tied up in their rituals and their rules, it keeps them strong. Why are they growing in numbers and power, while we are fading? We have turned the rituals that used to be our strength into rigid rules for keeping the hierarchy in its place."

"Is that something your father said?"

The girl shrugged. "It's what everybody says around here. Only through strength like that of the Curicuiriari will the Enclave survive."

Teora stared for a long time at the small head on the pillow. She couldn't believe it. "Are you thinking what I'm thinking you are thinking?"

A pixie smile. "Maybe."

"Corquée? You're only twelve years old."

"Thirteen. And he's only eighteen. It will take him five years to build up his Remuda enough that he can marry, and there I'll be, eighteen, at prime marrying age."

"So, you'll send Amand off to give him a horse."

"That's right."

"Won't the Haven people be upset?"

"Well, they would, but it won't really matter, because we'll have it all arranged ahead of time. The Temple doesn't approve of all these people having sex and then not getting married. But we'll be getting married; no problem."

"And you have this all figured out in two days. Perhaps that head wound went deeper than we thought." She put her hand on the girl's forehead. "Maybe you're delirious."

"I'm not. And I'm also not a silly little girl falling in love with someone from a story. I had already decided I never wanted to marry one of those hero-types. I only changed my mind after I met Corquée."

"And what does he have to say about this?"

"I haven't told him yet."

"When are you going to let him in on the secret?"

"Tomorrow."

"Tomorrow!"

"Yes. I have an appointment to see him. He's coming here after breakfast, before you leave for the Temple."

Teora tried to keep her voice level. "Aren't you afraid you'll scare him away?"

"I don't think so. I've studied the ways of the Riders, and they are quite businesslike about that sort of thing. Of course, usually the mother does the talking, but I want to do this myself. That's the advantage of being outside their culture, you see. I can make all sorts of changes, and people will forgive me because I don't know any better."

"Hastar, you are so far ahead of yourself that you scare me."

"I scare you? You are the most powerful being in this land right now, you and your Partner, and everyone is starting to realize that enough to start worrying. I don't scare you."

"Not right now, you don't. But some day…"

"Good. If you're going to have power, people have to be a little afraid of you. Not your friends, I mean, but the others, the ones you have to boss around."

Teora shook her head. "I hope you haven't got your heart set on this, Hastar. I mean…" She couldn't go on. This little girl seemed to have things arranged in such a mature way, how could she know?

Hastar reached out and took Teora's hand. "Could you help a bit?"

"Of course."

"Well, it has occurred to me that it might be a bit of a shock if I tell him straight out. Could you maybe, in a sort of subtle way, sort of introduce the subject to him, maybe tonight, so he can think about it? Then when we talk tomorrow, he'll be able to say his mind more clearly."

Teora breathed an inward sigh of relief. "Of course. I'll be very subtle."

She gave Hastar's hand a reassuring pat and went out on her mission. Given time to prepare, Corquée could find a way to let the girl down gently without hurting her feelings or breaking her heart. Or offending her family.

She found the Rider with the horses. Sure enough, he was sitting on a fence rail watching a youth walking a horse around on a long tether. As she approached, Corquée called out some instructions and the lad reversed the horse's direction. Teora swung up on the rail and waited.

"Well, Teora, what do you think?"

"I don't know much about horses. He's very pretty, in a skinny sort of way. Except for his off forefoot."

"That's what I meant. What do you think's wrong with his gait? And it's not the foot, it's the hock."

She watched a bit longer. "You're right. The hock isn't flexing far enough. Have you had a closer look?"

In answer, Corquée jumped into the corral and went over to the horse. He checked the whole leg over, then invited Teora to do the same.

"Feel the tension in the muscles there. He's protecting it."

Teora agreed. "He strained it, and it stiffened up on him. A bit of heat and some light exercise tomorrow will probably fix him up."

The Rider nodded. "And no riding for a week, or until he stops favouring it."

The boy nodded, thanked them profusely, then took the horse away.

"I'm sure Carlin could have told him the same thing, but it's good for our people to be helpful."

Teora jumped back up on the fence so her face was level with the Rider's. "I have something that might not be helpful if you don't handle it right."

"What's that?"

"What do you think of Hastar?"

He grinned. "What a kid! I've never seen anything like her. She is just too smart!"

Teora nodded. "Too smart. She was telling me all about the Curicuiriari marriage traditions. She seems to know a lot about your people."

"That's for sure. She knows things I don't even know. I mean, they're traditions from the women's songs, you know, but still, it's impressive."

"I sure hope her face isn't too scarred."

He tossed his hand in a dismissive gesture. "That scar? It's nothing. In my people it would be like a badge of honour."

"It would?"

"Sure. Anyone with a tale like that for the story fire, and the scars to prove it? It would bring the boys running."

"Oh."

"Sure. She's very pretty, you know. All that blonde hair, those big eyes. And she rides well, too."

"You would notice that."

"Of course. No Rider would ever look at a girl who couldn't ride."

"Corquée! She's only thirteen years old! You haven't been looking at her...like that, have you?"

"Teora, don't be silly. Of course not. But some day she'll be something to look at, and I can't help but notice that."

"Oh."

"What's this all about, anyway? You seem awfully protective all of a sudden. Did she tell you we were meeting tomorrow?"

"Yes. She did."

"She didn't happen to let on what it was all about, did she? It's all a big mystery to me." He turned and faced Teora. "Wait a minute. This is all coming together. All this about marriage rituals. Is that why she wants to talk to me?"

"My horsey friend, you aren't slow yourself." Teora dropped her smile, laid a hand on his arm and stared straight into his eyes. "Corquée, you'll be kind, won't you? You won't hurt her? Find a way to let her down easy."

"Let her down? I certainly will not!"

She sat bolt upright. "You won't?"

"Most definitely not. I'm going to listen very carefully to everything she has to say."

"You are?"

He laughed. "Teora, why are you surprised? It would be a very good match for me."

"Wouldn't your people object?"

"Some would, but most wouldn't. Our people admire the grand gesture, the bold attack. If I were to sneak around and sleep with one of your women without the proper rituals, there would be a big uproar. My sister would have been in serious trouble if she had been sneaky. But she wasn't. She did what she wanted to, out in the open. But I wasn't around to fulfill my part, and she got caught out. Bad timing isn't a sin.

"Teora, things are changing. We Curicuiriari are not going to be able to maintain our way of life forever. Did you know that in the Joined Kingdoms there are great trains of wagons pulled by steam engines that can travel across the prairie as fast as a horse can walk? We can't stay where we are. We have to move ahead. Joining with your people is one solution. You have the cattle; we have the horses to herd them. A man on a horse can take care of five times the cattle that one of your Herdsmen can. Especially in the dry areas where the cattle spread out. If Carlin used Riders, he could run three times the cattle he does now, using that land we rode through, and don't think he doesn't know it.

"If he had a guarantee of influence with our people and he could depend on us, he would start building his Herd next spring. If he could get some of Barozon's bloodline, he'd be away ahead."

"So, you think this whole thing is a good idea?"

"Teora, that girl is thirteen years old, and she has this all figured out already. Can you imagine what a head for business she will have by the time she's twenty?

"And besides which, I like her. She's the spunkiest kid I've ever run across. And those eyes!" He whistled appreciatively. "Five years from now, I'm going to have to marry her to hold on to her!"

Teora cuffed him along the side of the head. "I think you're awful. But you may get what you deserve."

"I hope so."

* * *

The next day, as Teora was leaving the house to mount for the journey, she caught the end of a most interesting conversation. Carlin and Corquée were standing outside the door, staring at the ground meditatively.

"...you understand my position. I'm not going to do you any good with your problems at the Temple."

313

Corquée nodded at this. "I understand completely. You don't get along with them too well yourself. Well, maybe we'll be lucky, and there will be a shakeup at the Temple."

Carlin shook his head dismally. "I've been hoping that for years."

"There are new things coming." Corquée looked up, saw Teora listening. "And here is one of them now." His smile was so wide that Teora knew how the interview had turned out. "How are you this morning?"

"Fine. And you, Carlin. What do you think of all this?"

The man shook his head. "I can't believe she did that. I guess that's what comes of teaching kids to be independent. At least she came to you for advice, first."

"I wouldn't exactly call it coming for advice. More likely for an ally. I guess I'm allowed to ask. Have you come to a decision?"

Carlin raised his hands. "Heavens, no. This is only an idea we are tossing around. A very good idea, but it could be approached in a number of ways, many of which do not involve my daughter's marriage. That's her way of seeing things at the moment. In five years many things could change, including her mind.

"But from a business point of view, it is nothing she hasn't heard me say often enough. Corquée and I will meet again, there's no doubt about it. Anybody with his accomplishments and my daughter's good will has access to my house at any time.

"In fact, that's one reason I have decided to ride into the Enclave with you. Come on, let's mount up."

He slapped the Rider on the back, and the bustle of mounting and leave-taking carried them away.

29. Conversion

As they neared the main town of Aeru, Teora moved Barozon beside Tourantij. "Time for more advice."

"On what subject?"

"What do to when we reach Aeru. It will be a very delicate situation and I want to be as effective as possible. Goianor has started to prime me with what he and his faction want. Carlin is free with his opinions. I need the outside point of view. Give me a rundown on what you know of the situation there."

For a while their mounts jogged along together. Then Tourantij spoke. "The Head Priest is a good man: tough. He is old, but full of strength. He seems only to be concerned with the good of his people. The problem is that he has been too strong for too long. A benevolent dictatorship is still a dictatorship. He has not delegated any authority.

"Those under him have followed his lead, but not with such altruistic motives. Each has created his own sphere of power, his own little empire. The motivation of all of them is to maintain their own domains instead of serving the Temple and the people."

"Is it possible to stay outside the political wrangling?"

"If your power is great enough. If you have to work within the system, it will be much more difficult. Then you will have to choose sides."

"I would like to avoid that."

"Then, from a military viewpoint, your best strategy is an immediate attack. You must overawe them from the first, keep them off balance."

"And the best way to do that is to strike quickly, before they have a chance to know what they are dealing with."

"And before Goianor has a chance to speak to the Head Priest privately."

"What is likely to happen when we reach Aeru? Will there be ceremonies like those at the Haven?"

"Probably. If you are willing to be put off, they will have you sent to your quarters to rest and freshen up. Then Goianor can make his report, and they can prepare for you. If you force a meeting immediately, you might get your licks in first."

Teora nodded, satisfied. "We go right to the Temple, head straight to the Altar. Keep them moving, keep them off balance." She glanced over at him. "I'm not sure I like the idea of a confrontation at the very beginning."

He shrugged. "Ask a soldier for advice and you get a battle plan. Do you have evidence suggesting anything else would work?"

"Not if Goianor is a true representative of what I'm facing."

"They chose him."

"They did."

She rode ahead to match paces with Carlin. "I need your help."

"Of course."

"When we get to the Temple, I want to go straight to the Altar. I do not want to be put off or turned aside. I want to meet the Head Priest as soon as I can. Could you help me to arrange that?"

He grinned, not a pleasant expression. "I saw you talking to your military advisor. A preemptive strike? Very good tactics."

"Confrontation isn't my style, but I see no other options."

"I have to agree."

She cocked an eyebrow up at him. "Says a participant in the battle."

"A fair assessment. But it's your choice."

"It is, and I have decided. You can help me?"

"You have only to ask. I will lead you to the Altar immediately. I will turn aside as many of those who wish to interfere as I can. If I cannot, you will have to take over."

Teora matched his roguish grin. "Barozon and I will lead. You follow right behind me and tell me the path. No one will give us any trouble."

As they rode on, Teora planned her strategy. Her experience with Goianor had trained her well. She knew that she must not give the slightest concession, not weaken in any way. She would be polite, even pleasant, but completely uncompromising. If the power of the Deity supported her, she would triumph.

However, as their distance from Carlin Wynn's ranch lengthened, her strange feeling of unease returned. Barozon swung his head from side to side, searching for an intangible enemy. Teora knew it was not as simple as that. She clamped down on the feeling and concentrated on today's problems.

As Tourantij predicted, they were met well out from the Temple by an officious Priest. Dust marred the bottom of his robe, and his breath was coming quickly, as if he had been walking fast. Teora stopped in front of him, gazing down affably from her high seat.

"Good afternoon, Priest. Are you here to escort us to the Temple? How considerate of you."

"Welcome, emissaries of the Haven. The Head Priest greets you. He will see you in the Temple as soon as you are rested. I am Sumner, and I am to guide you to your quarters, where you may freshen up from your journey. Please follow me." He started off, aiming towards a side street.

Teora let him go for several steps. "I thank you, Priest Sumner, but we have not travelled far today. We are not tired from the road, and we will be quite happy to see your Head Priest now."

She moved Barozon off along the route Carlin had told her led to the Temple, leaving the priest and his retinue to scramble to get ahead. When he came even with her, she could see that he wished to speak, but she ignored him, making a point of scanning the buildings on either side of the street. They were similar to those in the Haven, mostly built of whitewashed adobe or red brick, thick-walled, low and cool.

When they approached the Temple, Teora could see that the main building was similar in plan to the Temple at the Haven, but on a smaller scale. When yet another group of Priests intercepted them, she knew which way to turn. She thanked them politely for their concern, but said that she wished to pay her respects to the Deity and give thanks immediately for her safe journey. She would go straight to the Altar.

Having taken the opposition by storm, she then slipped off Barozon's back and paced with dignity into the Altar Room. It was smaller than that at the Haven, but with enough space for a medium-sized congregation and certainly enough for her party and Barozon. The Head Priest sat in his chair of state, his robes slightly disarrayed as if he had arrived in a hurry. The place to his left, where the Priestess and the Consort usually stood, was vacant.

I wonder what that means?

The Head Priest was an imposing figure when he rose to his full height, up on his dais with his robes and headpiece. He welcomed them cordially and formally, offering the hospitality of the whole of the Enclave for such distinguished guests. He then had chairs brought and bade them be seated, taking advantage of the pause to take Goianor aside, talking quietly and rapidly.

But Goianor shook his head emphatically and did not lower his voice. She had never expected to see him speak forcibly to a superior. "It was impossible, Rioran. Everything we have heard about the political troubles in the Joined Kingdoms is true. Teora and Barozon could be the solution we have been searching for. I have spent over a month with them, and I tell you, the hand of the Deity is moving in this matter.

"Not moving in the ways we expected, to be sure. But moving, nonetheless. We are in a time of change, Rioran, and if we cannot bend with the wind, we will be snapped off like dead twigs."

The Head Priest waited, his eyes measuring Goianor. "I am moved by your confidence, Goianor. I have seldom seen you support any cause so forcefully." He turned back to Teora.

"Goianor speaks well of you, and your Partner is a superb animal. I must conclude that the Haven has done its best by us. At least we can start working up our breeding charts, to place the Consort's seed where it will do the most good."

Teora nodded. "It is to be hoped that placement will be as widespread as possible. I would not see the Consort's seed concentrated unevenly, especially for reasons which have nothing to do with a breeding program."

Rioran raised his eyebrows, then glanced pointedly at Goianor. The Priest stepped forward, the vein in his forehead showing.

"Please excuse Teora's misunderstanding, Head Priest. She has already been subjected to some subtle political pressures."

Teora rose from her chair and advanced as well. She spoke as quietly and calmly as she could but allowed no compromise to creep into her voice. "I need no one to excuse me, Head Priest Rioran, and I doubt I misunderstand. I was sent here because you have serious problems, and not only those of genetics. On my journey, the Deity has seen fit to try me in Her own ways, to the point where Priest Goianor recognizes Her handiwork. However, do not expect me to wave my hand and painlessly cure your malaise. There will have to be changes. Changes come hardest to the leaders of the old ways. I sympathize with you and will try not to upset your routines.

"But remember. Something must be wrong with your ways, or I would not be here. Prepare yourselves for change, as Goianor suggests. And no one more than yourself, Head Priest Rioran."

The Head Priest stood still, his face working. Teora could see astonishment, then rage, building. As his mouth opened, his hand rose, and she could see the intent.

Now was the moment. If the Power of the Deity was within her, to call upon at need, never would her need be stronger. She brought back all the other instances when she had felt the power, allowing the emotion to build within her. She remembered the wolves cowering before her, the pirates of the Log Jam frozen at her command and the raw challenge of Barozon as the blood of his hereditary enemy dripped from his horns.

And nothing happened.

Time froze. Her mind spun frantically. *Where is the Power when I need it? Deity, please!*

Slowly, ever so slowly, the Head Priest's face darkened in anger, his eyes boring into hers. She felt his power filling the room, the support of all his priests behind him.

He is the strength of Aeru. In her heightened awareness she could feel the power rolling off him in waves, but something unbalanced it. The feeling of wrongness that had nagged at her for many days surged. *This is wrong. I must not confront power with power. Aeru does not lack power.*

She searched the feeling again, holding it up to the dim light of the Deity that permeated the Temple. *That's it! The power is too strong. The faith is too weak. That I can deal with.*

Faith. She reached within herself for that sense of sureness she had felt when Linea had blessed her. *I don't need the Deity's help for this. Power comes from Her, but faith comes from the People.* She spread her inner sense wide, searching for faith like hers.

Then joy surged through the Temple, the presence of the Deity countering the power that boiled within its walls. The two forces met and joined, creating an aura of rightness so strong it was nearly visible. Teora felt a glow of relief. *I am truly Chosen for this task, and the Deity is with me.* As the Head Priest's pointing finger centred on her, she raised a finger of her own, moving it delicately from side to side. Smiling gently, she opened her palm in a gesture to halt, and shook her head, just a little.

"It is not for you and me to argue, Head Priest. We must work together for the good of the Enclave and the goals of the Deity."

The Head Priest froze, his eyes bulging in surprise, his hand falling slowly back to his side. Teora's smile widened, pleased for him. Whatever his faults, if he had been unaware of the Deity's presence, he would not have been worthy of his position. Now he fully understood. It was up to him to bend or break.

Goianor again proved his usefulness. "As you can see, Rioran, the Haven has done well by us. There can be no doubt that she has been Chosen for this duty. It is our challenge to help the Chosen to help us. I have discovered that this is not always easy."

The Priest continued to speak in this vein, filling the gap, allowing the enormity of the situation time to sink into the Head Priest's mind. As he spoke, Teora allowed the presence to drain from her, leaving her slightly intoxicated, relaxed, satisfied. She felt a stir of sympathy for this man, who probably felt that he was doing the right thing for his people, empathy for his frustration when nothing went right, pity for the awareness he must have of his own failure.

When Goianor paused, she spoke again before the Head Priest could gather his thoughts. "I am here, as you have requested. There is no rush. These things will not be fixed in a day or a month. I will not destroy your way of life with a wave of my hand. Perhaps we could, for the moment, concentrate on the simpler problem? We should begin to organize the breeding schedules as soon as possible."

The Head Priest was recovering. His face had regained its normal colour. His voice was calm, although Teora could detect a tremour in it. "A sensible suggestion, Chosen of the Deity. But that is a task for the specialists. Please give your Partner's heritage lists to Goianor, and he will start the matching process," the old man's face twisted wryly, "fairly, and in a widespread manner, according to correct breeding procedures."

He turned back to Teora. "But perhaps you and I, Lady, should speak of more serious things. Alone."

Wondering what was coming, Teora nodded graciously. As she passed Barozon's papers to Goianor, she raised an eyebrow, but the priest could, or would, give her no hint.

The Head Priest strode towards a nearby door. It opened as if by magic before him. He stopped and motioned Teora through. She found herself in a neat, comfortable room with a well-used desk and chair. Soft eastern light poured through a spacious window, and leather-covered chairs grouped around a table. Following her in, the

Head Priest turned and motioned, and the door closed softly but firmly behind him.

Teora stood waiting, wondering what to expect. To her surprise, the man took her hand, leading her in a courtly manner to the table, seating her, then himself. He gazed a moment deeply into her eyes, his wrinkled hand still holding hers. With a shock, it came to her how old he must be. Also, his eyes glistened, and a tear hung on his eyelid, ready to fall. He shook his head, as if denying the emotion, but his voice trembled.

"My Lady, you must forgive an old man his weakness. You have little idea what this day means to me."

She had no response. All she could do was wait until he explained.

"You are very young. You cannot know how it has been. I have tried for decades to make a difference, and I have failed. My people are dying. The Great Experiment is failing, and I can do nothing. I see the primitive tribes flourishing and my Herds dwindling. I once thought I had the fire and the iron in my soul to lead my people out of this decline. It has been many years since I discovered that I did not. Since then, I have tried my hardest, but it was not enough. Many nights I have prayed for more power, for more faith, but it was never enough. I see my land, my people, and I feel an emptiness. I look within me, and again, a void. My faith fails daily and, try as I can, I can do nothing to regain it."

Teora shook her head. "It is not possible to try to regain faith. Faith is, or is not. Trying makes it worse."

His old head shook in time with hers. "How well you know." His chin came up. "But that was yesterday. Today, with a gesture of your hand, you have cured my faith. I have never felt such belief, even on the day I became Head Priest. I can never doubt again. I know I am alone no longer. The Deity has waited long and long, but She has answered my prayers."

Teora shook her head again, once. "I hope your faith in me is justified. I have no idea, at this moment, what I am going to do for you and the rest of Aeru. As I said outside, the events of this journey have proved to me beyond doubt that the Deity is taking a hand. What role She has for me, I do not know. All I can do is try. And I can give you no assurances. I have felt your need ever since I set foot on the soil of Aeru. I feel the need for change, and I fear it will be a painful change."

"Painful?"

"All change is painful. Even one as young as I am knows that. I have no idea how the pain will come, but already I can give you a taste. Although I have felt the need flowing from your land, there was one place where the need was muted. One spot where there is balance and rejuvenation. Do you know where that spot was?"

The old head shook slowly. "My dear, you do not know how you drive daggers into my heart. You have no idea how you bring my own inadequacies home to me."

"You already know?"

The Head Priest rested his hands on the table as if gaining strength from the heavy wood of the surface, pausing to organize his thoughts. Then, staring through the window, off into the hills to the east, he began.

"Once, many years ago, I made a choice. I made the only choice I could make. I had begun to realize that I did not have the personal power to drag the whole of my people out of their lethargy. At that time, an opportunity was granted to me to make a huge change. I could take a new path, hoping that it would lead to success, dreading that it would bring quick disaster. Or I could hold to my old ways, hold firmer, become more determined to use my old skills to help my people as best I could."

The old man's eyes swung to Teora's face. "At that time, there was one who could have been my successor. One who had the strength of mind to lead after me. I could have trained him, used his strength, his fire, to shore up my weaknesses."

The eyes held hers, but the Head Priest's body seemed to droop. "But I could not. Perhaps I was already too old, too set in my ways. The price he asked was too great. I could not change as he would have had me change. Instead of embracing him and the new ideas he brought, I branded him a rebel and drove him from me. I strengthened my fortress against him and all the newness he stood for. I made change my enemy, blamed change for our problems.

"And now you come to me, bringing the change I have feared. You come to me imbued with the power of the Deity, telling me that my way was wrong. You enter my Temple with my enemy at your side and tell me that he will be the saviour of my people. It is a hard blow you deal me, Teora of the Haven. It is a terrible thing to realize that your life's work has been for nothing."

He shook his head, wondering. "I told myself I hated him. I despised everything he stood for. And then his wife died. And I ached for him with every breath. But I could do nothing. What can you do at a time like that?"

"You might have used it as an excuse to mend fences."

The Head Priest shook his head, smiling fondly. "Not with Carlin. His heart was broken, but his strength doubled because he cared even less than before what happened to him. He became more outspoken, more deviant. I tell you, if it had not been for his daughter, he would have broken loose, and I would have had to destroy him."

"His daughter?"

"Yes, his concern for her led him to some caution, I believe. And then he hired a nurse, and the nurse became his wife. With his new son, he became calmer, less reckless. Still, he was a thorn in my side until schooling time came, and he removed his children from the possibility of my influence. I was relieved and let him go willingly. Since that time, I have been too concerned with my problems here to worry about him, and he has been satisfied to spend his time solving his own difficulties. And now you are going to bring him back, aren't you? He is our only hope?"

Teora shook her head. "I wouldn't say that, although his vitality would aid us greatly. In fact, his daughter may fit that role better."

"Hastar! I heard she was injured. How is she?"

"Recovering well enough. The bear ripped her scalp open, but we got it sewed back pretty well. When we left, the fever was subsiding and she was getting back to normal, if putting everyone on their ear is normal for her." Teora took in the old man's fond look. "Why do you smile?"

"You probably did not know. Hastar is my great-granddaughter. My daughter's only child went off and married my enemy. I labeled her as wrong-headed as her husband, and a traitor to me as well. What has Hastar done to disturb things now?"

"I'm afraid you may think that she has betrayed you even worse. She has taken it into her head to contract a marriage with one of the Curicuiriari."

Teora watched with concern how the old man would take this news. To her surprise, he nodded slowly. "That is the way it would be. That is the kind of thing her father would approve of." He smiled, then began to laugh, a hoarse chuckle that turned into a cough before it faded.

When he could speak again, Rioran continued. "Why am I blaming her father? That is exactly the kind of thing that her mother would have done. Did do, actually. And for all the right reasons, I suppose you will remind me. Tell me. What is she like? I have not seen her for years. Is she pretty? Is she as bright as she once was?"

"Oh, she's pretty enough, even with the injury. She's brighter than any child has a right to be. Imagine, arranging her own marriage at the age of thirteen!"

He laughed delightedly. "Oh, yes, I can see her mother in her. Bright and headstrong."

Teora considered this. "She's not that headstrong. At least not in the stubborn sense. She knows that she is doing the right thing and can't see why everyone else doesn't agree. I suppose that's one definition of headstrong. Of course, if she turns out to be right, that sort of changes things."

"Oh, yes it does." The Head Priest slapped his knee. "I can't wait to see her. And of course I will, won't I, now that her father is to have a position of power."

Teora snapped alert. "I didn't say that! I have just stepped through your door. I have made no suggestions on how to solve your problems."

He sighed. "You see? The disadvantage of wielding such power. I do not have to consult anyone. If I decide something is right, I order it, and it is done."

Teora shook her head. "If you really want to know, that may be what is wrong with your system here. From what I understand of government, that's not very healthy."

Again the wry smile. "You have come to me with the solution to our problems, but you will not let me implement it, because that is part of the problem?"

"That's one way to put it. We had better go very slowly in this area. Of course, it wouldn't hurt to let Carlin know that we are ready to listen to him."

The Head Priest leaned forward, and she could see the enthusiasm come back into his eyes. "Correct, but we must do it slowly or we will create a new division."

"Yes. There must be many in your Temple whose power is based on your old system. Unless you are willing to throw them out, you are going to get a lot of resistance."

"People such as Goianor. That is where you come in, Teora. You have impressed him; you will move the rest of them, where I may not."

"What if they aren't as perceptive as you? What if they can't feel the presence of the Deity in me?"

He laughed and rose to his feet. "You underestimate yourself, my dear. That is like saying they are not sensitive enough to feel a sledgehammer blow to the head."

He put an arm around her, leading her towards the door. "Come, Chosen of the Deity. We have work to do."

A circle of faces blanked in astonishment as the two entered the main audience room together. The Head Priest observed this reaction, and Teora could feel the tension through his arm before he dropped it from her shoulders. His head rose above her, and the formality rang in his voice.

"The Chosen has persuaded me beyond the shadow of a doubt that there is much change coming to us all. It is a challenge, a struggle, but I have great hope in its outcome, greater hope than I would have dared, when we sent Priest Goianor on his mission.

"Change is a terrible thing. The only thing that makes it bearable is the hope it will bring success. Will the new order be wonderful enough that the pain was worth it? I do not know, my people. I only know that it is our only chance. The sole other path leads downward to oblivion, to the death of the Great Experiment of the Aeran Enclave. The Enclave may change, but it will not die. It may not be what our ancestors envisioned, but it will exist to praise the glory of the Deity, and that is all that matters.

"Goianor, take our guests to their quarters. Carlin, if you have continued business with the Chosen, you are welcome to remain. Teora, is there anything else you require?"

"There is. When will I meet your Priestess and your Dancers?"

The Head Priest shook his head. "We have no Priestess." He paused to regard the group. "No, no, you who gaze at me in astonishment, I speak no sacrilege, and in your hearts, you know it. How can you think that girl is Chosen by the Deity, when you have felt the power that Teora brings with her? We have had no Priestess for years now. We have some lovely girls who Dance well enough and grace our ceremonies with their beauty, but not one Priestess." He shook his head, then raised it again.

"Perhaps that will be the sign. Perhaps when we have changed enough, the Deity will again shower her blessing on her Priestess. We can only hope." He turned to Teora. "Our 'Priestess' is at her parents' home today. We will send for her immediately, of course.

"And now I must leave you. As you may guess, we have much to organize. The Temple Council will meet in two hours. I suggest you all do a lot of thinking before then."

His voice took on the ceremonial tone. "Chosen of the Deity, you are thrice welcome to Aeru. You bring the double-edged sword of turmoil and hope to us. Despite my trepidation, I thank you."

With a nod that was almost a bow, he spun around and, followed by his advisors, swept from the room.

Teora turned to Tourantij, making an exaggerated wiping motion across her forehead with her sleeve.

He grinned. "I don't know what happened in that little room, but you seem to have made an important ally."

She nodded, her eyes seeking Carlin. "Your politics are quite involved here. With personal relationships, I mean."

The man's eyes held hers, then dropped. "I have been too proud, I know. He is a good man. His intentions cannot be questioned, but I could not bend to his will."

She laid a hand on his shoulder. "And he could not bend to yours. It is not unusual, among the strongest of men. He would like to see Hastar."

His head came up. "He would?"

"Of course! He is an old man, and she is a great favourite. He was most concerned when he heard of her injury. He sounds quite proud of her. Apparently she is much like her mother."

"Oh, she is, that."

She pulled him around and started towards the door. "Then he will see her. Come, let us inspect our quarters. I could do with a bath!"

30. Bureaucracy

Barozon pawed the earth, watching the dust float into the morning sun. He felt good. For a long, long time, he had been walking, always walking, with no Temple and only people and horses for company. Now it was changed. He was in a Temple pasture; he could feel the aura. It wasn't much of an aura, very faint and weak, but it was there. And there were cattle all around. Lots of cattle. Besides the smell, he could feel them, and they needed him. He paced, restless.

Soon I will go to them. Soon. Now if only Teora would come and Dance. He jogged around the pasture once, checking its confines. *Of course, I would never break a fence. I am much too well-mannered for that. But there is a great need. If it gets stronger...Teora is coming. She is happy!*

"So, are you comfortable here? Got enough grass to eat?" She leaped the stile and ran over to him, rubbing his ears, running her fingers through the curls on his neck. "Want a bit of exercise?"

She slipped up on his back, and he joyfully began his warmup turns. Soon they were into the routines, the hot sun and the dust ignored, swinging together through the moves, stretching the unused muscles. They had practised often on the trail, but it could never be quite as good as in a spacious Temple paddock.

This was no practise session. Teora simply ran through the Dances without stopping. There were plenty of rough spots, but they didn't matter. There was only the Dance, the beautiful movement and Partnership.

Teora was enjoying herself so much that she lost track of her surroundings. She continued to Dance, but it finally came to her that no one was watching. Normally she would have gathered a crowd of curious stable workers and Herdsmen. Someone must have given the word not to bother her. Well, she would fix that. Performance was part of her life. Anyone could watch, any time. It would be good for them.

 Then she noticed a slim figure pasted against a nearby shed, almost out of sight. As she Danced, Teora kept an eye on the person. *Someone with enough desire to disobey the strict Temple rules might be worth knowing.* Teora continued her routines, the small audience adding to her enjoyment. She pulled Barozon into a series of intricate maneuvers, one of their best performance closers.

Her audience – a girl in Dancer's clothing, tall and slim like Linea, but with light curly hair – moved forward, watching intently.

Teora let loose a bit more with some showy flips at full gallop. The next time she rounded that side of the pasture, the girl was at the fence, her eyes wide. Before she could move, Teora made a sliding dismount right in front of her.

"Good morning. Did you like our Dancing?"

The girl's face froze. She glanced right and left, but her head did not move.

"Aren't you supposed to be here?"

The wide eyes flicked around again, as if seeking escape. "Oh...yes. Rioran said I was supposed to watch you."

"Oh. Good. Where's everyone else?"

"Oh...they're not allowed. Only me... I guess."

"And what's your name?"

"Oh...I'm sorry, I didn't introduce myself. I'm Rebiema. I'm...the Priestess."

It was Teora's turn to be wide-eyed. This timid thing was the Priestess? Then she remembered herself. Scrambling over the stile, she presented herself with a formal greeting, giving the Priestess her full due.

The girl was taken aback but, forced to follow through the ritual, she gained confidence in the familiar pattern. When she had finished, she actually smiled timidly. Teora returned the smile.

"And Rioran sent you out to watch me."

"Yes. He said that would be easiest."

"And was it?"

The frizzy head dropped, then the girl looked up. "Not really."

"Then he must have had some other reason to do it. Probably wanted us to get to know each other before the formal stuff. So let's get to know each other. Do you want to meet my Partner?"

She could see by the glow in the girl's eyes that she had hit the right note. Together they entered the pasture.

Barozon waited eagerly. His ears flicked forward; his head swung from one to the other. His feet shifted. *She is a Dancer. Will she Dance with me too?*

Rebiema read his movement, her eyes shooting to Teora's face.

Teora nodded. "Don't hesitate. He is a marvelous Dancer. You will have no trouble."

The girl squared her thin shoulders and gave the signal. As Barozon started his turn, she ran alongside, then swung up on his back. After a brief hesitation, she righted herself with a nervous laugh. "He is so tall!"

Teora sent out a cautious message to her Partner to go easy, but it was unnecessary. As the girl got into her stride her confidence increased, and her lithe body swung through the moves easily. Gone was the hesitation, the shyness. This girl had won the competition to become Priestess, and her technique showed it. To Teora's critical eye she did no really difficult moves, but her style was consistent and her moves more fluid and graceful than those of most Dancers.

When she had finished, Rebiema and Barozon stood in front of Teora, both breathing heavily. The girl's proud carriage spoke volumes. "He is beautiful!"

Teora laughed, stepped forward to rub her Partner's ears. "Most people don't use that word to describe him, but I know what you mean. He loved Dancing with you."

"Did he? Did he really?"

Teora regarded the girl. She was beginning to see her task here. "You are a Dancer. You don't need to ask me that."

The girl hesitated. "Oh...I'm sorry..." Then she noticed Teora's encouraging smile. "I don't need to ask, do I? We had a great Dance together, didn't we, fellow?" She, too, reached out to touch the great head fondly.

The two stood companionably close, fussing over Barozon, which he enjoyed immensely. "How long have you been Priestess?"

"Only five months. I still don't believe it, sometimes." The girl's voice dropped. "I really wasn't the right choice, you know."

"Not the right choice! How could that be?"

"Oh...I'm...I'm not the right person for the job." Rebiema turned an earnest face to Teora.

"I know that Aeru is in trouble. We need someone who is forceful, strong-minded. Someone to lead our people. I'm not a leader. I'm sure you can see that already. I'm too shy. The only thing I can truly do is Dance." Her head came up. "I really can Dance."

Teora laughed, but inside her mind was whirling. "Oh, yes. You can Dance all right. Barozon knows that."

"But that does not make me the right Priestess. That's why I'm glad you came. I mean, I've enjoyed being Priestess, but I know I'm not doing a very good job, so..."

"Wait a minute right there!" Teora's voice cracked in surprise. "I'm not here to become your Priestess!"

"You aren't? But that's why they sent for you, isn't it?"

"Rebiema, I was sent to bring help. I suppose if I decided that what Aeru needed was a new Priestess, then that is what I would have to do. But nothing has been decided yet. I've only been at the Temple a day. Having seen you Dance, I don't think there is much question of taking your place."

She stared forcefully at the girl. "You are not the wrong choice. I may know what the problem is."

"You do?"

"Yes. Your Partner must be the best bull of his generation, and you are the best Dancer. You have been chosen by the Priesthood of the Temple to be the Priestess, and he to be the Sire of the Herds. But you have not yet been Chosen by the Deity."

"I haven't?"

Teora shook her head. "If you have to ask that, you haven't."

She reached out, took the girl's hand, placed it on Barozon's head, with her own hand covering it. "Feel this."

As she had done the day before, Teora reached inside herself for the feeling of the Deity's presence. She only needed the glow, the feeling of faith, such as Linea had given her back in the Haven. She stared into Rebiema's eyes, watching the realization dawn. Then she let the feeling slide away.

The girl stood, riveted, for a long time. Then her eyes dropped. "I see. It all becomes very clear, now. That is what it feels like to be Chosen."

Teora nodded. "At the Haven when the Priestess is Chosen, she feels it automatically. For me, it was not as easy. I have come by my Choosing through trial, suffering and great need. Because of this my powers are much stronger. For some reason, you have not had that experience. This is not your fault. There is something wrong here. I can feel the crying out, the need. Can you feel it?"

"I...I don't know. There has always been something. That is why I competed. I would never have had the nerve, otherwise. But I felt a need, and I had to do whatever I could, no matter how small. But I thought that was just me. I'm glad you can feel it too."

Teora clapped the girl on the shoulder. "You see? You are the right one for the duty after all. Only you are sensitive enough to feel the need of your Land. What we have to do is get the rest of it straightened out."

"Can you do that?"

"I have no idea. Remember, it isn't only me. Rioran is trying his best, and after all, the Deity has some interest here, as well."

She considered Barozon. "He's had enough exercise to last him for a while. Do you want to introduce me to your Partner?"

The girl's quick smile clouded as suddenly. "I...I'm not sure. Maybe we should ask Rioran."

"Rebiema, I am beginning to see your problem here. You shouldn't be asking the Head Priest anything of the sort. He should be asking you. You seem to be always second-guessing yourself. Someone has taught you to control your impulses."

"Of course. My impulses always seem to get me into trouble."

"Trouble with whom? With the authorities, I bet. Did one of your impulses ever get you injured, ever hurt anyone else?"

The girl was insulted. "No! I would never do anything dangerous."

"But our impulses are the channel the Deity uses to reach us. Surely you can feel that when you Dance with your Partner. The glow, the rightness of it."

"Oh, yes. That's why I love to Dance. I can never get that feeling anywhere else."

Teora chuckled. "Wait till you fall in love for the first time."

"What?"

"Oh, I remember my first crush on a boy. I didn't Dance for three weeks, just mooned around at home, or draped over Barozon's neck in the pasture. He was very good about it, as I recall. Barozon, I mean. The boy never even found out."

"I guess I never have been in love like that."

"When it comes, you'll know. Now, do you want to introduce me to your Partner? I can tell you do. If Rioran should object, though I see no reason why he would, you must stand up for yourself." That ought to be easy enough, with Teora to back her up and take the blame if necessary.

331

Rebiema's face brightened. She turned to say good-bye to Barozon, then fairly flew over the stile. Teora followed at a more sedate pace, grinning to herself. *I will have to foster a quiet rebellion, here. At least part of my job will be fun.*

The meeting with Dembe went beautifully. He was of only medium size by Haven standards, but beautifully proportioned. He did not seem overly strong to Teora, and when she Danced with him she was careful not to let her extra weight throw him off stride. When Rebiema worked with him, Teora could see how well the two were suited, and why they would have won any Competition in this small enclave. Even at the Haven they would have attracted serious attention.

The formal meeting went well, too. When Rebiema greeted her in the ceremony, Teora allowed a trickle of her faith to flow through the girl's hands, the reverse of the usual process, but the sudden brightness and strength in the Priestess' eyes was worth it.

Immediately after the ceremony Teora buttonholed Tourantij to sound him out on some ideas. They had supper together and talked far into the night. Again she was impressed by his political acumen.

With his assistance and the obvious nature of the problem, it only took a few days to get a preliminary idea of what was wrong.

As prepared as she could be, she asked for an audience with the Head Priest. Again, they met in his working room. This time he sat behind his big desk, and she pulled up a chair to one side. After a few pleasantries, he looked expectantly at her.

"I am beginning to get a feeling about your problems here in Aeru, and I'm afraid you won't want to hear about it."

"Teora, surely you know that I only want the best for Aeru. I will listen to anything you say, no matter how difficult it is for me to hear, personally."

Teora put a hand on his, where it lay on the desk in front of him. "You must understand that this is not all your fault. This problem has been in the making since long before you came to your position of power. In fact, the reason that you came to power is that your style suited the development of the power structure that had developed.

"What is wrong here is the imbalance of power. In the Haven, we have the Priesthood and the Priestess. We also have the Head Councillor, who has complete control over the running of the city. These three are almost equal in power, and they balance each other. Here, it seems that the Priesthood runs the Temple as well as the city.

"That is your first problem. There is no place for a strong and able secular leader like Carlin. He must fall in line and join the Priesthood or become an outcast.

"Worse still, this extra power concentrated in one body has overwhelmed the Priestess and taken over her functions as well.

"This is the most serious part of the problem. Because of the weakness of her situation, your Priestess has not developed the faith to accept the position. As you are aware, she has never felt the presence of the Deity. Rebiema is an obvious Chosen. Her Partner is a beautiful animal, although not powerful. She is a very sensitive girl, very aware. Their Dancing is a perfect representation of the bond between the People and the Herds, but it lacks the faith that keeps us all together. She lacks the presence of the Deity, and she will never open herself to receive it as long as she looks to the Temple and to you for permission to...eat lunch or anything else."

Rioran digested this. "You tell me the things I do not want to hear. The girl was the obvious choice. Her lack of confidence is her weakness, and I sought to shore up her power with my own. In doing so, I have weakened her further."

Teora's heart went out to him. "Your honesty with yourself is cruel, Head Priest. Do not allow this self-criticism to hamper your confidence. You are the only one with both the strength and the ability to carry Aeru through this difficult transition. If you fail, then others below you in the hierarchy with less ability and none of your motivation will take over, and you know what they will do."

"Only too well. They will attempt to consolidate their power in the worst way possible."

"Yes. Power with no purpose other than power itself. If it comes to a direct conflict, I will need the full power of the Deity to overcome them. And I represent our faith, not our power. I'm not sure that the Deity would support me in such a destructive action. I am not sure I would even try to fight.

"I don't need to tell you that Aeru is at a crux of its existence. You have reached the point where either the problem is solved or the Deity allows the Experiment to fail. If those below you take over, it will be too late. I may have to return to the Haven in defeat and leave Aeru to its own fate.

"So do not be hard on yourself. Don't think of it as trying to make up for your own mistakes. Consider it the opportunity to make up for two hundred years of mistakes."

The old man laid his other hand on top of hers. "I can see more and more the Deity's reason for sending you, Teora. Every time I feel Her presence flowing through you, I am rejuvenated. What do you suggest I do about Rebiema?"

"Very little. She is denying the very source of her faith in order to keep on your good side. I will encourage her to make her own decisions, and I hope you will take her independence in good grace. If she makes mistakes, let her make them. She must try her new wings to strengthen them. Then some day she may even fly."

"Is that possible?"

"I don't know if she has the strength. She has all the other qualities."

"I noticed a difference in the ceremony."

"One step only. The rest may take time."

"We don't have much time."

Teora was surprised. "I am in no rush. I thought I made that clear."

"Teora, do you know how old I am?"

"Oh."

"Yes. I don't have a whole lot of time left, and if you say I am important to all this, we had better get moving."

"Then I guess we had better."

31.   Ball of Fluff

"This is very frustrating." The Head Priest threw a sheaf of papers on his desk.

Teora concurred wholeheartedly. "It's like wrestling a haystack. Every time you think you have something to grab onto, you end up with a handful of loose grass."

Rioran slapped both hands down on the desk. "I should be able to do something. I have known this system all my life, I have thrived on it. What can we do? No, Carlin. I know what you are going to say. Throw them all out. I cannot do that as long as there is a chance that they will cooperate."

Carlin grinned, then frowned in his own frustration. "I see your point. Throwing them all out wouldn't help much anyway. Their underlings would be happy to slip into the old places, continue the old routines. And we can't get rid of everyone. We need some knowledgeable, trained people and there are no others in Aeru. What is the soldier's solution?"

They all turned to Tourantij, who sat, staring out the window. "I know nothing about Headquarters organization. I only know that, given a chance, it will grow like a weed, and the only solution to weeds is to root them out completely."

"Like a garden that is so heavily invaded that the best thing to do is clear it out completely, then start fresh? We cannot do that here, Tourantij. We have no new seed."

"I know, Rioran. An unfortunate metaphor, but the point remains."

The Head Priest scanned around the table. Teora caught his attention and flicked a glance at Rebiema, sitting quietly at one corner.

He turned his smile on the girl. "What do you say, Rebiema? How does this seem from the point of view of the Priestess?"

She sat straighter, red creeping up her cheeks. "I...I have been listening." She glanced at Teora, who nodded encouragement. "I don't know anything about what you are dealing with...but I do have something I should say."

The Priestess looked around. "I don't have anything to do with the power of the Temple, so I cannot help you with this problem. But Teora has made me see that my position, my duty, rests with the faith of the People. Their faith in the Deity, and also their faith in our ability to do what is best for them."

She took a deep breath. "And I know we are failing. How can the People depend on us to help them, when they see the power of the Temple being used for the wrong purposes? We are not helping them. We are driving them away. You don't know how frustrating it is for me. Teora has shown me what the presence of the Deity can do. I felt it in her the first day I met her. Now, when I search for it, I feel the faith in my Dancers, in some of the Priests, even in myself, but I can do nothing to make it grow. I just don't know how!" The girl's fists were knotted on the table in front of her, and tears glistened in her eyes.

Then the tension left her shoulders, and she glanced around the table. "But you do know, don't you? You're all feeling the same thing."

Rioran nodded. "Perhaps not as deeply as you do, my dear, but yes, we are feeling the same frustration, and I thank you for putting it into words for us."

The Priestess bowed her head to hide her blush, and the Head Priest turned his attention to the rest of the meeting. "Does anyone have another idea? Even an outlandish one that might give us a start?"

Tourantij rested his forearms on the edge of the table, his fingers laced together. "Let me try another suggestion. Why don't you make a list of all the tasks that need to be done and give someone the task of designing an entirely new system to do those tasks? A system with completely new departments, a minimum of paperwork and an emphasis on getting the work done. Make up descriptions of each position as thoroughly as possible. Then have each worker make up a list of his own skills and talents and match them up to the tasks. You might even have them bid for positions, or something of the sort. It would start you off fresh, anyway."

Carlin slapped the table. "I like it! That would get rid of the 'It won't work any other way,' line we always get."

Teora agreed. "We could ask for input from everyone, but only after our own organizational plan is finished."

Rioran finally nodded. "This will give the opposition time to regroup. We can't make any changes until the plan is finished. It might take months. It should, if we do it carefully."

Tourantij shook his head. "It might not work that way. If we challenge each department to come up with an organization of its own, with the threat of our plan hanging over them, they might do a lot of it for us."

Rioran gave his wry smile. "I have little hope. I suspect they will use it as a means of creating more committees and wasting more time."

Carlin matched his grin. "But at least that will keep them busy, thinking that they can stay in control. There have been shakeups before, and they have always weathered them. I'm sure they believe, at the moment, that sooner or later Teora will go home, Rioran will die or give up, and all will go on as before."

"Then let them believe it. We will come up with an organization plan which will knock them back into reality."

Teora spent the next month prying into every corner of the Temple and the town, trying to get an understanding of what exactly the Temple was responsible for. Carlin had to return to his family and responsibilities, but Teora had her Herdsmen, when they weren't out helping with the Herds, and Tourantij, who showed increasing enthusiasm with the project. When she quizzed him about this, he responded casually.

"I'm enjoying myself. I like the people here, and I would help them if I could. Besides, the problem intrigues me. They have the same difficulty, back in the Joined Kingdoms, you know. If we develop a solution, or even some techniques that help, it would be very handy to take it home with me."

So, she spent more and more time with the Soldier, and confirmed her opinion that his education and training had prepared him for much more than a soldier's life. His sophisticated grasp of organization helped her immensely in understanding the giant ball of fluff they had to control.

* * *

However, the ball of fluff had thorns in it. Teora was walking down a deserted hallway in the Temple one evening when she met Goianor. For a change he seemed glad to see her.

"I've been meaning to talk to you, Teora."

"Certainly. What about?"

"Well, it's a rather delicate subject. Perhaps we shouldn't discuss it in a public hallway. Oh, hello, Sumner. I was about to talk to Teora about that point we were discussing the other day."

Sumner smiled down at her. "Of course. In that case, I'd like to join you. My office is in the next corridor."

This was beginning to seem too coincidental; Teora followed, very much on her guard. They were very polite. Too polite. Goianor seated her, then went to stand at the side of Sumner's massive desk. She couldn't help but notice that her chair, while marvellously soft, lowered her considerably. Smiling sweetly, she leaned back and made herself comfortable.

"What can I do for you gentlemen?"

Goianor glanced at Sumner, received a nod of encouragement and started. "Well, Teora, you know things have been rather upset around the Temple since you got here. You haven't had a chance to see us when we are working smoothly. I assure you, when it is allowed to work, our organization functions exceptionally smoothly."

She nodded pleasantly. "I'm sure it did."

Ignoring her use of the past tense, he forged ahead. "So you agree that the system runs well. If that is the case, why are we changing it?"

Teora took a moment's thought. They had been over this material several times with the higher-level Priests. Goianor knew the answer to that question as well as she did. What was he getting at? She decided that since he had asked a rhetorical question, there was no need to answer. She waited, keeping a politely inquiring facade.

After a moment, Goianor continued. "If there is no need to change, and we are changing, we have to consider the reasons for the change." He started to pace up and down the office now, as he got enthused with his lecture.

"Now, Teora, if you had studied government systems as I have, you would realize that whenever there is something happening in a system that doesn't benefit the system, then whatever is happening is to the benefit of someone. Usually, it is someone in the system, and often someone at the top. Now, if we apply that technique to this situation, we find a strange coincidence.

"Up until this time, Rioran has led us with strength and ability, no one can deny. However, he is getting old. Out of nowhere his worst enemy, who also happens to be the father of his great-granddaughter, reappears on the scene. And suddenly we have all these changes happening.

"Now, if we again apply our technique, we ask ourselves who is most likely to benefit from a complete shakeup of the system. And the easy answer is, a person from outside who wants to create a place for himself. At the top, without putting in the time and effort to earn that place."

He ended his pacing behind Teora's chair, where it would be awkward for her to turn and look up at him, so she didn't.

"Do you see how our arrival could have been exactly what they were waiting for? How they have been able to use you to get what they wanted?" He moved in front of her, leaning back in a relaxed manner on Sumner's desk, palms up, hands spread wide, inviting her agreement.

When she did not disagree, he leaned forward. "The only question is how to get us out of this situation. Without causing more damage, without upsetting the people of Aeru more than they are already. Do you have any ideas?"

She stayed leaning back in her chair, now gazing across at him. She could see in his eyes when he understood that their roles had changed. Now she sat at her leisure, and he stood in attendance. She maintained the feeling by speaking in a conversational tone. "So, you two have decided to divide your opponents and you have chosen me as your victim, because I am the youngest and the stranger and thus the most susceptible to your arguments."

She sat up, businesslike. "Let me get this straight. You want me to stop supporting Rioran and help you resume control. The threat you imply is that, if I don't, you will go to the people and stir up trouble."

She shook her head sadly. "Goianor, I thought you were smarter than that. Surely you can see which way the wind is blowing in Aeru. Remember what you told Rioran about change. If you side with the dead twigs, you will be snapped off."

She checked her anger but allowed her voice to rise. "I thought someone with your political ability would see the advantage of taking the winning side. You could be of great use to us. We have youth and enthusiasm. Once the Head Priest is gone, these young people will need wisdom and experience to guide them. Now you have jeopardized all that. How can they ever trust you?

"Now I have a return message, and you can give it to the rest of your little group of schemers. The changes will happen. Tell them they are in, or they are out. None of this manipulation and politicking will be of any use. Tell them!"

He bowed. "And that is it. Capitulation or replacement."

"That is correct, Goianor."

"Do you really think that you can throw out all of the Temple hierarchy, and the whole system will not come crashing down around your ears?"

Teora continued to hold the man with her gaze. "Is that more rebellion, or are you honestly trying to help?"

"I am trying to help, Teora. I find it difficult to believe that you will be able to function, and you should know this. The workings of the Temple are much more complex than even you know."

"Goianor, I accept your intent, and I will answer in the same vein. In the first place, I believe that a large amount of the work these people do is concerned with keeping their places in the hierarchy, and not with producing anything useful. Secondly, once Rioran starts a purge I doubt if you will find you have much support. Those in the under positions who have been waiting their chance will see this as an opportunity to gain their own power, and they will desert you. Thirdly, this is all a bluff. I do not believe that the older Priests will jeopardize their positions. They would rather stay and work under the new system than be thrown out. As long as they realize that our position is not a bluff and we are quite willing to carry out our threats, the conflict will end. Tell them this, Priest Goianor, and remember, as you tell them, the power that supports them."

She turned to the door and left. As she strode away down the hallway, she shook her head. *That ought to make them think about any further opposition.* She shuddered to consider the chaos if they had the backbone, but she hoped they would not.

But there was still something wrong. *Our purpose is righteous, but we are matching strength against strength, as Aeru has been doing all these years, to such a poor result. What happens if the Deity feels the same way? What if I have to ask for Her power, and She refuses me?*

I can bolster everyone's faith as I bolster Rioran's power, but it won't last. They must have their own faith, and I doubt that the Deity can dump that on them.

I can't help but feel that something else is missing, but maybe that's just my inexperience. I hope so.

340

32. The Power of the Priestess

Her hopes were dashed several days later when they met with Rioran in his office.

"We are not making the progress we should."

Teora grimaced. "Do I need to ask why not?"

The Head Priest shook his head. "Resistance, overt and covert, heel-dragging and petty politicking. Despite all our work, nothing has changed."

Teora sat, stunned by the Priest's pessimism. She glanced over at Tourantij. "Any ideas?"

"Have we completed our preparations? All the surveys done? Our organizational plan laid out in detail?"

Rioran nodded.

"Then what's the problem? We seem to be on schedule. We didn't really think they would roll over that easily, did we?"

The Head Priest slumped. "We expected, at least I expected, to drag them reluctantly into a new, more successful era. But we haven't moved them at all. The way they are acting, I get the impression that they still think they can win."

Teora frowned. "But not all of them. Only the worst, the leaders."

"It is hard to tell. The leaders control contact with their followers."

"Which is one of many problems that our new plan corrects." She nodded firmly. "It is time to move ahead. We had hoped to use persuasion, but they would not be persuaded. We need to set a deadline. What do you say, Tourantij? If we confront them, will they fold?"

Tourantij leaned forward. "Consider the big picture, the historical perspective. Most people with any true ability and faith have long been ousted from the Temple. This is a large part of the weakness of Aeru. Those left are completely concerned with power and the exercise of power. Once you prove your strength they will toady under as they always have. They cannot fight the years of habit. They do not have the strength."

Teora met Rioran's eyes and raised her eyebrows very slightly. He hesitated, then got the message, turning to Rebiema, who had until now sat with her usual poise, saying nothing. "Priestess, what is your opinion?"

She firmed her back. "Head Priest Rioran, you know I have no experience with what you are trying to do, but I will support you in any way I can. The People of Aeru need this. They need something that the Temple is not providing for them. I am not giving them what they need, although I am learning. If we do not provide the People with the help and reassurance they need, what good are we? What good is a powerful Priesthood, if that power is not used for the good of the People and the Land? What use is a Priestess who cannot give her people faith? Where are the leaders of the people, who should stand up for them and tell the Temple what they need?"

Her fingers shook as she brushed a lock of hair over her shoulder. "I am doing my best to change. Everyone must." She nodded to Teora. "The Chosen has shown us the way. It is our duty and our privilege to follow."

She sat back, her eyes searching the faces that confronted her. Then she straightened again, and waited.

Rioran nodded. "I agree with you, Priestess. This is the time for action. I will announce the new plan, and let the Deity decide what happens next."

Teora controlled her growing elation. *At least one of my plans is working.* She gave the Priestess a simple nod of respect between equals.

Tourantij was likewise serious. "That was well spoken, my Lady. Balance is needed."

Teora felt a pang of fear. *And now it comes down to me. I must not help her anymore. I, too, am a factor that upsets the balance. I have brought her this far, and now she must stand on her own. If she fails, then I have failed. I will have failed them all.*

They all rose, silent, and left the room.

The announcement went out at noon, and in mid-afternoon came a request for a meeting. They considered this a bad sign, but they had made the challenge; now they must see it through. Teora, Tourantij, and Rebiema joined Rioran in his office ahead of time. He was dressed in full Head Priest's regalia, complete with his ceremonial Herdsman's staff and heavy cloak. Rebiema was in the ceremonial costume of the Priestess, of finest embroidered silk, but of simple design because of the need to Dance in it.

Teora sat and regarded the two of them. "You certainly look the part."

Rioran glanced at Rebiema. "We will soon find out if we deserve to wear these garments."

She held her head high. "The Deity will decide. I have prayed that our cause be right."

"Yes, She will. I have prayed for Her support. She will support us as She always has. We have the Power to do Her will, and our enemies will soon realize it." He turned to Teora. "Chosen, are you ready to do your part?"

Teora had listened to this discourse with mounting dismay. Now she was forced to say the thoughts that had been roiling in her head. "I'm not sure."

All eyes turned to her.

"Oh, I'm sure you are right. We have the right and the power to do what we are planning. But think about it. This has a good chance of success, but it is exactly what we should not be doing. We have allowed our enemies to force us into their kind of conflict."

She raised her hands in a helpless gesture. "We are solving the problems caused by two hundred years of centralized power by taking more power to ourselves. What makes us think we will do any better than all before us?"

Rioran steepled his fingers and stared at them. "I am probably the wrong person to be answering that, because of my notable failures in that exact direction. But my experience, slanted though it has been, is that there are times when showing weakness is a very bad idea. And this is definitely one of them. Certainly, it is good to allow discussion of different ideas and to try for consensus. But knuckling under to a display of power by an adversary whose main talent is the abuse of power is a fatal mistake."

She nodded miserably. "I know. I can't help but wonder if we're saying, 'This is wrong, but we need to do it just one more time'."

"And then one more time, and then one more, and soon you're in the habit." Tourantij's lips twisted. "But do you have a better plan? I have to agree with Rioran. Now is a very bad time to show weakness."

Teora nodded, thinking furiously. "A main argument is that I am the source of your power, and soon I will be gone. Thus, if you can accomplish this without using my power, it would prove them wrong, and it would mean Aeru has the ability to solve its problems on its own."

The Head Priest considered that. "I agree, that would be the best solution. But if you have to? Will you help?"

"Of course I will try. I'm sorry, Rioran, but I can promise no more than that." She slumped back in her chair. "When I took on this task, I didn't know if I had it in me to complete it. The Priestess at the Haven persuaded me that I was Chosen and therefore I would. I have since learned it isn't that simple. If I ask for the Power of the Deity, and She decides I'm about to use it for the wrong reason, She will not help me. I have had that experience already, and I know the truth of it. And that is the question today. If you ask me for Her power, will She allow me to use it, or will She deny me?"

"You must have more faith than that, Teora."

She shook her head. "But I do have faith. I believe in the Deity's power. How could I not, when She has allowed me to use it on numerous occasions? The problem is that we are depending on that power to get us out of our predicament, and I am unsure whether using my power is the correct way to solve our problem. So, whether it is because I am not certain, or whether the Deity decides it is a misuse, we must not count on my use of Her power to get us through this meeting. I'm sorry. I know I'm letting you all down. I will do my best, but you can't count on me."

Rioran glanced at Tourantij, then at Rebiema. "We have heard the message. We must bow to the Chosen's experience." He straightened. "Then it is up to us. Priestess, you and I and your Partner represent the Goddess and her Consort, Their power and the People's faith. Teora is right in that. It is our duty to face these problems and solve them ourselves, with no outside help if we must. Are you ready?"

Rebiema turned dark, wide eyes on Teora, a look of utter desolation on her face.

Teora's heart went out to her, but she could not let her down. "Rebiema, you told me that you became a Dancer because you could feel the need of the People. You worried because you did not have the power. Now is the time when the People need you the most. Your power is weak, but your faith is strong, and faith is the duty of the Priestess. Now is your moment, Rebiema. Now you must become the Priestess you were destined to be. I cannot do that for you. It must come from within. Feel the need, Priestess. Stand up for your People in their hour of need."

Rebiema's back straightened, and her lips pressed together. She placed a hand on Teora's shoulder and squeezed. "Thank you, Chosen. I will do all I can. I will do everything in my power to protect the faith of the People." Then she turned, beckoning to the Head Priest. "We must do what the Deity demands of us, no matter what the result."

He offered her his arm, and the two of them left the room.

Teora sat a moment, a bitter taste in her mouth. She glanced at Tourantij.

He gave her a lopsided smile. "If it's any consolation, this is exactly what they need."

"I know. But if they fail and I can't help them, what then? I will have failed doubly, because my mission will be a failure, and I'm the one who let them down in their need."

"I'm not one to be advising you on religious matters, but if they fail, then maybe that is what the Deity wishes to happen."

She shook her head. "That's one thing I'm sure of. We can't sit aside and expect the Deity to do things for us. We have to make our own decisions and take the consequences. Otherwise we don't deserve Her help."

He shrugged. "Then you have it easy. Go in there with them. Give them all the moral support you can, on your own. If you feel that the Deity's Power is needed, try. If it works, then it was meant to be. If it doesn't, then it's the Deity's decision."

She thought that over. "It doesn't work that way. I'm responsible for deciding. If I decide wrong, and help them win in the wrong way, then it's all on my head."

He rose. "And if you do nothing and they fail, then it's all on your head. I'm in favour of action, myself."

She dragged herself to her feet. "And so am I. I just wish I knew if..."

He put an arm around her shoulders and squeezed. "End of wishing. End of thinking. Time for battle. Get in there and do your best. Nobody asks more." He turned her to stare down into her eyes. "Not even you."

She nodded mutely and turned out the door and made her way down the hall to whatever awaited.

* * *

345

The Head Priest received the delegation in the Altar Room. To his left, the Priestess sat, her Partner behind her. To his right, Teora stood aloof, her power in check. At least Barozon played his part: head up, nostrils wide as the Priests entered.

If the culprits had dreamed of discussion and compromise, their hopes were quickly shattered. Teora could see how Rioran had attained his position. He did not wait for them to speak; he did not ask what they wanted. He was regal, powerful, and disdainful all at once.

"You have been given my instructions. As you can see, I have the backing of the Priestess as well as the Chosen of the Haven. We expect nothing but complete compliance. Refuse to cooperate, even in the smallest way, and you leave immediately."

Sumner, the leader of the rebels, stood forward. Teora could see his intent, and shook her head. He had never forgiven her for the embarrassment of her arrival, when she had left him stumbling on the street. *Well, those who cannot learn will have to go.*

"With all respect, Head Priest Rioran. You may have the power now, and you do a marvellous job of leading our people. But you are old. The Representative from the Haven will soon leave us to our own devices, and we all know that the Priestess has no real strength..."

Power surged off to Teora's left. Rebiema rose from her throne, her face icy cold, her body rigid. Slowly she approached the Priest, her hands clenched by her sides. Her Partner stalked beside her, his sides heaving with each breath. She stopped for a long moment in front of her antagonist, and Teora could feel her gathering power about her. *Real power!* The Deity's presence flowed into the Temple, slowly at first, but increasing.

"Priest!" Her voice was low, but it carried to everyone in the building. The man jerked to sudden attention as her tone penetrated.

"Priest!" She paused again. "Anyone who speaks with such disdain of the Chosen of the Deity can be no Priest of Hers. Anyone who is that unaware of the Source from which his own power comes cannot wield that power for Her good."

As she spoke, she paced forward, and he gave way before her. She forced him back until he came up against a pillar and cowered there with no way to escape her wrath.

"How can you consider yourself a Priest when you deny her Chosen? Do you now realize your mistake? Do you realize that you have taken the path directly against Her desires, the path from which there is no return?"

She paused as her power built again. "From this moment, only your perfect behaviour will allow you a place within the territory of the Aeran Enclave. One slip and you will be banished completely. For the moment, the mercy of the Deity is upon you. You have one hour to remove yourself from Her Temple. You may NOT return!"

She held him motionless, then turned from him with a swirl of her robes. Laying a hand with exaggerated gentleness on her Partner's shoulder, she turned him and moved him back to his position. Then she sat, gracefully and slowly, in her chair. As she passed Teora she shot her an amazed glance, and Teora nodded in response. In the long pause that followed, Teora could see the girl's hands shaking, but she maintained her poise.

Sumner slowly straightened himself, made one last, wordless plea to Rioran. The Head Priest simply made a gesture towards the Priestess, then ignored the man.

"Now, my friends, and I still consider you my friends. Together we have ruled this Enclave for many years. It turns out that we have been mistaken. How difficult do you think it was for me to accept that fact, when I have been the leader of you all? I have given you as much opportunity as I could to change your minds, but now I must ask for your decision. We must move forward with those who will join us. We must leave the others behind. There will be no more banishments if you make your choice now and stick to it." His glance was directed at Rebiema, still sitting regally in her chair. "But I do not suggest that anyone have a change of heart at a later date. It could have quite disastrous results.

"You will make up your minds today. I will receive you individually in my office to accept your decisions at any time during the afternoon. If you do not come before the evening meal, I will assume you have decided to leave us. Positions will be found for you elsewhere. I am sure there are a few haciendas that could use someone to oversee the cattle and keep the books in his spare time."

The Head Priest rose to his full height, towering over them on his dais. He bowed formally to Teora, then Rebiema and turned to the exit. As they followed, side by side, the Priestess shot a glance at Teora. Teora returned the look briefly, then kept her eyes straight ahead.

Once out of the room, the formality collapsed. Rebiema turned to Teora, wonder in her eyes. The Head Priest faced them both. "Rebiema, what happened to you?"

The girl turned to him. "I have never in my life dared to speak like that to anyone, but I felt it, Rioran. I could feel the Power of the Deity in me. I could not sit still and allow him to say those things. For a moment, I didn't know what to do, what to say, but then I said to myself, 'What is best for the people of Aeru?' And after that I just went and did it. Did I act rightly?"

The old man glanced across at Teora. "It is not for me to say, my child. He made a challenge to you, and you answered it. What you did was your choice, and you must accept the consequences. The question of rightness is between you and the Deity who gave you the power."

The girl turned to Teora. "But you said..."

Before she could answer, Tourantij's chuckle brought their heads around. "Teora, you disappoint me. Let me guess. Even after all your experience, you thought faith and power were two separate things."

Teora closed her gaping jaw, her face burning. "But...oh. I see."

"Yes. Priestess Rebiema, I believe I have heard you bemoan your lack of the power to bolster the faith of the people?"

The girl smiled. "It seems the Deity has heard my prayers." She turned to Rioran. "And will this make our problems worse, as Teora has suggested?"

The Head Priest smiled. "The Deity does not seem to think so. You certainly made my job a whole lot easier. The whole question of bluff and counterbluff was resolved with the least possible fuss. I suspect I will receive a large number of penitents in my office this afternoon."

Teora nodded. "But will they stay converted?"

His face became grim. "They have no choice. They have been warned, and I will act as Rebiema did without hesitation. They know that of me. If, at some later time, Teora and I am gone, they have no doubt that there is still power here to maintain the threat."

Rebiema's timorous smile firmed. "There certainly is."

33.   Stampede

After that, the plan progressed as smoothly as possible, with a notable lack of resistance. Rebiema continued to grow, and even demoted a Trainer to Herdsman.

"He was always too mean to the youngest and weakest Trainees. He only had the position because of his contacts with the Priests. He brought out the worst in the Dancers, and we'll do much better without him."

Rioran had only one comment: "It's your area, and your decision."

Teora would have been ecstatic, but something was bothering her.

"Rebiema, you know that feeling we talked about when I first came here? The feeling of need?"

"Yes, I remember."

"Do you still feel it?"

"Yes. Stronger than ever. I've been meaning to talk to you about it, but we were too busy getting the Temple organized. I thought that would help."

"It hasn't, at least not yet. I don't know if Sumner and Goianor have actually been stirring up trouble, but I doubt it. Our work at the Temple can't have had any calming effect on the people yet. At this stage, it has probably caused more upset.

"It's their faith that is fading. They need to feel that the Deity is there, taking care of them. It will be a long time before the reform of the Temple changes enough for the average person to even notice it. I hope it won't be too late."

Rebiema nodded. "Has that feeling been bothering you?"

"Even more than before."

"So, we have solved the problem in the leadership and the Temple, but not in the most important place: the People."

"It's logical."

"Maybe the Week of Gathering will help."

"I hope so. If it doesn't, we could have a problem."

Rebiema shot Teora worried glance. "What kind of problem?"

Teora shook her head slowly. "I wish I knew. I just wish I knew."

At the end of months of hard work, it was a relief to know that a holiday was coming up. The gathering and marking of the new spring calves had to be done. Since there were no fences, all the scattered animals had to be collected and separated into their respective Herds. Then the calves were tattooed, and the Herds were sent home. By this time next year enough animals would have wandered far enough that it had to be done all over again. Once the job was done and before everyone took their Herd home, a great ceremony ensued, with parties, Dancing and a great Thanksgiving at the Temple. It was, after all, the one time that most of the population of Aeru got together, and no one would miss the opportunity to enjoy it.

Teora had spent some of her time working with the young Dancers, and they were eager to show off their new skills. The Priestess was less enthused. Teora had been working with her as well, though not publicly. Rebiema's Partner was an amiable beast, and he and Barozon had no problem working in the same pasture. It was easy to make it look like the two of them were helping each other, rather than Teora teaching Rebiema. The Priestess had such natural grace that it was easy to give her a few of Linea's favourite moves, which she learned quickly. It was more difficult to build her confidence to the point where she would perform them. Her usual style was to practise and polish each new move for months before showing it to anyone, the reason for her beautiful but limited repertoire.

The week of Fall Gathering was a hot and dusty one. People were on their feet from sunrise to sundown, either working with the animals or feeding the workers. Teora asked Rebiema and the other Dancers to be out and around as much as possible because the presence of the bulls had a quieting effect on the Herds and was much appreciated by everyone. Teora's own Herdsmen and their dogs were in great demand because of their skills. She tried to concentrate them where they were most needed, where injuries or illness prevented the smaller families from coping. It was also an easy way to make friends among the secular leaders, with whom she had little contact otherwise.

As they neared the end of the week, excitement began to build in everyone. A wave of anticipation rose. Work went even more frenetically, with impromptu contests of speed and skill that bordered on dangerous. Rebiema, too, did not seem happy.

Teora thought perhaps it was the anticipation of the celebration. "Are you tired? Perhaps you shouldn't be out here so long. You and

Dembe haven't been hardened up like Barozon and I have, with all our weeks on the trail."

The girl rubbed the back of her neck. "I'm not tired, Teora, just out of sorts. It's like I have a headache but there's no pain. Something is nagging at me."

"That's how I feel. Something is building up, and you and I are feeling it. It's the need that I felt when I first came here. But now it is stronger, much stronger and growing. Do you think it will be a problem?"

Rebiema frowned thoughtfully. "There has been a Gathering every year and nothing has gone wrong. Usually there is a heightening of expectation near the end, but not quite like this. Maybe the need has been there other years, but now we're feeling it together. After all, what's different from last year?"

Teora nodded, but both of them were unsatisfied with their solution.

The next day was the celebration, but Teora couldn't really enjoy herself. She went through the ceremonies and led the parade with a proud Rebiema beside her. She Danced well, but not spectacularly, and she was proud that the pupils were a credit to her and themselves.

But still the feeling built. By the end of the day, she could see its effect on Rebiema and the other Dancers as well. The normally sensitive Priestess snapped at the youngest Dancer, reducing the poor boy to tears. Dembe was restive, and Barozon's attention was wandering.

Teora endured it all as if it were a hot day in a sandstorm, waiting for all the people and Herds to disperse and everything to get back to normal.

When the first storm clouds edged over the peaks to the west, she groaned. There was nothing worse than a thunderstorm with an edgy Herd. Combined with the emotion that charged the air around the city, the situation could be lethal.

At least now she could take action.

The ceremonies were almost over, and many were glancing westward and muttering to each other. Teora rode Barozon to the front of the Presentation platform and called out over the noise.

"People of Aeru. I don't need to tell you how dangerous this storm can be. To your Herds, all of you, and quickly."

She caught a glimpse of Corquée in a mass of horses nearby. "Any Riders with herding experience, please help where you can." The Rider saluted her, then he and his friends galloped off to the western edge of the city.

Teora and Rioran gathered the Dancers and Priests together. "Rebiema must return to the Temple of the Consort. That is her place in time of need. But the rest of the Dancers must be seen. We must ride around the Herds, helping to calm them. Keep your Partners under the strongest control you can. A panicked bull would be disastrous. If there is anyone who feels he or she might not stay in control, please go with Rebiema. She could use the support."

They all faced her, eager to be working. "I thought so. Move to your positions. Do not expose yourselves to any danger, but be seen, be there to help. Head Priest Rioran and all your people, pray to the Deity to strengthen us."

The tall old man nodded. "Our place is at the Temple. Come, my friends. May the Deity assist us in our need."

With that final word they parted, and Teora moved Barozon down the street to the west. She didn't know what she could do to stop a storm of this size, but she was going out to meet it. As she rode, she could feel the pressure build, and it frightened her. The need was there, but the fear was there too, ready to take over at any excuse.

They reached the edge of town as the first lightning bolts crashed into sight, reaching down to the foothills, and the thunder muttered after. She stood on a low hillock with Corquée and several other Riders, surveying the Herds in her sight for any sign of trouble.

She noticed a swirl starting off to the left. Corquée saw her pointing, motioned two of his Riders off to assist. Then the thunder rolled again, and an outburst of frightened bawling sent three more off in the opposite direction.

The storm swirled and the cattle responded; the rest of the Riders mounted and spread out to help. Finally Corquée bared his teeth in her direction, shouting over the rising wind. "Only me left, Teora. Where should I go?"

"Better stay here. If a real stampede starts, it's a different story. We have to get to the leaders and turn them, and you've got a better chance than most."

He nodded grimly, knowing what it meant to run his horse through that mass of heavy bodies and churning hooves. They sat together, watching the storm approach.

Corquée glanced at her. "This hill isn't the best place to be waiting for a lightning storm."

She glared up at the black clouds. "The Deity will decide that."

Lightning struck again, closer this time, and the thunder followed immediately. Teora could feel the fear building, both in the people and the Herds. She knew that this wasn't going to last. The storm wasn't even on top of them, and she could see by the stirring of the Herds that something was going to turn loose, and soon. It would need only one more close strike of lightning...

A horrendous crash boomed directly overhead. Teora felt a lurch and realized dimly that Barozon had gone to his knees beside her. He stumbled up again. Teora, her ears ringing with sound, stared around in a daze. Corquée's horse was down, and he was at her head, coaxing her to her feet, shaking his own head as if something was stuck in his ears. She tried to see more, but all her senses were washed out by the sudden scream of panic that rushed in from all sides. It slammed at her until she could hardly refrain from beating her fists on her head in sympathy.

All the need and fear from the whole Enclave crashed on her, all the pent-up yearnings of a people without hope. A wash of sound, and the bellowing of the whole Herd underlaid by the stamping of thousands of hooves, echoed the roll of the thunder.

Teora's head reeled, and she clutched Barozon's mane for support, but her Partner, picking up on her anxiety, shifted away, and she tripped and lost her hold. As she stumbled to her knees, she knew that this was her moment. This was what she had been sent for. Aeru was calling to her in its time of need, and she was failing.

The dazzle of lightning blasted her eyes, and she covered her head with her arms. Mightier than the noise came the craving inside. As it built within her, she could feel the yearning change towards disappointment and anger. The people needed help, and if they did not receive it, they would act on their own. What action they would take, no one knew, but it would be violent and bloody. The Herd was already in motion, not unified yet, but swirling in masses, bawling and crying in the eddies of dust.

The desperation surged through her, and she fought the urge to leap on Barozon's back and scream down into the oblivion of massed horns and hooves.

With an effort, she wrenched herself to her feet. The success of the action steadied her, and she reached out again for Barozon's shoulder.

Steeling her mind, she called to him for help: for the strength of his back, the cool solidity of his horns. His nose swung around, and one large brown eye, pink-rimmed, stared at her for a long moment. His head rose, and he snorted a challenge at her.

They are only cattle. They need us.

She caught hold of her emotions, strove to focus her wits, and the thought came to her. *This is what I told everyone else. I must be strong enough to act, or the Deity cannot help me.* She reached out and leaned on the base of his horn, lifted her head to see the swirling cloud of the storm descending upon the city, as the Herd began to form into one heaving mass. *But it is not for me to do alone.* She sent out a questing, a search for the power of the Land of Aeru, for the faith of its Herd and its People. *I can only help you if you will help yourselves.*

Then faint and far off, she could feel Rebiema, gathering the security of the Temple about herself, reaching out with growing strength for anyone in range, giving of herself in comfort and hope. Then, softer still, tiny glowing points of each Dancer and Partner, out among the Herds. The firm presence of Rioran and the Priests gathered around him underlaid the whole pattern. This steadied Teora and made her understand what she must do. She swung up on Barozon, feeling his warm strength and support. Feeding on the thread from the Priestess, she called out for all the Faith the Land could give.

Up it rose, like a golden light from out of the soil around her, filling her with an incredible sense of strength and peace. Her feelings shot upward until her eyes were on a level with the highest thunderheads. Barozon stamped his feet and the thunder rolled. Lightning played from horn to horn, crackling and raising the hair on his neck. She felt she could reach out and squeeze the clouds until rain poured from them, could hold her hand out and stop the lightning.

She listened to the cry of fear like a mother to a child in a nightmare. She fed the tiny points until they pulsed with faith in the Deity. She joined each one in a network of golden strands and laid it like a blanket over the whole of the city and the Land, until the thunder muttered softly like the stamping of a distant Herd on the move, and the lightning was only the flickering of the sunlight on the peaks. Finally, the wind calmed, and the clouds ceased their turmoil, rolling in orderly fashion across the sky. Then the rain came, not in a downpour, but soft and soothing, filling the parched Land. Quiet descended with a single moment of peace.

And then, seeping back up from the city, came a wash of the purest joy. The animals and the people cried out their relief to her, their gratitude, their adulation for her, and she basked in their praise. The Temple glowed pure gold in a shaft of late afternoon sunlight, and Teora could feel the steadying blaze of Rebiema's belief, holding firmly there with her Partner.

Then the whole scene began to fade. Teora's soul drifted earthward, and the great outpouring of emotion was gone, sinking into the soil with the new rain. She shook her head and gazed around. She and Barozon stood on the hillock, alone except for Corquée, who, drenched but smiling, sat his horse staring at her.

"What was that all about?"

She shook her head. It wasn't the kind of thing you could explain.

"You did it again, didn't you? But big this time. Really big! I could feel it. We were about to have the biggest stampede in the history of the world, and you just reached out and patted the whole Herd on its head and calmed it down. The people too!" He shook his head in wonder. "Teora, are you real?"

"What do you mean, real?" Her voice quavered, broke.

"You know, I mean really a person. Normal people can't do things like that, in case you haven't noticed."

She stared at him, hoping he was joking, knowing he wasn't. "What do you say, Corquée? Do you think I'm a real person?" She could not keep the plea out of her voice.

He smiled. "Oh, yes. You're still the Teora we know and love. But you've got to stop playing with the gods. Scares us mortals right out of the saddle."

She smiled shakily back. "I'm having trouble dealing with it myself, right now. I think I'll have to quit."

"Good. Right now, though, I figure your best place would be at the Temple. Your Head Priest is the one to help you out. He's supposed to know about things like this."

He pushed his horse ahead, nudging Barozon's shoulder around, and herded Teora and her Partner towards the town. People were out in the rain, not rejoicing, just walking or talking quietly. They glanced at Teora, then away, but she could feel their eyes following her after she had passed.

Aerans thronged the Temple Plaza, but they flowed from in front of her like the rain, and she gained the main doors easily. There she left Corquée and went inside with her Partner. The Head Priest was waiting, and he led them, dripping wet, to the central Altar.

He smiled down at her. "There may be no need for you to communicate further with the Deity. For me, it would ease my soul to thank Her for what She has done this afternoon." He prayed briefly, while Teora and Barozon stood dumbly waiting.

The he slipped around the Altar and pulled some folded cloths from behind it. "Come, now. Let us get you and your Partner dry and we can talk about it."

One on each side, they rubbed Barozon down. The familiar actions and the rhythmic motion calmed Teora, but the memory of the experience kept coming back to her.

Rioran was watching her, a faint smile on his face. "Reliving it?"

"Umm...I suppose I was. It is very difficult to let it go. I held all those people in the palm of my hand. I was the Deity, and they all looked to me for help and guidance. I was their protector, keeping them from the destruction of the storm. I was the storm, all that violence, to destroy or not as I chose. I was the Herd, all that power, to trample anything in my way. It was the most incredible feeling I have ever known. Of course, how could I have known it?

"I was a god, Rioran. I know what it feels like to be a god!

"And it scares me to death. How can I ever be a normal person again? How can I worry about little things like finding love or starting a family when I know what it feels like to have thousands of people depending on me? How can I ever be satisfied with the love of one man, when I have felt the adoration of a city? I don't want to be a god, Rioran. I just want to be me again!"

The sobs wracked her body, and she huddled into herself, her misery a burning ache inside her. The old man sat beside her, one arm around her shoulders, the other hand stroking her hair. After a long time, she regained control of her breathing and sat up straighter, turning her tear-stained face towards him.

"I'm sorry, Rioran. It has been so long since I could let down with anyone. I...I don't know what I'm going to do, that's all. I know it sounds silly, but I wish my mother were here. She always knows what to say when I get like this. Not that she would have any solution, I'm sure. It's not every day that your daughter gets to be a god. But she would make me feel better about it, at least.

"I know. She's not here, and I had better grow up and handle my problems on my own."

The old man stroked her hair one last time. "You don't have to handle this on your own. I am honoured to be here." He held his palms up, an inviting gesture. "After all, it isn't often that a god comes along and asks my advice. But since you have, and it isn't fitting for a mere mortal to give advice to the gods, I am going to give you back some of your own words. When you first came here, you told me all about change. You told me how hard it was going to be."

She nodded. "All change is painful. And now it's my turn. I guess I had better listen to the rest of the lecture. I am supposed to tell myself that sooner or later I will get used to it, and that some day I will look back and say that it was all worth it, and how silly it will seem, how upset I am right now. How am I doing?"

"You have covered the usual platitudes. They are all true, you know. You are a strong woman, Teora, the power of the Deity aside. She does not choose the weak to do Her bidding. What use would you be if you were not able to wield Her power without breaking? I would like to think that the Deity is gracious enough not to use you up, then throw you aside like a broken tool. My faith is stronger than that."

"And mine should be as well. I suppose you are right." She sighed and took both his hands in hers. "Thank you, Rioran. With all my heart. There is no one else I can turn to. The others all depend on me too much to allow them to see me weak."

The old man turned his hands over, grasping hers firmly. "Teora, that is the mistake I made, thinking I was the only one who had the strength. Depend on your friends all you can. Make a conscious effort to confide in them. You will be surprised. You have some exceptional friends."

"I know, but how can I expect them to deal with this, when I can't? How can I live a normal life with all this power in me? I'll be afraid to get angry in case I kill someone."

"Do you really think you would? And even if you wanted to, do you think the Deity would allow the misuse of Her power?"

"I suppose not."

"Do you consider you were in control of all the power and faith of Aeru tonight? That the Deity just dumps it on you and goes away?"

Teora thought that over. "Then the Deity is doing the work and I am merely a tool in Her hand. Exactly as Barozon took control when we attacked the bear, I don't have any choice. I have no control over the situation and can take no credit for the solution. A humbling concept."

The Priest shook his head. "I don't believe that you are a puppet. There are different types of power. For example, there is the Deity's power that you could call on, at any time you needed it during the journey."

"Like with the wolves. And I may lose that, now that I have fulfilled my mission."

Rioran nodded doubtfully. "That is possible. But there is the power that you will never lose, such as that which comes between you and Barozon, which is part from each, making a whole which is more than both of you."

She thought with fondness of Barozon: his sense of humour, his strength. "Yes, I have that."

"And never forget your faith. That will always keep you strong, more than any power you may be given temporarily."

She smiled wryly. "And at the bottom, I suppose, is whatever natural talent I possess. Such as it is."

"Do not diminish your own abilities, Teora. Without your strength, hardened by the trials you have endured, you would not have been able to do what you did today."

"Thank you for putting it all into perspective for me."

"Part of my duties." He gestured across the Temple, where Rebiema and Dembe stood in the doorway. "Now, I suspect the feast will begin rather late, tonight, but it will be no less joyful for that. Aeru has a lot to celebrate. Let us join our people."

The Head Priest strode to the main door. The Chosen and the Priestess swung up onto the backs of their Consorts and followed him into the crowd.

34.   Flash Flood

"I think we're going to get wet."

Teora glanced over her shoulder at the clouds gathering over the western peaks. "Probably."

Rebiema shook her head, frowning. "We need to hurry."

Teora shrugged. "I don't mind a bit of rain."

"This doesn't look like just a bit of rain to me."

"What do you mean?"

"It's the time of year. We get some wild rains in late winter. Sometimes there is flooding."

Teora's memory kicked into gear. "Flash floods? Are we in any danger on this trail?"

"I doubt it. We don't have to go through any low spots. That's the reason I took this path."

Teora grinned at her companion. *This is no longer the timid soul I met last summer.* "Glad to know you're taking care of us." She raised her voice. "Radman, Mayna, we'd better pick up the pace. Rebiema says there may be flooding."

The two Herdsmen nodded, glancing around at the terrain. They had no trouble keeping up with Barozon's usual pace, or anything a whole lot faster, for that matter. "Do you want to turn back?"

Teora glanced from Mayna's worried face to Rebiema. "I don't think so. It's important that we put in an appearance at this hacienda. They have had a series of serious setbacks, and our presence will be a great boost to their morale."

Rebiema nodded. "They live in low country."

Teora shot her a sharp glance. "Are they at risk?"

"We will have to wait until we get there, but with Hansa gone there may be no one at the hacienda who knows the dangers."

Teora thought briefly. "Radman, I want you to run ahead and check on them. You understand the possibility of flash flooding if that cloud opens up over the mountains. Tell them we are coming, but start evacuation to high ground if needed."

The Herdsman nodded and without a word was sprinting up the trail. Teora nudged Barozon to a faster pace, wishing she had brought more help with her. It had seemed such a simple journey, visiting a family who had run into some bad luck lately, with the deaths of some prime stock due to illness, and the injury of the head of the family, who was now in the Temple infirmary under round-the-clock care after a fire that had burned one of the family's storage sheds.

They broke out of a jumble of rocks, and the hacienda came in sight. It was in a pleasant valley with a clear stream running past the buildings. But two dry washes opened into the same valley and the boulders strewn at their mouths suggested that once in a long while a large force of water erupted from them. With a nervous glance at the mountains, Teora and Rebiema jogged down to the buildings.

Radman had already gathered a small and worried group about him. He reported as soon as Teora arrived.

"They think the house is safe, and they could be right. Any water coming down the valley is going to run through the low part, over against the east bank, there. And that's going to be a problem."

Teora scanned the area. The eastern edge of the valley was steeper than the side they had come down, and bent away out of sight below the ranch house. "Why?"

"Because around that corner is where their whole herd is pastured."

"Can we move them quickly?" She looked down at Hansa's wife, Ayla, a pleasant, round-faced woman with two small children clinging to her skirts.

The woman shook her head. "I couldn't do it without help. They've been jumpy since the fire, and we could lose them all."

Teora stared at the mountains, where the black clouds were shedding a grey pall of rain onto the rocky slopes. "You had better risk it. You have help, now. Send all your people with me. We'll move the herd, not too far, but away from the lower side of the valley. You had better move your household stock out of the ranch yard and get them to high ground in case."

The woman began to give orders, and soon Teora was leading a grim-faced band of ranch people down the valley. As they walked, she reassured them. "There doesn't seem to be a lot of lightning. The herd won't spook if we are careful. We'll start them moving slowly with the Priestess in front. They should follow the Consort willingly, especially with Barozon and me behind, giving a push where it's needed."

They grinned at that, regarding his long, sharp, horns.

"You spread out on either side to keep them from straying. Mayna and Radman and the dogs will be on either side at the rear to keep any from turning back along the side. Keep it slow and gentle. We're not going to get flooded out in a hurry, if it even happens."

The faces brightened even further, and they all went purposefully to their appointed positions. As Teora expected, the presence of the two bulls controlled the Herd easily, and soon a wide swath of cattle strolled across the valley towards the higher land on the western side, grazing as they travelled. It took over an hour to complete the job, and Teora watched with growing anxiety how the clouds gathered, pouring rain against the buttresses of the peaks.

She breathed a sigh of relief when the herd was finally contained in a natural pocket in the hillside, guarded by a few of the herding people. Gathering her group, she headed back up the valley towards the hacienda.

When they reached the buildings, everything seemed in order, but Teora wasn't satisfied. "Is this area clear of livestock?"

The rancher's wife nodded. "We have moved them up to an old corral near the trail. Would you like to come in and sit down?"

Teora's eyes scanned the area. "I know this may sound overcautious, but perhaps you should move up to the valley wall as well. If a serious flood comes, there is no telling how much time we would have to escape."

The woman hesitated, looking around at her home.

Rebiema laid a hand on her shoulder. "We will keep watch, if you want to put things in order."

The woman smiled in gratitude, then scurried into the house.

Teora grinned at the Priestess, then called to the Herdsmen. "Radman, will you go up near the mouth of that first draw and keep your ears open? You can signal us if you hear any water coming." As he jogged off, she had another thought. "Stay on high ground!"

He waved a hand without turning and continued. They watched him cover the distance to the canyon mouth and climb rapidly to the upper edge. He turned and waved an "all clear" signal, then settled down to wait.

Teora glanced around, disturbed by the strangeness of it all. Bright sunshine, the ground as dry and dusty as it had been for two weeks, and here they were preparing for a flood. It seemed ridiculous, but the black cloud ranging along the mountainside gave the light a strange, brittle colour, and Teora shivered despite the heat.

A whistle brought their heads up. The distant figure on the hillside was waving and pointing at the second canyon mouth. Teora couldn't see anything, but a gesture sent Mayna sprinting into the house. She exited a moment later, towing a protesting Ayla firmly by the arm. Radman gave a "wait" signal, and they all stood, wondering what he heard or saw.

Then Teora, with the height advantage that Barozon's back gave her, saw it. The waters of the stream began to darken and boil, and soon it was rushing along frantically, its colour a dark, muddy brown.

Teora's eyes turned to Radman, but he gave no further warning. They watched for a few minutes, but the stream grew no further. Shrugging, she grinned at the woman. "False alarm, I guess. Do you need to go back inside?"

"Well, there were a few more things I could have moved upstairs..."

She was interrupted by a shrill whistle from Radman that brought every eye to him. He waved his arms frantically, pointing up the canyon where he stood, then to the high ground in the west. Before anyone had a chance to move, a great spray of water rose from the ground up the hill behind him, and he whistled and waved again, urging them further.

"Everybody move!" Her words were unneeded, as the group around her dissolved into running figures. Holding Barozon back, she motioned Rebiema ahead, and both bulls started their cumbersome gallop. As they ran, Teora watched the mouth of the canyon. There seemed nothing there, and the great spray had disappeared.

Then a rumbling sound drifted over the thunder of Barozon's hooves, and around the corner of the canyon churned a mass of water, almost the height of the canyon walls, racing towards them.

She urged Barozon to greater speed, and they bore down on a younger ranch girl who was flagging. "Up here!" Reaching out an arm as they thundered by, she swung the girl up behind her. "Grab a strap and hold on!"

Ignoring the girl's bumping and bouncing, Teora glanced back again in time to see the water erupt from the canyon's mouth, spreading in all directions as it came. The main mass of the water, however, stayed in line with the canyon and shot across the valley in a brown stream, striking the steep side of the far wall with tremendous force, sending spray shooting high in the air.

Leaving the confines of the canyon had robbed most of the force from the torrent, but still the water poured forth, slowly spreading over the land. A veritable river ran along the eastern side, its current rising inexorably towards the farm buildings.

She heard splashing. Barozon had blasted through a small dirty creek where there had only been dry grass minutes before. More rivulets trickled everywhere, but none seemed threatening. One more large puddle and they were on dry ground, Barozon panting as he heaved himself up a low rise to safety.

They sat, all three of them breathing rapidly, then Teora turned to her passenger. "Well, I guess you didn't really need a ride after all."

The girl's eyes were wide. "Thank you ever so much! I might have drowned!"

Teora laughed. "I doubt it." She pointed back down the trail where they had run. The builders of the hacienda had chosen their site with care, and while the water rushing down the valley swirled to the east of the property, the land to the west, especially where the trail was, had stayed mostly dry.

"Oh. Well, thanks, anyway. It was an exciting ride!"

Teora grinned and gave the girl a hand down. "With any luck, we'll be able to stand here and watch it all run past. These floods never last long."

They all turned and watched, fascinated, as the water poured along. Rebiema dismounted and spoke to Ayla.

"Are all of your people here?"

The woman checked. "Yes, Priestess, everyone is here." She paused, her eyes searching the valley. "Thanks to you people. Is the Herd safe?"

Teora nodded. "They are even higher than we are."

"Thank you so much. I don't know what we would have done, with Hansa being injured and not here. Have you seen him?"

Rebiema smiled gently. "Yes, I have seen him every day, and transformed many prayers for him to the Deity. He was in a great deal of pain, as you know, but there seems to be little infection, thanks perhaps to the new medical ideas of the soldier from the Joined Kingdoms, Tourantij Niverdahl. We are giving your husband a strong painkilling medicine which the Curicuiriari use, and he is getting some sleep, which is very important."

Tears appeared on the woman's cheeks. "Oh, thank you, Priestess. It has been hard. It is good to know that you are helping us. I don't know what we would have done..." She dissolved into tears, and Rebiema took her gently in her arms, cushioning the older woman's head on her shoulder. After a moment Ayla recovered herself and straightened. "I'm sorry, Priestess."

"No, don't be. I understand." She smiled gently, patting the woman on the shoulder. "What's the good of being Priestess if someone doesn't cry on my shoulder once in a while?"

The woman smiled tentatively and reached up, covering Rebiema's slim hand with her work-roughened fingers. The smile strengthened, then the woman's back straightened, and she turned to regard her home.

Once again, Teora felt the glow of faith rise from the Land and surround her. It was faint and gentle, swirling around the Priestess and the woman she comforted like the waters of the stream, now nourishing the fields they had threatened moments before. *My winter's task has been successful; Rebiema is now a Priestess. The Temple is functioning smoothly on its new course. I am free to go home.*

35. Departure

Something woke Teora, and she watched the early morning sunlight glow on the adobe wall of Hastar's bedroom. Adimé had been embarrassed to put an honoured guest in with her daughter, but the house was so full it was the only chance for Teora to have even that much privacy.

Hastar. That was what had woken her. She glanced over, and sure enough, the girl's bed was empty. Feeling guilty, she checked the mattress, finding a trace of warmth that showed it had recently been slept in. Then she dressed in her travelling clothes, washed her face and wandered outside to see what was happening in the new day.

Sure enough, over by the horse pens two familiar figures stood close together, his arm draped casually over her shoulders, her arm around his waist. Teora wondered how to handle this. If cruelty is to come, best it comes from your friends.

"So, Corquée. How is your Remuda growing?"

This had the intended effect on the Rider. His arm dropped as if the girl was hot.

Not Hastar. She tightened her grip. "Five mares and two stallions in four months, all top-quality animals. And one gorgeous gelding." She grinned and shook her head. "We aren't too sure if that was meant to be a message."

"Corquée, isn't this a bit dishonest? Do these girls know that you already have other plans? And how did you...you know..." she was trying not to embarrass him "...I mean, you didn't have time, did you?"

He gave his usual expressive shrug. "It works out. I gave out more horses than that for my sister before she made up her mind. Most of those girls don't really want to marry me. Just the fame, you know. A week or so, and they go on with their lives. Don't start worrying about us Riders, Teora. Our rituals have been working for us for centuries. Please don't even consider changing them."

They all laughed at that, as the big metal bar in front of the kitchen clanged, calling them for breakfast.

Hastar shook her head as they walked towards the hacienda. "I can't believe how many people felt it was necessary to come and see you off."

"It helps that your great-grandfather came. There are a lot of people who think that any time he and your father are together, it's a good idea to be listening."

"You're right about that. You should have heard them last night. It could have been a Council meeting, the things they were discussing."

"And they let you listen in?"

The girl grinned. "It's my father's house. Who would send me away? He and Mother certainly wouldn't, and no one else wants to offend him."

"Why? He has no position in the new organization."

"No official position. Of course, he is the father of the Head Priest's new secretary."

"Hastar, you're not taking that seriously, are you? It isn't official."

"Yes, I am, and it doesn't need to be. It's going to be wonderful, working with Rioran. He said I have to call him that in the Temple, because otherwise it would sound funny." She smiled impishly. "I still call him 'Gramps' at home, though."

In the doorway they joined the Haven Herdsmen, who had been saying their own good-byes. Obed had formed an attachment with an Aeran girl, and would help Daegal, who was staying to work on the reform of Herdsman training to turn out some younger, abler trainees. Replacing them were four young Aerans who were coming to the Haven for training: three as Herdsman, one to be a Priest. Sabba and Tourantij had become a tight unit, spending most of their time together, so she and Mayna were both in the homeward party.

Teora and her people ate breakfast quickly to make room for the other guests, who drifted in as they rose. As Teora left the building she noticed Corquée and Hastar together again.

"I'll be glad when he's out of here for a while."

She turned, to see Carlin in the doorway behind her. "I thought you approved."

"Oh, I do. But this part of the plan isn't scheduled yet. They need some time away from each other to get things straight. They may have all their lives together, what's the rush?"

"Try telling them that."

"Exactly. I'm not worried, though. Corquée is smart enough not to do anything stupid, and Hastar won't let him, anyway. They need to build that remuda."

Teora laughed. "She is probably in better control than he is. Still, Amand had better start looking for a good horse."

Hastar's father shook his head ruefully. "I suppose he should."

The Herdsmen were lining the animals up for the journey. Carlin checked them all over. "Got everything you need?"

"And more. We've been treated so well that we've been hiding things so we won't hurt the feelings of people who gave us gifts we have to leave behind."

"Not taking a Priest this time?"

"After the last trip, we thought we might do better without. Tourantij is quite capable of handling the organization, and we have enough representation from the Deity."

"No argument there."

"What have you done with Goianor? I didn't see him around the Temple lately."

"I didn't do anything, but I gather Rioran is using him as a test. Any situation where he succeeds means there is a problem."

They shared a laugh, and then the rest of the party spilled into the courtyard along with the Head Priest, casual in his "ranch clothes" of heavy dungarees and embroidered shirt. Soon they were all mounted and ready to leave. The speeches and ceremonies had been taken care of with Rebiema at the Temple yesterday. This was a considerably less formal and noisier parting. Finally they lined out, to shouted farewells and cheers.

Barozon was glad to be on the road, trotting a bit when the horse in front of him opened a gap between them. He huffed and shook his horns at Spar, who nipped playfully at the bull's forehoof as he limped about his usual rounds. The dog was going with Tourantij, because, as Daegal said, he was much too independent to ever make a good herding dog.

Corquée was soon out of sight ahead. He was going to move quickly and take a big swing to the south to check out the new Land. He would join them in two days, 'give or take,' in Rider fashion.

Sure enough, in the evening of the second day he came splashing across the river to where they were camped. Samira looked like she had been ridden hard.

He was so enthused he couldn't wait for supper to be over to talk about it, although he glanced at the cooking fire with interest. "It's a beautiful place, bigger than we thought at first. There's good herding all along the mountains. Even some places for crops, down in the flats near the streams, with long grass and stands of trees. I saw wild cattle, tall, scrawny, tough beasts with long, shaggy hair, and short, upward-pointing horns. There are bears, and I saw some sign of mountain lions. Farther south it's drier and flatter, perfect for us. I don't know why the Curicuiriari haven't used that area."

Teora agreed. "I don't understand why someone hasn't taken up that land, if it's that good."

"Accessibility."

They turned to Tourantij. "What do you mean?"

"Mountains to the west and east, and there is a true desert to the south, between here and the Haven. That's why the Aerans went east of the mountains. Until the Log Jam cleared up, there was no way to get there except through Aeru, and they weren't interested because the land seemed to get drier."

"But now?"

"We keep our mouths shut and get back here quick with enough of a settlement to claim the area."

"How about our transportation?"

"Flat-bottomed steamers can get up the river almost this far, for part of the year at least. The path to Aeru is easy, now that we know it's here." The soldier nudged Corquée. "In fact, I suspect our Rider friend would like to try it."

Corquée nodded enthusiastically. "I thought I'd skip back to the Wynn ranch, talk to them about it. I could catch you in another couple of days." He glanced anxiously at Teora, who shook her head.

"And incidentally discuss it with Hastar? Sorry, Rider, but you have a job here, and it isn't messenger boy. Besides, poor Samira deserves to rest at Barozon's pace for a couple of days."

At his disappointed frown she relented. "I tell you what. We'll send a dispatch back from Tanish. I had thought of doing that anyway. It wouldn't hurt to set up some form of communication over this trail. You can send Hastar a letter that way." She read his face. "I'll write it for you."

Four more days and they were in Tanish. A lot had changed since they left, but a lot hadn't. A big new pier and warehouse perched on the shore, raw wood cooking in the sun. Someone was making a try at sorting through the great piles of logs, but they didn't seem to be making much progress. Out in the bay, wood floated around, but no serious hazard to a slow-moving ship. The shoreline was still piled high. Over against the south shore, though, several big rafts tied together with stout cable were moored. On each raft several of the huts she recognized from the day after the storm sent up cheery plumes of smoke. As they came near, Tzevi appeared, running ashore across a boom of logs with his usual skill. He made his ritual approach to Barozon, but then surprised Teora.

"Hello, Teora, Chosen of Deity."

"Hello, Tzevi. You have learned our language."

"Must learn. Work with merchants."

"Selling logs?"

He made a rocking motion with his head. "Sell some. Take some. Whose logs?" He grinned and shrugged with his shoulders and both hands.

"That doesn't sound right. I'm going to have to work on this." Then she realized he couldn't understand her. "I will help. You wait."

"Thank you, Teora, Chosen of Deity."

"Teora. Just Teora, please."

"Thank you, Teora. Thank you, Barozon."

She smiled and swung her Partner's head towards the new warehouse. Anyone of authority would be there.

Inside, the building was huge and mostly empty. A scruffy-looking man rose hastily from the chair he had leaned against the wall and approached her, one hand on his pistol butt.

"What can I do for you, Lady?"

She motioned for Radman, who had moved forward, to relax. "I'm looking for whoever is in charge here. Is he around?"

The man nodded politely enough. "That's Wendell. He's in the office. I'll tell him you're here, if you like."

Only after he left did she realize that he hadn't asked who she was. *Probably not necessary in this town, now that I think about it.*

Wendell was more than glad to see her. "Madam Teora, you don't know how good it is that you returned! Would you and your people like to come into the shade? Do you need a place to stay?"

Teora was taken aback by this barrage of enthusiasm. "Yes, I suppose we do need somewhere to camp."

He swung his arm around the huge space. "There you go. Lots of room. Unfortunately. Bring them all in – horses too. We don't have much to offer, but at least there's a sanitary, and the roof keeps off the sun and rain."

He bustled around, seeing them all settled.

When Teora was satisfied that everything was under control, she sought him out.

"Wendell, I don't want to be blunt, but you sound overly happy to see us. What's the problem?"

He smiled and led her to his office and living quarters: simply three rooms walled off in one corner of the warehouse. "Right to the point. What a relief. Things aren't going as well as they might, here, as you can see. Our warehouse is going to waste, there's an ocean full of wood out there and I can't get any of it. That Priest they sent out from Aeru was worse than useless."

Teora nodded. The man had been selected by Sumner's people and had returned during the political wrangling, partly because of his failure to deal with the situation in Tanish, but mostly because he wanted to protect his position in the Temple. "What about the locals?"

"The townspeople are a pretty useless bunch, and the natives try but I can't talk to them."

"Tzevi seems to be learning our language."

"Yes, that part is getting better, but it's difficult to tell them what kind of wood I need, and to pay them for it. They bring any old stick and I have to bargain with each one separately for each piece of wood. Plus, I'm sure they've been selling me the same pieces twice while I was trying to find someone to put the wood in the warehouse. Is there anything you can do?"

"I don't know, Wendell. I think the best thing is to get you and Tzevi together and work it out. You must have worked with primitive people before?"

"I haven't."

"Then we'll have to bring in the experts."

"Experts?"

"Sure. Tourantij has dealt with just about everybody, and Corquée, well, he's as primitive as they get, sometimes."

It didn't take long to gather the group together, along with the scruffy guard. Wendell introduced him as Tugen, his foreman, although foreman of which crew wasn't immediately obvious. Teora proceeded to outline the problems. Corquée had one quick answer.

"You have to show them what you want."

"How?"

"I don't know. Make pictures. Draw the sizes of logs on the wall or something. Nail up samples of the kinds of wood."

"That sounds fine."

"Get Tzevi to bring all his people here and tell them all at once."

"I can do that. Can he?"

Teora turned. "Tzevi, can you bring your people here?"

"Bring people? Yes." He made to get up.

"Not yet. Wait." She reinforced it with a hand on his shoulder. "Now, what about moving the logs into the warehouse?"

"Pay them for delivered logs." Tourantij gestured to the big waterside doors. "Not in the water, in the warehouse."

"I thought of that, but I couldn't get them to understand. Plus, they never show up with enough people to move a log on land."

"We can cope with the first problem when we have them all together. Can you build something to lift the logs out with fewer people?"

"I don't know what."

"A ramp with a carriage and a rope with a purchase."

Teora regarded the soldier. "Could you say that in words the rest of us can understand?"

"A wagon with a rope. Roll the wagon down under the log in the water. Pull on the rope and haul it up the ramp. A block and tackle makes it easier. You've got one on the wall over there."

Tugen was immediately enthusiastic. "We could also use the wagon to move the wood around the warehouse. I could make it out of the wood left over from the building."

"Now, what about payment?"

"What do you have to pay them?"

"They have no need for coins. I'm using standard trade goods: knives, pots, axes, jewelry."

Corquée nodded. "Same solution. Draw a picture of the things you'll trade on the picture of each size of log. Then when someone comes in with a log, you go to the picture wall, you point to the size of log he brought in, he points to what he wants. If there's a question of the quality of the log, you can have different payments listed, like a 'good, medium, poor' price."

Teora had a thought. "This system would work for the townspeople too, wouldn't it?"

"If they wanted to work."

The others had ideas that all had to be explained to Tzevi in simple words, and in the end the merchant was satisfied. As the others left, he motioned Teora to stay behind.

"Teora, thank you for your help , but there is a larger problem."

"Is there?"

"Yes. There is no organization in this so-called town. We have obeyed your instructions not to meddle, and so far there has been no problem, but this situation is not going to last. Especially if what we have organized today works out. As long as the trade goods are in my warehouse, Tugen and I can guard them. Once they get spread around, theft will begin, and there is no one to stop it. Tzevi seems to be able to control his people, but the rest? Not the cream of society, here. We could have chaos."

Teora considered. "Can you arrange a message back to Aeru?"

"Certainly. There are a few trustworthy locals," he grinned wryly, "as long as they get paid after the deed is done."

"Good. I'll mention your problem to them in my dispatch. The Aerans have their own problems right now, but if you can keep things going for another month, we'll try to get them to send someone with better organizational skills this time."

"And a strong hand."

"That, too. But remember. There's nobody to give anybody any authority. This town belongs to no one."

"Don't I know it."

They camped out in the warehouse for the next two days, helping out where they could. Teora talked to as many of the locals as possible, trying to figure out what their problems were and searching for solutions. She was frustrated at her inability to create any answers that would last with no organized authority to enforce them. She was more strongly aware of the need for someone to take charge before an undesirable element like the town's last leader took over instead.

36. Return Voyage

Tourantij had already made arrangements by letter from Aeru, and soon their ship arrived: a slim, fast, freighter, with both steam engine and sails. Winds were light, and they made a quick, uneventful run down the coast under engine power, a real letdown for Teora, who had learned to enjoy the sound and movement of the sailing ship.

At the Temple in Coalantha, they were greeted warmly by Dezter, who seemed very pleased with the way things were going in general, and with himself in particular. He did not remark on the lack of a Priest in their party, and in turn Teora refused to ask about recent political developments. Teora and Sabba enjoyed the same luxury apartment for the night, a pleasant change from the plain and rugged cabins on the steamsailer.

The next morning, Teora took Barozon for a stroll around the town. The atmosphere had definitely improved since her last visit. There was a lack of patrolling soldiers, and the populace moved freely, if slowly, about their business. Children played in the streets and followed parents on their errands. When she reached the road to the castle, she noticed another change. In contrast to the bustle of the town, this street was empty. Looking up at the castle, she could see no signs of activity in the windows, and smoke from only three of its many chimneys.

Curious, Teora followed the litter-strewn road up to the castle. The wind blew dead leaves along the street in front of her, making Barozon skittish. The main door to the fortress was open, a line of debris along the bottom showing that it had not been moved lately. No one challenged her entry. Leaving her Partner in the main courtyard, she climbed the steps to the throne room. This door was open as well, but this time a single soldier stood there, not precisely at attention, but at least not slouching. He was an older man, his face not shaven recently. He regarded her as she approached, then dropped his pike wearily across her path.

"It's you, back again."

She waited. *Will he let me in?*

"Haven't you done him enough harm? Or are you only here to gloat?"

Teora felt her face warm. "I come as I came before, to do no harm, but to right the wrongs that have been done."

The man regarded her closely, then slanted his weapon aside. "I suppose you might believe that. Maybe you oughta take a see the results of your charity."

Teora waited, but he would say no more. Mentally shrugging, she moved past.

The inside of the castle was cool and dim, and she could barely see the dais at the far end of the room. Her eyes grew accustomed to the faint light as she walked forward, and she could make out a dark blot in one corner of the huge throne. A human figure hunched into the corner of the chair, arms pulled tightly around knees that supported his chin.

She stood for a while, but his eyes showed no recognition of her existence. She sat on the end of the bottom step and waited, watching.

It was cold in the throne room, but she forced herself into patience. It was a long time before the eyes focused, the head swung towards her. Kilyan's voice seemed to come from a long way away.

"I don't get many visitors these days. What do you want, girl? May I assume you're actually going to talk to me?"

She did not answer, merely waited.

His laugh cracked in his throat. "Not that anyone wants anything from me recently. Which is good, because I have nothing to give. It's all gone. All of it. Gone." His voice faded, and she could see the vacant stare returning.

"All of it? Are you sure?"

His head swivelled towards her. "Do you question me, girl? The lord of this realm? Who do you think you are?"

She waited for a while. "You asked me that question once before."

A puzzled crease appeared between his brows. "I did?"

"And you didn't like the answer."

He stared at her, and she could see the memory return, along with a certain amount of life. Then the shoulders slumped again. A long sigh escaped him.

"Oh. You. I should have expected this. I suppose you have come to check on your handiwork. You and your friends down in the Temple. I must admit I made a mistake, there. I never realized how powerful that bunch of old fuddy-duddies was." His eyes regained some of their sharpness. "But they weren't powerful, were they? They were just an average group of scheming priests until you came along. Who are you, anyway?"

"I am the Chosen of the Deity. Who I am is not important. What I represent is. I represent the idea that there is something above and beyond man, that there is a power and a purpose for what we do, which keeps us from acting in a narrow, selfish way. It is necessary for all to have faith in this. Most do, most of the time. The occasion arises when more belief is required. Then someone like me comes."

"And there was a need here?"

"You thought you could do what you liked with no consequences. You were acting as though as long as you were strong enough, nothing could bring you down."

"I suppose I was."

"Do you believe now?"

"Do I believe?" A half sob. His hand swept the cold air of the decaying room. "Look around you."

"You don't have to die, you know."

"There are few options as palatable."

"That would be a waste."

"More wasteful than this?"

She shrugged. "You don't seem to have much to do here. On the other hand, you must have a certain amount of ability. You haven't lost that."

"Ability? Oh, I had ability, all right. The ability to get myself into a lot of trouble."

"Don't think of it as trouble. Think of it as an opportunity to gain wisdom."

"An easy thing for you to say."

Her voice sharpened. "I have paid for my wisdom, in my own way."

His shoulders slumped even further. "I'm sorry, my Lady. I'm sure you have."

"So have you gained wisdom?"

His head rose. "If you are asking whether I believe that there is a 'power and a purpose for all we do' that is beyond the control of any man, I suppose I would have to say that yes, I did gain wisdom. For all the good it will do me."

An idea was beginning to form in Teora's mind. "Here, perhaps it would do you no good. What if you were to find another place, one where your ability could be useful?"

He stared at her suspiciously. "Useful to whom?"

"Useful to some who need an able administrator, a spokesman who knows the ins and outs of diplomacy."

"And where would this person be, who needs such a spokesman?"

"Not one person, but a people."

"And you want me to go and lead these people? What's in it for me?"

"The chance to be other than this." Her hand swept the gloomy room.

"And aren't you afraid that I will create another empire with these new people as my soldiers?"

She smiled gently. "Some things are beyond even your abilities. Besides, you have gained wisdom."

He shrugged. "It sounds better than anything that has come up lately. Will these people accept me?"

"You would have to work your way up to a position of trust. A letter from me would help."

"A letter, you say." His voice rose in a harsh croak. "Aelfon. Come here. I need you. Aelfon! Where is he?"

With a patter of metal-shod feet, the old guard from the doorway appeared, out of breath from the short run. "Is there a problem, my Lord?"

"No, Aelfon. I need a pen and paper. The young lady is going to write me a letter of reference. Now, doesn't that sound nice of her?"

The old retainer stared up at his master, expecting a joke. Seeing no response, he moved over behind the throne, returning a moment later with a light writing desk, which he proceeded to fuss over, opening several bottles to find ink, wiping the rust from an iron-nibbed pen, going through a mess of papers before discovering a clean one.

"Don't rush, Aelfon. When hope comes to the destitute, we like to savour the experience, stretch it out, in case it should prove groundless. Take your time."

"Hope, my Lord?"

"Yes, Aelfon. The young lady brings us hope as once she brought us disaster. Ironic, is it not? She is sending us on a journey, I gather."

Teora paused in her writing. "A sea journey, my Lord."

A ghost of a smile crossed the grey features. "There you are, Aelfon. My hopes are already being ground down by reality. I never did get along well on boats. I don't suppose it is a long journey?"

"You may have heard of the Log Jam in the Ayanna River."

"Ah, of course. Our penance is not over yet, it seems."

The old soldier's gruff voice intervened. "I heard, my Lord, that the Floating Island busted up in that big storm last year."

"And I was never sure that it even existed. Isn't that typical. We have a choice, young lady, to believe in a myth or a reality that is even more disappointing."

Teora scrounged through the desk for a piece of moderately clean blotting paper. "The floating island is gone but the people of the island have survived. They are the ones who need your help." She folded the paper, leaving it unsealed. "This is your introduction. Notice that I make no promises on your behalf. Go to the raft village on the south side of the riverbank. Use my name. They can't read this, but you can use it with anyone else if you need to." She handed him the paper.

"And remember your newfound wisdom."

He held the letter between them. "I don't know if I should thank you for this, my Lady."

She grinned. "There will be times, I suspect, when you will wish you had never seen me. But they will pass."

His grin disappeared. "There have already been plenty of those times, Teora, Chosen of the Deity. But they may pass."

She regarded him. *He knew my name all along.* She nodded. "That is more than I could have hoped. You have a chance."

"A chance is better than what I had when you walked in a moment ago."

"It is better than what you had the first time I walked in."

He shook his head. "Perhaps, perhaps not. At the time, I would have argued with you."

"I'm sure you would have. And now?"

He shrugged, tapped the paper on the throne thoughtfully. "Only time will tell, I suppose." He spoke in a crisper tone. "I don't suppose you know of a ship headed north, do you? Of course you do."

As she exited the huge gateway with Barozon she had mixed feelings. Knowing what she knew now of Temple politics, she wondered how much responsibility Kilyan bore for the former conflict. All she could do was hope that her action today had in some way evened the score.

Strolling down the street, she was overcome by an aimless feeling. She had accomplished what she could. What would her life hold now?

She was bounced out of her reverie by the appearance of a familiar stocky figure. "Teora! How good to see you and your Partner. He's as beautiful as always."

She couldn't help but smile. "And still ready to perform his duties, Vachel. I gather your bargaining with the Temple has not gone well?"

Vachel shook his head, his smile disappearing. "The price was too high, in both money and groveling. I'm not sure your actions here have worked out altogether well."

"In what way?"

"Before you came, we had a power struggle, but the sides were balanced, religious and secular. Now the balance has been disturbed and the Temple is, quite frankly, becoming difficult."

"I have seen no evidence of that."

"You wouldn't. You're the source of their power. They'll be treating you like...well, like someone special. Which you are. By the way, thanks for what you did up at the Ayanna River last summer. Our salvage operation is going to pick up a lot of cheap wood."

"What did I do?"

"I heard it was you that broke up the floating island."

Teora broke out laughing. "It seems gossip has exaggerated my role a bit. I was there, and that was all. In fact, our ship could easily have been sunk by the pressure of the logs. All I did was straighten up the social problems that arose."

He nodded, seeming unconvinced. "And, if you don't mind my asking, what are you doing up at Kilyan's castle?"

"A mission of mercy."

"The same mercy you showed him before?"

"As it happens, I gave him a task to perform. Did you know him well? Could you work with him?"

Vachel shrugged. "He thought he was a hardheaded businessman, but mainly he overused his political powers to make his enterprises successful. If you knocked some of that out of him, I could probably make him see reason."

"Well, you might get the chance. I've sent him to Tanish. They need some administrative help there, and he was wasted here."

The stocky teamster regarded her quizzically. "You sent a former Lord of the Land to be a small-town Head Councillor? On whose authority?"

Teora threw up her hands. "It wasn't like that. I told him about a place he might be useful. I didn't make him do anything. It was his choice."

"Some choice."

She glared up at him. "It was more choice than he had before I came."

He nodded sagely. "I suppose. You've certainly changed since I saw you last. You have done some personal growing, as the Riders say."

"It happens."

"So, what do you have planned for me?"

"Nothing. Why would I?"

"Really? Nothing?"

His confidence piqued her. "All right, since you are so sure, I will find something. If you're doing business up at Tanish, be very aware of the political balance there. The original people of the town, the natives from the raft and the new businesspeople make a difficult mix, and if things aren't handled carefully, it could get messy. Can you do anything to help?"

He grinned. "I knew it." He lifted his hands in a defensive gesture. "It's all right. I don't mind. I had thought of going up there with a span of oxen. I'll keep in mind what you said. May I use your name if I must?"

"I don't know why you would. As you correctly pointed out, I have no authority at all anymore."

"There are different kinds of authority, Teora, Chosen of the Deity."

"In case you didn't know, I'm done with that. My mission is complete."

He smiled down at her gently. "I don't know anything about religion, Teora, but I don't get the impression that being Chosen is something that just goes away."

She couldn't help but respond to his smile. "Well, it hasn't kept everyone, from friends to casual acquaintances, from telling me what I should be doing, now."

"I'm sorry, I suppose I presume too much."

"Actually, I'm glad you did. I'll see things with a new eye when I get back to the Temple. If you're right, I might have to put my finger back in and stir the pot again."

She rested a reassuring hand on his arm. "And don't worry. If Barozon's services are available, I'll put in a good word for you. That's all you really wanted, wasn't it?"

He tilted his head. "If you want to put it that way, go ahead. Now, I have business to take care of, and you have a Temple to put in order. I'll take my leave."

She shook her head as he strolled off, whistling tunelessly. She continued to the Temple, wondering what he had really wanted. If the Temple was overstepping its bounds, what could she do about it? The best place to find out was the top.

When she got to the Temple, a meeting with the Head Priest was not hard to arrange. Once the formalities were over, she got right down to business.

"Head Priest Dezter. I know the last time I was here, I was new to my situation, and I was willing to follow whatever you wanted. That has changed."

"What do you mean?"

"I mean that the situation has changed. I have changed. I have gained a good deal of wisdom, and along with it a good deal of power. I assume you have read your letters from Aeru?"

The Head Priest glowered at her. "Yes, I have. I have heard from the Head Priest and also from other sources. It seems you have played merry havoc, meddling with things you know little about."

Goianor. Teora wondered which one of the young Priests he had persuaded to carry a personal letter in secret. "Then Goianor also warned you that, should I choose to meddle, I definitely have the ability to mess things up, whether I know what I'm doing or not?"

That set him back a bit. "He did speak of your abilities in the strongest terms."

"I assume you are also aware of the success of my mission, and the good favour I will be in when I reach the Haven?"

"I have been informed officially by the Head Priest of Aeru that you are in especially good repute. With the Head Priest of Aeru."

"Which is to remind me that it is a long way from Aeru to the Haven? Still the same games." She rose from her seat, paced away, came back to stand in front of him.

"I give you no orders, Head Priest. I make no threats. You assume that I tell you of my success to frighten you. You fear I come to threaten you, to make you do things I want. You could not be farther from the truth. I am here to give you information that might stop you from continuing to make certain mistakes. I merely wish to point out that things are changing.

"There will be changes in the administration of the Temple. Not because I make them, but because they are coming. They have happened in Aeru, they are happening in the Joined Kingdoms, and the Haven will not escape them.

"You have not maintained your position for so long without political skill. Surely a man of your astute nature will recognize when the winds of change are stirring. Surely, if you wish to maintain your position, you will try to change as well.

"Think, Head Priest. If the change is coming and I was against you, what would my best move be? I would leave you alone, and you would be blown away like a bit of dirt in a sandstorm. But I am not willing to do that. It would cause a great deal of trouble for the Temple. I am merely doing my duty by helping you. If you can find some other, subtler motive, then your mind is more devious than mine."

The Head Priest sat looking at her. For a long while, he seemed at a loss for words. Then he smiled slyly. "This wouldn't have anything to do with my judgment against your friend the Rider, would it?"

"Of course it has. That was when I first realized the basis upon which this Temple is run. I would like to thank you for that, actually. Having experienced the effects of a rigid, top-heavy organization once, I recognized it immediately when I saw it again."

"A rigid, top-heavy organization, is it?"

"Mainly, yes. Too many people with too much concern for their own personal power, not enough for getting the job done. Too many meetings, too much paperwork, not enough action. Too many decisions based on maintaining the structure instead of finding a fair outcome. Too much interference with the secular government, not enough religious guidance. Too much power for the wrong purpose, not enough faith. I know it is difficult to change. I only wish you to consider these things. You will know from your communications with the Aerans that a major sweeping-out was necessary. Given a timely warning, perhaps you can avoid that here."

She set both hands on his desk, leaned over him. She fleetingly wished she could give him a touch of the Deity's power, then rejected the notion of even trying. If he couldn't see the nose on his face, he didn't deserve to survive.

"And don't think that I am giving you time to make plans which will further entrench your old ways. That is what the Priests in Aeru thought. See where it got them."

She backed away, let her hands drop. "I am giving you no orders. I have no authority to make you do anything. I am only trying to help you with a timely warning. I hope you can see it as such."

The Head Priest folded his hands under his chin and stared at her over them. Finally, he nodded, slowly. "I do believe that you think you are doing this for the best. I have no reason to doubt your commitment to the Deity. Therefore, I will take what you say seriously. I make no guarantees."

Teora was satisfied. It was more than she had hoped for. Whether he was only playing safe or actually believed her, the fact that he had heard her out meant that he had a chance. Otherwise, she doubted that he would survive long. *I hope the people of Coalantha will not suffer too much more for his mistakes.* She thought of one last point that would get to him.

"I know you have the glory of the Deity in mind. You are also aware that there is a weakening in the power of the Joined Kingdoms. From what I have heard, the Kingdoms have the same problems we have. If we can cure ours first, we have a chance to take over some of that power, to regain some of our former glory."

She disliked the words even as she said them, but the priest nodded sagely, and she knew she had tugged the right line. He was deep in thought and barely noticed her leaving.

Tired of the politics and the close confines of the Temple, Teora harnessed Barozon and rode back into the town. She could tell from the sideways glances that everyone knew who she was. They seemed friendly enough, and she guessed that their memory of her deed overshadowed any antagonism they had for the Temple hierarchy.

She was considering checking a few shops for gifts for her family when she heard her name.

"Teora! Teora!" A lithe figure ran out of an alleyway, jogging along beside Barozon, eager face turned up.

"Natanya! How are you? Would you like to come up?"

The girl nodded, grabbed a strap and swung up, landing breathlessly behind Teora.

"That was pretty good! Have you been practising?"

The small face lost some of its animation. "Not as much as I'd like. But they can't keep me away all the time."

Teora filed this away. "How is your mother?"

"Oh, she's fine. She doesn't know you're here, I bet. I heard it at the Pastures and I came in right away."

"Can I go visit her?"

"Sure, she's home making dinner. Turn left at the next corner."

The home was a humble one for a Priest, and not new, but it was well cared for. Noleta greeted Teora with surprise, but recovered quickly and invited her in.

"What will your Partner do? He can't stand in the street."

"I suppose that's what we train young Dancers for. Natanya, is there a pasture nearby?"

"Yes, down at the end of the street."

"Good. Take him down there and keep him occupied. If he tries to come back, it's because I called him."

The girl's eyes were shining. "Can I ride him?"

"How else does a Dancer move a bull? Were you thinking of carrying him?"

Natanya giggled, then ran and clambered up on Barozon's back. She kicked her heels on his side to turn him. With a disgusted snort, he strolled away.

"Have fun, you two."

"I have a feeling they will. Is it all right for her to take him off like that?"

"If she hadn't been here, I would have left him there alone. This way she can keep him from getting bored."

Noleta led the way into her house, and soon the two were gossiping like old friends, their previous experience having brought them closer together. Teora learned that Noleta's husband had returned safe and sound, and was doing better in the Temple, partly because of the children's fame and partly because he was learning to keep his mouth shut. They still weren't completely happy, though, as Teora could see from the lines around the woman's mouth, and the odd comment she picked up.

Their conversation was interrupted by a man's anxious voice, calling from outside. "Noleta! Noleta, come out here. Quickly."

Noleta grinned. "That's Jalil. I can imagine what he's upset about!" The woman walked out, and Teora followed.

"Noleta, what is Natanya doing...Oh!" The Priest, short, bearded and stocky, was fairly hopping up and down in confusion.

"Jalil, this is Teora. She dropped around for a visit."

"Teora! Oh, that explains everything." He gestured down the street. "I gather that's Barozon, then, as if it could be anyone else."

Teora laughed. "That's him, all right. Shall we go and see what's happening?"

As they walked towards the pasture, Teora pulled the two to the side of the street. "Let's watch for a while."

They stood, partially concealed by some bushes, and watched the scene in the pasture. Barozon was plodding patiently in a circle, and Natanya was doing mounts and dismounts, clumsily trying to reach the tall back in one swing, usually failing. Each time she fell, he would stop, turn his head around and snort at her. She would talk to him, get up gamely, and they would try again.

A small crowd had gathered, mostly children, and they were watching, spellbound. Then a taller head appeared, splitting the watchers. It was a man in the cloak of a Temple Marshal. He walked right into the pasture and waited until the girl saw him.

Both parents stepped forward, but Teora stopped them. "She's not doing anything wrong."

The Marshal cocked an eyebrow up at Natanya, sitting high on the mighty hump. "Now what are you about, young lady?"

She stared down at him with injured dignity. "I'm Dancing, of course." Then honesty compelled her to continue. "Well, just practising."

A smile tugged at the corner of the man's face. "And who said you could practise with this bull?"

The girl thought a moment. "Well, I suppose you don't have to ask anyone permission to Dance with the Consort of the Deity. If he agrees, who is going to complain?"

Noleta stifled a gasp of dismay, but Teora again held her arm. "Good answer!"

The Marshal stepped forward, holding out his hand for Barozon to sniff. "So this is the famous Barozon, is it?"

"Of course!"

"Well, I'm sure he knows what he's doing. Don't let me hold up your Dancing." The Marshal turned and started away, then noticed the three standing there and directed his steps towards them. He was shaking his head as he approached.

"I guess I've been put in my place, haven't I?"

"I'm sorry. She should have been more polite."

He held up his hands in a negative gesture. "I shouldn't have interrupted. I knew full well who she was Dancing with. I just wanted a chance to meet him." His eyes shot towards Teora and away again, quickly, but Jalil noticed.

"I suppose you would like to meet Teora as well? Teora this is Taima, one of our best Marshals."

The man shrugged and blushed. "I do all right I guess."

Teora grinned. "Well, when it comes to dealing with unique situations, you improvise quickly."

He returned the grin. "You know, before I was halfway out to her, I knew she wasn't doing anything wrong. She seemed so serious, and so...well, so right out there. Just like the other Dancers do." He turned to Jalil "So she's going to be a Dancer, is she?"

The Priest shrugged. "I'm not sure. It's hard to get training, you know."

The man was indignant. "Well, it shouldn't be. Not for one who has natural talent like that." He stood watching her with a proprietary air. Then he broke his pose. "Well, I've got to keep on my watch schedule. An honour to meet you, Lady Teora. And Barozon as well."

"A pleasure, Taima. Perhaps we'll see you again."

"I hope so. Good night." He turned and walked away.

Teora's eyes followed him. "It seems not everyone in the Temple finds you dangerous, Jalil."

A quick glance to his wife let him understand that Teora knew all. "Oh, I have plenty of friends like that. If I last another twenty years, I might get ahead some."

Teora patted his shoulder. "I doubt it's going to take anywhere near that long."

He stared at her, startled, trying to read her expression.

"This situation can't last. You have heard the news from Aeru?" She knew that the Temple grapevine would be efficient. "The Enclave isn't the only place with problems that need solving."

Further discussion was cut off, as Natanya noticed them and brought Barozon over for a creditable off-shoulder dismount in front of them. She turned and formally acknowledged her audience, then threw her arms as far as she could around Barozon's neck. Then she turned to Teora, her face alight.

"Thank you so much. He's wonderful!"

Teora laughed. "I agree. I'm sorry to take him back, but I have to return to the Temple. Your mother invited me to stay for supper, but they're having some sort of state banquet tonight. Say good-bye, and I'll be off."

While the girl was hugging Barozon once more, Teora turned to her parents. "Even more, now, you have to get her training. Who should I talk to at the Temple?"

The Priest looked at his feet. "Well, Teora, I don't want to seem ungrateful, but we don't believe in that sort of pulling of strings. I mean, we would like her to get training, but..."

Teora shook him by the sleeve. "Noleta, talk to him. Make him see some sense. If it's his pride, not wanting to ask for favours, don't worry. This is my job. If I see a potential Dancer, I can demand that she gets training, and the trainers will comply gladly. Not because I command it, but because they are always searching for good Dancers." She turned to Jalil. "If you don't believe in pulling strings, you are never going to be a very good Priest. Part of your job is politics and you had better get good at it. We need people like you."

He still wasn't convinced. "I know about the politics, but it's not right to pull strings for my family, you know, use my influence to get my daughter put ahead."

"Those are good scruples, but no one is asking for her to get any more than she deserves. And if someone is pulling their own strings to make her get less than she should," she swung up on Barozon and regarded the three, "they are going to get them snipped off. Very quick, and very short!"

She smiled at them. "I'm sure you know the practice schedule, Natanya. Show up for every practice. Don't miss any. That's part of your training. Say hello to your brother for me. If he wants to drop up to the Temple tomorrow, I'm sure Sabba and Nipha would be glad to see him."

She said her good-byes and jogged Barozon back towards the Temple. When she was putting him into the pasture, she inquired about the Dancing instructors. They were easy to find in their quarters nearby. They were an old couple, with a comfortable, relaxed manner, but still with the slim bodies of Dancers. Teora broached her subject immediately.

"What's the situation with Natanya? Has she been training?"

They glanced at each other. "Well, sort of."

"Well, yes..."

Teora glared. "...and no, you mean."

They nodded unhappily.

"What is the problem? Has anyone given any orders that she shouldn't Dance?"

Again, a negative. An uncomfortable communication passed between the two, then the man spoke.

"Teora, we have no problem with training her. But what's the use? When the time comes to qualify for a Partner she will fail, and it will be all a lot of heartbreak for nothing. It would be better for her if she didn't even start."

Teora forced her voice to remain calm. "And why should she fail?"

Their eyes dropped.

"Don't you have any say?"

They sat up straighter. "Of course." Then the man slumped. "But somehow it never works out. There's always a perfectly good reason why the list gets changed, and there's never any way we can complain. But I can tell you, right now, that no matter how hard Natanya works or how good she becomes, somehow, when the list for Partners comes out, she will not be on it."

Teora turned away, paced a few steps, reminding herself that these two poor souls were as much victims as Natanya. Then she walked back to them. "It may have been that way, but not this time. She will be coming to practice. Train her as you would any other promising young Dancer, no more, no less. Because her father is a Priest there must be no hint of special favours, you understand."

They both nodded.

"When the time comes, you make out the list, and make it fairly. I have every confidence that her name will be on it, but it might not. Things change, especially with children, and I will not be upset if you think she is not the right type of person to be a Dancer. But I will be very upset if her name disappears from the list after you have made it. And I expect you to inform me. I know I might be far away at the Haven, but you can expect a lot more communication back and forth in the near future. I may even be back myself. Let me know," she allowed her voice to sound grim, "and I will take whatever steps I need."

Having made her point, Teora lightened the mood. "Barozon liked Dancing with her, she can't be that bad."

The woman's face lightened. "She Danced with the Consort?" Then she grimaced. "Her mounts are terrible."

Teora laughed. "That they are. Of course, he is rather tall for her. Her dismounts seem quite good, though."

They fell to discussing technicalities, as Dancers do, and Teora parted a while later with smiles and reassurances that Natanya would get a fair deal, no matter what.

Teora had only one more job to do. Just a pleasant suggestion, no hint of a command, in the ear of the person in charge of the Partner lists, that Natanya was going to be a great Dancer someday. Whatever his loyalties, he was far enough up the chain to be able to take a hint. It was easily accomplished, but Teora was disgusted. *All this work, all this time wasted, and for what? To make sure something happened that should have occurred automatically if the system was working properly.* She would have words for the leaders back in the Haven. Aeru wasn't the only place with problems.

37. Home

It was an easy trip through the mountains. They stopped at Vachel's logging camp for one serious breakfast before the ascent and loaded up their water sacks at every spring, but no precautions were necessary. They travelled through the last days of spring, and water was running everywhere. The heat had not yet attained the smothering weight of summer. Two days of steep climb, and they were on the long, slow slope down to the flatlands. At the avalanche site a new route had been cut through the slide area. At least someone was taking care of the trail.

Aided by cooler temperatures, the wind at their backs and plenty of water in their bags, they made good time across the flatlands. No dust obscured the air, and Teora could see that there truly was a lot of life, both plant and animal, in the area that was "not a desert."

At the bottom of the Plateau, they were greeted with great respect by the shepherds who lived in the rocks. It was difficult to tell, because their hosts were naturally close-mouthed, but it seemed that rumours had been circulating all winter about Teora's escapades.

Tourantij rode ahead of Teora as they ascended the trail to the Rim. He glanced back frequently, showing concern, but without the tense control he had needed on the outward trip. At the top, he was even able to joke about it.

"Would you like to take a peek over the edge, Teora?"

She grinned back. "No, thanks. Once was enough for me. Unless you need me to?"

"No, that's fine. I'll finish this assignment as I am. Thank you for your concern." The sincerity of his smile told Teora that the gratitude was for more than today.

As they rode out across the plateau, Teora was dismayed to see that the drought still held the Haven in its searing grasp. Even this early the grasses were browning, and the streams they crossed were mere trickles, as they had been for the past few years.

The trip across the plateau seemed short. Barozon's pace had increased as he became hardened to travelling, and they reached the Haven early in the afternoon. Unsure what the protocol was, Teora decided to go straight to the Temple of the Consort.

She got there before news of their approach. Leathad's stall was empty, and she passed an undecided minute before a surprised junior Priest found her there and hurriedly went looking for Linea.

The other two young Priests who came to entertain her were almost comical in their inability to think of anything to say. She took pity on them and asked them about general happenings in the Haven recently. They gratefully filled her in until Linea appeared, riding Leathad. She did not wait to dismount, calling out in a very un-Priestess-like shout as soon as her head appeared over the edge of the ramp.

"Teora! You're back!"

Teora made a show of regarding herself. "Seems like it."

Linea brought her Partner straight over to Teora and turned her dismount into a firm hug. Then she released her sister and checked her over critically. Uncertainty crossed her face. "It's good to have you back, Teora...Chosen." She hesitated again. "I...we weren't expecting you this early."

Teora regarded the Priestess, her concern breaking her formal mood. "What's wrong, Linea? Has something happened while I was away?"

Linea smiled tentatively. "Something has happened, Teora, but not here. It has happened to you. I have spent over a year as Priestess. I have learned a lot about transforming prayers and dealt with many people, some holy, some not." She glanced at her sister, bit her lip and continued. "I have never felt anything like the aura you carry about you, the aura of the Deity. Never anything close."

"But Linea, I have no power anymore. I have not felt the smallest twinge of it since I left Aeru."

Linea stared into her eyes, probing. "Perhaps. I feel no power emanating from you, such as I feel from the Head Priest." She hesitated. "But there is still something there, like the residue of great faith, the feeling...this sounds silly, but the feeling you get in an old, old Temple. The feeling of the presence of the Deity."

Teora nodded and smiled with the reminiscence of the day she held a Herd in her palm, a people in her heart. "I'll tell you all about it."

She put an arm around her sister's slim shoulders. "But something I do know; we can talk to each other. Chosen to Chosen, sister to sister. None of those rules apply to us now, do they?"

Linea laughed. "You are so different from when you left. Then you came to me, trying to be the determined old Teora, but seeking assurance that you were doing the right thing. Now you march in and start telling me what rules we need to follow. If I wasn't so glad to see you, I think I'd be jealous."

"Linea, don't be jealous, please!"

"Teora, you do what you do best, and I'll do what I do best, and I'm sure there will never be any competition between us. In fact, I can't think of two more different people who could both be good at the same job!"

They laughed together and strolled, arm in arm, over to talk to Leathad, but not for long. With a rush of feet, officious clergy surrounded them, all anxious to take part in Teora's welcome home. Sharing a wry smile, the sisters allowed themselves to be swept apart by the torrent of officialdom.

Two hours later the ceremonies over, and Teora finally, gratefully, made it home. Her family had been there to greet her and had been honoured as well at the ceremonies, but it wasn't the same. Now she could collapse with exaggerated exhaustion on the old horse-leather couch with her mother close beside her, Sovestin standing beside them, grinning from ear to ear.

"Was it as hard as you expected, dear?"

Teora smiled weakly. "Immeasurably harder, Mother. Until you have been dying of thirst, you never really know what it's like."

"Dying of thirst!"

"Well, we never actually ran out of water, but we were worried enough to take very short rations. That and the dust and the heat, not to mention the wolves and the bandits. No, I had no idea what it would be like."

Her mother scanned her face, concern wrinkling her forehead. "Was it that terrible, then?"

Teora laughed. "No, Mother, it was glorious! It was an experience I will never be able to repeat in my lifetime, and it was wonderful.

"They were right to send me, Mother. I am completely suited to that sort of thing. Even when I was thirsty, dirty, hot, and uncertain what to do next, I still felt good, somewhere down inside, because I knew it was right that I should be there."

Sovestin sighed, and his smile faded. "I wish I could be Chosen like that."

Teora beckoned to him. "Sov, come here."

He hesitated.

"Sov, I am your Big Sister, and you will do what I say. Come here. That's right. Now sit down here," she put an arm around his shoulders, held him firmly to stare into his eyes, "and listen to me. This has nothing to do with being Chosen. This could happen to you as well as anyone else. When you really believe in your purpose, and you go ahead and do it in spite of everything, then you feel that way.

"And it doesn't matter, in the end, whether you win or not. It only matters that you do the right thing, and you stick with it. Do you understand?"

He grinned. "Sure, but if it's all the same to you, I'd rather win."

She slapped his shoulder hard enough to make him wince. "Well, some things haven't changed much!"

Their laughter was interrupted by a light tap at the door.

"Who could that be? I was sort of hoping to get some time with you before I got called away again."

"That's Dinnan's knock." Sov jumped up. "I'll let him in."

As he strode out, Teora raised an eyebrow to her mother.

"Dinnan visits here often. I think he found it more convenient to pump all of us for information, rather than only Sov." Her mother's smile indicated that the Priest's presence had not been unwelcome. Just then Sov returned with Dinnan and another man.

What kind of information has this up-and-coming priest been gathering here?

The newcomer's name was Hadar, a very influential mover in the higher circles of the Haven's ruling group. He looked the part: greying, distinguished, conservatively dressed. Something in the familiar way he moved into the room and how close he stood to her mother brought Teora's senses alert. A meaningful glance at Sov brought a confirming wink.

"Mother! Have you been taking my advice?"

This barb brought a blush to her mother's cheek. "Daughter, I'm sure you know Hadar," was all she managed to get out.

"Of course I do. It is a pleasure to have you visit us." She left it at that, just on the friendly side of neutral. Let him establish his position in his own way.

"Teora! I am glad to finally meet you. The real you. I have heard so much about you, all of it good, by the way. If I hadn't seen you Dance many times, I would have been afraid you would turn out to be a myth."

What kind of flattery is this? "You have seen me dance many times?"

"I most certainly have. I was one of your greatest supporters before you took up training Linea instead. How could anyone miss such talent? Come, now, no false modesty. I saw it, as did many others."

She nodded. That was nothing she could argue with. It just wasn't something she wanted to discuss.

"But that is enough small talk. I am pleased to see you because you bring some of the most exciting news we have heard in a long time, I am sure. Please forgive me for breaking in so soon, but..." He made an appealing gesture that she could not ignore.

"I'm sure you are welcome, Hadar. I am also sure that I will not hold out too long without giving my news." He had been given enough of her attention. "Especially with Priest Dinnan standing there with his tongue hanging out."

The Priest grinned easily and reached out to take her hand. "Welcome home, Teora. I'm glad you are not coming to haunt me."

His hand was large and firm, with unexpected calluses. She was puzzled, then remembered their parting conversation, long ago. "So now you are taking credit for the whole thing, are you?"

Dinnan's laugh rang through the house. "Without us pushers and prodders, how would you movers and doers ever get anything done?"

"Considerably quicker and easier, I suspect."

"You begin to understand, Hadar?" The aside from her mother brought Teora's attention to the fact that their conversation excluded the rest of the party. "She has already put you in your place and insulted the priest twice, and she has only been home half an hour. I shudder to imagine what damage she has worked at the Temple."

"Don't worry, Mother. I haven't even written up a report for them, just given them a general sketch of the situation. They kindly allowed me to come home for the evening. I'm to meet with Head Priest Aolan and Head Councillor Rhondona tomorrow afternoon to discuss the details."

Manora stood up, dusting her hands together. "So! We must eat. Teora can entertain us with stories of her travels while I prepare the meal, and we can talk serious business afterwards."

Teora absorbed this casual arrangement. Dinnan was playing host, pouring drinks, while Sov brought appetizers from the kitchen. Hadar sat comfortably, chatting with Teora while it was all arranged. It could have been a family, the way they functioned smoothly together. She reconciled the homey atmosphere with the status of the members. *A new power clique is forming in the Haven, a group to be reckoned with. Hmm.*

After dinner they all sat comfortably, considering the brandy that Sov had poured. Teora had a moment's disorientation. This was so different from the past months: civilized, sane. And yet it was similar. The same feeling, the same camaraderie.

Dinnan regarded the group. "How many times over the past months have we all sat here, this very group, and longed for this moment."

Teora looked at him in curiosity. "What moment?"

He grinned awhile, then became serious. "Your mother should answer that."

Teora rounded on her mother. "What have you been planning?"

Manora laughed. "Not planning. Hoping. Me more than the others, perhaps. It is truly enough to have you back here, whatever the outcome of your mission." She sat forward, all business. "But ever since we heard your reports, we have been dreaming. Longing for the day when you would return, to put meat on the bones, so to speak."

She glanced to Hadar, and he took up the narrative. "We saw this as an ideal opportunity for the Haven, Teora. A chance to expand, to cover new ground, to rejuvenate ourselves, at a time when the Joined Kingdoms are falling into decay. Some day, there could be a new power rising in the north, Teora. A new style of government. A clean, sharp, wind from the peaks, to cut through the soft, cloying odours of decadence which clog the Joined Kingdoms to immobility. Your ideas gave us the germ of that chance. We wanted to talk to you, to see whether it was all feasible."

Teora took this in, her mind whirling. Only one aspect jumped to the surface. Without considering, she spoke it. "And where do you see yourself in this clean, sharp wind, Hadar? Near the cutting edge?"

The man sat back, his mouth open, glancing helplessly to Manora. She smiled gently. "As close to the front as we can get him, Teora. Do you see anything wrong with that?"

It was Teora's turn to pause, wordless. "I...I'm sorry, Mother. I didn't mean to be critical. I mean...I mean, after all, why shouldn't he?"

Sovestin laughed heartily. "She's done it again, Dinnan."

The young Priest laughed as well. "Don't be hard on your sister, Sov. It's a beautiful technique."

"Technique?" Teora frowned at the Priest. "What technique?"

Sovestin and Dinnan laughed again. "She's a natural, all right. She does it without even noticing."

Teora was beginning to get angry. "What are you laughing at? What have I done?"

Dinnan calmed himself. "I do apologize, Teora. You know that you have been the topic of many of our conversations. The stories told about you begin to create a persona which is not exactly you, but more your legend. It is a shock, and a bit of a triumph to us, when something you do proves our conjectures."

Teora decided to be mollified. "And what typical trick have I pulled now?"

"Well, you have this habit of missing the game completely and jumping straight through to the end and scoring anyway."

"For example?"

"Let's assume, for sake of argument, that we were all playing one of those twisted bureaucratic games here, and we had decided to sound you out on your support for Hadar in some political move he was making. We have it all planned out: who will open the subject, who will drop what hint, whose job it is to lay on the flattery, who will make the decision as to whether we have had enough success to make a direct request. Don't be so shocked. This sort of planning is what makes diplomatic meetings go smoothly."

Teora nodded. "I see. And I spoiled your fun by jumping right to the main point without allowing you to make all the planned moves."

Hadar leaned forward. "Yes. It is an effective move, but few have the nerve to play it as it must be played, boldly and cleanly. Usually, only one in complete command of the situation uses that gambit. One who tries it but jumps to the wrong conclusion ends up looking very foolish."

Teora shook her head, confused. "But I wasn't playing a gambit. I was trying to get to the centre of the problem, so it could be solved."

They all laughed. Sovestin slapped her shoulder. "That's what we mean by a 'natural'. You do the right thing without even thinking about it. Makes you extremely difficult to manipulate."

Teora turned to Manora. "Mother, where is he learning language like that? Why is he learning it?"

Her mother gestured around the room. Both Hadar and Dinnan were regarding her proudly. "You mean you think this is a good idea?"

"I do, dear. Your brother is never going to have the advantages you had, or be given the power that you have. He has to be more conscious of his talent, to use it to its fullest."

"I understand." She smiled at her brother. "Actually, since you put it that way, I must say I am impressed." She looked at her brother; his haircut was positively normal. "I never thought of the Tall One learning politics, but why not?"

Dinnan placed a friendly hand on the boy's shoulder. "Sovestin has been of great use to us. He shares your ability, Teora, to understand what motivates people. He also seems to be good at using that knowledge to influence them."

Teora and Manora shared a grin. Sov had always been good at manipulating family situations. Amazing that the skill should have positive applications. "Are you going to turn into a political priest?"

Sov laughed. "I'm not going to be a Priest."

Hadar nodded. "He's much too interested in how the organization works. He has been of great use to me, finding information, running messages, performing minor tasks. In the process, he has developed his own network of acquaintances. When he reaches sixteen, he will be competing for a lower position in civic service. And he will get one, easily."

"Because he has friends in high places."

Hadar laughed easily. "Don't pretend to be so disgusted, Teora. Not because of your mother or me. Because it is a sure thing that some of the members of the interview panels will know him. They will already have seen him at work, passing messages, helping out, and they will know that he is bright and reliable. We do not need to pull strings, and we would rather not. It is better for him to work his way up. It is going to be easy enough for him, and more because of what his sisters have accomplished than anything to do with Manora or me."

As the evening progressed, Teora watched Hadar closely. He could never replace Teora's father, but he certainly was good for her mother. Teora pushed him harder for ideas, fascinated by his knowledge of different government systems. She couldn't help but notice that Sovestin was equally interested. As the evening wrapped up, Teora knew things were well at home. If she had to leave again, they would miss her, but they would survive.

And I'm already thinking of leaving again. Hmm.

* * *

Aolan sat back, reflecting on Teora's report. She had been talking steadily for over an hour, interrupted only by infrequent questions from the Head Priest and Head Councillor and supporting details from Tourantij.

"Well, Teora. It seems you have exceeded our expectations."

She felt a warm flush on her cheek.

Rhondona gave the ghost of a smile. "And you seem to have exceeded your mandate as well."

A touch of guilt brought Teora down to earth. "I did?"

The older woman rocked her hand in a 'yes/no' gesture. "In a sense, you did. We sent you to bring spiritual relief to the Aerans and new blood to their herds. We had no expectations that you would turn their Temple hierarchy upside down."

Teora was stunned. "But I...but I thought I was sent to help them. That was where they needed help. I realized my inexperience in that area, but I had already spent too much time telling people that I was the wrong person for the job, so I went ahead and did my best."

"If we had meant to help them with their organization, we would have sent an experienced bureaucrat with you."

"And, with no disrespect to bureaucrats, that would have been about as effective as sending a grizzly to take care of the calves. Bureaucrats were the problem, not the solution."

The Head Priest, who had said little until this moment, surprised Teora with a hearty laugh. "Which proves to us the wisdom of our original choice. Or to be more exact, the wisdom of the Deity and her Choice."

The Head Councillor smiled as well. "I cannot argue with that. In broader terms, Teora, you did what you were sent to do. You were given no guidelines. We set it up that way on purpose. Not knowing what problems you would find, we had to give you the freedom to work as you saw fit. We hoped that, with the guidance of the Deity, you would succeed."

"And with considerable assistance from Tourantij."

Rhondona regarded the soldier, nodded slowly, then straightened her back in a businesslike fashion, the thoughtful look leaving her face.

"Now, Teora. Since you have made such good use of the freedom we gave you, give us your opinion on some of the plans we have.

"First, we feel it would be good to approach the Aerans about giving us some of their cattle. We are aware of the need to expand our own bloodlines, and their records indicate new developments in their breeding programs. Some of the bloodlines they took with them originally have developed differently from those left behind."

Teora nodded. "Interbreeding with wild cattle, especially in their early years at Aeru. Their records have suspicious blanks in places. The wild cattle are very hardy, although spare by our standards. Again, I am not an expert," she glanced at the Councillor with a smile, "but they have some new lines that could benefit us."

Rhondona's smile acknowledged Teora's irony. "This fits in very well with some plans we had in the making. We were also considering a deal with a cattle breeder near Coalantha."

"Vachel Yamil?"

"Yes. Do you know of him?"

Teora and Tourantij broke into laughter. "Let me guess. The deal has something to do with a sharing of bloodlines, specifically Barozon's."

Aolan stared at them, perplexed. "Is that unusual?"

"Oh, in this case, it wouldn't be unusual at all. He only tried every trick he could, both times we passed through, to get that very thing. He does have superb stock of his own to contribute."

Rhondona smiled. "We will remember that when we are dealing with him. And while we are on that topic, tell us about the Temple at Coalantha."

"Another area where I exceeded my assignment, I suppose."

The Councillor nodded to the Head Priest. "Our assignment, perhaps, but it would seem that the Deity allowed you much more latitude." Then, more seriously, "Tell us about what you found there."

Teora described the situation as well as she could, especially the Ceremony of Exclusion, the political feelings surrounding it, and her final solution to Lord Kilyan's problems. She wondered if they would consider that she had overstepped her boundaries there, too, but they listened without comment until she turned to the topic of how Corquée had been treated.

At that point, the Head Priest's brow furrowed. "It sounds as if Goianor was using the authority of office to exact personal revenge. The priest's job was to maintain the morale and spiritual integrity of your group. In borrowing the Temple's authority, he proved his inability to handle that job on his own."

"His friends in the Temple don't see it that way."

"Which condemns them as well. I will check into this. The Rider's reputation should not suffer."

"Thank you, but I doubt if he cares much what we think of him."

The Head Priest grinned. "Another free spirit, I gather."

"As are most of his people."

"True. But he might not mind receiving the remainder of his pay. Please go on, Teora."

Teora completed her report. She only touched on Jalil and Noleta's problems in a general way, because she thought they would be solved if the rest of the situation at the Temple improved. When she had finished, Rhondona and the Head Priest glanced at each other in a meaningful way.

Teora glanced from one to the other, puzzled. "Is there anything I missed?"

The Head Priest frowned, but then his brow cleared. "A point of clarification only, Teora. We have received messages from Head Priest Dezter, as well. What did you do to him?"

What has the man reported? "I only talked to him briefly on our way back through Coalantha. Is there a problem?"

"You only talked to him briefly, and now he is writing to us, suggesting that we need to review all our policies, to put new life into our organization? Dezter, who has spent the last twenty years walking backwards gazing at 'our former glory'? I don't know, Teora. You seem to have an electrifying effect on the people you meet."

Rhondona's eyes shot to the Head Priest. "Should we be worried too?"

Aolan considered, then turned to Teora with a wry smile. "So, Chosen. You were sent to do a job and, having done it well, you don't know how to stop. Is there a message there for us, here at the Haven? Will you soon be telling us that we are running things all wrong?"

Only his smile kept Teora from gasping. "I hadn't thought of it that way." She turned to Tourantij for his supporting nod. "But it seems to be happening everywhere. From what I can gather, many of the problems of the Joined Kingdoms stem from the same weakness. Aeru had it seriously. Coalantha has some of that, although I only saw one specific problem, so my experience was limited. I...well, I never saw any of those problems here. But maybe I wouldn't have seen any, before my eyes were opened. I don't know."

The others laughed gently at her uncertainty but soon sobered. The Head Priest's brow wrinkled. "Good administrators can make a bad system work well. The Haven has some talented people running things, if I say so myself, but perhaps we have become complacent. I know that the centre of the religion is expected to be a hotbed of politics, but have we allowed this to overwhelm us? I don't know the answer to that, but it is a question that needs some thought."

Teora thought back to her first days in Aeru. "Aeru had a bad feeling about it from the moment I entered."

"You mentioned that in your reports."

"When I had time to work it out, it was a feeling of imbalance. Too much power to the wrong purpose, and not enough faith. The Land and the People could feel it, and they were helpless to do anything."

"And you solved it by...?"

"Well, it's complicated. I tried to help the Head Priest, but he had too much power already. I encouraged the Priestess to take power at his expense to restore the balance. Then I boosted her faith in herself so that she could feel the presence of the Deity and become Chosen. It was enough to prepare them for the crisis, when the Deity helped us bring the faith of the people back into the formula, as the Temple and the Dancers are supposed to do. Then there was the complete lack of lay leaders, which solved itself once the people involved realized their purposes coincided."

"And what do you feel here?"

"Nothing. There is no need crying out to me." She grinned. "I suppose that's a good sign. Everything must be balanced."

Rhondona leaned forward. "Teora, thank you for a fresh viewpoint. It is not often that we receive that kind of criticism."

"I didn't mean to criticize…"

"I know you didn't. Don't worry, you are not dealing with Dezter here. I hope we are open-minded enough to listen," she paused to smile slightly, "without you having to turn your persuasive powers on us."

Tourantij's soft comment floated into the pause. "Unless, of course, she already has."

The two stared at him, blank looks on their faces. Then understanding dawned, and both turned their attention to Teora, as if considering her in a new light. A humorous glance passed between them, and Rhondona shook her head, as if in awe. Teora followed all this, puzzled.

Then Aolan leaned forward, changing the subject. "Tell us more about Jalil. Yearly reports from his superiors have not been enthusiastic."

Teora thought a moment. "I can't give you an unbiased opinion, as I have only met him briefly, and I have become friendly with his wife and daughter. It would be fair to say that he is too idealistic. His convictions do not sit well with his superiors, but he has many friends in the lower levels. Even his friends admit he is poor at politics, although I get the feeling he has learned a lot recently."

The Head Councillor sent a strange glance at the Head Priest. "So, he has high principles and tells them freely, no matter who is listening?" There seemed to be some private message passed between the two, because the Priest's eyes dropped as if he was embarrassed.

"And he is surprised when people get upset with him, because it should be evident to everyone that he speaks the truth?" Again she glanced at the Priest, and Teora caught a glint in her eye.

The Priest slammed his hands down on the table. "Then I suppose there may be the slightest chance that he might learn a bit of subtlety, some time down the road?" He was smiling, too. "That he might make a place for himself, even a high one, some day? Despite what his friends told him, years ago?"

By now Teora and Tourantij were smiling too, having caught on to who they were talking about. The Head Priest must have been too idealistic himself, once. Hopefully some of it remained.

"I suppose." The Councillor turned seriously to Teora. "Is he satisfied in Coalantha? Are his family happy there?"

"I doubt it. There is too much frustration, too many unhappy memories. If you had seen Noleta when she brought the children to be Heralds for the Exclusion..."

Another glance passed between the two leaders.

"Could you work with him?"

Uh-oh. Where is this heading? "Of course. In what capacity?"

The Head Councillor shrugged expressively. "We are not sure yet. Simply one of several ideas we have been considering." Then her face became more formal, and she turned to Tourantij. "You have been silent until now, Officer Niverdahl. Teora speaks highly of your knowledge. Have you anything to add?"

Teora gave the soldier an encouraging nod. She hoped he would see that he could speak frankly here, must speak frankly if he were to help. After a moment's thought, he answered in measured tones.

"Haven should be looking northward to expansion and new horizons, following the example of the Aerans, many years ago. The centre of the Joined Kingdoms is losing its power, and the periphery will become more important. The Magali will become a serious threat, with the Kingdoms' troops withdrawn. This means that the Aerans and their allies, the Curicuiriari, will also rise in importance."

Rhondona's eyes narrowed. "There have been rumblings that the Joined Kingdoms want the Herds of Haven to move south for protection. It is an idea that might tempt some. A chance to be nearer the centres of power, to have more effect. What do you think of that?"

He smiled. Teora remembered seeing that predatory look on his face, just before the wolves attacked. "The power brokers of the Centre want the source of religious power under their thumbs. I counsel you not to fall in with that plan. You would simply join them in their long slide into stagnant decay.

"With the power of the Deity behind you, the Haven could resist, but I would not like to organize a defence based on this isolated plateau. We could hold out indefinitely, but we would also be effectively cut off, and therefore unable to act in the broader field of the Land. There is a definite need to expand the Haven's power base, to cover more territory, with more population, transportation, and natural resources."

"And Aeru is such a place."

The soldier nodded tentatively. "They would be good allies, but do not consider moving in with them. They have their own ways and their own problems, and they have been independent too long. It would be better to find new territory, with no preconceived patterns to struggle against."

"Thank you, Tourantij. You have given us something to think about." A silent communication passed, and the priest stood up. "I have some business that requires my presence. Would you accompany me along my way, Officer Niverdahl?"

This was a not-too-subtle invitation to leave Teora alone with the Head Councillor. Tourantij, with a private grin for Teora, made a polite bow over Rhondona's hand and left.

After a moment, the older woman spoke. "What kind of assistance did Officer Niverdahl provide?"

It was Teora's turn to smile indulgently. "What do you know about Ser Niverdahl?"

Rhondona shrugged. "Very little. A mercenary, good at his profession. The name is uncommon. I suppose he could be related to the Niverdahl family in the capital."

"That's about all I know, too, except I'm not convinced he is playing a solo hand. There is little doubt as to his breeding and education. He is well versed in politics as well as battle. It was his analysis that allowed me to understand the underlying problems in Aeru. He was the expert who gave me information on bureaucratic procedures and their problems."

"With an accompanying contempt that most battlefield soldiers feel towards the pen-pushers back at headquarters?"

Teora shrugged, grinning. "Probably."

"Do you have any idea what his personal plans are, now?"

Teora's smile widened. "Whatever they are, I'm sure they include Sabba."

"Good, good. We may find him useful again, and it will help that he has ties to us. Did you notice that he has already thought about defending the Haven?"

"I'm sure he thinks about defending any place he visits. He is very good at his job."

"I thought I detected more enthusiasm."

"Probably. We have discussed this situation a great deal."

"And you don't think he's really a mercenary, working for himself?"

"I know that's the impression he gives, but it doesn't ring true. He mentioned keeping an eye on the Magali."

"Then he's on some kind of assignment."

"It's possible." Teora shrugged helplessly. "That's all I can tell you. It's only an impression I get. He doesn't try to hide it; he just doesn't say anything."

"Thank you very much, Teora." The Head Councillor rose. "You must know how grateful we all are. You have done a great service for the Deity and Her people, under conditions of considerable hardship."

"Don't thank me, Rhondona, I would do it all again."

The older woman had taken her hand. Now she held it tighter, gazing straight into Teora's eyes. "Do you really mean that?"

"Of course. Believe me, no one who has felt the presence of the Deity flowing through her could ever regret it."

"You may be asked to serve again. In similar circumstances."

"I had hoped I would. Frankly, I would find the Haven rather confining if I had to stay here."

Rhondona smiled. "I'm glad you feel that way. We will talk more about this later. Thank you again, on behalf of all our people." Still holding Teora's hand, she led her to the door and sent her away cordially. When Teora glanced back from the end of the corridor, she was still standing there, still smiling.

38.   The Future

A month later, Teora sat and regarded the group gathered in Rhondona's office: The Head Councillor, Head Priest Aolan, Hadar. *These are the ones. This is the driving force in the new direction for the Haven. What do they want with me?*

"So, Teora." Rhondona steepled her fingers. "Once Barozon has made his contribution to the bloodlines of the Haven, you will have some choices. If we create a new Dispersal, would you be interested?"

"Of course."

"And who should we send with you?"

She swung to face Hadar. *Now I know why I was invited, and where I fit in the hierarchy.* "What kind of question is that?"

He shrugged. "A hypothetical one, it could be argued, which is becoming less and less hypothetical."

"Do you really think so?"

"It is a logical solution to a great many problems. We here at the Haven have the luxury of considering politics in the long term. We do not have to worry about staying in power or being awarded a position in the next Assembly of Lords. Thus we have a certain objectivity." He smiled. "We only have to worry about being useful to the Deity to keep our places."

Hadar deferred to Rhondona, who leaned forward, her hands now flat on the desk in front of her. "Our analysis is that the Joined Kingdoms are far from dead. They may be stagnating, but it will be many years, even centuries, before they lose their great strength. But we must plan for that eventuality. A new Enclave would give us the expanded power base Tourantij speaks of. We have a chance to become influential in the growth of Tanish, and at the same time to protect its citizens, both physically and spiritually. Thanks to you, we already have an agent in a place of power there."

"We do?"

She grinned. "Oh, yes. Your friend Kilyan has sent a report already."

"Sent a report to whom?"

"Kilyan feels that he has been assigned the agent of the Haven in Tanish. He has sent his first report to the Temple and intends to report as regularly as possible. He requests guidance and some indications of the policies he is to follow."

"You have seen this report?"

"Of course, although it is not available to everyone yet."

"What did he say? How is he doing?"

"Generally, he is doing well. He had no trouble establishing his credentials, I gather. It seems that your name was enough. He is working with both the townsfolk and the natives from the Raft. The townspeople frustrate him by their lack of ambition and intelligence. More success with the natives, despite the language barrier. Apparently someone called Tzevi is of great assistance."

"Good. Tzevi is the leader of the Raft People and sort of a shaman as well."

The politician nodded. "That makes some of the report clearer."

"How are they dealing with the outsiders? Have many shown up?"

"Few who are organized. He does ask for guidance in dealing with Vachel Yamil. Apparently, the logger is moving his operation in quickly before the wood disperses. Kilyan says he has allowed this, as long as the local people benefit."

Teora nodded, pleased. "That is something I didn't think of until later. I'm sure those two will keep an eye on each other. If either one gets out of hand, we will know as quickly as possible."

Hadar shook his head. "It still takes too long to get information of that sort, especially in the dry season when the desert is impassable. We need a centre of authority much closer. A Temple in the town some day, even."

Teora raised a cautionary hand. "But that is no place for our new town. There is no good grazing. The only water is near the river."

"Exactly. You must be inland and south, where Corquée found the grazing lands. You'll need a good town site there. We can send engineers and builders. Some will be pleased to go. We have done little building here in the Haven the past few years. We will send a basic group of appropriate breeding animals, but most of your stock will have to come from the Aeran Herds.

"You won't have an Enclave at the beginning, only a small settlement. You won't need a Head Priest for years, not until you have a real Temple, and I can tell you right now, there won't be much support from us in the Haven to build one. We can't afford it, especially with the drought. If the rains are scant this fall, I don't know if we can support you at all."

"You expect us to build our Temple with the profits of our own operations. That will take many years, and we will need an experienced religious leader."

"Experienced, but not too old. We have read all the reports, from Goianor, Dezter, Rioran, others. Even they agree with us on one point. Youth and vigour are necessary. The old ways are changing, here and in the Joined Kingdoms. If they cannot change as we have, they are doomed as well. It is best that the Deity has Her hand spread out over new territory. Dinnan is too young to be the leader. There needs to be someone with a bit more experience, a mature man with a family, for preference. Perhaps Jalil might be our man. Although I have thought he might be useful in Tanish as well."

Teora suddenly picked it up. "Dinnan. You're sending Dinnan with us?"

"Is that a problem?"

The thought of those electric blue eyes brought a strange feeling over Teora. "No, no, not at all. I thought he would be more interested in, well, I don't know…Wait a minute. How much of all this is his idea?"

Both leaders laughed. "Don't be so suspicious, Teora. He has been part of our planning, as he should be. That's all."

Rhondona broke into the silence that followed. "Of course, there will have to be a Priestess."

Teora nodded. "Will you hold a new Competition? That will be interesting. Could I help?"

"Teora, have you noticed? We seem to have a surplus of the Chosen already."

"But I have lost my power."

"Really? Have you tried to use it lately?"

"I had no need."

"So, try now."

She sat there, remembering the feeling of the Deity's presence, the golden glow that would encompass her, the power that she could reach out and… *and what?* She shook her head. "It is not something you turn on for fun, or to prove it to yourself. I have faith. If the Deity wants me to do something and I need Her power, then She will send it. If I don't need it, I guess I'll do it on my own."

Again they laughed. Rhondona answered Teora's perplexed frown. "Teora, you are such a strange blend of modesty and confidence. You have been Chosen. Giving you the name of Priestess at the new Enclave will change nothing."

The Head Priest nodded. "It might even make the situation easier for you to accept. I understand how difficult it has been for you, being given power but no guidelines to follow. You may find the strictures on the Priestess confining, but they will also allow you to relax and not feel responsible for everything."

Rhondona smiled. "Yes, Teora. You will no longer have to be Big Sister to the whole world. Just to your congregation."

"You've been talking to my mother."

"We most certainly have. And with your sister, and also with your brother, who gave us some most interesting insights."

"How much of this did you have planned before we even got home?"

Rhondona turned to the Head Priest. "That's how the boy said she would react." She returned her attention to Teora. "I know you like to be the one with the ideas at the beginning, but we have been seriously considering the reports you sent at the end of the summer, ever since they arrived in the late fall. We had several possible plans, but we were waiting to get your personal impressions before we made a choice. It seems that one possibility meshes quite closely with your ideas. That makes it the obvious plan to follow."

Teora nodded. "I see." Then she looked up anxiously. "It's not that I need to be the leader..."

"No, Teora. We understand that. Some of us have the urge to organize others. There is nothing wrong with that, as long as it is channelled to a proper purpose. If there were not people like us, who would run things? Some people have the urge to control others. That is not the same thing, and it is not a good scenario."

"People like us...?"

Rhondona gestured to her office, its cupboards, filing cabinets, and piles of papers. "You don't think I do all this out of altruism, do you? I love this position. I love making everything move smoothly, getting people to work together. I love looking out on my city knowing that I have had a great deal to do with its success in recent years. There's nothing wrong with that, Teora."

"Oh...I know. But I never thought of myself as...well, you and I..." She stumbled to a confused halt.

The older woman smiled. "Get used to it, Teora. When you are no longer Priestess and the power of the Deity does not come at your command, this will sustain you."

* * *

Later that evening, Teora rode Barozon out to a small rise north of the Pastures of the Haven, and the two of them looked down over the Herd and the City. She thought of taking the trail again: the heat, the dust, the boredom, the danger. Yes, she would miss her soft bed at home, and a hot meal whenever she wanted to cook it. But now she would be part of something new, something that would help the Followers of the Deity to survive in this new world that was coming.

A warm glow filled her. Part was an echo of the Deity's presence, part the knowledge that she had done the right thing and was about to do more. She sat there enjoying the sensation until her Partner stirred under her. She chuckled and turned his head back towards his Pasture, his huge feet kicking up dust that floated away on the ever-present wind.

The End

If you enjoyed this story, please take a moment and post a review at your favourite online retailer. Even a simple star rating would be helpful to both readers and the author.

About the Author

Brought up in a logging camp with no electricity, Gordon Long learned his storytelling in the traditional way: at his father's knee. He now spends his time editing, publishing, travelling, blogging and writing Fantasy, Sci-Fi and Social Commentary, although sometimes the boundaries blur.

Gordon lives in Tsawwassen, British Columbia, with his wife, Linda, and their Nova Scotia Duck Tolling Retriever, Josh. When he is not writing and publishing, he works on projects with the DIVERSEcity Community Resources Society and is a staff writer for <indiesunlimited.com>

More from Gordon A. Long

Other Titles by Gordon A. Long available at <amazon.com>

Science Fiction

"Factory 4-80" Freighty 1
"Outback Rebellion" Freighty 2
"Asimov's Laws" Freighty 3
"Occam's Razor" Freighty 4
"Slivership" Freighty 5
"Centauri Triangle" Freighty 6
Coming Soon
"Plague Jumper" Space Opera

Fantasy

"Ocean of Grass" Petrellan Saga 1
"Waves of Stone" Petrellan Saga 2
"Path of Water" Petrellan Saga 3
"Zoysana's Choice" The Petrellan Saga 4
"The Innkeeper's Husband" Petrellan Saga 5
"Mercenary's Dream" Petrellan Saga 6

"Out of Mischief" World of Change 1
"Into Trouble" World of Change 2
"Mountains of Mischief" World of Change 3
"The Trouble with Tents" World of Change 4
"Queen of Mischief" World of Change 5

"A Sword Called...Kitten?" Romantic Comedy with an Edge
"The Cat with Many Claws" Sword Called Kitten 2
"Cloud Cat" Sword Called Kitten 3

411

Other Genres

"Storm Over Savournon" (A Novel of the French Revolution)

"Why Are People So Stupid?" Social Humour with a Point

Online

Look for Gordon's books, selected reviews, poetry and short stories:
<airbornpress.ca>
Gordon's opinions on humanity "Are People Really That Stupid?"
blog:
<http://airbornpress.ca/arepeoplestupid/>
Find all his reviews and his ideas on writing at
"Renaissance Writer:" <http://airbornpress.ca/newdir/>